THE PIEDMONT CONSPIRACY

by James Washburn

MADISON BOOKS

Lanham • New York • London

Published by Madison Books
4720 Boston Way
Lanham, Maryland 20706

3 Henrietta Street
London WC2E 8LU, England

This is a work of fiction. Any resemblance between
characters in the novel and actual persons,
living or dead, is purely coincidental.

Library of Congress Cataloging-in-Publication Data

Washburn, James.
     The Piedmont conspiracy / by James Washburn.
          p.   cm.
     ISBN 1-56833-075-8 (alk. paper)
     PS3573.A7867P5   1996
     813'.54—dc20   96-31200
                                              CIP
     96/12

ISBN 1-56833-075-8 (cloth: alk. paper)

Distributed by National Book Network

*This book is dedicated to the friendship between the authors
and the love, support and encouragement
from their families and friends.*

PROLOGUE

The lovers stirred. The man sighed, then raised himself up on one elbow to look down at the woman, her pale skin contrasting with the rich black of her hair. Michelle was exquisitely beautiful, he thought with a smile.

It was morning and daylight was creeping through the wooden slats of the lovers' shuttered window, but Simon Zeisman was not just waking. He had a problem, a sudden and very serious one. He had slept little this night, though he had left his Vatican City apartment to lie in the arms of the mistress he loved.

Michelle Campagna's apartment was in the quiet and conservative Parioli section of Rome. Yet Zeisman could sense, though he could not hear, the guns of war booming in the south as the Allies continued the blistering counteroffensive that had caused the fall of Mussolini and the occupation of Rome by Nazi Colonel Hauptler's troops a month ago.

Zeisman knew why Hitler had chosen the infamous, Jew-hating Wolfgang Hauptler to govern Rome; even Zeisman, the civilian head of Vatican finance, had to fear such a man. For Zeisman was a Jew, and Jews were not safe anywhere in Hitler's Europe. Not in Germany, not in Poland, not in France . . . not even in Rome!

Michelle turned in her sleep and nuzzled against the dark hair on Zeisman's broad chest. He kissed her gently. There was a tight feeling in his gut as he thought of Hauptler's threat—delivered only yesterday to Malachi Solomon, Chief Rabbi of Rome—to deport ten thousand Roman Jews if they did not contribute ten million dollars to the Third Reich's war effort. Hauptler had told Rabbi Solomon that it was simple; each Jew would be ransomed for a thousand dollars. That was the deal.

"The war has left us little," Rabbi Solomon had said that day in Zeisman's third floor office in the Vatican City. "Hauptler has given us three

1

weeks to raise the money, but I couldn't raise it in three months! Not as things are now. But you can, Simon. You are the only one who can. You can get the Vatican to help. The Pope trusts you."

Yes, it was true that the Bishop of Rome, Pope Pius XII, trusted Zeisman. Both the present Pope and his predecessor had trusted the Vatican's chief investment adviser. In the fourteen years since Mussolini had paid the Holy See ninety-two million dollars in cash and Italian bonds for the Piedmont States—the Papal States—under the Lateran Treaty of 1929, Zeisman had doubled its value through shrewd investments. He had accomplished this in spite of the worldwide depression of the thirties and Hitler and Mussolini's war in Europe.

Zeisman had listened to the rabbi's plea and promised to intervene with the Holy Father, even though he knew that the Vatican Treasury, which had been in sorry shape before the Lateran payments, still lacked liquidity. In spite of Zeisman's investment success, the Vatican's cash income was meager. Most of its support came from dividends on the Italian government bonds that were a part of Mussolini's settlement and "Peter's Pence," the contributions made to the Holy See by Catholics around the world. Unfortunately, the war had reduced the latter to a mere trickle.

Looking down at Michelle's angelic face, so peaceful and relaxed as she slumbered, he knew he had to find some solution to the Nazi threat. Zeisman gazed upon her soft features with adoration, his look tracing the face he knew and loved so well. Merely contemplating the dark of her eyebrows, the pale peach color of her cheeks, the curve of her petite chin made his heart feel serene and filled with love. She alone was worth ten million dollars, he was sure.

Zeisman faced a dilemma such as he had never before known. He was responsible to the Vatican and, in that capacity, could not recommend depleting its treasury even for a very just cause. But he also had a duty to his people, for he and Michelle were both Jews, as was their daughter Deborah. She was their love child, born outside of marriage, and Zeisman worshipped his beautiful twelve year-old.

As he concentrated on how to balance these needs without compromising either one, Michelle whispered, "You're so grim, darling. Do you need some time alone? I'll leave and take Deborah . . ."

Zeisman silenced her with a fiercely loving kiss, his hands going automatically to her delicate breasts, which were covered only by the wispy material of her pink nightgown. In spite of his pressing problem, he found it easy to make love to Michelle a second time. Or perhaps it was because of his problem that his passion rose like a tidal wave of lust, making him forget, for the moment, that so many lives depended on him.

He reached for her and tenderly slipped the nightgown straps from her shoulders, as his mouth visited her breasts to kiss and caress them. Michelle moaned with pleasure and Simon could feel her open herself to him—body and soul—as his hand moved, ever so gently, to the delicious flesh between her legs. He touched her, softly, in a way he knew would give her great pleasure and she reciprocated by placing her hand on him in a place that only a lover's hand can roam. He moved his body closer to hers as he prepared to take her and she prepared to take him, and soon the two became one as they expressed their love through the physical melding of their bodies.

"I love you," Zeisman called out, as he felt his pleasure rise to the greatest of heights. "I love you more than anything, Michelle."

Michelle was not his first woman, nor was she his "official" woman. He was still legally married to Pina, who was more of a distant memory than a wife. Pina lived on Zeisman's estate in neutral Madrid, but it was Michelle who lived in his heart. She was his first real love. He was certain of that.

He vowed to himself that after the war—this *cursed* war, he amended—he would finally divorce Pina, the Vatican be damned, and marry Michelle. He wanted so to spend his life with her, and to legitimize their beloved Deborah.

After their lovemaking, the two lay peacefully in each other's arms. Zeisman stroked Michelle's hair, and she nuzzled her face into his brawny shoulder. She glowed with love and joy.

"I love you so, Mr. Vatican Banker," she cooed, "even though your bosses don't approve of me."

"Don't say that, Michelle. It isn't you they don't approve of. It's . . . you know, divorce. But soon . . ."

She kissed him apologetically. "Silly, I don't care about marriage. It's enough that I have you, and you've given me our lovely Deborah. If you can't get a divorce, at least we can be married in our own way. But something is wrong, Simon. I sensed it when you arrived last night. You slept poorly. I know you did."

Zeisman shook his head. He couldn't talk to Michelle about the Hauptler threat. There would be panic among Roman Jews if they learned of it. For that reason, Rabbi Solomon had sworn him to secrecy.

"It's just . . . a problem with the young bookkeeper at the bank, Michelle," Zeisman improvised. "The young monsignor—Massara. He's smart, maybe too smart. He despises Jews no less than the Nazi Schickelgruber, I think."

"Bookkeeper?" she repeated, for she knew Massara was more than that.

"Monsignor Massara won't be happy until he's a cardinal and in charge of the Vatican's investments," Zeisman declared, "but it won't happen while I'm around. The Pope has the final say, and he won't go against my advice."

"Then, my wonderful Pope-adviser," Michelle said with a twinkle in her dark eyes, "why do you fear that he would disapprove of your divorce?"

Zeisman's answering smile was bleak. "In investments," he said, "the Pope knows I have no peers. But in matters of the soul . . . well, that is something else entirely."

Later that day in his office in the Apostolic Palace, Zeisman had an idea. In spite of the war, emissaries of the Pope were free to travel to and from America. If one of these emissaries could carry a personal request for aid from the Pope to his good friend, Archbishop Martinson, the money might be found in the United States.

When the Pope heard Zeisman's proposal, he agreed, and a papal emissary was in New York within days, discussing the problem of the Jewish ransom with the capable Martinson. The archbishop's most earnest desire was to be a cardinal, and he quickly realized that delivering the ten million dollars would go a long way toward helping him achieve his dream.

Unfortunately, America was also at war, and American Catholics faced the same financial constraints as the rest of the world. The Church could not raise the ransom money in so short a time. But Martinson knew where to turn. Joel Rosenblum, the Jewish financial adviser to a strong, but quite unsavory, Italian organization could, perhaps, arrange a loan on short notice. A meeting between the papal emissary and the lender was scheduled within hours.

Neither Monsignor Vincenzo Massara nor his superior, Monsignor Ambrosiani, were informed by Zeisman of the mission to New York, but Massara learned of it anyway—through one of a select group of powerful cardinals who had intimate access to the Pope. A year earlier, these same cardinals had been secretly responsible for the young Massara's appointment to the Istituto per le Opere di Religione—the Vatican Bank.

Under the cardinals' orders, Massara convinced both the Pope and Ambrosiani that it would be inappropriate for Zeisman, a Jew, to deal with the Nazis on the Jewish ransom. "The Nazis might betray a Jew," Massara said, "but if I handle the transfer of funds, they'll know they must honor their commitment."

The Pope agreed and officially instructed Zeisman to permit Massara to complete the transaction if the emissary were successful in raising the money. When he learned of the Pope's instructions, Zeisman became incensed and stalked into Ambrosiani's office.

The priest was sympathetic, but not very helpful. "There is nothing I can do about it, Simon. You can, of course, ask the Holy Father to change his mind, but I see little to be gained. If I were you, I wouldn't get involved with the transfer of blood money to the Nazis. It's an abomination!" Still unsatisfied, Zeisman was nonetheless forced to accept Ambrosiani's advice.

A day before Colonel Hauptler's deadline, the papal emissary returned from America with a satchel containing ten million dollars. Zeisman was greatly relieved when he watched the emissary hand the bag to Massara, but he left the room in disgust when Massara insisted on counting the satchel's contents before giving a receipt.

Zeisman, who had postponed a trip on Vatican business to await the emissary's return, now spent a happy weekend with Michelle and Deborah. He never dreamed it would be their last together.

Monday morning he prepared for his business trip to Milan. Just before he left, Zeisman reached for his daughter and hugged her dearly. The young girl climbed on his knee and wrapped her arms around her father's neck. He softly patted her head and gazed at her beautiful face, admiring the dark eyes, which were set in a soft, peachy complexion like her mother's, and the long dark hair, which came from both sides of the family. Zeisman was on the stocky side, with large facial features and broad shoulders; his daughter took after her mother more with her soft features, long legs, and a trim torso. Even at her young age, she was turning into quite a beauty.

"I'll bring you back a gift," he promised Deborah. "Something special, just like you!"

"What about me?" teased Michelle, hugging her lover and daughter together.

"What would you like?" he replied with a happy laugh.

"Just you," she said, suddenly serious. "Be careful," she begged. "The Germans are everywhere, and it won't matter to them that you're the Vatican banker and adviser to the Pope."

But it was Michelle Campagna who was in danger, not her lover. Zeisman delayed his return to Rome until the morning of October 21, a day after Michelle received unwelcome visitors just as she was about to go to the market.

"You will come with us," the unsmiling Nazi SS officer ordered as five rifle-carrying SS thugs pushed past her into her apartment.

"Where?" Michelle replied dazedly. "I don't understand. Where are you taking me?"

"You are under arrest, Fräulein. Where is your daughter?"

"My daughter?" Michelle repeated, numb with fear. "I have no daughter. You must have the wrong place." Thank God, she thought, that she had sent Deborah to stay with her friend, Simonetta, while she went out to market.

"You are Fräulein Michelle Campagna, mistress of Simon Zeisman," the officer declared. "You have a daughter named Deborah. Now tell me, where is she?"

"No," Michelle said, "I have no daughter." She backed away from the officer, but two burly Nazis seized her and held her fast as their superior approached, his hand upraised.

"We will see about that," the SS officer declared. He slammed Michelle against the plaster wall and pummeled her with his fists until she was weak from the abuse. He ceased only when she feigned unconsciousness. Michelle silently prayed for her daughter's safety as she was dragged from her apartment and forced into the back of a truck with six others.

That evening, the SS men returned for Deborah, but Simonetta had already learned of Michelle's arrest and had hidden the child, sensing the girl was in danger.

Upon his return to Rome, Zeisman was stunned to learn of the arrest of Michelle and ten thousand other Roman Jews. In a rage, he stormed into Massara's office at the Vatican and demanded to know what he had done with the ransom money. Massara told him that he and Rabbi Solomon had personally delivered the money to Colonel Hauptler a week earlier.

When he could not reach Rabbi Solomon to verify Massara's claim, Zeisman went to Colonel Hauptler's Rome headquarters. The Nazi military governor refused to see him and threatened him with arrest if he did not leave immediately.

In desperation, Zeisman went to the Pope, who dispatched his secretary of state with a horrified plea to stop the arrests. The pontiff sent a copy of his plea by special messenger to Colonel Hauptler's superior in Berlin. The man, a dissident Nazi general who would later in the war attempt to assassinate Hitler, telegraphed Hauptler a direct command to halt the arrests immediately, a command that Hauptler obeyed.

But the intervention came too late. Not one Jew rounded up and shipped to northern Italy, then to camps in Germany, was ever seen again—alive or dead—including Michelle Campagna.

Zeisman's daughter returned to him several weeks after her mother's arrest and disappearance, but it was impossible, under the circumstances, for Zeisman to keep Deborah, as much as he wanted his child to be with him. He arranged for Roman friends to care for her.

Colonel Hauptler—or so he later claimed—never received the Jewish ransom money. And the money was never seen again.

There were those who suggested that the missing Rabbi Solomon had absconded with it, but a shepherd discovered his partially decomposed body in early November hanging from a beam in a derelict barn outside Rome. An apparent suicide, Solomon had left no note.

ONE

The early morning sun glittered brightly off the waters of the Hudson River far below Elliot Bradford's high-rise apartment on Riverside Drive at West 108th Street, but the sight did not cheer the tall, bearded man as he stood, looking down on the city from his picture window. Not today. There was precious little that would make Bradford smile today, for it was three years ago this afternoon that his wife Nancy and his two boys, Scott and David, were killed in a bizarre automobile accident.

Three years!

Elliot Bradford—known simply as Brad to Tom Sumereau, his partner at FINVEST, and almost everyone else he'd ever been introduced to during his forty-seven years—was especially lonely each March 2, though none of his days since the deaths of Nan and the boys had shown much sparkle. Only his work kept him reasonably sane, and he was thankful for that. He wondered sometimes how he would have managed now if, like his father, Tom Bradford, he had been a nine-to-five blue-collar man working with his hands in a Michigan auto factory.

Bradford's face twisted into a scowl. Not since his father's death from cirrhosis of the liver, shortly after Brad's return from Vietnam in 1972, had Brad been able to drive a General Motors car and look at the instrument panels that had been his father's assembly line responsibility. His father had been a widower—Brad's mother had died a few years after his birth—so Brad had suddenly found himself orphaned. He had come to the conclusion that his father's boozing was understandable, though it had led him inexorably to the grave.

Bradford turned away from the window and drained his coffee cup. He silently walked into the kitchen, put the cup in the dishwasher, and picked up his briefcase. He was about to leave the apartment when he remembered Nancy's silver crucifix. He had bought it for her on their first wedding anniversary to replace the one that she had lost during their honeymoon in Hawaii. Nancy had worn the new crucifix every day after that. She was clutching it when she was found dying in her car after the accident on the Northern State Parkway on Long Island.

Returning to the bedroom of the large, well-furnished apartment he had shared with Nan, Scott, and David, he took the crucifix from his dead wife's jewelry box, which still sat on the larger of the two dressers in the master bedroom. He stared at the shiny object for a moment, then sighed as he dropped it into the pocket of his blue-gray wool suit.

It was cool outside, but Bradford was hardly aware of it as he crossed upper Broadway and then turned left at the next block, Amsterdam Avenue. He headed for the huge Cathedral of St. John the Divine, a landmark no one could miss at West 112th Street between Amsterdam Avenue and Morningside Drive. Beyond the big Episcopal church was the smaller Roman Catholic one, Notre Dame, at West 114th Street, where Nancy and he had attended masses with their sons. Nancy was the Catholic in the family, not he, but he had never tired of wishing her "Peace" at the appropriate time during the mass with a loving kiss.

Notre Dame was large, though not as spacious as St. John's Cathedral down the street. Like St. John's, it drew worshippers from Columbia University and the nursing schools nearby, so all daily masses were well attended. It was early when Bradford walked through the big doors of Notre Dame, about twenty minutes before the beginning of the mass, but already there were a few people on their knees in the front pews.

Bradford paused in the dimly lit entrance to dip his fingers into the font of holy water at the wall, consciously imitating Nancy's routine. Then he walked to a rear pew and sat, fixing his gaze on the big cross above the altar. Reaching into the pocket of his suit jacket, he took out Nan's crucifix, held it in his hand, and thought of her. How often had they sat together in this very same pew? He'd lost count long ago, yet for one moment, he would swear he felt her body next to his and for that one moment he felt alive again.

Now he knelt and slowly repeated the words to the Lord's Prayer, his only concession to religion. He believed in God, more or less, but he didn't believe there was any "right" way to worship God or that there was any "true" religion. As he prayed, he watched a priest appear through the sacristy door. The priest stopped for a moment to survey the congregation, then approached several worshippers in the front pew. He could not hear the priest's benediction.

Bradford's heart beat faster as he concentrated on finishing his prayer for Nancy and the two golden-haired boys she had borne him in the first two years of their marriage. God, he had loved them so! He swallowed the lump that he suddenly felt in his throat and had to blink to clear the mist that had come to his eyes.

The priest was moving down the side aisle toward him when Bradford murmured a quiet "Amen" and rose to leave. He had nothing against priests but he had nothing in common with them, either. Moreover, he was uncomfortable in their company, perhaps because of what he had done while serving with army intelligence in Vietnam.

As he retreated from the church, he wondered if there was any real point to his annual visit. If the spirits of Nan and the boys had survived the death of their bodies, could they see him only from inside the church? He shrugged at the question as he reached Amsterdam Avenue and began looking for a taxi. He realized it didn't matter if Nan could *see* that he missed her; what mattered was that he felt infinitely better for having observed his yearly custom of visiting her church and saying a prayer for her.

As he walked south on Amsterdam Avenue past St. John the Divine, Bradford smiled at the sight of a young boy tugging on the leash of his stubborn dog, a small one that looked like a collie. His own boys had almost had a dog; Nan had wanted to raise a puppy with them, and Brad had been visiting pet stores trying to decide what kind of dog to get when suddenly there was no longer any need.

"Going my way, Mr. Bradford?"

Bradford paused and turned away from where the pup was squatting at the curb. Beside him was a checkered cab and behind the wheel was the familiar figure of Danny Taylor. Brad kept no car in the city, though FINVEST had several he could use if he chose. He preferred to use taxis to travel to and from his office and had struck arrangements with several different drivers over the past few years, Danny among them.

"How'd you find me, Danny?" Bradford asked, climbing into the back of the cab.

"I remembered from last year," the cabbie responded. "You told me about going to Notre Dame every year when you asked me to pick you up there last March 2nd."

"Well, thanks for thinking of me. It's not too easy to find a cab this time of the morning. I meant to ask you yesterday, but it slipped my mind."

The cabbie grinned into the rearview mirror. "No sweat. I've got a great memory and anyway, you're the best tipper I got, so I'm not about to lose you, even for a day."

In spite of his wistful mood, Bradford was warmed by Danny's banter. He always wished he could find Danny when he frequently had to grab a cab for a quick trip to the offices of one or another of FINVEST's growing list of New York corporate clients. Most New York cabbies were unhappy philosophers who as often as not left Bradford depressed or annoyed. Not Danny, who was always in a good mood and jabbering about one or another of his six little kids in Queens.

As Danny concentrated on maneuvering the cab through the post-rush-hour morning traffic, Bradford pulled his mind away from the depressing anniversary and thought about his scheduled lunch with Jack Sands at Transnational Industries, FINVEST's richest and best client. It was going to be a touchy meeting because Brad would be delivering a financial report that would alarm Jack. It contained strong evidence that a TNI subsidiary was swindling its parent out of substantial amounts of cash.

FINVEST was an unusual, but effective, company. It was a super-corporate financial investigative firm that had offices all over the world, linked by a satellite computer system that gave all FINVEST's employees on-line access to information and made possible instant telecommunication between offices. The name of the firm was a marriage of words that represented their area of expertise: financial investigations.

Bradford and his partner, Tom Sumereau, had conceived the idea for the firm and founded it a dozen years ago as a partnership. Although the business was incorporated now, Sumereau and Bradford still held all the stock. Sumereau was the company's chairman and Bradford its president. The firm was prospering, thanks to the systems devised by the ingenious Sumereau and the organizational and motivational abilities of Bradford.

Suddenly thrown to the floor of the taxi by Danny's quick stop to avoid a big, black Cadillac limousine that cut in front of them without warning, Brad was jolted back to the present.

"Sorry about that, Mr. Bradford," Danny shouted. "You okay?"

Brad nodded as he regained his seat and brushed himself off. "I'm glad you keep a clean cab, Danny," he said jokingly. "With all the wild drivers in this town you never know when you're going to wind up on the floor."

"My fault," the cabbie said. "I shoulda figured the Caddie was gonna swing in on me. He got cut off, too."

Brad liked Danny's not blaming the other driver, as most cabbies around New York were prone to do. If Danny were no more or less capable than most, he was, at least, more honest.

The gold lettering on the frosted glass door read ELLIOT BRADFORD, PRESIDENT." When he was younger, Bradford had swelled with pride each time he looked at it. Now, he unlocked the door to his private office and pushed through it without a second glance. As usual, he was the earliest one in the office, so he went to the lounge area where there was a small refrigerator and a Bunn coffee maker for the staff and made a pot of coffee.

He was sitting at his walnut desk going through the TNI report when Linda Hamilton, his personal assistant, joined him. In truth, Linda did much more than a secretary; she scheduled his entire life and ran personal errands. She took care of Brad's minutia, freeing him for more leveraging work.

"Anything you need to finish that report, Brad?" Linda asked, eyeing the papers in his hands. They had worked and reworked the data collected by FINVEST investigators in Europe these past eight weeks, and Brad had made two three-day trips to Europe to confer personally with the team. Still, Brad was a perfectionist and would not deliver a report that had loose ends.

"Yeah, Linda," Brad replied sourly, looking up. "Give me the name of the pigeon at Plymouth Films who's on the payroll of Cinema Services. We think we know who he is, but I'd like to give Jack Sands a name. I want to be specific."

"But Ted Mangini in Los Angeles says none of the Plymouth executives are living over their heads any more than usual, and there is no sign that any of them have an out-of-control drinking or drug problem that could be causing them to steal."

Bradford nodded, finished his coffee and placed the empty mug on his desk. He knew that Linda would bring him a refill as soon as their conversation ended. "Someone is squirreling away a nice chunk of profits from Plymouth and TNI, Linda."

"There is an interesting article in today's *Wall Street Journal* on foreign distribution of American films, Brad. It's buried under the papers on your desk. I circled the article. It says films draw overseas pretty much the way they do here."

After Linda had filled his coffee cup and left him alone with the TNI report, Brad read the article. He was not surprised that the industry was concerned about the possibility that European film profits were being skimmed by distributors. It was precisely for that reason that TNI had hired CSI, Cinema Services, Inc., to be a watchdog over the foreign distribution operations of Plymouth Films and later had hired FINVEST to quietly check on CSI.

Brad had suggested the move to Jack Sands last Christmas when he was a house guest at Winterhaven, Sands's chalet in the Green Mountains of Vermont. They'd been enjoying a few drinks and a hot game of rapid-fire chess—Jack's favorite indoor game—when Sands casually mentioned that theater receipts in Europe had not improved after CSI was retained. In fact, they had actually taken a sharp downturn. Now Brad knew why and in just a few hours he would share his explosive information with his old friend.

The faint, but distinctive scent of Linda's Opium perfume—a Christmas gift from him—made Brad swivel his chair to face her even before she spoke.

"Have you decided what you're going to do about Frank Bartlett yet?" she asked.

Bradford frowned and shook his head. Bartlett had served with Bradford as an intelligence officer in Vietnam in 1969. Frank had been rough, tough, and smart then, but he was a disaster now. He was an admitted and reformed alcoholic, but had never disclosed that he'd been both using and modestly dealing in drugs until fairly recently. Although he had never been convicted of the latter, he easily could have been, according to Brad's information. Bartlett was apparently clean now, but he could never meet FINVEST's rigorous standards.

Frank had shown up last week when Brad was in London conferring with Tony Phipps, director of FINVEST's British operations. He'd wanted to see Brad about working for FINVEST. Tom had interviewed him and Linda had secured a personnel sheet detailing his current situation and history. They had also run him through a detailed check, and the results precluded a future for Bartlett at Brad's company.

Brad had taken Frank out to lunch yesterday. Mostly they'd talked of the old days in Nam, Frank tacitly reminding Brad that their service together constituted a bond between them—at least it should. Back at the office, Brad had confronted him with the facts in his report. "Where and when did you start using drugs?" Brad had asked without rancor.

"Drugs?" Frank's mouth had dropped open, and it didn't take an expert psychologist to recognize the guilt on his face.

In the end, Brad had not reached a decision, promising Bartlett only that he would try to help.

"I'd like to help the guy out, Linda," Brad said now. "He's really up against it. He was a good man once. How good he is now, I just don't know. What's your feeling?"

Linda had proved in the past to be an excellent judge of character. "He's on the fringe, I'd say. Shaky risk at best. Taut and tense as a violin string when I spoke to him. He didn't even make a pass at me."

Brad smiled at the last, but knew Linda was simply trying to take some sting out of her assessment, which was not far off. Still, Brad wanted to give Frank a second chance, not because of the special sense of loyalty always felt by former war buddies but because the man seemed to be making an honest effort to rehabilitate himself.

"We can't use him here, Linda," Brad said, "but I think I can get him a job with Les Sawyer's detective agency. Les needs good people, and Frank used to be one of the best. I think I'll give it a try."

Brad had no trouble arranging an interview with Sawyer for Bartlett and closed out his morning just before eleven by reaching Frank at his hotel. He warned the man that Les would get a copy of Frank's record, and he would have to walk "a straight line" with Sawyer.

"I owe you one, Brad," Bartlett declared gratefully, his voice cracking with emotion.

Feeling better about things, Bradford took a taxi over to Columbus Circle, home of the glittering glass-walled skyscraper housing TNI and its chief executive officer, Jackson T. Sands. During the cab ride across hectic Manhattan, Bradford relaxed for the first time since Linda's appearance in his office earlier. It would be good to see Jack again, he thought—in spite of the explosion FINVEST's report on Cinema Services was bound to detonate. Brad's fingers went to his short, brown beard and tugged idly at the curly hairs as he thought of the free-drinking Irishman who had become more than just a good friend and personal patron saint over the past twelve years.

Jack was as warm with his family and friends as he was capable as the head of the billion dollar TNI. He was a loving husband to his wife Ellie and adored their only child, twenty-two year old Holly Sands.

Holly, a stunning blonde, had been a precocious child and perhaps was an even more precocious young woman. Strong-minded and sometimes short-tempered like her father, she had a tendency to demand what she wanted out of life. She often quarreled with her doting parents—about the usual stuff—yet still spent a good deal of time around them rather than running around with people her own age. The family divided its time between an upper-East Side townhouse where Brad was a frequent visitor, their chalet, Winterhaven, in Vermont, and a condo in the Florida Keys.

Jack had treated Brad as family almost from the beginning of their friendship. Nancy had liked Jack, too, and it had been Jack's paternal counsel that had helped Brad get through the tough times after her death.

The cab's arrival in front of the TNI building interrupted his thoughts. As he paid the cabbie and strode into the lobby, Brad didn't notice the fat man watching him from near the lobby newsstand. The man's cherubic face was partially concealed behind a section of the *Daily News*. As Bradford walked past him and entered an express elevator, the fat man closed his paper without haste, tucked it under his arm, and walked rapidly toward the same elevator car. He reached it just in time to join Bradford and nine others, delaying the closing of the elevator doors as he entered.

None of the other occupants of the car gave each other a second look—none, that is, except Bradford and the round man in a black cashmere overcoat who stood on the opposite side of the car. Bradford's inspection was quick but thorough. As always, he was simply looking for a potential mugger, a breed he did not really expect to find in the middle of a business morning on a busy elevator. Because of his background in army intelligence—and as a New Yorker—he was trained to spot those criminal types.

While studying the innocent features of the round man, Bradford's scalp prickled as he wondered if he knew him. The man was staring straight ahead, but Bradford sensed that his eyes were not as disinterested as they seemed.

Were his senses deceiving him? Bradford wondered. They rarely had in the past. Once, back in Saigon, he had been attacked in a crowded bus by a Vietcong assassin. The man had trailed him through the city's streets and Bradford had not noticed him. But once in the bus, Bradford's sixth sense warned him just before the assassin lunged with his knife. That vigilance had saved his life. But this was not Nam, and no one had reason to attack him—unless it was for money. As for the fat man, chances were he was an off-duty chef, Bradford decided, looking at the wide girth that an expensive coat couldn't camouflage. Besides, muggers rarely wore cashmere. No, Bradford was certain the man was harmless. He relaxed and raised his soft brown eyes and watched for his floor number like the others in the car as the elevator ascended.

Bradford got out at the nineteenth floor, but in spite of his last judgment about the round man, he did not immediately turn in the direction of the TNI executive offices. Instead he stopped as if he were uncertain of the direction he should take. Not until the doors of the elevator closed and the two pretty young women who had preceded him out of the car had disappeared down the corridor did Brad make a move in the direction of the TNI suite.

After reassuring himself, Brad subsequently began to review his presentation of the report in his attaché case. Plymouth Films, the Hollywood-based production company TNI owned, was sixteen million dollars short in overseas profits despite a run of successful films. Cinema Services was supposed to be making sure their European theaters were not falsifying attendance in order to short Plymouth. Instead, Cinema Services was making private deals to get a cut of the skimmed profits. This confirmation of Jack's suspicions surely would not please him, and Brad was prepared to meet Sands's fiery temper.

Brad reached into his memory to recall another Sands explosion. It had been two winters ago at Winterhaven when Holly's behavior ignited her father's anger. They'd all been enjoying the warmth of a blazing fire in the living-room fireplace and cups of Irish coffee when Holly, then twenty, had suddenly batted her emerald eyes at Jack and announced her intention to seduce Bradford and then marry him. She had illustrated her statement by leaping onto Brad's lap in an attempt to carry out her first objective immediately.

Knowing of the private hell Bradford had gone through since his family tragedy, Jack had lost his self-control, yanking his aggressive young daughter off her prey. Then he verbally caned her as only an Irishman could. Not that it mattered to the impetuous Holly; she let her father's sharp words roll off her like the fine spray of a shower and stood defiant.

"If Brad doesn't want me," she declared hotly, "let him tell me himself!"

With all eyes on him, a red-faced Brad tried to defuse the situation. "Another time, Kitten," Brad told her, speaking in a tone he would use with a child. "But I sure am flattered by the offer!" Then he turned to Sands and calmly encouraged him to relax about the situation. "Don't blow up, Jack. I'm flattered that she thinks I'm worth seducing."

Holly behaved herself after that, and Sands's anger vanished.

Now, as he pushed his way through the door to TNI's reception area, he met the almond eyes of an attractive dark-haired Asian woman at the reception desk. Recognizing Brad, she flashed him a bright smile. "You can go right into Mr. Sands's private dining room, Mr. Bradford. Lunch will be served in roughly ten minutes."

The fat man Elliot Bradford had pegged as a chef who liked to sample his own culinary wares got out of the elevator one floor above TNI's floor. A frown wrinkled his forehead as he watched the elevator doors close behind him. He did not leave the bank of elevators in the thickly carpeted hallway and, instead, caught the next elevator back down to the lobby and exited the building. Today's preliminary task was completed.

So, Frank Bochlaine thought, Bradford was personally delivering the FINVEST report on its investigation of CSI's operations in Europe. It was a good thing Bochlaine had learned of it. He wondered if the count or Nicholas had yet received the message he had intercepted from their FINVEST spy.

Bochlaine's face lost its cherubic appearance. He didn't like either of the Aspis people. But tonight Bochlaine had a job to do. Tonight he must keep his appointment with Sands, learn what was in the FINVEST report Bradford was delivering, and then act accordingly. After the meeting, he might pay a call on Bradford, who was a bigger problem for Bochlaine's employers. What, Bochlaine wondered, would Bradford do if he learned the truth about the accident that had wiped out his family three years ago?

Just then pangs of hunger made his huge stomach rumble loudly.
There had been a time when the big man could afford to indulge his
appetite. He was an Olympic weightlifter then, and needed every calorie
he could pack in to build his muscles and keep up his strength. Although
he no longer worked out, his Olympic-sized appetite had never dwin-
dled. Now, layer after layer of fat padded his body, and the muscles of
yesteryear were buried somewhere deep inside his massive flesh.

Across Broadway near the New York Coliseum was a small Italian
restaurant he had noticed earlier. He joined the hordes streaming across
West 59th Street as the light turned red for cross-town traffic. As the
morning expired, thousands of hungry office workers were already leaving the huge office buildings lining Broadway and Eighth Avenue in
search of nourishment. Once inside the restaurant, Bochlaine eased his
huge frame into a wooden booth meant to hold four. He refused the
plea of the waitress that he move to a two-person booth. He did not
point out that he weighed as much as two normal-sized persons and
needed the extra space, but she finally saw that she could not move him
and reluctantly took his order.

"They're robbing you blind, Jack," Bradford observed. "It's as simple
as that." Brad's eyes never left Sands's as the two men lunched at the
meticulously set table in the paneled TNI dining room that adjoined
Jack's office.

Sands scowled as he stared at the report on the table next to his plate.
He squinted a little as he saw the black cover and clean, white FINVEST
logo, the weathered creases of his face tightening into furrows of concern beneath his bushy white hair. Then, aware of Brad's scrutiny, he
turned away and stared silently out the window at his right. If he'd been
standing before the glass and looked down, he'd have seen a stark, still-
wintry Central Park nineteen floors below, its grass covered by a layer
of snow.

Sands's reaction—or lack of one—to the revelation of CSI's thievery
astonished Bradford. The aging Irishman should, at the very least, be in
a rage right now—on his feet and stalking around the blue-carpeted
room. Sands knew every four-letter word in the book and was not
averse to using them. But now he sat mute in his armchair at the head
of the long table, strangely unruffled.

Before Bradford could break the silence, a stocky, aging black man in a well-worn tuxedo emerged through the door at the far end of the room and stood between Sands and his guest.

"A Compari and soda, sir?" the wizened old man asked Bradford with a smile. He had a file card on Elliot Bradford that listed all Bradford's food and drink preferences, and he had checked it over carefully when he learned the identity of today's guest.

"Make it vodka on the rocks, Jesse," Bradford returned. "I could use the lift."

Sands nodded in response to Jesse's inquiring glance, and the waiter brought an Irish whiskey in a tumbler without ice along with Bradford's vodka.

As they drank, Bradford studied Sands without looking directly at him. His host was idly folding and unfolding his beige linen napkin on the table in front of him, searching for answers in the soft crevices of the cloth. How very much Jack had meant to FINVEST and its two partners, Brad thought. Were it not for Sands, he knew, FINVEST might well have been stillborn, for it was Sands who had put FINVEST on the business map.

Brad and Tom were investment bankers who'd had it with working for other people. Two smart young guys with courage and brains, with contacts and computer expertise, they knew they could grow a company once they landed one big fish—and Jackson Sands had been that fish.

Years ago, when they opened their office on Third Avenue, Bradford and Sumereau had a suite that contained two offices and a small reception area where their secretary would work—when they hired one. Before the secretary came on the scene, Sands visited their office. Then TNI's controller, he had received FINVEST's card announcing they were in business as "confidential corporate financial investigators."

Sands, Bradford thought now, must have found it amusing as the two young associates, fresh out of the Wharton Business School, postured and tried to convince him that they knew their way around. Jack had given no indication that he was anything but impressed until he had suddenly shut off Tom's sales pitch in its unexciting, albeit fact-filled, middle. Then he asked them if they could become "a sort of specialized Dun & Bradstreet" for TNI. What he wanted, he said, was to get all the competitive information he needed, quickly and with a minimum of bullshit. When I call you and tell you at nine o'clock in the morning that I need to know everything there is to know about XYZ Industries—who runs it, how solvent he is, who's his banker, what he might take for it, and so on—I want you to deliver a report within forty-eight hours. Maybe ninety-six hours if the outfit's in Europe. Can you guarantee me that?"

FINVEST couldn't do that—and neither could any other firm in the world—and Bradford spoke up and told Sands so, over the sounds of Tom's choking unhappiness. But Sands then surprised them again.

"Wonderful!" he told them. "I'd be on my way out of here right now if you'd tried to bullshit me, gentlemen. Now tell me the truth—how soon can you set up to service me the way I need to be serviced? To give me what I want as soon as it can be dug up? Time is money, you know, and wasting it has a snowballing effect in terms of corporate dollars."

"We're just starting out, Mr. Sands," Brad said. "If we had enough money . . ."

"I'll see that you get what you need, Elliot," Sands broke in, "I'll give you a retainer."

"Then I'd say we can arrange things in about a month," Sumereau said, swallowing hard at what was happening.

"Make it two weeks and I'll send you a $10,000 retainer by messenger this afternoon. No, let's make it twice that—$20,000. You have to be hungry to do a really good job, but if you're too hungry, you won't do the job right. You can charge me, say, $1,000 a day for the work you do for us at the start, and I'll see to it that you always have an advance on your expenses in your bank account."

"Which will, of course, be in one of your banks?" Bradford suggested with a knowing grin.

"You catch on quick, Elliot," Sands said with a laugh. "That'll help establish your line of credit, which you'll sure as hell need."

More than twenty-four million dollars of TNI business moved to and through FINVEST in the next ten years. Sands originally became TNI's president, then its board chairman as well, and FINVEST opened offices all over Europe to cope with Sands's continuing investigative demands as well as those of other clients. Bradford and Sumereau moved to new quarters on Fifth Avenue, a few blocks away from their principal client, and Bradford often walked the short distance to Columbus Circle when he was in a hurry or could not get a cab immediately.

Sands took a shine to Bradford that went far beyond the business relationship that he established with Brad's firm. Had Tom Bradford been alive, he could hardly have been more supportive of his son than Sands had been during the trying times that followed the accident that made Brad a widower. Brad had broken down and wept on Jack's shoulder the day of the funeral and the gruff Irishman had shed tears, too.

Sands was the only person in the world who called Brad "Elliot."'' It seemed right and natural for him to do so. After Bradford's return from two tough years in Nam, nightmares featuring three South Vietnamese traitors he'd killed when they tried to lead him into a Vietcong trap had haunted him. It was Sands who had finally all but psychoanalyzed him and helped him through the remorse he had suffered since his return to civilian life.

Brad became the son that Jack Sands never had. By the same token, Jack Sands was, in Bradford's mind, his adopted father.

At last Jack spoke, breaking the oppressive silence in the ornate dining room. "I may want you to sit on your report for a short time, Elliot," he said. "But run it by me in simple terms here and now so I don't have to read it."

"Cinema Services is up to its ass in a three-way steal, Jack. Somebody at Plymouth Films is involved, but we haven't fingered him yet. Cinema's field people are sleeping with the foreign theater owners as sure as TNI is bigger than a bread box."

Sands smiled thinly. "More," he urged, finishing his tumbler of whiskey. "How are they doing it? How are they covering up?"

Bradford admired the way Sands cut to the core of things. He stood and began to wander around the dining room as he gathered his thoughts.

"First, you have to understand that the motion picture business is like Ali Baba and the Forty Thieves. Every so often they've got an Ali Baba, but mostly it's just thieves."

Sands didn't laugh, which didn't surprise Bradford. He knew Jackson T. Sands as a shrewd but scrupulously honest businessman who admired cunning and grace but could not abide thievery, whether private or corporate. "Sometimes I have to deal with big corporate crooks, Elliot," Jack had often told Bradford, "but I never have to like it. Given a choice, I'll take incompetence over dishonesty any time—and you know how I hate incompetence!" Bradford knew very well indeed.

"Theater owners," Brad continued, "are no exception. Maybe there are a few here and there who won't knock down a couple of hundred tickets a week—a thousand if they're doing a really good business—but they're the exception. Any theater owner who can skim a thousand tickets a week is a helluva high roller. He can pick up more than two mil a year—and it's tax free!"

"Which," Sands said now, "is why we hired Cinema Services—to make sure our Plymouth Films Division didn't get silent-partnered by the theater thieves. If they do their job, Cinema Services is well worth their ten percent of net profits. They're supposed to save us at least ten percent of gross by keeping the skimming to a minimum." Sands flushed, his blood pressure rising as he saw the picture more clearly. "What you're saying, Elliot, is that Cinema is dealing with the theaters that skim, then splitting with the owners and our Plymouth people?"

"Somebody at Plymouth," Bradford corrected. "Whoever's taking a cut there. It's probably only one or two people and they're not top level. They're supposed to cover up the difference between domestic and foreign receipts, because that's how we can tell there's skimming going on. We get a more honest count in the States because it's so easy for us to hire people to do head counts when we want them. Because we know the proportion of US theaters to European ones—and, with very few exceptions, American films tend to gross about the same elsewhere as domestically—we can estimate pretty accurately what the foreign take should be."

"And it's off by sixteen million?" Sands continued to show remarkable restraint as he leaned back in his big black leather armchair and met Bradford's eyes.

"Whoever was supposed to cover up the shortfall in foreign markets by fiddling with domestic figures blew it somehow, Jack. The only difference it made, once we got on the scene, was that it made it easy for my people to measure the shortage. Once we started checking theaters it wasn't hard to see what was going on—or how. Cinema's field people aren't terribly genteel, by the way. They strong-armed some theater owners into dealing. The threats they used were sweet ones—like blowing up little sections of the theater when they're filled with people!"

Bradford paused to light a cigarette offered him by his host, who then lit a long snub-nosed cigar for himself. Then Brad offered a grin and said, "You're taking this awfully goddamn well, Jack. I expected you to reach for a nitro by now to calm the explosion."

Sands shrugged. "I don't like what you're telling me, Elliot," he declared, "but TNI's on the verge of unloading Plymouth, and your report gives me a problem I hadn't figured on. Right after your people began checking on Cinema Services an offer came in that will let us turn a tidy profit on Plymouth's sale."

Now Bradford understood Sands's silence, for Jack had obviously been grappling with the knotty problem of whether or not to conceal FINVEST's report from the buyers of Plymouth Films. "They'll have auditors looking over Plymouth's books, Jack," he said gently. "Why not let them have the report? Not only are you playing things honest and aboveboard, but I believe you'll justify an even higher price by doing so since your buyer will know the profits ought to be even higher than they have been. We both know, after all, that the skimming can be stopped, now that we know it's happening."

Sands sat bolt upright, his eyes lighting up. "Sonofabitch, why didn't I see that right off? Elliot, you are smart. Remind me to send you and your sidekick Tom a bonus when we dump Plymouth. You earned it with the work of your green eyes and by realizing that I could use your report to help me sell the operation."

Bradford smiled at Sands's use of "green eyes" for financial (green) investigator (eyes). Though Brad had never heard the term used by anyone else, either in or out of the business, he liked it. "You'll release the report to your buyer then?" he asked.

"You're damn right I will! What's more, I'm going to scare the hell out of those crooks from Cinema Services tonight by having a copy made to stick up the ass of a certain Mr. Frank Bochlaine, their rep. He's due here at 7:30, and by 7:40 he'll be running out of here with his tail between his legs. You've just given me enough ammunition to level the bastard!"

Bradford frowned. "The name sounds familiar somehow, but I'm afraid I can't place it, Jack. Say, be careful what you tell this Bochlaine, old-timer. Don't want a lawsuit on your hands, do you?"

"Who the hell are you calling old, Elliot? Anyway, no one will hear me when I tell the sleazebag off, so I won't need a lawyer."

"I'd take it a little easy on Bochlaine anyway. Get him pissed and he might just cut you down to size. You're not a young oil roustabout anymore, and Ellie and Holly wouldn't like it if somebody had to carry you home in pieces."

"Stow it, Elliot. I can still throw a pretty good high hard one—and I'm not talking about a baseball. When I was working the oil fields of West Texas, I threw a lot of them, and damned few ever got blocked. I remember once when we'd just brought in a gusher and worked like hell to cap it, I had to deal with two of the biggest, toughest fellas you ever saw."

Bradford relaxed, as he laughed at Sands's penchant for recalling his former oil field days. He made his first million, Sands was fond of telling his close friends, at a time when he didn't know where he'd get his next pint of Irish whiskey. A rig hit the black gold with only two days left on its lease.

"Those two fellas," Sands related, "were the husband and big brother—and I mean big—of this sweet little redheaded oil field olive I was sleeping with. They saw red when she told them to bug off and came into my arms for an oil kiss. Well, it took me almost five minutes to bring down that pair. The husband was a goddamn California red-wood—eleven feet tall and a couple of yards wide. I kicked him in the balls and he didn't even lose his grin. I finally knocked him for a loop with a railroad tie."

Bradford laughed his way through Jack Sands's rollicking story as Jesse delivered their entree, salmon in a beurre blanc sauce. Though Brad had heard the tale before, he loved the flair with which Jack told it—a flair that was evident throughout Jack's life, both personal and business. Everyone who knew him liked the big Irishman; there was something about him that was just plain hard to resist. To know Sands was to love him, and no one loved him more than Bradford.

While Elliot Bradford lunched with Sands and Frank Bochlaine filled his enormous stomach not far away, a tall, slim, good-looking man leered at a pretty, dark-eyed Alitalia flight attendant from his first-class seat as the jet streaked across the Atlantic toward New York.

"Can I get you anything, Mr. Criscolle?" the well-proportioned woman asked in Italian, pausing in front of the man who sat alone in the sparsely populated first-class section.

Nick Criscolle, whose mustached, rough-hewn face spoke of charac-ter but not of his love of violence, money, and women, let a smile show as he nodded agreeably. "Are you good at mixing drinks, Rosa?" he asked her.

The attendant threw back her head and laughed. "How did you find out my name?" she returned. "It's not on my uniform."

"It's my business to know things, Rosa. I also know you'll be laying over in New York for twenty-four hours. It just happens that I'll be in the city for a day. I'd be tickled if you'd fix me a drink or two at my place. It's gorgeous and so are you, doll."

Criscolle focused his icy blue eyes on the woman, who could recognize that he was a VIP as well as fit, trim, and handsome. What she didn't know was that Criscolle's employer, Aspis S.A., had a special relationship with the head of the government-owned airline. With a simple telephone call, Criscolle could arrange a vacation for her—or a permanent furlough without pay.

The passenger's crisp assurance and flattering words were not unappealing to Rosa, nor was his VIP status. "It just so happens," she said, "that I once worked in the East Village as a bartender." She giggled and switched to English—flawless, though slightly-accented English—as she added, "but if I go out with you it won't be to work, Mr. Criscolle."

He took the hand she'd been resting on the edge of his seat and brought it to his mouth for a charmingly European kiss, a satisfied look crossing his face. "I'm Nick, Rosa, and we won't be going anywhere. My place is nice—damn nice. It's only a little smaller than that Trump guy's and it has a better view. I like to enjoy it when I'm in the city, and have my guests enjoy it, too. My car will pick you up about nine."

"I'm staying with . . ."

"I know who you're staying with and where, amore mio," he said with a grin. "Just be ready when my car comes for you."

Criscolle's grin grew wider as the beautiful flight attendant's face reddened. She then backed away, turned, and walked quickly down the aisle to the rear of the plane. His eyes lingered for a moment on her pleasantly wide backside and the provocative swing of her hips as she hustled away. She would provide him with the evening's fitting finale, he thought, glad to have the pleasures of her flesh to look forward to that night.

With that taken care of, he turned his mind back to the problem of FINVEST. Elliot Bradford and his financial sleuths were increasingly annoying to Criscolle's interests—Aspis's interests. The latest report they were delivering was another nail in the coffin that the New York-based investigative firm had been constructing for itself since first crossing the path of Aspis. A coffin Criscolle would soon start lowering into the earth!

In mid-afternoon, with a few flakes of snow swirling in the air over Kennedy Airport, the Alitalia jet landed smoothly. Criscolle whisked through customs and climbed into the rear seat of a gleaming red and white Lincoln limousine. His New York chauffeur and gofer, Dominic, a swarthy Italian-American from Brooklyn, was behind the wheel. The scent of Obsession cologne hung heavy in the car.

By four o'clock Criscolle had learned from a friend of Aspis that Bradford had delivered the FINVEST report on Cinema Services. The scheduled meeting between Sands and Frank Bochlaine at seven-thirty that evening surprised him. He wondered what the hell Bochlaine was doing in New York.

TWO

The early March sun was unusually bright and warm when Bradford emerged from the TNI Building on Columbus Circle. He decided to skip the half dozen cabs parked in front of the building in favor of a leisurely walk to his office in the Corning Glass building on 56th Street and Fifth Avenue.

Frank Bochlaine. The name Sands had tossed at him nagged Bradford like the face of an old friend he'd long forgotten. He couldn't shake it as he picked his way through the thinning after-lunch crowds inhabiting the sidewalks of mid-Manhattan and headed across 58th Street. Once there had been substance to the shadow of the name. He was sure of that. But not now.

Waiting for a traffic light to change, he deliberately wrenched his thoughts away from Bochlaine's faceless identity. His unconscious was far better equipped to dredge up facts about the Italian than his conscious mind. He reflected on his lunch with Jack.

Jack's mood had changed abruptly for the better when he'd seen the positive effect FINVEST's report would have on his sale of Plymouth Films, and that could not have pleased Brad more, both personally and professionally.

Reaching the FINVEST lobby, Bradford nodded at Anne, the perky receptionist, as he strode briskly toward his office at the far end of the suite.

Linda Hamilton sat in the armchair beside his somewhat cluttered walnut desk going through a sheaf of notes she had made on telephone call slips. "Lots of people want you, Brad," she said. "Want to go through them now? There's nothing here that will shake the earth if you put it off. You look like you're into some deep stuff."

"Frank Bochlaine," he muttered. "I know that name, Linda, but I just can't place it. He's associated with Cinema Services, but I know that I've seen the name somewhere else. I'm sure I have."

29

"Want me to run the name through Max, Brad? I can find out any-thing there is to know about him in a minute if he's in our database."

"Do it," Bradford agreed, walking to the large, curtained window to look down on the ant-sized people creeping along the sidewalks far below. Max was the pet name he and Tom had given the FINVEST com-puter system, which linked all FINVEST offices by satellite and stored an enormous amount of esoteric information. The name stood for "Maxi-mum" and was entirely appropriate because the system had a spectacular capacity for tracking down some of the oddest details.

"Tom called, Brad," Linda added before leaving. "He's at Business Machine Corporation with Walter. The job BMC has for us will buy us another mainframe or two, he says. He'll be there until tomorrow, so you can reach him if you need to. He left a number with Olga."

"Leave him alone. It's hard enough trying to estimate a job without interruptions. Did Tony check in from London before they closed up shop for the day?"

"Only by computer, boss," Linda said. "He told Max to tell you he's meeting with a pair of gorgeous sisters over dinner tonight—that you should eat your heart out."

Bradford shrugged, but did not smile. Anthony J. Phipps, Managing Director of FINVEST Ltd., London Branch, was a super-efficient investi-gator with a steel trap of a mind. Because Phipps was also a great admin-istrator, the London branch was one of FINVEST's best. But Phipps was also a notorious womanizer and a joker, with a personality and charm that was a cross between James Bond and Monty Python. Tony's mem-ory was often nearly as good as Max's—at least the Englishman liked to think so. Brad suddenly thought of a way to capitalize on his colleague's computer-like brain. "If Max can't come up with Bochlaine, Linda," he said, "try to reach Tony, will you?"

Linda nodded, then disappeared through the connecting door be-tween Bradford's office and the sealed-access computer room that could only be reached through either Brad's office or Tom Sumereau's on the other side. It had been Tom's idea to minimize the possibility of anyone gaining access to the FINVEST computer or the paper files locked in a large wall safe. The files contained the most important and confidential reports FINVEST made to its best clients, including TNI.

Bradford sank into the supple leather of his high-backed swivel chair and went through the telephone messages. Confirming that nothing was urgent, he leaned back and listened to the clicks Max made as Linda keyed in the comments that instructed the computer to search for information on Frank Bochlaine of Cinema Services.

Moments later she returned to tell him the bad news. "Bochlaine's not in the computer, Brad. And Tony doesn't answer his home computer code or the telephone. I guess he really is trying to keep up with a pair of British nymphs." She paused, her eyes dark. "Maybe that's what you need, Brad."

"Forget it," Bradford said defensively. "I'm not in need of a woman—or two for that matter. Tom's always trying to match me up with one or another of his wife's friends, but I like my life just as it is."

Linda's look was understanding and compassionate. After all, she herself had slept with him once, about a year after his wife died, and she knew firsthand that he simply was not interested in conquering women. It had happened during one of those late nights at the office, when the tired boss and his tireless assistant fell into each other's arms after a long week of hard work. Passion flamed for a few moments in time and then disappeared like a rainbow after a storm.

Their lovemaking was adequate but uninspiring. It wasn't that Brad was a bad lover, it was just that the lover in him seemed lost to a ghost, and Linda wasn't up to wrestling with that ghost in bed. The brief affair never affected their office relationship. In fact, it had been long forgotten. Brad was a considerate boss and Linda was a very efficient member of the FINVEST family, someone Brad trusted implicitly.

As Linda left, Bradford's eyes went to the photo in the silver frame on his credenza. The faces of his sons looked up at him, each of them expressing the innocence of youth. They were handsome faces, very much alive. It seemed the cruelest of life's jokes that their father had already outlived them both. His heart hung heavy in his chest, and sadness swelled in his throat as he remembered his two boys.

Brad had often agonized over what might have happened had he not taken an unexpected business trip to Washington the weekend Nan and the boys had planned to visit friends in Southampton on Long Island. Nan had gone anyway and made it out there without incident. But she never made it back.

Nan had been a good driver. Maybe she was even better than he, for much of Bradford's traveling was by plane between New York and the foreign cities that housed FINVEST's offices. He knew the roads of Rome as well as those of New York. Better in fact.

No, he finally decided, his presence in the car with Nan and the boys that day would only have resulted in his death as well. He would not have minded that. Not then and not now. Death was neither his favorite subject for conversation nor a great concern of his, not since his father's death.

He had always taken risks with a reckless abandon, never worrying about the results. But that was before he'd met Nancy Reardon and realized that she was the one for whom he was destined. He had wooed her with an inspired passion. That passion, he believed, had died along with Nancy. He hadn't felt it surge through him in so long that he doubted if it ever would again. Until the accident, their lives together had been a perfect combination of great love and joyous idyll.

Their car, a small station wagon Nan relished using to tour the countryside, had struck a parkway bridge abutment head-on. The police said afterward that there had been no witnesses to the accident. It appeared that the car skidded, changed direction, and simply was unable to stop on the slick highway surface. Nancy had died before emergency crews arrived. She had been found clutching her crucifix, but both boys lingered for a time before dying of massive internal injuries. The memory of his loss, and his visualization of the details, always gave Brad a cold, clammy feeling, as if he were being swallowed by death itself.

Bradford shook these familiar thoughts out of his head and began working his way through the calls before him. It was 6:15 P.M. in New York when Tony called.

"Are you alone?" Bradford asked. "Can we talk?"

Tony laughed. "Fear not, Brad, my loves live down the hall, and I'm to go to their playpen, old boy. What can I do for you? Do we have some sort of little problem?" The Englishman knew that Brad wasn't interested in patter with a late night call such as this.

"Bochlaine, Tony. Frank Bochlaine. He's some sort of consultant to Cinema Services, but his name is not mentioned in our report to TNI, and it's also not in Max. I know that name. Fill me in if you can."

If there was anything to Bradford's shadowy memory of Bochlaine, Tony would find it. He never forgot anything. He could quote—or sing, if he'd downed enough ale—long passages from Shakespeare. Or "Lucy in the Sky with Diamonds." Or even the London telephone directory.

There was silence on the line for a moment as Phipps aimed his mind in the right direction. Finally he spoke. "Bochlaine? He's a fringe figure in the Cinema Services picture. We didn't make him on any of the dirty stuff in our Plymouth Films study, although I have heard a few things about him."

"Such as?"

"Depending on whom you listen to, his firm is said to be seeded with Mafia money, Pahlavi gold, or Madame Nhu's diamonds."

"Cinema Services—primed with Mafia money?" Brad shook his head in confusion. "There was no mention of that anywhere in the Cinema Services report, Tony."

"First, brother Brad, what I'm telling you is strictly rumor. Second, it's not Cinema Services that's primed with Mafia money or whatever, it's their parent company—an international firm of wheeler-dealers known as Aspis. They're a god-awful mysterious kettle of Roman fish, I can tell you that."

"Aspis?" Brad had heard the name, but, like Bochlaine, could not recall any details. "Tell me about it and how it ties in with Bochlaine."

"No doubt there is a bloody lot to tell, but I don't know much for certain. Some of what I know is fact, but most is just conjecture."

"Just identify what's fact and what isn't, Tony. And try to connect the Bochlaine name."

"Well, I've heard Aspis is behind International Commodities, the out-fit that specializes in swap operations with Eastern Europe. They're also supposed to be backing Pratt & Woodward, the commodity trading company in Philadelphia, and Central African Mining."

"Out of Zambia," Bradford broke in. "Yeah, I've heard of that outfit, Tony. Gold smuggling is involved there, or you don't know a woman from a cow."

Tony chuckled. "My twin Sophias are anything but cows. They're five-six, a hundred and fifteen or so pounds and have legs right up to . . ."

"Aspis, Tony. The women are your problem."

"Yes, Brad. Aspis is also behind the Omega Bank and God only knows what else. As I said, its participation in enterprises all over the world is shrouded. I've run across them here and there, and a few years ago I checked them out—more out of curiosity than anything else. I found out the company was chartered in Liechtenstein just after the Allies finished off Hitler. Called themselves Piedmont, S.A., then. Changed their name later for unknown reasons."

"Who are the principals?"

"Who the bloody hell knows? All the stock was issued in bearer form and held by attorneys of record. Until the '50s their main business was fund management for a select clientele—whose names are not on record anywhere I can find. Then they began expanding into other fields, buying this firm, investing chunks of capital in that—it's all a ruddy complex puzzle and impossible to figure out."

"What does their name stand for?"

"Well, I'm not really sure, but I can say it's not an acronym. The dictionary says it means shield, and there is a species of horned viper known as Aspis."

"Nice, sweet images," Brad said. His sarcasm came despite his discomfort with Tony's information. "What about Bochlaine, Tony? Is he an Aspis principal? Who is he? What is he?"

"With Cinema Services he's no doubt some sort of watchdog. But he's in the Aspis upper echelon of management, though it's hard to know for certain. Aspis is involved in some exceedingly shady operations, I think, but I've heard nothing to tie Bochlaine to any of them. As I said, we found absolutely no indication of Bochlaine's being involved in the Cinema Services shakedown and conspiracy."

Tony fell silent for a moment, then continued. "About three years ago was the last time I actually ran across his name in print. He was, by the way, a player in the negotiations of construction contract settlements for the Watergate complex way back when. Aspis was behind the construction of Nixon's least favorite building, and they indirectly own part of it, but there was a long dispute over the final contractors' bills. The fact was the building leaked!" Tony's smooth baritone escalated as he spoke the last line, finally breaking into a very non-English half-giggle.

Bradford, deep in thought, paid no attention. "Anything else you can tell me?"

"I understand he's fluent in several languages and was once an Olympic weightlifter. He's a huge man. They say his hands are as big as baseball gloves."

Brad's brow furrowed. A big man? Something tugged at his brain cells. But he came up blank.

"Bochlaine was in Panama, I think," Tony continued, "when Aspis jumped into the banana business and buggered World Fruit. Their baby was commodities."

"Christ!" Bradford interrupted. "Commodities Management Inc.—CMI?"

"That's the one. Remember?"

"How could I forget CMI, Tony? And now I recall where I came across Bochlaine's name before. He was involved in that case. On CMI's payroll, wasn't he?"

"He was, but we never found anything dirty about him."

"Bob Walters, Tony. My God! That was the deal that caused Bob to do a swan dive out of the thirty-fourth floor of the Pan Am building two weeks after we laid it out for him in our report."

Tony began talking about Walters, but Bradford wasn't listening. Beads of perspiration formed on his neck as thoughts began taking shape in his brain. "Look, Tony, I've got to go now. First thing in the morning put out a request to our sources in Europe asking for all available information on Bochlaine and this Aspis organization. Got that? I want preliminary reports within twenty-four hours."

Bradford hung up, his eyes on his watch. It was quarter of seven. Forty-five minutes from now Bochlaine was due at Jack Sands's office. Bochlaine, who was involved in the TNI-Plymouth-CSI affair just as he had been in the World Fruit-CMI one. Was it important, or just an isolated coincidence?

Brad, alone now after Linda's departure, unlocked the computer room and went to the locked safe to get the files on CMI and World Fruit. To his surprise, neither file was there. They should have been but they weren't. Perplexed, he went through every file in the drawer on the off chance that they'd been misfiled. They had not. Where could they be? he asked himself. Those files were sensitive and weren't supposed to be taken out of the computer room by anyone but Tom or him—or someone else acting under their orders. If either Tom or he had reason to remove the files, they would have left a memo saying so. And there was no memo.

Returning to his desk after locking the computer room door, Brad called the small FINVEST office in Panama City, which conducted investigations in Central and South America. Two minutes later, he hung up, more perplexed than ever and disgusted as well. The Panama office, which had conducted the CMI investigation, had somehow misplaced its copy of the World Fruit-CMI report!

All available copies of the report were missing. What had happened to them? What could possibly have happened to them, considering FINVEST's strong security? Bradford swallowed hard. Could the missing files have been stolen by a FINVEST employee? His mind refused to accept the possibility, and he quickly veered toward the name that had started his current train of thought.

Bochlaine. How had Bochlaine been tied up in the CMI affair? Bradford strained to recapture his memory. Walters, World Fruit's president, had screamed long and loud about CMI's dirty dealings in the banana export business in competition with World Fruit. Bob commissioned FINVEST's confidential report and two weeks after receiving it packed it in with his crazy swan dive.

Brad considered it astonishing, for when he'd left the man, Walters had not seemed at all suicidal. He had been furious over CMI's thievery and chicanery, but his rage hardly suggested an impending suicide. CMI's improprieties, as Brad recalled, would be costly for World Fruit because they were legal—or at least would be hard to prove illegal. But that fact again could cause Walters little more than embarrassment and anger. In the scrawled suicide note he left behind—undeniably in his handwriting—Walters had not mentioned CMI, writing only of "business pressures he could no longer cope with." Had those pressures been connected with the shadowy Bochlaine? Had Bob tried to deal with CMI—threaten them—and run into the Italian?

Brad glanced at his solid gold Patek Philippe watch. Seven o'clock. Bochlaine was due in Sands's office in just a half hour. And Jack had told Brad he planned to give the Italian hell. Had Bob Walters done the same thing? Brad had a dim memory of Bob telling him he was going to use the information FINVEST had given him to "make those people a little more reasonable." But then, suddenly, Bob Walters was dead.

The day after Walters's suicide Brad had gone to see Milt Farr, the executive vice president who ultimately succeeded Bob. Farr did not disagree when Brad explained that Bob's death "doesn't make a whole lot of sense." In spite of the company's losses, Walters's position was solid with the firm; both men agreed on this. He had done a capable job over the years, and CMI's manipulations were not, of course, Bob's fault, nor did they in any way reflect badly upon Walters. Then Farr, who was oddly defensive about the whole affair, pointed out that Bob's ego was sensitive—super-sensitive. Farr believed that once Bob became convinced he had failed the company, and would lose prestige because of it, he had decided he had little choice but to kill himself.

Christ! Brad thought. It kept coming back to Bochlaine. What was it Tony Phipps had said about the man? That he had hands as big as baseball gloves? That . . . suddenly another thought leapfrogged over the last. Tony's description of Bochlaine. "Huge," Tony had said. Big enough to be an Olympic weightlifter. The man in the elevator! Even with an overcoat on he looked immense. Could it have been Bochlaine?

Now Bradford stopped his rush of thoughts and tried to think rationally. Bochlaine had an appointment with Jack this evening, so why should he show up early? To find out where he was going later? That could be, although there seemed to be no real reason to do so. But even if that were his purpose, why hadn't the man gotten out of the elevator at the right floor? Had he recognized Bradford? But what difference would that have made? He had nothing to fear from Brad—nothing except the report.

Bradford felt a trickle of telltale sweat on his neck again. Ever since he was a callow youth he had sneered at danger and engaged in all sorts of potentially injurious activities. He had climbed mountains, dived off cliffs in Mexico one summer, and done some hang gliding in Europe. The only evidence of his fear had always been his telltale sweating. In his youth he sweated all over his body, but when he was in Nam, the sweating had been like a sixth sense and was confined to his neck. He experienced it only when something wasn't right, when he was face-to-face with danger, real or imagined. He had felt it in that Saigon bus, and it had saved his life. He had felt it other times when nothing had happened, yet he'd never stopped trusting it.

Was Jack in danger? Brad couldn't be sure, but suddenly he was on his feet, his mind made up as he headed for the office door. Maybe Bochlaine was no threat to Jack at all, but Brad would feel better if he was there with Jack when the fat man arrived.

As he flew out the private door of his office and ran to the bank of elevators, Brad patted the left side of his suit coat to be sure his .38 was there. He had started to carrying the weapon after two men had tried to rob him not long after Nan's accident. His army training, rusty though it was, had helped him disarm his assailants, but the attack convinced him that he should get a permit for and carry a gun. He had done so, but had never had to use it.

It took him less than a minute to reach the lobby. Linda had left him a well-lit elevator, its door wide open, locked in place with a special key Brad had requested when they'd moved into their Fifth Avenue building. He frequently worked late at night and wanted no unseemly surprises from marauders hiding in a darkened elevator summoned by the routine push of a button.

A snowflake or two hung in the air when he burst out of the building. He glanced right and left, but no cabs were in sight. Not expecting any at this hour, Brad took off at a steady half-gallop up the street. As soon as he could, he darted between the cars on Fifth Avenue and continued north toward West 59th Street. As he ran, his breath formed small transient clouds in the near-freezing chill of the early March night. Even in a city where the weird and bizarre were as much the rule as the exception, Brad drew looks of surprise from overcoated New Yorkers. After all, only an exercise freak—or someone fleeing the law—would run through Manhattan at this hour and in this weather, with or without a coat.

Brad ran by the appraising look of an attractive young woman curbing her French poodle, then veered out of the paths of three husky young toughs in leather coats and gold chains who loitered near the entrance to a hotel. The effort of running was strenuous even for a man like Brad, who was in good physical condition, but it calmed him somewhat. He told himself that he had nothing solid to go on, no concrete reason to worry that Jack Sands was in danger. This whole thing was likely to be a wild goose chase. And yet . . .

Again he felt sweat on his neck. He was right to worry.

At the TNI building's front entrance Brad paused to catch his breath, then cupped his hands against the glass so he could see through the door. He didn't bother trying the doors, knowing they'd be locked at this hour. New York was a jungle at night, with predators always ready to hurt the unwary.

Brad desperately searched for the lobby guard. But the main desk in the large rotunda, staffed during the day by several information clerks, was now unattended. The huge, gray marble desk was lighted by a lone sixty watt bulb, which cast just enough illumination to show Bradford that the guard wasn't there.

The man had to be around somewhere, Brad thought. He produced his set of office keys and began rattling them against the doors. No one answered him. As he banged his keys on the glass, he began trying the doors one at a time. He was surprised to find the very last one open, but didn't stop to reflect on his good fortune.

He rushed in and immediately heard the sound of rock music coming from the guard's portable radio. Turning, he saw the radio resting on the top of the information desk and crossed over to it. An open sign-in book rested on the marble counter. It was dated on the top of the two facing pages. There were no entries on either.

Brad did not pause to become the first signer. Instead he crossed the lobby to the bank of elevators, where he found a single elevator lit and apparently working. Inside, he punched the button for the nineteenth floor and waited impatiently for the stainless steel doors to close. When they didn't do so immediately, he began bouncing up and down to make the weight-activated microswitch spring the elevator into action. At last it did.

The elevator was fast and reached the nineteenth floor in just seconds. As the doors slid silently open, Brad thought about getting his .38 out of its holster inside his jacket but didn't follow through on the impulse. The lobby was deserted, so he moved quickly down the corridor and through the portals bearing the legend "TNI EXECUTIVE OF-FICES." There was no one at the reception desk now, though the area was brightly lit. Brad's watch said 7:15.

The door to the anteroom of Sands's office suite, which included the private dining room where he and Jack had eaten earlier, was wide open, the lights on. Bradford's heart was pounding in his chest as he reached the closed ebony door to Jack's office. He leaned against it and listened. He heard the sound of muffled voices—one voice, actually. It was not Jack's.

Was the voice that of Frank Bochlaine? Was he berating Jack for the allegations contained in the FINVEST report? Brad concentrated on the voice, trying to make out what was being said, but without success. The office was not soundproof, but its thick carpeting absorbed the sounds within it as did the expensive velvety wallpaper.

He debated what to do because nothing out of the ordinary seemed to be happening inside. No shouting, no angry voices, nothing that would even suggest that anything was going on other than a simple business meeting. Brad was suddenly glad he had not burst into the room, gun in hand, making an utter fool of himself. He silently exhaled the breath he hadn't even realized he'd been holding in, then backed away from the door.

But he stopped in his tracks as he heard Jack Sands's deep voice bellow loudly, "The hell I will!"

Returning to the door, Brad put his ear against it again. Jack Sands was no longer talking. What was happening inside? What were they discussing now? What was it that Bochlaine had said to cause Jack's seemingly angry reaction? Brad was tempted to knock on the door and fling it open to see for himself. Again, he discarded the idea.

Still, not completely satisfied that all was well, he moved away from Jack's door and walked swiftly along the wall to the dining room door. Perhaps, he thought, he could hear more clearly through the door that connected the dining room to Jack's office, since the desk was not far from that door.

In seconds he was listening to two voices arguing. The voices came in loud and clear.

"No one will believe this."

"Quit fighting it, Sands. Now write your name on that, or . . ."

"So you can?"

"Sign it!"

Brad's forehead furrowed as he tried to understand the exchange of words he'd just heard. Then he heard a thud as if a heavy object had just struck the desk.

The noise galvanized him into action. "Jack!" he yelled as he reached for the door handle. "Jack! It's me—Elliot Bradford!" He turned the handle just as he heard the roar of a pistol shot. The sound made him light-headed with fear. The door was locked.

"Are you all right, Jack?" Brad began to pound wildly at the door. Then he paused at the sound of a loud click across the interior of Jack's office.

The outer door! Brad yanked his weapon out of its shoulder holster and thumbed off the safety catch as he sprinted across the dining room and burst through the door. He found the anteroom still empty.

Bradford's gun barrel followed his eyes as he made a quick search of the open area before him, but there was no one in sight. Jack! The name thundered in his brain. He wasted no time, running to the outer door of Jack's office. The knob turned freely and now, as the door opened, he heard the same click he'd heard seconds before. He shoved open the door, his gun in firing position, his body to one side of the opening.

As the door swung open, he froze at the sight before his eyes. Jack was there, slumped over his desk. Brad raced across the room toward the motionless body. Fear that the scene before him meant the death of his longtime friend drained Brad of his vitality and he began to feel nauseous. There was a gaping, bloody hole in the left side of Jack's head and blood and pieces of gray matter were on the wall, the carpet, the desk—everywhere.

Brad seized Jack's left wrist to seek his friend's pulse, and that's when he saw the gun in his hand. A gun that made it look as if Jack had killed himself.

No! Brad took a step backward after finding no pulse. This was no suicide. There was someone in here with Jack. Someone who . . . who was still in the building.

Turning away from the devastating sight at Jack's desk, Brad fled the office like a sprinter, crossing the empty anteroom to the corridor leading to the elevators. A glance told him the killer was not using an elevator, for the only one in service was the one Brad had taken up to the nineteenth floor, and it had long since returned to the lobby as it was programmed to do at night.

The fire stairs. Brad's eyes were already searching for them and he quickly found the red exit sign in the far corner, partly masked by the leaves of a potted ficus. He crossed to it, pulled the door open, and hesitated for just a second at the top of the steel stairway to listen. Immediately he heard the clatter of hurried footsteps on the stairs below. Brad hurled himself down the first section of stairs like a man possessed, taking the steps two and three at a time as he leaped from place to place like a kangaroo and used the metal banister to keep his balance.

Somehow, incredibly, the war was on again. He was back in Nam fighting for survival. As then, his thoughts were not of the dead man he'd just left behind, but of the enemy ahead—a vicious, cruel enemy who might even now be lurking just yards in front of him, waiting to execute Brad as he had Jack Sands.

Brad had no choice but to chance the ambush. He had to, for Jack was the closest thing to kin Brad had and now he was dead. Dead. The word was obscene, and Brad had the heady urge to scream it out at the killer below.

But he didn't. Suddenly he was flying through the air—he had misjudged a leap and slammed into a cinder block wall. He grunted in pain, but bounced off and regained his balance without loss of time. On the next floor, he lost his balance again and this time sprawled on all fours, jamming his shoulder into the landing wall amidst a blinding bolt of pain. He forced himself to get up and plunge onward, his eyes searching the poorly lit stairwell for a look at his target. Impossible.

At the eighth floor he had come to within two floors of the killer and was getting an occasional fleeting glance at the shadowy figure, but that was all. At the sixth floor he stopped briefly and leveled his .38 but found it impossible to get a clear shot at the killer below.

Another floor and Brad knew he had lost the race. There was one more possibility, he thought. But just as he had the thought that he might get a look at the killer outside the building if he continued to narrow the gap, the fingers with which he pushed on the railing to propel himself downward were suddenly stung as if attacked by an angry bee. He glanced down and saw that blood was streaming from an open wedge of flesh atop two of the fingers on his left hand. Only then did he realize that the killer was firing up at him with a silenced weapon.

Brad leaped to the next landing and took the following flight of stairs in long, lazy hops, ignoring the throbbing pain in his right shoulder and the flow of blood from his hand. Twice more the man fired up at Bradford, the first time taking a chunk out of the wall behind him, the second time hitting the iron railing.

By now Brad had given up the notion of firing at the killer, but he still hoped for a look at him. There was only a single floor and two flights of stairs between them now. If the killer was not quick when he exited the fire door . . .

Suddenly he heard the clang made by the metal bar of the street-level fire door as the killer shoved it open. Brad made his final turn and all but flew down the remaining steps. No more than three seconds passed before he reached the metal door and shoved it open. Holding it in front of him to guard against an attack, he peered out. No bullets greeted him, but neither did he catch the sight of a fleeing killer. He searched the square outside, but saw only a young couple walking arm-in-arm toward the TNI building.

Bradford stood there for a few moments, letting the cool air outside the building clear his head.

THREE

A quick check of the downstairs lobby told Bradford the guard was still missing, so he returned to Sands's offices. The sight of the lifeless body of his dear friend and patron forced him hesitate in marveled disbelief. He had to close his eyes against the vision of the already-stiffening corpse that had until only a few minutes ago been a living, breathing, warm human being named Jack Sands. Only the sight of the stark white bodies of Nancy, Scott and David in a Long Island morgue three years ago had filled him with such horror.

Still a little winded, his shoulder throbbing since his collision with the cinder block wall, Brad produced a handkerchief to stanch the flow of blood from his fingers. Then he moved to Jack's desk and an icy chill washed over him. For lying on the desk a little to Jack's left was a blood-splattered piece of TNI stationery. Jack's Mont Blanc pen lay on the paper as a paperweight.

Brad moved around the desk to read the letter. It was in Jack's familiar writing, though it seemed a little less flamboyant than the Irishman's usual style. But as he read it, Brad found its words incredible, for it was a suicide note:

> *Dearest Eleanor and Holly,*
>
> *You can't imagine how difficult it is for a soggy old Irishman to do what I'm about to, but I have to, although you're better off not knowing why. The simple fact is that if I were around to talk about it, you'd all be damned ashamed of me and I wouldn't blame you. So good-bye, my loves.*
>
> *Always and in all ways,*
>
> *Jack*

A cold rage swept over Bradford at this evidence that the killer had so cleverly planned to make Jack's murder look like a suicide, even including the note and planting the gun in Sands's left hand after shooting him in the left temple. Jack Sands was a southpaw.

Bochlaine? Had the fat man come early? Was his recent, unannounced visit a prelude to murder? Its purpose to check out the premises to make certain he could escape undetected? If Bradford hadn't come, Jack's death would surely have seemed an open and shut suicide to anyone who discovered the scene.

Jack's death.

Brad's granite-hard features turned pallid as the enormity of the tragedy sank in. Jack was dead. There'd be no more black Irish jokes, no more tall stories about his days in West Texas, no more weekends in Vermont, no more long talks about life and . . .

Brad collapsed in an armchair near the desk and fought to keep from fragmenting. Stronger men than he had broken when they saw their best friends torn apart by grenades or mortar fire or automatic rifles. And the love of a best buddy paled beside Brad's affection for his "adopted" father.

But there were decisions to be made and Bradford soon found that making them here—in the presence of the lump of dead flesh that had been Jack—was not easy.

He should call the police. Or should he?

He thought about it. If he called in the NYPD, he'd quickly be embroiled in a bloody mess in which he would come up the main loser. He was the only witness to what had happened—the only contradictory evidence to Jack's seeming suicide. Would New York's homicide detectives believe him in the face of the overwhelming evidence that Jack had killed himself?

Bradford stood and surveyed the scene again. There was no sign of a struggle, and the note on the desk was in Jack's own hand. Whoever had killed him had not signed in at the visitors' register in the main lobby. Apparently, the killer had successfully concluded his confrontation with TNI's CEO.

The guard. Where was the guard? Had he been killed? Not likely. But where was he and what had been done to get him out of the way? Brad decided he had to find out about the guard before deciding if he should call in the cops. A trip back to the main lobby took less than a minute because he had held the elevator at Jack's floor by jamming the doors open. Now he made a careful search of the lobby and soon found the guard unconscious sitting on a toilet seat in the men's room.

There were no telltale lumps or bruises on the man's head, so it appeared that he had been drugged. Certain drugs, Brad knew, could even erase the guard's memory of having been unconscious.

Whatever the cause of his blackout, the guard was beginning to make noises and would soon come to, so Brad left him where he was and returned to the front doors. The door he had entered through earlier was now locked.

That's when he made up his mind to let Jack's body be discovered by someone else. Reporting the murder himself meant getting involved with detectives he didn't have time for. He'd also have to give the police good reasons for all sorts of things that were at best difficult to explain: why he was on the premises, what he had expected to find, and how a killer might have entered and rendered the guard unconscious—and why anyone would want to kill Jack in the first place.

Brad knew some answers, but could not easily prove them. He had a compelling idea that the man from Cinema Services, Frank Bochlaine, might be Jack's killer, yet had absolutely no evidence. Furthermore, Brad could not put the police onto Bochlaine without divulging confidential information contained in the FINVEST report he'd delivered to Jack. Once he'd mentioned Jack's scheduled meeting with Bochlaine tonight, the cops would surely want to know why they were in contact.

No, Brad could tell the police what he knew to be the facts of the case at almost any time. For now, he needed time to pull things together in his mind. Time to figure out what to do about Bochlaine.

Whoever the killer was, he was efficient. He had used Jack's own gun—Brad recognized it because he had obtained it for Jack after his mugging three years ago. And there was a smell of burnt gunpowder on Jack's left hand, so no doubt Bochlaine had placed the weapon in Jack's hand, held it against Jack's temple, then used his finger to pull the trigger after first immobilizing Jack.

Jack's gun would bear only his fingerprints, for Bochlaine would almost certainly have worn gloves. The note was the final, damning piece of evidence. Chances were Bochlaine's very presence in America might be questionable, though it mattered little, for no one could place him at the murder scene. No one but Bradford.

Clever? Diabolically so. Even with Brad's intervention, the killer was likely to get away with murder.

Now Brad frowned, remembering that he had announced himself to the killer before pursuing him down the fire stairs. Would Bochlaine remain in New York long enough to silence him, too? The man might. Brad hoped he would, for right now his greatest desire was to stand chin to chin with the fat man and make him talk. Though pursuing Bochlaine might well sacrifice his own life, Bradford knew it was what he had to do. He owed it to Jack. And, whatever else he might be, Brad was no coward. In Vietnam, he had risked his life for his men more than once. To risk it for Jack was no less reasonable and no less necessary.

Could he kill Bochlaine if he had to?

A picture drifted into his mind—a picture of Jack Sands standing beside the fireplace of his study listening to Brad spill his guts about the Vietcong spies he had killed in Nam, executions that had tortured Brad for some time after his separation from service even though they were "necessary." Jack had given him a perspective on them that had sustained him. Jack had given him so much!

Brad could do what he had to, he knew that. But for now he had to regroup and prepare. And get the hell out of here before the guard came to or the police showed up.

Brad left through the fire door to the street. Alert for a possible assault, he dashed along the edge of the skyscraper, then dodged across West 59th Street and began looking for a cab. He found one after walking a few blocks and was able to reach Riverside Drive twenty minutes later.

Nick Criscolle was not in the best of moods when he returned to his high-rise apartment after a busy early evening. After dispatching his chauffeur, Dominic, to pick up Rosa, the pretty flight attendant from Alitalia, he took the elevator up to his floor, took off his gloves, and made a telephone call.

"I need Bradford's schedule," Criscolle told the woman who answered his call. "I want to know everywhere he plans to go, whether it's to a meeting at Macy's with the goddamn mayor or a flight to London to see his man Phipps there. Got that?"

"He doesn't tell us everything, Nick," the woman replied, "but I'll give you everything I can learn."

"You'll get it all, honey, if you don't want to find yourself sleeping with the fishes!" he snapped.

The woman made an indistinct noise over the phone. "I'll call you when I have something to tell you, Nick. Anything else?"

"Isn't that enough?"

In answer the woman said a stiff good-bye and hung up.

Criscolle had to smile. She was a spunky bitch, he thought, and he liked those kind. A lot. The woman at FINVEST had been on the Aspis payroll since the beginning of the CMI investigation. She had earned her pay, but Nick had never succeeded in luring her into his New York bed. Not that it mattered much. He had his fill of women and always had.

Criscolle's real appetite was for young girls—around eighteen or nineteen. Whether he was in Rome, New York, or anywhere else in the world of Aspis, he'd go out of his way to secure one for an evening of fun—his kind of fun. He never hurt them badly, but he always hurt them in some way. That was the only way Nick Criscolle knew how to express himself to women. Sometimes they enjoyed his games, sometimes they didn't, but they always remembered the experience. They never cried about it afterward, for one menacing look from Nick assured their silence.

He was all business most of the time, though. The uncle who'd arranged for his early posts with Aspis expected him one day to inherit the top spot from Count Vignola. And he would grab it—nothing was as certain in his mind as that—whether or not the count liked it or approved it. He was tougher than Vignola—a lot tougher.

Criscolle made a face at his reflection in the large mirror over his living room fireplace. The Aspis credo, as laid down by the count, was to look clean no matter how dirty its linen might get. That wasn't Criscolle's style, though he was living with it for the moment.

The door buzzer sounded and Criscolle's spirits soared—his woman for the evening had arrived! A moment later he wore his most civilized smile while showing the flight attendant the view. An hour later Nick was hardly civilized as he surveyed the beautiful, squirming captive he'd just finished binding to the king-sized bed in his playroom.

Rosa was naked, her lush body an inviting sight to Criscolle's eyes. Her large breasts heaved with her labored breath and her broad hips wiggled as she fought against the restraints that held her down. She hadn't been exactly sure what he meant when he invited her into the bedroom for some "adult games and home movies," and now she was finding out firsthand. Although she was nervous, she was not yet frightened of her captor—she had taken her clothes off willingly, and she didn't know the truth about the man who was about to gag her to stifle her screams.

He was the same man who, as a child, enjoyed killing cats and other animals. He had been a teen who went on wild rampages of robbery and, eventually, rape, with a neighborhood gang of young hoodlums from a decrepit neighborhood in Brooklyn where too many kids dropped out of school by sixteen and were arrested for the first time by seventeen. And now he was a grown man with a twisted libido who could only feel joy by causing pain. And Rosa was his playmate of the moment.

Naked, Criscolle knelt on the bed and pressed the gag into Rosa's mouth. "I want you to scream," he said. "But I don't want anyone to hear."

With that, he leaned over and began to softly, sweetly caress her full, firm breasts and tenderly kiss the rising tips, which made Rosa relax and surrender until, suddenly, he viciously grabbed the large dark nipples of each breast between his fingertips and pinched hard. Rosa's body jolted upward but was pulled back by the restraints; a look of pain and fright crossed her face. Perspiration began to slide down the crevice between her breasts. Nick laughed out loud.

"Now," he announced for the benefit of the microphone of the videotape unit that was on a tripod at the foot of the bed, "the fun has just begun. Wait till later, baby. I'm gonna make you a star and then I'll show you the reruns. And if you're a good girl and let me have my way, I'll make sure your mother never sees the tape. Otherwise, I'll flood Italy with prints and sell the tape to cable TV. Nod, baby, if you read me loud and clear."

Rosa blinked back the tears and nodded in the affirmative. There was nothing she could do but succumb and try to ward off greater harm. Little did she know it was the best thing she could have done—she was so cooperative that Nick thought she was too easy. He sent her home in his limo just an hour later; she was still walking on her own two feet.

Not all of the women who crossed Nick Criscolle's path came away in such good shape. Unfortunately, his rugged features framed by wavy, dark hair that fell below his collar at the nape of his neck and a good cash flow lured women to him unremittingly; and he had no reservations about taking what he wanted without permission—even if it happened to be a woman's body.

Bradford got little sleep after leaving Sands's office.

Early the next morning, he showered to ease the soreness of his body and cleaned and rebandaged the bullet wounds on his fingers. Then he accessed his computer terminal and typed out a message to Tony Phipps in the London office:

WHAT NEWS ON BOCHLAINE? REPORT NOW.

Tony's response was almost immediate. He sent a two-page memo containing a complete biographical sketch on Frank Bochlaine, including his physical description—320 pounds, five-foot nine, rosy cheeks, large hands and forearms, enormous strength. Bochlaine won a bronze medal as a weightlifter in the 1964 Summer Olympics, spoke four languages—English, Italian, Spanish, and French—and had been a corporate officer of Aspis since 1974.

The report was necessarily sketchy since, Tony pointed out, no one except Aspis itself had a complete rundown on Bochlaine's activities. Bochlaine's office was Aspis's main office, located in Rome. His superior, who seemed to carry no corporate title, was an Italian count—one Raffaele Ernesto Vignola. There were only rumors, Tony wrote, that Vignola was Aspis's number one honcho, but they looked "pretty damned credible." There was also street talk that suggested that Aspis had occasionally "held hands with" the infamous Cosa Nostra, if they were not actual lovers.

But street talk, Bradford thought, studying the report, was not evidence.

Neither Aspis nor Bochlaine, Tony's report continued, had ever been caught in illegal activity. Aspis's burgeoning empire was so shrouded in mystery it could have been worth anywhere from ten or twenty million to a billion dollars or more. It had offices in a few capitals—New York, Hong Kong, and Zurich as well as Rome—but conducted large portions of its dealings from the offices of wholly and partially owned banks and other subsidiaries all over Europe, the Far East, and Latin America. Aspis's overseers were always on the move, it seemed, and that was the case with Bochlaine, who had been a consultant with Cinema Services and served similarly with a number of other Aspis-owned companies around the world in the past ten years.

But Tony's information did not connect Bochlaine or Cinema Services's mother company directly or indirectly to any past dirty dealings that might have involved violence. The only violence in sight was the suicide of World Fruit's Bob Walters, and there was no evidence that it was murder.

Bradford keyed a code into Max and fed the names Tony had mentioned in his report to the computer, looking for additional information. Vignola's name produced only the obscure fact that the Italian count was a frequent visitor to the Vatican and had been received on occasion by several cardinals and, once, by the Pope. No help there.

Tony had said Nicholas Criscolle was an Aspis lieutenant of Vignola and that he worked out of Rome. Max found Criscolle in several files FINVEST had established over the years, but Aspis was not a part of any of the files. Were the companies affiliated somehow with Aspis? Did Aspis own them? If so, what difference did it make?

By seven o'clock Brad was bone-weary again, his mind filled with information dredged up by Max. He sat in the antique wing chair in his living room and stared out through the window at the Hudson River far below. But his mind was not on the view. It was on the quiet desperation in Ellie Sands's voice when she'd phoned him at eleven o'clock last night.

"Brad? The police are here. They say . . ." Ellie's voice had cracked, then trailed off for a second before resuming. "Oh, God, Brad! They say Jack's dead. That he killed himself!"

"No! That can't be, Ellie. I saw him today at lunch."

Ellie had begun to sob. "I don't know how," she wailed, "but suicide, Brad! They claim he did it himself. Shot himself right there in his office. Oh, God, I think I want to die!"

"Easy, Ellie," Brad said, trying to comfort her. "Tell me about it."

He had listened as Jack's wife blurted out everything she knew, then told her, "Jack wouldn't kill himself. Don't you believe it for a minute." It was both what Ellie wanted to hear and the truth, though it couldn't help her much and Brad knew it.

"They showed me a note. It . . .," Ellie couldn't continue and finally quieted.

"Do you want me to come over? I can be there in twenty minutes."

Ellie hesitated for a moment, then said, "Come tomorrow morning, Brad. I'll get through the night somehow."

"How's Holly?"

"She fell apart when the homicide inspector told us. She's in the bathroom right now pulling herself together. We're going to the morgue."

Bradford knew someone would have to identify the body, even though Jack had been found sitting behind his desk in his office. "Why don't you go tomorrow, Ellie? What's their hurry?"

"It's not their hurry, Brad. We want to go now. Maybe . . . maybe it's all a big mistake. Maybe it wasn't Jack that was killed at all. Maybe." Again Brad heard her muffled sobs. He wished there was some way he could comfort her. He knew, intimately, her pain.

After Ellie's call he had turned on his television set and watched a late news bulletin that mentioned the apparent suicide of the CEO of TNI, but the commentator did not identify him. The body had been discovered by cleaning personnel shortly before eight o'clock.

Now Brad shook off the memory and stared sightlessly out his window, still finding it hard to believe the events of last night.

Was the man he chased down the fire stairs Frank Bochlaine? In his mind, Brad conjured up the rosy-cheeked, cherubic face of the fat man he had noticed in the TNI building elevator just before noon. He wished Tony Phipps had come up with a photo of Bochlaine. If Bradford's guess was correct and Bochlaine had been in the elevator with him, there had to be some significance to the Italian's earlier visit.

Brad's expression was woeful as he rose from his chair and went to the kitchen for a fresh cup of coffee. As he poured it, he thought about all the early morning cups of coffee he had shared with Jack Sands, both in Vermont and here in the city. What would his life be like without Jack? Only Ellie and Holly could possibly miss Jack as much. Brad now remembered that he had promised to be at the Sands's brownstone on East 87th Street by ten, so he took his coffee to the desk in his study, the apartment's spare bedroom, and flipped on his computer.

He typed out a message and e-mailed it to Linda Hamilton at the office, informing her that he'd be with Eleanor Sands this morning and wouldn't get to the office before eleven.

Then he punched out the code of FINVEST's Rome office and instructed Murray Jolles, the officer in charge, to find out if Frank Bochlaine had booked a flight in or out of Rome during the past three or four days. Jolles, once an official in the Italian government after serving as an officer of the Banca di Roma, was so well-connected in Italy that there was little he could not accomplish if given time to do so. He spoke English like an American and French only a little less fluently than a Frenchman in addition to his native Italian.

"Also," Bradford typed, "there is an American named Nicholas Criscolle with the Rome headquarters of Aspis. See Tony's report from London and have someone good check Criscolle and Bochlaine out. Send all information ASAP by encrypted e-mail. If you can confirm that Bochlaine is in Rome, I will fly there later today, so your fastest reply is needed. End."

Was Bochlaine back in Rome? Or was he still in New York—perhaps even now stationed nearby waiting to gun down Bradford? Wherever he was, Brad was determined to find him. He kept a suitcase in the office containing a change of clothes for emergency trips and would use it without hesitation if Murray confirmed that Bochlaine had returned to Rome.

Now Bradford keyed an addendum to Linda, telling her to expect a communiqué from Jolles about Bochlaine's whereabouts. He told her to make a reservation for him on a flight to Rome if it turned out that Bochlaine was indeed there. He did not explain to his assistant the reason for his interest in Bochlaine or his need to follow the Italian to Rome.

A call to Tom Sumereau's apartment went unanswered, and Brad wondered if Tom had yet heard the news about Jack. Tom's wife, Jane, a museum curator, was an early riser who usually left by seven o'clock for work, as did Tom. Since it was nearly eight o'clock, Brad decided they must both be on their way to work by now, Tom to BMC where he was busy securing the information he needed for a FINVEST quote and Jane to her office at the Guggenheim.

At last Brad left the computer console, put on his suit coat, and went downstairs to wait for Danny, whom he had contacted earlier. The taxi pulled up in front of the high-rise shortly after Bradford emerged from its entrance.

It was only a little past nine when Brad's cab reached the Sands's brownstone. There were no tears in Eleanor Sands's eyes when she greeted Brad in her doorway, his name on her soft, wide mouth.

"It's all right, Ellie," Brad murmured as the tears finally came, and she retreated into the house with him close behind. He wrapped his long arms around her, and she buried her face against his neck, releasing a torrent of words and tears.

"How could it have happened, Brad? How could he be dead? My Jack. Our Jack! He had everything to live for. *Everything*. Oh, Brad. Brad! Tell me it's not true, that the body I saw last night wasn't really Jack, that it was really a nightmare. Tell me I'm going to wake up soon and find Jack here with me again, alive and well. Tell me."

Brad wished he could, but of course could not. "I'd gladly take his place if I could," he told her. "You know how I felt about him."

Ellie was ten years younger than her husband and some people might have called the honey blonde "well preserved." In her mid-fifties, she had a youthful face and figure, with a youthful attitude to match. She was a classy and cosmopolitan dresser who had learned to imitate her style from the pages of upscale magazines like *Town and Country*, but you could tell she had a soul made of concrete from a lifetime that had endured more tough spots than easy rides. The seventh daughter of an Irish immigrant steelworker in Pittsburgh who died before any of his children reached a tenth birthday, she had been born poor and lived that way for many years. Her father's premature death left Ellie's mother to fend for herself and her brood and somehow raise them as decent human beings. Ellie never let life beat her; Jack used to say his wife had "good old-fashioned Irish spirit and spunk." When Jack Sands had introduced himself to his future wife, Ellie had been swept away by a man who spat in the face of life and wrestled it at every opportunity. After they were married, she had never had to worry again about creature comforts, love or security.

Until now.

On the way over in the cab, Brad had cautioned himself not to expose what he had witnessed the evening before. Not yet. It would do her no good. Later he would tell her the whole story.

He regarded her tenderly. She was soft, yet determined; bright and open and direct, yet inoffensive; honest, yet tactful. Alive and glad of it. But now things had changed. A part of her very being was gone—ripped from her grasp suddenly, violently. Horribly.

Ellie fell into Brad's embrace as they stood for a moment in the foyer of the town house. He held her as sobs slipped from her throat and she mourned her loss. For the first time, Brad had to play the rock for Ellie and Holly; it was a responsibility he welcomed in one way, and feared in another, if only because his own pain was so deep.

"I know what it's like to have the guts ripped out of your life, to lose someone so special that you think you'll never get over it," he comforted. "But you know what—you make it through, and things get better somehow. But I won't lie to you Ellie—you never forget, and you can never totally let them go. And you shouldn't have to."

He hugged her as her sobs grew louder and then, suddenly, she stopped weeping.

"He was such a great man, Brad, such a powerhouse. He'd flip if he saw me spending my time all red-eyed and mopey. At least I still have our daughter; he would want me to be strong for her." Ellie pulled away, straightened her posture and dabbed her eyes with a handkerchief redolent of jasmine.

"Where is Holly?" Brad asked.

Ellie said nothing as they walked side by side into the large, airy living room with its plush yellow and maroon draperies and comfortable decorator furnishings that Ellie herself had chosen. "She's upstairs, Brad, crying her eyes out," Ellie said finally. "She'll be down. I told her you were coming. I don't . . . can't find the right words to say to her." Her eyes seemed to add a plea: Would you calm her somehow?

He understood. "I'll see what I can do."

"I know you will, Brad. She loved her father dearly, though she fought with him—with both of us for that matter—quite a bit. And she loves you, too. Worships the ground you walk on."

Brad knew that all too well, because from the time she was a teen, until the time she turned twenty, Holly had stalked him like a predator. But in the past two years, she'd taken a more subtle approach to try to turn him on—bringing home dozens of college men, some for weekends at Winterhaven, when she knew Brad would be there. Ah, the stunning young Holly had learned the ways of a woman and attempted to set off Brad's jealousy alarm. But Brad still saw her as a kid, his little Kitten, sort of a sister because her dad is—was—like Brad's adopted father.

But there was no denying that Holly had blossomed into a beauty— with wide green eyes and a bright smile. Her soft features, pale skin, and curvaceous yet slight body provided a sweet mixture of all-American-girl-next-door and sultry vixen. She, too, had been blessed with a fiery Irish spirit.

"Brad?" Ellie's eyes were imploring as she looked up at him. "Jack. He didn't do what they claim. I know he didn't. Jack is . . . was brave as a lion." She held herself ramrod erect, tense with nervous energy, yet more in command of herself than Brad had thought she would have been.

"No, Ellie," he replied in a near whisper, "I'm sure he didn't kill himself."

"Brad!" Puffy-eyed Holly Sands stood in the wide doorway of the living room, her pink velour robe wrinkled all over as if she'd slept in it. Holly's tear-stained face was without makeup except for the remains of her lipstick when she ran across the room to Brad, throwing herself into his arms.

Holly tore at Brad's emotions even more than did her mother, for Holly, though she was not a typically spoiled jet-setter, had never known the kind of adversity Eleanor Sands had. "Easy, Kitten," he said, stroking her soft yellow hair as she sobbed against his neck. "If Jack were here right now he'd chew you out for crying over him."

She pulled back and met his eyes defiantly. "You're right, Brad," she declared, "but only because Daddy was so unselfish. Only because he was so much a man he couldn't stand to see a woman cry around him. Especially Mom or me. He'd have done anything to cheer us up. I remember once he tried to stand on his head to turn my crying into laughing. He miscalculated and fell over and hurt his nose. Then I cried for him."

A half-smile now appeared on her face at the memory, like a rainbow among the rain clouds. But it died a quick death, overwhelmed as it was by the grim reality of her father's fate. At last she calmed, her green eyes met Brad's again, and she said, "Give me a reason Daddy would kill himself, Brad. Just one good reason; I just don't understand."

"I don't blame you," Brad said. "Neither do I. And as I told your mother, I'm just as sure as I can be that he didn't."

"The police are sure he did," Ellie said. "The young lieutenant, Burke was his name, kept asking us both to tell him why Jack was depressed enough to do such a thing."

"Why are the police so dumb?" Holly broke in. "Daddy wasn't depressed. He was happy. He had no reason to shoot himself—none at all.

Why can't they see that? All they're good for is chasing speeders and writing parking tickets." She dissolved into tears akin to her anger.

"What exactly did Burke say, Ellie?" Brad asked.

"That there was no indication that it was anything but a suicide. It was Jack's gun, and he had powder burns on his hand, the lieutenant said. Jack's fingerprints were on the gun, too. Does that mean there's no doubt that he pulled the trigger?"

"It supports the suicide theory, Ellie. But people don't kill themselves without a motive, and Jack didn't have a motive."

"I don't believe Jack could have written that note," Ellie said. "It's just . . . well, not what he'd write. If he was really going to do himself in, he'd have said so. He didn't mince words."

"Do you think that someone killed him, Brad?" Holly asked, her eyes searching his face. "Was it murder?"

Brad hesitated. "I believe it was, but it's going to take a lot of proving in the face of the overwhelming suicide evidence."

"The cops aren't going to prove that," Holly said.

Brad could feel the eyes of both mother and daughter on him, weighing his resolve to verify what they all felt in their hearts. "I know," he said. "That's why I'm going to try. It's the least I can do for him and for you."

"But how? If the cops can't or won't do it, how can you? You're no detective."

"Maybe not, Holly," Brad told her, "but I used to be in army intelligence, and there are more than a few associates who think I'm a reasonably smart guy. My business is private investigations—more or less. Of course, they're financial rather than criminal and mostly involve companies and not individuals, but the technique is the same."

"Where would you start? Do you have any clues? Is there something you haven't told us about Daddy's death?"

Brad recognized the anger in Holly's expression and quickly reassured her. "I know your Dad was supposed to meet with someone last night around the time he died, and I intend to locate him to see what he knows about what happened."

"Who is he, Brad? Do the police know about him? Is he missing? Has he run away?" Holly was full of questions.

Brad parried them all. "I'll answer all your questions, Kitten," he said, "after I find the guy. As for the police, I'll toss this in their lap after I question him. Meanwhile, don't say anything to Burke or anyone else. All right?"

Eleanor Sands looked at Bradford searchingly, but did not ask the questions that seemed to be on her lips. Neither of them noticed the new respect for Brad on Holly's face or the gleam in her eyes.

Brad reached his office just after eleven and was greeted by Olga Xirau, Tom Sumereau's personal assistant, in the reception area. "You just missed the police, Brad," Olga told him. "Lieutenant Burke wanted to question you about your lunch date with Jack Sands yesterday. I'm so sorry. I heard what happened. It's in all the papers."

Bradford bit his lip as he read the sincere regret on the face of Tom's aide, whose normally bright smile had turned into a sympathetic frown. "Is there anything I can do?" she asked.

"Thanks, but no. Is Tom in yet? Did he talk to Burke?"

Olga shook her head. "He's still at BMC. He'll be in about noon, but I told Lieutenant Burke that he wouldn't be here until late in the day, around the time you were expected."

"Good thinking, Olga. That'll give me time to figure out what to tell him if he wants to know what Jack and I were talking about over lunch."

"Did our report on CSI have anything to do with his suicide, Brad?"

Brad shrugged. It would do no good to discuss his suspicions with Olga. He wanted no flak from anyone while he was running down the one clue he had to Jack's death. "I need to talk to Tom," he said, dismissing the woman. "Ask him to see me the minute he gets in."

Linda wasn't in her office, Brad noticed as he strode past it. In his office he found a message from Murray in Rome. Bochlaine, Murray reported, had flown to New York under his own name Monday and was booked on a return flight today. Murray had not yet located the fat Italian's residence.

The postscript Linda had written let Brad know that she had booked him on an afternoon flight to Rome and had already faxed a note to Murray to meet him at Leonardo da Vinci International Airport at six o'clock A.M., Rome time.

Rome. Brad turned to gaze out over the New York skyline as he thought about the ancient city. The Holy City it was called. Brad had been there often, but just once since Nan's death. He could have gone there more frequently, but he avoided it because of its resplendent Catholicism, which was painful as it reminded him of Nancy and the boys.

Now the death of Jack Sands was forcing him to go back, and he wished he wasn't. Bochlaine, he knew, might be impossible to find. Or the man might refuse to talk to him. Perhaps the Italian might even add Brad to his list of corpses. This was no means an impossible contingency.

Perhaps, on the other hand, Bochlaine was as innocent as a newborn babe and had nothing at all to do with either Jack's death or the suicide of Bob Walters. If so, the trip to Rome was an impetuous journey designed by Brad's tortured mind simply to get him away from New York at a difficult time for him.

And yet . . .

A thought now struck him. Had Linda pulled the files on World Fruit and CMI and forgotten to replace them? Were they in her desk? Brad was more than curious about that and now went to his aide's office and opened her file drawer. Quickly he went through the files contained in it. Nothing. A further search of the rest of her desk produced no more, and he returned to his office. He was just finishing a short conversation with Jack's personal lawyer and financial adviser, Al Spencer, about the funeral and Ellie's financial state when Linda came in.

"I just can't believe Jack Sands committed suicide," she declared after Brad had hung up the phone. "Did he give you any hint that he was on the verge of killing himself, Brad?"

Brad again suppressed the urge to refute the idea that Jack had killed himself. Instead he shook his head and asked, "Do you have any idea what happened to our files on World Fruit and CMI?" His voice was cold rather than casual as he had intended it, but Linda didn't seem to notice.

"They ought to be in the computer room safe, Brad," she replied.

"They're not. Have you seen them recently? Or pulled them?"

"We haven't done any work for World Fruit since Milt Farr took over as president after Walters's death. I haven't had any reason to pull the files." She hesitated. "Maybe they're misfiled. I can check."

"Do that, Linda. And ask around the office about them. They must be here somewhere. Were there any calls?"

"Jack Sands's daughter called. She sounded pretty upset and who could blame her, poor kid."

"I was with her and Eleanor earlier. What did she want?"

"She forgot to ask you to call her when you've talked with the man you mentioned to her. She didn't give me his name. I told her I'd remind you to call when you got back from Rome."

"With luck I might even get back tomorrow night, Linda. By the way, I just got through talking to Al Spencer. He's going to give the office a call when the funeral arrangements are made. Put it on the fax to Murray in Rome as soon as it comes in. Okay?"

"No problem. Oh, Les Sawyer called. He said to thank you for sending Frank Bartlett to him. That you shouldn't worry about him. Les seems to think Bartlett will be a solid addition to his firm."

"I'm glad for both of them and I hope to hell he's right," Brad declared. That was the only good thing that had happened in the last twenty-four hours.

"Who is this Bochlaine you're going to Rome to see, Brad?"

"He's a special rep with Cinema Services. Jack mentioned to me at lunch that he was supposed to see Bochlaine last night. I just want to find out what Jack may have told him, since he may be the last one to have seen Jack alive."

Linda's raised her left eyebrow at the unorthodox nature of Bradford's mission. "Shall I arrange for a cab, or will you take a company car?" she inquired.

"A cab will be all right. And by the way, keep my Rome trip and Bochlaine's name confidential."

Linda looked as if she was about to ask why, but did not.

Not long after Linda's return to the office, Tom Sumereau arrived. A somewhat shorter, slightly rounder figure than his tall, wiry partner, he ambled into Brad's office. "I can't believe Jack's dead, Brad. Did he seem depressed when you saw him? How did he react to the report on Plymouth Films and CSI?"

"He was just fine, Tom."

"Christ!" Tom declared, staring across the desk at his partner. "Did you see the papers? The *News* put a picture of the TNI building on its front page—with a white arrow pointing to his window and two-inch headlines happily informing the whole damned world that Jack just blew himself away. They even got a picture of the interior of Jack's office, showing with a white tape body outline how he was found with his brains blown out."

Brad shrugged. He had seen the paper and there was nothing to be done about it. Suicides always made banner headlines if they were spectacular enough or if the person was well-known.

"What happened to your hand?" Tom asked now, noticing the bandages on his partner's fingers.

"Scraped them," Brad said noncommittally, watching Tom rise and walk over to the wet bar on the far wall for a Perrier. Sumereau poured them each a glass and brought the two glasses back to Brad's desk, then sat after handing Brad one of them. As Tom raised the glass in mock salute, Brad delivered a bombshell. "Jack didn't pull the trigger."

In the tense silence that followed, Tom quickly rose and returned to the bar. "Jesus," he muttered. He opened a half-bottle of Remy Martin poured about three fingers in a snifter and gulped the cognac. He punctuated his swallow with a coughing fit. Then he looked hard at his partner. "How the hell do you know that? How can you know that? Not unless . . ."

"I was there, Tom. I was outside the door when he was killed, and I'm positive he didn't pull the trigger, because he wasn't alone. He was murdered."

Sumereau downed the remainder of his drink and poured himself a second while Brad related what had happened at the TNI suite last night. When Brad finished describing his chase after the killer, Tom said, "The guy shot at you? That's how you scraped your fingers?"

In answer, Brad pulled off the bandages and displayed the scored finger tips. "I was lucky, Tom. They'll be healed in a day or two. Jack's wound was fatal."

Tom shivered. "They play for keeps, don't they? Why didn't you run all that by the police? Why let it stand as a suicide?"

"Mainly because the only man who knows for certain that it wasn't suicide is Bochlaine, and he's not likely to admit it to anyone. Not if he's the killer. I figured he probably would take off for Rome right afterward, and I was right. That's why I'm booked on a flight to Rome this afternoon."

"Maybe he's not the killer, Brad. It's possible that he's innocent or that he arrived for his appointment with Jack after seven-thirty, not before."

"I doubt it, but if he did, he'll talk to me when I run him down in Rome. If he won't talk, and I can't force him to talk . . ."

"Hey, you're not going to do anything rash, are you?" Tom broke in, fearing his partner's potential rage.

Bradford's answering smile was bleak. "I've dealt with killers before. In Vietnam I made a spy spill his guts with my bare hands. It wasn't my idea of a party, and I have no thought of doing the same with Bochlaine, guilty or not."

"Do you think our report could have caused Bochlaine to murder Jack?"

Sumereau was plainly nervous about the possibility, and Brad understood why, for Tom was the "Mr. Soft" of the company, the opposite of Brad, who had always been a fighter, not afraid to risk his life in a war no one wanted. Tom, a computer wizard, had an agile mind no less wise than the computers he fiddled with, but he was not very physical. Brad skied, sailed, played tennis and racquetball, and could chase a murderer while toting his own .38. Tom could play as bold a game of chess as any man short of a grand master but looked silly playing ping pong. Tom lacked the stomach for guns or war.

"What I think isn't important, Tom. The facts are that FINVEST has done reports for World Fruit and TNI, both of them dealing with thievery by subsidiary companies of this Aspis outfit. As near as I can tell, these are our only contacts with Aspis or companies it owns. In each case the CEO of our client has, within days of the delivery of our reports, apparently committed suicide."

"Of course there is no way we can know for sure whether the suicide of Bob Walters was real, but I'm sure that Jack's was murder. From what I know of Bob Walters's character, I'd be surprised now to learn that Bob really did himself in, though I suppose it's always possible."

Tom finished his second drink. "Our missing files on CMI and World Fruit could mean trouble. We could have a mole working for us. It's something we've never considered before." He stretched his fingers into the shape of a tent and looked over them at his partner. "What are we going to do about that?" he asked gloomily.

"Nothing for the moment. But don't tell anyone what I've just told you. And be more careful than ever before with the data we handle. Especially anything I tell you about what I learn in Rome. Don't trust anybody."

"What about that cop? He'll be showing up again, from what Olga says."

"Tell Lieutenant Burke I had to go out of town on business. Don't tell him where. I've typed into Max a complete rundown on what happened last night and what my conclusions are. It's entered under my private code and only you and I can call it up. If anything should happen to me in Rome, pull it out of Max and deliver it to Burke right away."

"For God's sake, Brad, don't talk like that! Nothing's going to happen to you."

Brad smiled thinly. "I hope you're right, Tom. But if the reports we made for Bob and Jack got them killed, who's to say we're not next on Bochlaine's list?"

Tom whistled. He looked far more worried than usual in spite of the slight buzz the liquor was producing. Watching him, Brad felt a wave of sympathy for his partner, who had a reputation as a worrier that went back many years. Tom could always find a dark cloud around the silver lining the office joke went. Right now he might have a real reason to fear.

Brad hoped he did not.

Across town Holly Sands sat before the dressing table in her bedroom and surveyed her image in the mirror. She had carefully applied her makeup and aside from her eyes, which were a little puffy, she decided, her face would do. Barely. She stood and crossed the room to her private bathroom, where she inspected her reflection in the full-length mirror on the door. She shrugged. Pretty, perhaps, but not beautiful. Although her creamy white legs and taut breasts were assets she could honestly appreciate, she often viewed herself as too short and too thin, rather underdeveloped instead of voluptuous.

Her father, she thought, had always conned her by telling her she was gorgeous and for a while she had believed him. To Jack Sands she was always "Princess" Holly, whose enchanted mirror would never deny that she was without question the "fairest of them all." She made a face now and pushed the thought from her mind, knowing that she had to, if she were to accomplish her secret plan of action.

A cab would soon arrive to take her to the airport, and she wanted to be ready. Her suitcase was packed, and she had removed her "mad money" from its hiding place in the bottom of her jewelry box so she would have plenty of cash as well as her credit cards.

But first there was her mother to contend with. Holly sighed at the thought. She loved her mother, but had wondered if she wasn't a little jealous of the attentions her father always paid her. Her mom was always chastising her for one thing or another. She still had not accepted that Holly was twenty-two years old—old enough to have affairs with men, to stay out all night on occasion, or even to get married.

It was not that Holly wanted to marry, though she had in recent years had affairs and stayed out all night. What she wanted was a life of her own, free of the restrictions that even loving parents placed upon her. She had for some time now been trying to muster the courage to leave the nest, but it wasn't easy. Her mother had openly discouraged her, and while her father had agreed in principle that she ought to go her own way and experience life independently of them, he kept postponing her leaving for one reason or another.

Holly's education had begun at various exclusive private schools during her father's business journey from the oil fields of Texas to important corporate positions in Houston, Los Angeles, and finally New York, and it had concluded with four years at Princeton—over the protests of Mom and Dad, who had wanted her to go to Vassar or Bryn Mawr.

She had enjoyed the years at Princeton, especially the last two, when she'd had an one bedroom apartment. Although Holly lived alone, her affairs had been few, not because she wasn't popular with the boys, but because she found most of the young Princetonians immature and self-centered. Their idea of a fine evening was to get drunk at the university's famed eating clubs and hit on equally drunk young women until one finally acquiesced to their crude advances. The finale was, of course, a night of bumbling passion.

A little booze was all right, but the sex was awful at best. It wasn't that she felt used or soiled afterward—simply disappointed. Not one of her lovers had that special combination of strength and sensitivity that she saw in her father or Brad, at least that's how it seemed to her.

More importantly, Holly had learned self-reliance at Princeton and felt certain she could make her way in the world if given a chance. She had majored in English and literature and could teach if she chose to. Or better yet, she could write. That was something she really liked to do. The trouble was—or so her creative writing professor had told her—she hadn't yet lived enough to write interesting prose. Her life had been "too much peaches and whipped cream and not enough hot peppers and shit on a shingle," he said. Did that mean she had to throw away her money and figure out some way to experience the hell of poverty or crime or punishment?

Holly had considered her college days as infinitely more positive and free than living a sterile life in New York with Mom and Dad. Her father's death had shaken her core, however, and viciously snatched Jack's presence and his fortitude from her. But she was determined to steady herself and get on with her life. Starting now.

Eleanor Sands was sitting at the desk in Jack's study trying to remember what Al Spencer, Jack's lawyer, had told her during his brief visit. All she really recalled was that the funeral mass would be in St. Patrick's Cathedral at noon Saturday, that arrangements had been made to bury Jack in the Rutland cemetery plot near Winterhaven they had bought together, and that Jack had left her "well provided."

"Mother?"

Holly's voice startled her, but her appearance surprised Ellie Sands more, for as she cleared her head of somber thoughts, she saw that Holly was dressed, had her coat on, and was holding a suitcase.

"I'm going to Rome, Mother," Holly said. "Brad's booked on a flight out of Kennedy this afternoon, and I've got a reservation on it, too. I want—I need—to help."

Ellie shook her head, doubtful. "How can you help him, Holly? And what about Daddy's funeral?"

"I don't know how I can help, but I've got to try. If I stay here, all I'll do till Saturday is cry. I've done enough of that already. So I'm going. I'm sorry that I'm leaving you right now, but I'll be back by Friday night. I'll be at the funeral. Don't worry."

Ellie's struggled to sensibly respond to Holly's news. The events of the past twenty-four hours were overwhelming and Ellen Sands felt helpless in their wake. Holly—going to Rome with Brad? "Did Brad say it was all right for you to go with him?" she asked her daughter.

"He doesn't know I'm going yet. But I'm sure he'll go along with it." She hoped she wasn't lying.

Ellie had risen as she and Holly talked and now she stood before her daughter. "I wish you'd change your mind and stay with me," she said softly. Any strength that Ellen might have had to refute Holly was gone. "I need you here, but I can understand why you want to go."

"It's not just want to, Mom, it's have to! I have to feel that I'm helping Brad find Daddy's killer, that I'm doing something to help Dad. I don't want to stay home crying when some crazed lunatic may be in Rome. I need to get away from all this. "

Ellie shook her head wearily. She didn't agree that Holly should go and would have argued the point more strongly, but knew it would accomplish nothing other than to upset both of them. There was a tinge of anger in Holly's voice already. She was as stubborn as her father was at his "Irish stubbornest," as he used to put it. She would go, whether or not Ellie agreed that she should. She moved closer to Holly and reached out to her. Holly moved inside her arms and they hugged.

"Call me when you get to Rome," Ellie said.

"I will. I promise."

"Do you have money?"

"Plenty, Mom, don't worry. And credit cards, too. The plane leaves soon, I've got to get going. Take care of yourself. I love you." Holly kissed her mother on the mouth and fought back the tears that threatened to spill down her cheeks.

Ellie Sands forced a smile. "I love you, too, darling. Much more than you could ever know. You were Daddy's Princess, but mine as well. And you always will be, honey, headstrong or not. Now get out of here right now before we both start bawling again."

Holly needed no urging. She fled, and her cab arrived in front of the brownstone minutes after she'd begun pacing the sidewalk.

Brad was preparing to leave when Linda flagged him down from her office. She was on the telephone. "There's a call for you," she told him, her hand covering the mouthpiece.

"Who is it?"

"A man, but he won't give me his name. He insists on talking to you."

"Tell him I refuse to talk to callers who won't give their names."

Linda uncovered the mouthpiece and relayed Brad's words. Then her eyes grew large as the caller identified himself. She covered the mouthpiece again and looked up at Brad. "Will you talk to Frank Bochlaine?" she asked.

FOUR

Bradford ran into his office and kicked the door closed behind him. Bochlaine? Would he talk to the fat Italian? You're damned right he would.

Picking up the phone, he murmured a quick, "I've got it, Linda," then waited until he heard a click on the line that told him she'd hung up before saying, "Bochlaine? Did you keep your appointment with Jack Sands last night?"

"Is this Elliot Bradford?"

"You know damned well . . ."

"Who was your commanding officer in army intelligence, Mr. Bradford?"

"Are you serious?"

"I must confirm your identity."

"My CO in Nam was Major Whiting—Andrew Whiting. Okay?" Bochlaine had surprised him with this one. If he really knew that Whiting was his superior in Saigon, the Italian had to have some hot connections. Information like that was classified and not easy to acquire, even years after the war's end.

Now Bochlaine spoke again. "You are familiar with me, Mr. Bradford? And the firm for which I work?"

"You work for Cinema Services among others, Bochlaine. And Aspis. And you were supposed to see Jackson Sands last night. I want to know if you did." Bradford's voice was icy, and he wished he could make it even more so.

"I will tell you, Mr. Bradford, but not until we meet. You will come to Rome, and take a room at the Londra Hotel near the Piazza Fiume. I will be in touch with you there."

"The hell I will, Bochlaine. I want some answers now. If you want me to travel all the way to Rome, you'll have to . . ." The sound of the telephone's click penetrated his consciousness. He was talking to dead air. Bochlaine had hung up.

Bradford yelled the man's name into the mouthpiece a few times before a dial tone reached his ears, then he slammed the phone down and cursed. If he had any doubts about his trip to Rome before, they were gone now. He had to go. And yet . . . was Bochlaine luring him there to kill him? When they met it would be in a place of the Italian's choosing and Bradford would have to be careful if he were to keep from meeting the same fate as Jack Sands. Under normal circumstances, Brad would stay at FINVEST's spacious corporate apartment in Rome.

He was deep in thought as he picked up the suitcase he kept packed and ready in his office closet and walked into Linda's office. "Book me a room at the Londra in Rome for the next two nights," he instructed. "If I don't need the second night, I'll cancel it when I'm there."

"Was that really Bochlaine, Brad?" Linda asked as she scribbled the hotel's name on a piece of scrap paper on her desk.

Brad nodded, only half listening to his assistant as he silently repeated his conversation with Bochlaine. "Tell Tom about the call from Bochlaine. I'm to meet Bochlaine tomorrow."

Ten minutes later Brad occupied the back seat of a cab whose driver had grinned enthusiastically when he gave Kennedy Airport as their destination.

As the cab sped over the Queensboro Bridge, Brad caught a glimpse of the bright red Roosevelt Island tram before hurtling east on Queens Boulevard. Brad again wondered how someone Bochlaine's size could have descended the fire stairs at the TNI building as fast as he had last night. If the reports on the Italian were to be believed, he was a muscle-bound weightlifter and would not be able to move with such agility.

Bochlaine's voice had been smooth and cultured, his English impeccable, but that was not surprising for a man who worked for an international firm and often had to deal with English-speaking clients, both in Europe and in America.

Aspis. Brad's thoughts wandered back to what Tony had told him about the firm. Was Bochlaine purely and simply an Aspis front-runner? Was Aspis, as Tony's reports had implied, in league with the Mafia? Or was it simply a super successful financial organization that had acquired several firms of questionable business ethics? If he got a chance to talk to Bochlaine, he hoped to find out more about Aspis.

If he got a chance to talk to Bochlaine. Was it a long shot? He hoped not.

The taxi now swung onto Van Wyck Expressway, a concrete highway that became so clogged with cars at certain times of the day that this part of Queens became a series of narrow, winding parking lots. Traffic was moving along briskly today, for the month was March, not June, and it was early afternoon, not rush hour.

The female cabbie sported dirty, stringy hair that cascaded over her right eye, covering half her face. She was not attractive, but she was chatty, as many New York cabbies were. Brad had long ago learned to parry talkative cabbies by simply nodding occasionally as they rambled on to demonstrate he was listening.

But this was not midtown Manhattan, rather a parkway that demanded a driver's rapt attention. Maria Gonzales, as her cab license and the horrible mug shot next to the meter proclaimed, seemed as a good a driver as most New York cabbies, but Brad knew he would feel a whole lot better if the woman stopped talking. He told her so with a smile on his face, hoping not to upset her.

"Don't worry, good-looking," she said grinning at him in her rear-view mirror. "I'll get you there in one piece." She put special emphasis on the last word, then giggled. Brad wondered if she went back to her garage at night and bragged about the men she'd leered at that day.

His wondering came to an abrupt end as automotive chaos unexpectedly surrounded him. A silver Lincoln came out of nowhere as Maria tried to change lanes and ease her cab toward the entrance to JFK. The big car cut her off and forced her toward the concrete median. The woman cursed loudly, fought the wheel, then lost control of the vehicle as the Lincoln swerved toward the divider and forced the cab up against the concrete. The cab flipped sideways atop the barrier, balanced in midair for an extended moment, and then plunged down the other side, roof first in the westbound lanes and straight into the path of fast-moving traffic.

Just as the cab landed upside down on the pavement the first of the westbound cars, a bright yellow Geo Prism, crashed into it and bounced back, only to be struck two cars from behind. A dozen other cars careened into each other, all going too fast to stop or maneuver around the obstruction, but one car—a brand new Acura—stopped cold at the end of the line. The anti-lock brakes earned the driver a full-force hit from the car behind him.

Maria's scream was lost in the sound of grinding, tortured metal as the cab slid on its roof across the lanes of traffic after being hit by the Prism. Now it was pummeled by a new line of cars. The next car to make impact with the cab was a classic VW Bug, whose driver was the first to die in the crash—squeezed between the accordioned front baggage space of his car and a rear engine rammed into the front seat.

Bradford hit his head and fell unconscious as the cab rolled repeatedly before it came to rest teetering on its side at the edge of the westbound lanes of the parkway. Then the battered machine fell back over onto its four wheels and lay still.

Minutes later Bradford blinked and opened his eyes wide as the memory of the accident struck him. Looking around him, he wondered dumbly what had happened to Maria, so he sat up and leaned forward to see if she was all right. He found her lying unconscious across the front seat, blood from a gash in her temple smeared over her upturned face. Reaching over, he grabbed her wrist and was relieved to find a steady pulse. As he tried to exit through a jammed door, a police helicopter landed nearby and two big officers hastily pried open the door using the jaws of life. They quickly extricated the driver.

"You need to go to the hospital, buddy?" one cop asked as they returned to the helicopter.

"Is anybody hurt?" Bradford asked, eyeing the wrecked cars strewn all over the road.

The chopper crew member shook his head. "There's a guy over there in a Volkswagen that hit you, he's bought it—dead as yesterday's horse race. My partner will get him out of the way, and I'll pick him up next trip. Your driver's okay, but she'll need some bandaging."

"I've got to make a plane, officer. Take the woman. I guess I can get to the terminal on foot."

The cop grinned. "You won't have to," he said. "I can have the pilot drop you right over there on the grass, in front of the terminal. Are you sure you're okay?"

Having been escorted to the airport after a paramedic declared him unharmed, a slightly dazed Elliot Bradford, his suit coat dirty and torn, carried his bag into the terminal building housing Alitalia. He made it to the plane just as the flight attendants were closing the doors and preparing for takeoff.

Hours earlier in Rome, a hulk of a man had kept an appointment. Graceful in spite of his size, Frank Bochlaine strolled the narrow winding walks that led through the courtyard of St. Paul's Outside-the-Walls. The setting sun, yellow and lush in the Italian sky, accentuated the richness of the mosaic saints on the church's exterior.

Bochlaine, realizing that he was early, slowed his pace and toyed idly with the wavering ends of the low hedges that lined the path. A few British tourists lingered by the doors to the centuries-old church, posing each other for a final photograph as they admired the beauty of the structure.

Bochlaine avoided them, taking a slower, more circuitous route to the door of the church. After a final look over his shoulder, he ducked into the cavernous building. Only a few worshippers were inside, all silently praying or meditating in the long wooden pews, their thoughts diverted occasionally by the distant chanting of monks. The fat man walked to the center aisle, genuflected and crossed himself. Then, rising quickly, he moved down the aisle toward the ornately carved confessionals that stood six across to the right of the altar. Four of the booths were vacant, yet he entered none of them. Instead, his eyes studied the closed door of the third double, coffin-like vertical box. As he waited, he manipulated an olive wood rosary in his stubby but powerful fingers.

Large ebony beads marked each decade of smaller beads, and the supplicant quietly recited an Our Father as he fingered the first large bead. He quickly followed it with the required ten Hail Marys. He had prayed nearly full circle on the five decades when suddenly he stopped, and stared down at the antique rosary from Jerusalem. Then he snapped the cord in two, pulled one large decade bead off and dropped it into his coat pocket. Careful not to lose any of the other precious sacramental beads, he retied the cord.

A penitent exited from the third booth, and Bochlaine jumped to his feet and hurried inside, sliding the rosary into his pocket. He had to turn sideways to squeeze his wide frame through the narrow confessional entrance. With great effort he managed to drop one knee to the hard, worn wooden kneeler. A soundproof panel, which had covered the screen of the booth when Bochlaine entered, now slid back.

"Yes, my son." The priest's voice spoke in mellow Italian with a deep, smooth bass that professed years of saying masses.

"Father, I have come at the direction of Saint Ignatius of Loyola." Bochlaine spoke in English, the seeming non sequitur issued calmly and with purpose.

Hearing the English words and recognizing the voice, the priest now leaned closer to the grill, dropped his voice, and continued in English. "What do you wish to report, my son?" he asked.

"Sands is dead."

The priest was silent for a moment. "Lord have mercy on his soul," he intoned. Bochlaine muttered "Amen."

"I am afraid they know about me, Father. For years they have tried to insulate me, but with the help of Suzanne Steelman, I have penetrated their curtain of silence."

"No one suspects she is Zeisman's granddaughter?"

"Not yet. Count Vignola trusts her implicitly, though they shield her, too."

"The Piedmont Papers are the key. You must find them!"

"I have searched diligently for them, but without success. They are not to be found—not in the count's office, not in his study upstairs at the Rome palazzo, nor in our files. With Suzanne's help I have been trying to invade the computer system, but it will take time."

"It must be done."

"I fear the papers were destroyed—or perhaps were a figment of Zeisman's imagination in the years before he died. Invented to soothe his conscience because he was unable to keep the Nazis from slaughtering his people."

"Take heart, Franco. Zeisman did not conjure up the Piedmont Papers. They are real enough. And if it weren't for Simon's financial acumen, the Holy Church would have lost the money Mussolini paid us for the Piedmont States. St. Peter's might now be a relic of the past. Without money to do what it must, the Church could not exist."

"But there is no other evidence that Aspis is in any way tied to Colonel Hauptler, or that the ten million dollars with which it was chartered was the missing blood money."

"Zeisman was certain of it. So am I. I pray each day that you, my son, will solve this riddle before I must leave this earth to meet our Father. I am almost eighty, so I beg you to fulfill this wish of mine. Find the papers and with them the truth. My heart is heavy with guilt over the past."

"I am meeting with Bradford, Father. I have already given him his instructions. He will come, I am sure of it. And then—"

"—he will be condemned!"

"He is already. Twice he has survived, although his wife and children did not. I must talk with him first, for he could be valuable to us."

"You're certain he will come to Rome?"

"You have my word. To make certain, I will call him in New York."

The priest, who was in 1943 a junior official in the Vatican Bank, exhaled a weary sigh. "Do what you must, my son, but whatever you do, you must protect Suzanne. Her grandfather would not be happy to see her again so soon."

"I will protect her, Father."

"Let us pray."

After their prayer, Bochlaine left the confessional without a backward glance. He had much to do, and nothing could be delayed. He had to reach Elliot Bradford and then speak to Suzanne in London, where Count Vignola had sent her earlier today. Later he would deliver a note to Bradford's hotel. The old priest, Cardinal Ambrosiani, remained in the church and prayed for resolution to the nightmare that had begun five decades before.

And Bochlaine had to eat, for his stomach was grumbling and confused from the time change since he'd flown back to Rome from New York.

Bradford was dozing in a window seat of the first-class section of the Alitalia jet when Holly Sands unexpectedly occupied the empty seat beside him. Holly had already been seated in an aisle seat at the rear of first-class when Bradford boarded. She had waited until the plane was aloft and well out over the Atlantic before summoning her nerve and making her way forward to Brad's seat. Now she turned toward him and looked down at his rumpled figure, willing him to open his eyes. He did not, so she used the opportunity to look him over with care.

Brad was, as she had long ago decided, an attractive man any woman would be proud to have, though he had never learned how to dress. If he were her man, she thought, she'd throw away all the clothes in his wardrobe. Give them to the Salvation Army! For they did him no justice at all. His conservative clothes made him look older. He preferred gray suits with white shirts or stuffy blue pinstripes. He should look as he was—young and virile.

His face, darker than hers, went well with his brown eyes and his short well-trimmed beard. He looked exhausted.

God, how uptight Brad could be sometimes, she thought. She had wanted him almost from the moment she'd first seen him. And she'd been barely fifteen then—home on vacation from boarding school. She'd lost him shortly thereafter to Nancy Reardon and for a time Holly was truly unhappy over her fate, although she had liked Nancy well enough. Eventually, Holly recovered; when Brad lost not only Nancy but also his boys, she'd cried for him and with him.

Holly had had a crush on Brad ever since she could remember, but she felt their relationship was based on more than that. They shared a lot of history. When Brad lost his wife and sons, Holly tried to comfort him. And she enjoyed the time they spent together when he was visiting the family.

Holly also remembered it was around her twentieth year that she got ever-so-bold with Brad and announced to Brad and her parents that she wanted him as a lover and a husband, in that order! That statement jarred everyone and she could not believe her impertinence after making the admission. Her father's wrath had been so intense that she withdrew from Brad, though she regarded him with more longing than ever.

In spite of her horror and fury over her father's death, Holly could not, as she looked at Brad's sleeping form, help but wish he belonged to her. If only he could see her as the grown-up woman she was! She would one day pen a novel—a love story—and use him as the male lead character, she thought. It was certain to have a happy ending.

"Brad," she said now, reaching out to touch his cheek with the fingers of her right hand. "Wake up, Brad. Please."

Brad's eyes popped open. As he recognized Holly, they formed the question he was already asking her. "Holly? What the devil are you doing here?"

"Going to Rome," she replied.

"What?"

"I'm going to Rome because you're going there to see the man you told Mom and me about. The one who was supposed to visit Daddy last night. The one who may have killed him." It sounded melodramatic when she said it, but that's exactly how she wanted it to sound.

"How did you know I was going to Rome?" A brief reflection provided him with an answer. "You found out from Linda that I was going to be on this flight," he said.

"Something like that. Then I decided the only reason you'd be going would be to see the man you told us about. Don't deny that that is the motive for this impromptu trip. You're not on your way to study the Vatican's art treasures."

Brad shook his head. "You've added it up right, Kitten, but you shouldn't have come. As you pointed out, this man is probably dangerous. Look, Holly, he may try to kill me."

"Then it's even more important that I'm here for you, Brad. I can go to the Italian police if you get into trouble. I want to help catch my father's killer," she declared. She leaned toward him and gazed into his eyes.

"Holly," he replied, "I'm trying to find out what happened to your father. I'm not catching a killer, I only want to talk to the man who might have been the last person to have seen Jack alive. Having you along is going to screw things up, dammit! I don't want to have to answer to your mother if something happens to you."

"Screw things up? Answer to my mother? It sounds like you're not planning to merely talk to the man. Listen, Brad, I'm a goddamn adult, whether you think I am or not! Mom knows where I am, so you don't have to answer to her anymore than I do. I'm going!"

Brad was as taken aback by the sudden fury of Holly's verbal assault as he was by her presence on the plane. He stared silently at her and noticed her hair and the womanly body under the black sweater she wore. Yes, she was older and more attractive than ever before, but would her maturity make her any more secure if they ran into a killer?

A thought struck him with considerable speed and force. He and Tom had spoken earlier about the possibility of them being in danger from whoever killed Jack Sands and whoever might have orchestrated Bob Walters's suicide. Could his taxi accident have been no accident? A vague memory of a red and white Lincoln flashed through his mind. He now recalled it had materialized out of nowhere. The car had cut them off and forced the cab up against the center divider and then over it.

Brad shook his head. Had he not blundered onto the scene in the TNI building, Jack's death would have been recorded as a suicide, as had Walters's before him. If Brad's hunch were right, that parkway incident had been designed to *look* like an accident; the outcome, he guessed, was supposed to have been his death. Perhaps the killers in Rome— Bochlaine and company—were prepared with another fatal accident for him. Having Holly along would be placing her life in as much jeopardy as his.

But he knew Holly would never agree to go back to New York. He had to dupe her with false tasks in order that she might stay out of harm's way.

"Don't try to figure out a way to trick me, Brad," she said now. "I'm not a dummy."

"I don't have to trick you, Holly," he lied. "What I have to make you understand is that I'm probably just as much a target right now as your father was."

Holly searched his face for signs of trickery. "You're serious?" she said, her features contorted by concern.

"You be the judge," he declared. Then he told her about the "funny thing" that happened to him on the way to the airport. Only when he pointed out the condition of his clothes did she notice the tear in his jacket and the grease spots. He hadn't had time to change before the flight and couldn't do so now because his clean suit was in his suitcase in the plane's baggage compartment.

The episode got her attention but, as Brad suspected, she resisted his suggestion that she take the earliest available flight from Rome back to New York and wait there for the results of Brad's investigation. Still, she agreed to let him keep his date with Bochlaine without interference from her.

The jet's landing at da Vinci International Airport, or Fiumicino as the Italians call it, was routine.

Murray Jolles, a tall, solid man with short, salt and pepper hair, met them while they were awaiting their baggage. He was surprised when he noticed Brad's companion. "I'm not sure we can get a second hotel room," he told them as he guided them to a large BMW 850 in a spot at the arrival curb. "And when Linda notified us that you were booked at the Londra, we promised the corporate apartment to a client for a couple of days. So we've got no room there, either."

"No problem," Holly announced. "We'll stay in the same room. It'll have two beds, won't it?"

Bradford gave Murray a black look but the man's grin remained as he slid behind the wheel and started the car. Brad got in the front with Murray while Holly sat in the back. Both were silent during the twenty mile drive to Rome.

They were almost to the Great Aurelial Wall around the outer city when Brad broke the silence in the car. "Did you find the man?" he asked Murray in a quiet voice.

"Bochlaine? No. He's sort of a mystery man, you know. He has a nice apartment, but I understand he's rarely in it. Always on the go to one place or another. I have someone keeping an eye on it though. He'll call me the minute Bochlaine shows up there."

"Call him off, Murray. I won't need him anymore. Do you have a car at the hotel for me?"

"A Fiat," Murray said apologetically. "If you'd rather though, you can have my baby here."

"The Fiat will be fine," Brad murmured as Murray piloted the BMW through the streets of the old city.

He knew from experience that the Fiat would be the more practical car to drive because the streets would be filled with frantic Italians behind the wheels of automobiles and angry green buses—all anxious to get to where they were going and vociferously impatient with anything or anyone who got in their way. And then there would be the flashy foreign cars driven by snooty Americans. The Fiat would get him where he wanted to go, would be easier to park, and raise no holy or unholy Italian wrath.

The Londra was neither the newest nor the oldest hotel in Rome. Eight stories high, modern windows and small balconies regularly interrupted its yellow stucco facade. As Brad and Holly walked across the light terra-cotta floor in the lobby to the dark marble reception desk, he was praying they had an extra room for Holly. She hoped they were fully booked.

"We need a second room," Brad told the mustached, balding desk clerk after giving his name and confirming that his room was ready for him. "For Miss Sands."

The clerk's bushy eyebrows shot up and he looked from Holly to Brad. "The beautiful lady is not your wife, Signor Bradford?" he said.

"Oh, that is too bad!" The clerk lost his smile. "I am sorry, but all our rooms are occupied. I might point out that there are two beds in your room."

"That's great," Holly said, as she grabbed the key to the room and headed toward the lobby elevators.

Brad stared after her, his lips pursed, ignoring the desk clerk, who looked like he was going to break his subdued silence with laughter. A bellboy had picked up Brad's bag and was following Holly. Finally, having muttered an oath, Brad followed the pair.

He and Holly were barely in the room, which was furnished in a contemporary, unspectacular fashion with tan leather furniture, when the phone on the writing desk rang.

Brad picked up the receiver and listened as the reception clerk informed him that there was a message that he had forgotten to give him. The desk clerk told him that the note was delivered by a priest, which Brad considered strange.

"Please send it up," Brad requested, his eyes on Holly, who had hung up her jacket in the closet and fallen backward on the bed in a weary heap. Her eyes closed, she was now lying still as if she were sleeping.

"This isn't a very good idea," Brad said, standing at the foot of her bed and staring down at her.

Holly opened her eyes and stretched in feline fashion. "It's the best show in town, Brad," she said. "Anyway, I'm not about to start walking the streets of Rome looking for a room. Do you want to?"

"Not exactly," he said, turning away. "I suppose we can make do."

A grin bloomed across Holly's face as she watched him take off his suit jacket, hang it up, and begin unbuttoning the white shirt he wore. "Why don't you wear colored shirts, Brad? Pastels are far nicer than white ones. And those dark gray and navy blue wool suits . . ."

"Why don't you pick up the phone and call your mother, Holly?" he growled. "Tell her you'll be home Friday. I know it's early in the States but call her anyway."

"Oh, no, Brad! I'm staying until you're ready to go home."

"With luck we can both be home by then, Kitten. The message the desk called me about is from the man I've come to meet. When I've seen him I'll probably be able to head straight back to the States."

She met his eyes, her expression doubtful. "You wouldn't lie to me, would you?"

"I'm a lousy liar, Holly. I doubt you'd believe any lie I told you any-way. Now call Ellie, please? And for God's sake, don't tell her we're sharing the same room."

Brad's message arrived as Holly reached her mother on the phone.

Though the note was unsigned, Bradford was sure it was from Boch-laine because it said nothing other than the location of the meeting place: THE SCALINATA DELLA TRINITÀ DEI MONTI AT 1000 HOURS TODAY.

Bradford knew the location well. The "Spanish Steps"—three tiers of stairs leading to the French church of Dei Monti—was a Roman tourist attraction.

"Brad?" Holly's voice penetrated his woolly consciousness.

As he met her eyes, she said, "Reassure Mom, will you? I told her you were here, but not that we have the same room." She offered him the phone.

Taking it, he made himself smile, though he didn't feel happy. "It's all right, El," he said. "Holly's not a little kid anymore. She'll be all right. I'll look after her. I've a feeling if she went to Moscow she'd wind up with the KGB waiting on her hand and foot."

Ellie was relieved. "You'll get her back for the funeral?"

"She'll be there and so will I, Ellie. And I'll make sure she stays out of trouble." He hesitated. "Any more visits from the police?"

"No, but reporters have been haunting the front steps. I'm afraid to open the door for fear of getting a foot stuck inside or a microphone shoved into my face."

"It'll blow over soon. Hang in there."

But would it blow over soon? He wondered as he undressed in the bathroom, put on a robe from his suitcase, and returned to a darkened room. As he climbed into bed he could hear Holly's even breathing. A nap would do her good. He felt tender and more forgiving of her unwel-come arrival, if only because of his "little sister's" obvious state of ex-haustion. For the first time since he'd realized he had company on the plane, he felt protective toward Jack's daughter. The flight to Rome, he thought, had taken her mind off her father's death and she seemed to be taking it better now. Good!

His body and mind weary from the events of the last twenty-four hours, Brad fell heavily asleep the instant he turned off his mind. He slept deeply until he was awakened by a sobbing Holly climbing into the bed beside him and burying her face in his neck. He learned from his watch that it was eight o'clock.

"Oh, God, Brad!" she cried against his neck. "How could he be dead? How could he?"

He hugged her to him and cuddled her. Both finally fell asleep. She was still sleeping peacefully when the alarm sounded at nine. That's when Brad looked down at the woman next to him and realized she wore nothing but a pair of filmy black panties.

Holly lay half on her back, half on her side and he couldn't help but see the firm breasts peeking out from under the blanket and sheets. He recalled her saucy insistence on that occasion when she announced to Jack and Ellie that she would one day manage to get Brad into her bed. She had, it seemed, finally accomplished this, though not quite in the way she had imagined.

In repose she seemed older and more mature than her twenty-two years, however much the past two days had revealed her vulnerability. Her body was young, but very much the body of a woman.

He squashed the last thought and was glad he had slept in his robe. Usually he slept nude, but that wouldn't have been right—or smart— under these circumstances.

Wrenching his eyes away from Holly's pert bosom, he tried to disentangle himself from her without disturbing her.

FIVE

"It's important and necessary," the tall, stately brunette declared, fixing an icy stare on the man behind the desk—Paolo Cislaghi, the swarthy Sicilian director of the London Branch of Banco Sanseli on Queen Street, one of the banks that was controlled by Aspis S.A.

"Count Vignola will require the information about the American firm FINVEST no later than Friday," Suzanne Steelman finished. "Were it not important, I wouldn't be here," she added as an afterthought.

"You'll remain in London long enough to carry it back to the count?" Cislaghi asked, fastening his perennially eager eyes on his visitor's lovely face.

She knew what was coming, but also how to handle it.

"Perhaps!" she said. "If I find I need to leave before Friday, you can send the information with your assistant, who will have orders not to open the sealed envelope. Understood?" She watched the man get ready to make his move.

Cislaghi, a young man in spite of his important position, was short and had a short man's appreciation for tall women.

Especially for the statuesque Suzanne Steelman. She was Count Raffaele Vignola's ward, but that made no difference to him. And she was also the most infuriatingly aloof woman he'd ever met—which only made him desire her more.

Every time their paths had crossed since Suzanne appeared on the Aspis scene, becoming first one of its computer experts and then Vignola's personal aid, Cislaghi had tried to penetrate the American woman's defenses. He was never successful. Once he had managed to get Suzanne to his London flat while his wife was away in the country, but the moment she realized his flat was empty, she froze him in his tracks: "I'm not a one-nighter, Paolo, but if I were, you'd be the last person I'd spend a night with. Take care of your beautiful wife and our profitable bank and forget your idiotic lust for me."

But Cislaghi was not a quitter and Suzanne almost laughed as he walked menacingly around his desk in the elevator boots he habitually wore. "Suzanne," he said, "I have tickets to the Royal Festival Hall for tonight to see one of your American operas."

"Take your wife—or one of your girlfriends if you prefer. I have other plans." Suzanne eluded Cislaghi's outstretched arms with a quick step backward, then made a graceful exit from the director's office.

Outside the bank building, she discarded the mask of tough aloofness she wore whenever she conducted Aspis business and let a smile appear on her face, which was tanned from frequent ski excursions to northern Italy during the past winter. Normally pale peach in complexion, the soft natural color showed through her tanned cheeks.

With a deep sigh she sucked in fresh air to clear her lungs from the stifling discomfort of Cislaghi's sexual harassment; as she walked she loosened up her shoulders and neck, which always tensed in his presence. Her dark eyes, punctuated by naturally dark brows were dramatic on a face carved of such soft features and skin; somehow the combination made Suzanne Steelman an especially appealing beauty. Her long legs and curvaceous frame added to the look. But it was her strong, self-confident nature that spoke truly of her power as a woman.

As she began walking, her eyes alert for a taxi, she laughed softly at the renewal of Paolo Cislaghi's campaign to bed her. He was totally conceited, she thought—a prime, male chauvinist pig. She wouldn't have slept with him if she could have borrowed someone else's body!

Suzanne's smile vanished at the thought that she would have let even Paolo have her if he could give her what she had been seeking ever since she received her inheritance from Grandfather Zeisman, including a letter from the old man that changed her life. In the letter her grandfather had cleared up the murky matter of her origin—Zeisman had never married her grandmother, though Suzanne's mother had been born just before World War II. He had outlived his mistress and their daughter, neither of whom lived to be forty.

The Nazis had killed her grandmother, and childbirth had killed her mother.

Zeisman had also told her the horrible truth of how his mistress was deported and died in a Nazi concentration camp because of someone's betrayal. The secret of the betrayal, he wrote, could be found in the Piedmont Papers, which would prove a connection between the ransom of Roman Jews and the formation of Aspis. Zeisman had begged her to search for the papers within Aspis itself.

If Cislaghi had the secret to the whereabouts of the papers, Suzanne would have curbed her revulsion for the little Sicilian and spent a week with him in bed. She made a face at the thought and the driver of the London cab that had pulled up beside her grinned.

"What's the matter, luv?" he asked, looking her up and down approvingly. "You get stood up?"

Suzanne's grimace was gone in a flash as she climbed into the cab. She liked cabbies here, for they were nice, though a bit flippant, the Cockney ones at times impossible to understand. American cabdrivers were far worse. They were leering and nasty, and always had their grubby hands outstretched, palm up, looking for tips they hadn't earned. Suzanne found Roman cabbies incredible, with their explosive, intolerant ways in the mess of Roman traffic. Had Caesar lived into the twentieth century he wouldn't have thrown the Christians to the lions but rather the cabbies and other Roman drivers.

"Bond Street, please," Suzanne told the driver, trying to avoid the usual small talk.

He gave her a chuckle. "You goin' shoppin? You'll be sorry if you do that, luv. Old Bond Street—and the New one, too, full of Arabs. Bid up the prices, they do." He pulled the cab away from the curb and asked if she was an American.

When she responded in Italian, he just shook his head.

On Bond Street, she browsed in Hermés's new boutique, but nothing caught her eye. She could afford to shop at any of the trendy Bond Street boutiques she wished, for her grandfather's legacy had left her well-off even without her Aspis income. But she despised the airs put on by the fashion centers and avoided them like the plague. And she was not really in a shopping mood, nor was she in Mayfair to shop.

Bochlaine had called her late last night at the Fountain House flat Aspis maintained near its London office on Upper Brook Street. Knowing where she was, he had been guarded and told her nothing more than that he needed to talk to her. She was to call him at two o'clock sharp— 1400 hours London time—at a number he gave her, probably a pay phone in Rome, since she knew his home and office numbers.

She knew Bochlaine was in trouble. The count had as much as said so when he initially found out about Bochlaine's sudden trip to New York. Suzanne herself was surprised by the trip, for Frank had not told her in advance that he was going.

She was not surprised, however, when she learned that Nick Criscolle took off for New York within hours of Bochlaine's departure. Suzanne was not privy to certain top-secret Aspis files, so she knew little about Criscolle except what she could see for herself or find out by snooping around and listening to gossip among the others who worked in Aspis's Rome office. She knew Criscolle traveled a lot. She also knew he was as cruel as he was handsome. He was close to Vignola, yet the count never talked about him or his duties. He was almost as much a mystery as the Piedmont Papers.

Bochlaine had been actively seeking the papers even before Suzanne came on the scene, though she hadn't known it. He had failed to find them in the nearly ten years he'd spent as an Aspis executive he told her when he'd hired her as a computer technician for the company. While she had not known of him, Bochlaine had known of her, telling her who and what her grandfather had been, her grandmother's name and fate, and the fate of her dead parents as well. It had been Frank who ultimately introduced her to Vignola and made it possible for her to attempt to gain the count's trust.

Vignola's personal interest in her had come quickly, although it was sparked by Suzanne's intense interest in him.

Bochlaine said the count was a snake and he was probably right, though she found Vignola a likable Italian in spite of his dark side.

As Suzanne lunched at Wheeler's, she opened the *London Times* she had bought earlier and read the headline: "TNI President: A Suicide in New York."

TNI? Suzanne tried to place that corporate name. She had seen a memo recently that had mentioned it and its president, Jackson Sands. Was that who had killed himself? Sands?

She read the entire story, which was not long in spite of its bold, blaring headline. And then the contents of the memo came back. It was about Cinema Services and a problem it was having with one of the companies that had contracted it—TNI. There was something about shortages in profits reported to TNI.

Suzanne's large, nearly black eyes grew wide as the name FINVEST landed in her conscious mind. FINVEST? The American firm of high finance detectives the count was interested in? This might be the reason for his interest.

Was the suicide of Sands somehow tied in? She resolved to put the question to Bochlaine when she reached him. In the meantime she ordered more tea and rechecked her watch to confirm that she had just twenty minutes before she put her call through to Rome.

ROME

The warm rays of the morning sun were filtering into the hotel room, filling it with light as Holly Sands awoke and found Bradford getting out of bed. He turned his back to her as he sat on the edge of the bed. "If you want to sleep some more, go right ahead. I won't disturb you."

Holly, well aware of her middle-of-the-nap change of beds, admired Bradford's back. Even through the robe she could tell he was strong. How often had she seen him in just a pair of swim trunks diving into the Sands's swimming pool in Vermont? Sleeping in his arms had been grand. Never had she ever felt as safe, as warm, as comfortable.

She had not climbed into his bed to fulfill her vow to seduce him. She wondered now if he thought that was her purpose. If her father had not just been killed she might have, but not this morning. Nothing had been further from her mind. She had just needed his protection, his closeness, his comfort.

She felt better, though she hadn't slept as much as she would have liked. She wondered idly whether being nearly naked had bothered Brad last night. Did it matter? She wasn't certain.

This was her chance to get him to notice her. She might never have another opportunity like it. How often she had dreamed of Brad's reaction if and when he at last saw her naked body.

Reaching a sudden decision, she sprang out of the bed and stood defiantly in front of him, sucking in a breath to make her breasts seem bigger than they were. She wore no smile of invitation, yet could hardly have been more inviting. Moistening her dry lips, she murmured, "Thanks for holding me, Brad. I needed that. And right now, I need you another way. I need to have you know I'm a woman."

Bradford, taken completely by surprise, met her eyes but did not look down at the rest of her as she urgently wanted him to.

"For God's sake, Brad, look at me. You don't have to make love to me. Just look at me!"

He jumped off the bed as if it were hot and stood, towering over her, as he dropped his eyes to her freckled shoulders, which were tawny brown from surfing last summer, then down to her creamy white breasts. She closed her eyes and began to shiver when his eyes touched her flesh, warming it everywhere. Did he like what he saw?

"Very nice, Kitten," he said, his voice cracking.

Her eyes snapped open again. "There's more to see," she said teasingly, dropping her hands to the edges of her nearly transparent black panties.

"I'll pass, Holly," he returned. "Don't do that."

"You don't want to see the rest of me?"

His eyes had dropped to her panties, but he raised them a split second later. "Any man would."

"Then be a man, Brad. You take them down. Now."

He sucked in a great breath of air, but Holly could see his indecision turning to desire. She moved closer, stopping just before she touched him. "Please, Brad." Only an inch separated them.

Holly closed her eyes again when she felt his hands slide down over her hips to reach inside the elastic holding the thin black nylon around them. His touch was torturous. Like an itch that scratching wouldn't help. When the cloth was on the carpet he straightened, but did not look down. Seeing his eyes, she was disappointed.

"Feast your eyes, Brad," she said. "Tell me I'm still a little girl—if you can." Still he hesitated, but she saw signs of the battle that had to be raging within right now—a fight between his conscience and libido. She didn't have time to glory in it, however, because he backed off a step and looked at the rest of her.

Her blood was boiling inside her body as he inspected all sixty-three inches of her. "Brad, kiss me. Just once pretend we're lovers, even though we aren't. Take me in your arms and . . ."

"No, Holly! Enough's enough. We're not lovers and aren't going to be. You're pretty—sensational, in fact, and definitely not a little girl. Okay? But no kisses. I'm made of flesh and blood, not steel."

She all but leaped into his arms as he tried to move away. "Kiss me, or I'll start screaming and tell the whole Roman world that you forced me to make love to you!" she threatened.

He brought her tirade to an end with his mouth, although the kiss he offered her was not sensual enough. Holly felt it was like kissing her father. She wormed her tongue between their lips and tried to get him to cooperate. Suddenly, without warning, he did, and the kiss became all-arousing. Her legs trembled.

He wrenched his mouth away from hers and fled toward the bathroom.

"Get dressed," he called back, "before I put you across my knee and use my belt on that pretty backside of yours."

"I dare you," she challenged. But she was a little bit glad he had regained his self-control. Just a little bit.

She knew she had gone too far with him. She would have to use all her wiles to get back on his good side. She was not, however, prepared for the Elliot Bradford who returned, fully dressed ten minutes later from a cold shower.

"All right, kiddo," he said, stuffing his wallet into his inside coat pocket, "here's how it's going to be from now on if you're going to stay until I fly back to New York.

"First, you're going to have your own hotel room while we're in Rome, and you're going to stay in it all night long. You're going to forget what just happened and start remembering that your father was like a father to me and that makes you almost my sister."

"Almost," she pointed out, "but not quite. Can you forget what happened?"

Brad nodded. "Yeah," he said, "and you better forget it, too. I have to go to meet someone now. When I get back we'll see about getting a room for you."

"You'll tell me what you find out?" Suddenly, Holly became concerned that Brad might refuse to confide in her.

Brad softened. "I will, but don't get your hopes up too high, Kitten. I may not learn anything."

Brad headed for the lobby of the hotel to use a pay phone to call Murray. As he inserted a gettone, the brass token that was peculiar to the Italian phone system, he was again wishing there were some way of getting

Holly out of his hair. She was damnably disconcerting, and she complicated matters a lot.

"You slept well, Signor Bradford?" the desk clerk asked solicitously as Brad walked by.

Brad was about to give him a dirty look for the inference contained in the remark when he realized that it was a different clerk than the one who had checked them in last night.

The Fiat Murray had left for him was in the hotel parking lot. Before starting the engine, however, Brad took a nine millimeter Beretta from the glove compartment, made certain it was loaded, and then placed the weapon in his right coat pocket.

Having now focused on his meeting with Bochlaine, Holly was far out of his mind as he swung the car out of the parking lot. As he maneuvered the Fiat through the heavy traffic on the Corso, then on the Via Francesco Crispi, he assessed the possibility that he was heading straight into a trap.

It could well be a trap, he knew, but if it was, why hadn't Bochlaine tried to surprise him back in New York after he'd killed Jack Sands? It would have made more sense. The fat Italian had to know he'd be on the alert now.

Was Bochlaine behind the wheel of the silver Lincoln that had tried to kill him on the way to Kennedy Airport? Had the telephone call been designed to lure him onto the expressway to kill him? Brad resolved to be ready for anything. He doubted that a sniper would be Bochlaine's style, though he could not be sure. More likely, the fat man would try to kill him at close quarters.

His thoughts were interrupted by his arrival in the vicinity of the Piazza di Spagna, and he seized the first parking space he came upon— one that forced him to park nearly perpendicular to the curb. He slowly squeezed out from the small car and began walking the several remaining blocks to the Spanish Steps.

Twenty minutes early for the meeting with Bochlaine, he took his time walking up the Via Condotti toward the Steps. The March air was almost summery compared to the blustery cold he'd left behind in Manhattan, but he hardly noticed.

His eyes glided over the spring fashions displayed on mannequins in the windows of the boutiques lining Rome's version of Fifth Avenue, but his thoughts were not on Gucci or Bulgari. Nor were they on the shapely derrières belonging to the attractive women window-shopping among the exclusive shops. He didn't even smile when he saw one adventurous Italian man sidle up to a slim, light-haired woman standing at the window of Ferragamo and pinch her bottom, then tip his hat as he walked away. The woman must have been Italian, for her only reaction was a dark look at the man before returning her gaze to the store window.

It was five minutes before ten o'clock when Brad reached the fountain at the foot of the Spanish Steps, whose only connection to Spain was that the Spanish Embassy had once stood here. The magnificent steps were built by the French and the three long stone flights led upward to the beautiful French church, Trinità dei Monti.

Brad now stopped uncertainly, staring far up the steps toward the twin-towered church that arose behind the obelisk at the top, almost a football field away. Where, he asked himself, would Bochlaine be? Hiding in the church? Or in the shadows of one of the adjacent buildings?

He stood where he was, looking for signs of trouble as he scanned the few dozen tourists who trudged up and down the dizzying steps on their pilgrimage to the church. None of the men he saw looked anything like the house with legs that Bochlaine was. Brad was sure he'd recognize the Italian when he saw him, for he knew in his gut that he would be the same fat man Brad had seen on the elevator in the TNI building.

Now he decided to climb the steps to the landing two-thirds of the way up, for it was large and open and afforded a far better view and more protection than his present position.

His right hand was buried in his coat pocket, his fingers holding the Beretta as he began climbing the stairs, his eyes scanning the area around him. None of the tourists paid him any attention as he reached the landing and again looked up and down the steps for Bochlaine. A glance at his watch told him he was still a few minutes early, so he turned and casually looked at the familiar earth-colored stucco of nearby Roman buildings.

On a day like this, he thought, with the air cool and dry and free of the clouds that frequently pelted Rome with rain in March, you could almost taste spring, though it had not yet arrived.

His eyes went to the west, where the dome of St. Peter's, an anchored golden ball, glistened in the sun. St. Peter's, the center of the Roman Catholic Church and home to its Pope. Nancy's Pope. Brad looked back toward the steps, another thought in his mind. Could Nan and Jack and the boys *see* him now from wherever they were? Was there some sort of secret dimension, a sort of corridor in time and space like that imagined by an old army friend of Brad's who was a strong believer in the transcendental spirit? Did the spirit have access to all things after death?

Shaking off the thought, he stared down the steps. They were drab now, but in only a month or so they would be one of the most colorful sights in all Rome due to the hundreds of baskets of flowers adorning them. He and Nancy had seen the Spanish Steps one spring and she had raved about it for months afterward.

Suddenly Brad saw a large figure far below him—the house on legs he'd been waiting for. But this one shocked him, for it was wearing the black cassock robe of a Jesuit Priest.

The man ascending the steps had a white rope serving as a cincture, a belt with four knots to signify the priest's chastity, poverty, obedience, and papal devotion, and a large, loose cowl covering most of his face.

Watching the lumbering approach of the huge man up the long, travertine stairway, Brad's nerves were taut, his thumb on the safety catch of the gun in his coat pocket. Was the robed figure the fat man who'd followed him into the elevator Tuesday? Christ! Had less than forty-eight hours passed since Brad had lunched with Jack? It didn't seem possible.

The priest was upon him now and stopped, his hands hidden beneath his robe. Bradford, his finger on the trigger of his weapon, knew that he might have reached his final moment. If Bochlaine had a gun under his robes, Brad's gun could not save him. The best Brad could do was retaliate instantaneously to bring down his adversary at the moment of his own death.

Not a happy thought, but it was a chance he had to take. He knew it and so, he thought, did Bochlaine. Brad's finger tensed when he recognized the cherubic face beneath the priest's cowl. It was indeed the man from the elevator.

The priest made a movement now as if to bring out his hidden hands and Bradford almost shot him. But then Bochlaine stopped, seeing the reaction in Brad's eyes.

"Do not fear, Mr. Bradford," Bochlaine said. "I have nothing in my hands. If I were a killer, you would already be on your way to meet our maker."

Brad did not relax his vigil. "You're Bochlaine?"

"Some call me that, Mr. Bradford." The priest's right hand now came into view—empty. His left hand followed it, also weaponless.

"You're taking a chance, Bochlaine," Bradford said. "I could kill you right now."

"You'd ruin your suit for nothing, Mr. Bradford," Bochlaine. "I'm not the one who killed your benefactor. I haven't killed anyone at all."

"You were there when I was on my way to lunch with Jack. I saw you. Why? Your appointment was much later."

"I had to be certain of my information."

"Certain that I was delivering FINVEST's report on Cinema Services? You've bought someone in my office, Bochlaine. Who is it?"

"Aspis has an informant in your office, Mr. Bradford, but I don't know his identity. Come with me. We must talk where we cannot be observed, for we are both in danger and even in Jesuit garb I am afraid I am not hard to recognize."

Bradford stared at him. Was he telling the truth? Could he be trusted? Did he plan to kill Brad after he'd lured him away from here? Brad's neck prickled a little, but there was no telltale sweat to warn him that he was on thin ice. "Where to?" he asked.

Bochlaine inclined his head toward the church above them, then led the way up the tier of steps, around the obelisk, and to the doors of the church. In spite of his bulk, the Italian moved easily.

Inside, Brad didn't have an opportunity to appreciate the ornate interior of the church. Bochlaine led him quickly past the entrance to a door that opened into a small cloak room. He locked the thick oak door after turning on a switch that operated a ceiling bulb and illuminated the place.

Bradford's hand remained in his pocket with his gun, but he was more intrigued by the big priest than he was fearful. There were no chairs in the small cloak room and Brad leaned back against the wall near the door opposite a row of hooks from which musty-smelling clerical robes hung.

"If you didn't kill Jack Sands, Bochlaine, who did?" Bradford asked, studying the big man's eyes.

A dark cloud that spoke of sadness touched Bochlaine's face. "I did not fly to America to murder your friend, Mr. Bradford. My most fervent desire was to warn him that he was in danger."

"How did you know?"

"It's a long story, my friend."

"I have plenty of time."

"The story is about Aspis, an evil organization, and Nicholas Criscolle, an evil man. Criscolle is a sadist and killer. *He* murdered Mr. Sands."

"You work for Aspis, too, Bochlaine," Bradford pointed out.

The Italian was pleased with Brad's daring. "I am a spy of sorts, Mr. Bradford, though I'm not a very talented one. I've made every effort since I penetrated Count Vignola's organization to be a counterforce against it."

"Why didn't you see Jack Sands sooner than you did if you only wanted to warn him? You could have even done it by telephone." There was accusation in Bradford's voice.

"I don't blame you for being unhappy with me for delaying, Mr. Bradford, but there were reasons. Now I can see that they were not very good reasons, but at the time they seemed valid."

"Tell me what they were."

"It was not enough for me to simply tell your friend he was in danger, for he would not have believed me. Why? He would have asked me, 'How do you know?' And it would have been a difficult question to answer, for it involves my mission in working for Aspis, the objectives I have that are entirely contrary to those of Count Vignola and Aspis. To have told your friend these things would have jeopardized my cause, and that cause is more important than life itself."

"Nothing is more important than the life your inaction forfeited," Bradford charged.

"When you've heard what I'm about to tell you, Mr. Bradford, you'll understand, though I can only hope you'll forgive me for not preventing your friend's death."

"You'll tell me?" Brad was genuinely surprised.

Bochlaine nodded. "I'll tell you far more than you should know for your own safety. I have no choice—it appears you can learn what I could not. In any event, it's now too late for me. They know about my attempt to warn Sands and my life is now in as much danger as yours— more, actually, since they need not make my death look like an accident or suicide. There is little chance now that I can find the Piedmont Papers."

Bradford met Bochlaine's eyes. "Why am I in danger?" he said. "Because of our discovery of Cinema Services's dirty linen? And what the hell are the Piedmont Papers? Did your outfit or Nicholas Criscolle have anything to do with Bob Walters's suicide?"

Surprise showed on Bochlaine's face. "You connected Walters's death with Aspis?" he said. He fell silent for a moment, his small eyes glittering like shiny marbles between the oversized flaps of flesh that served as his eyelids and eyebrows. "You are a formidable man with a quick mind, Mr. Bradford. May your efforts somehow succeed where mine have failed."

Bochlaine began a long, rambling story. It had its beginnings with the Nazi threat fifty-three years ago to deport Rome's entire Jewish population, the inability of the Vatican to help, the raising of the ransom money in America, its apparent payment to Nazi Colonel Hauptler, the ultimate deportation of the Jews in spite of it, and finally Rabbi Solomon's suicide. He explained Simon Zeisman's intimate involvement with the whole situation and said that the top Vatican financial adviser had not only made finding the Piedmont Papers his life's mission but also made sure the mission would carry on after his death.

Bradford's mind processed the information quickly. "Could the rabbi have stolen the ransom money?" Bradford asked.

"Unlikely. Nor is it even a remote possibility that Rabbi Solomon hanged himself. Zeisman knew him intimately and emphatically denied that it was suicide. The rabbi, he said, would not have compromised even a single life for money or any other material pleasure."

"Then?"

"That is the rub. After the war, Zeisman learned of the formation of a financial services corporation known as Piedmont S.A. It's capital was almost exactly equal to what the Jewish ransom—ten million dollars— was. Zeisman made inquiries and expended a small fortune of his funds trying to find out exactly who owned the firm, but without success. There were no firms like yours around at the time, Mr. Bradford."

"Piedmont changed its name to Aspis in the early fifties," Bradford now broke in. "I know that. But tell me—what made Zeisman connect the ransom money with Aspis? I don't see the connection at all. And what happened to Hauptler? Did he escape Nuremberg? Did Israeli intelligence exterminate him? What?"

"Hauptler is in prison in Italy—the last Nazi still alive and incarcerated. After the war, he claimed that he never ordered the Jews deported. After his conviction, he admitted privately that he did—after the ransom went unpaid.

"However, Cardinal Massara—then a priest assigned to the Istituto per le Opere di Religione, the I.O.R.—was with Rabbi Solomon when he delivered the money to Hauptler."

"Let me get this straight, Bochlaine. Are you suggesting that Aspis was started, using the invested ransom money, on Hauptler's behalf? What good would it do him if he's still in prison?"

Bochlaine watched Bradford's brow furrow as the American concentrated on the problem. Would Bradford make the connection before receiving the final clue?

Fully a minute went by before Bradford looked up at Bochlaine, a quizzical look on the American's face. Then the look changed to one of total disbelief.

"My God!" Bradford exclaimed. "No matter how I twist it around in my head it always comes out the same. Massara. The priest at the Vatican Bank. No one but Hauptler is alive to refute him and who would take the word of a convicted Nazi killer against that of a Catholic priest—a cardinal? Yet it's almost impossible to believe. A cardinal of the Catholic Church wouldn't have stolen that money!" Bochlaine's story, Bradford thought as he stared at the fat Italian, led straight off a cliff—a cliff on Vatican Hill.

"Zeisman's attention was attracted to Aspis by the initial capitalization of the company, Mr. Bradford, and because it was clear that the company's director—who was not and is not named in its papers of incorporation—is Count Raffaele Ernesto Vignola."

"Count who?" Bradford frowned. "Did I miss something somewhere?"

"Count Vignola, director of Aspis operations and my superior until very recently, is the half brother of Cardinal Massara," Bochlaine said with a wan smile.

"Holy shit!"

"Exactly."

SIX

The Rome headquarters of Aspis was an ornate, three-story palazzo surrounded by a high stone wall with a gate to keep out interlopers, both during and after the business day. Aspis's widespread organization did business in every major city in the world, and some of their offices were located in billion-dollar skyscrapers, but Rome was home and all major policy decisions were made here.

Count Vignola, Aspis's director, was a slightly built, well-dressed man with a hawkish, swarthy face partially covered by a Vandyke beard who was used to power and knew how and when to exercise it. He had helped found Aspis years ago, and it was Vignola whose connections had turned it into a very private financial empire performing a host of different, and valuable, financial services.

Each day Aspis managed billions in cash, carefully bought and sold securities and companies, washed money, made loans from huge cash deposits in banks it owned, and kept all its records entirely secret. While the records were fed into the gigantic Aspis computer system at their sources, they were available for recall only by permission—and such permission had to come from Rome. Aspis had already created and broken great financial institutions, manipulated commodities markets, and brought down banks.

It had also, here and there, snuffed out a life or two. Like those of Jack Sands, Bob Walters, and Elliot Bradford's family.

Today, Count Vignola's displeasure over recent events showed in his expression as he regarded his aide, Nicholas Criscolle, Aspis's contact with the American Mafia, across his uncluttered desk.

"I don't know how the hell Bradford got out of that cab alive, Count," Criscolle declared. "He should have been taken care of by the accident."

Vignola, for the moment, said nothing. Bradford and his FINVEST financial sleuths were, he thought, becoming more than a mere annoyance. But the American and his firm would be dealt with soon, one way or another.

"Bradford's in Rome right now, Count. Would you believe I almost bumped into him at the airport when I flew in last night on our courier jet? What a lucky son-of-a-bitch! He was going out the door when I saw him."

"He's more than lucky, Nicholas," the count said as Criscolle bit off the end of a cigar and lit it. "Bradford is clever. He has an efficient organization and a sophisticated computer system. Our people in Tokyo say it's almost as good as ours."

"It won't do him no good when I catch up with him." Criscolle said. "And that's gonna be soon. He's the only one who knows Sands didn't kill himself."

"But he hasn't informed New York authorities, Nicholas, so, for the moment, I want you to defer action on Bradford. He can wait. And as you know, it is much too soon after Sands's demise for another death. When you dispatch Bradford there must be no hint that he was murdered. You know my policy about such things."

"Yeah. Kill only when it's necessary. I know it by heart, Count, but I don't fuckin' like it. The bastard's too goddamn smart and his outfit's dangerous."

Count Vignola shot Criscolle a disapproving look. He was a gentleman and was not used to, nor would he tolerate, gutter language. Criscolle could speak like a gentleman when he chose to, but all too often lapsed into the street talk from his youth in Brooklyn—much more often than the count would have preferred, though he did not usually comment on it.

Criscolle had some other habits the count didn't like, either. Among them was his treatment of women. So far, no permanent damage had been done to the organization because of it, but only because of the count's continuing protests to Criscolle that he exercise care. The count was glad Criscolle wasn't causing enough trouble to stir up any public outcry, for he was an important associate and performed necessary tasks for the organization. Nicholas had done his services so well for seven years that he had made himself more or less indispensable to Aspis. He did whatever violent work had to be done and he did it when and wherever it was necessary, at Count Vignola's bidding.

"Agreed," the count said, eyeing Criscolle. "FINVEST is more dangerous to us than the American CIA. Bradford and his people know what they're doing and do it very well. Too well, as you know.

"But there are many ways to get at FINVEST, Nicholas. Eliminating Bradford will hurt his company badly, but FINVEST will survive that loss. Bradford's partner is more than capable of continuing its growth."

"Why don't I arrange for Sumereau to have a heart attack, Count? There's a new drug around that'll fool even the best pathologists. The beauty of it is that it stays liquid. After it kills you, all traces of it are washed out of the body in the urine when it releases after death. It's just about impossible to detect."

Vignola was annoyed and showed it with a shake of his head. "We can't kill everyone involved, Nicholas," he declared. "You must learn to curb that impulse you have for . . . eliminations."

"Eliminations? That's a good word, Count. I like it."

"And I don't like unnecessary eliminations, Nicholas.

"I'm well aware of FINVEST's capabilities and I can assure you that I won't allow them to continue to focus on us. I've sent Suzanne to London to obtain certain information that will tell me how we can squeeze FINVEST like a grape—through its capital structure, of course. I intend to break Bradford's company financially and that will guarantee what an elimination cannot."

"Suppose you can't find your financial lever?"

Vignola shrugged. "There are always financial levers," he said. "But, if necessary, I shall just loose some other dogs."

"Mad dogs like Nick Criscolle? You can say it, Count. It don't matter. There's madness in everyone. It shows up more in some than in others, but it's always there. It's in me, in you—in some of those holy bastards in their holier-than-thou city across the Tiber."

"God have mercy upon your soul!" Vignola declared angrily. "You, Nicholas Criscolle, are no one to speak ill of the Holy See!"

"The Holy See? Horseshit! I'd call it the Holy Don't See." Criscolle chuckled at the red-faced rage of Vignola.

He enjoyed arousing Vignola's ire and often went out of his way to do so. One day, Nick would no longer have to put up with the lily-livered little count, but would occupy the chair of power. He couldn't wait to see himself in it. Returning to the problem with FINVEST he told Vignola, "Anyway, I won't go after Bradford until after Sands's funeral. But then he's had it—got it?"

"Wait until I give the order," Vignola replied. "This organization is mine and as long as you're a part of it, you'll carry out my orders."

"Fine, Count," Criscolle said with a grin. "Provided you give me the go ahead by Saturday, that'll work out okay. But if you don't, I'm gonna to do what has to be done. Bradford's no dummy and shouldn't be put off. I wouldn't be surprised if he wasn't meeting with Bochlaine right now. Probably pumping him for information. He sure as hell didn't fly to Rome for his health. And your fat friend called Bradford at his office in New York, you know."

Vignola's eyes narrowed. He had made a mistake in not getting rid of Bochlaine a long time ago, he realized. Having an innocent in the front ranks of Aspis had been and still was a good idea, but it had recently become all too apparent that Bochlaine was not the fat innocent he portrayed himself as. Criscolle was right about that. What the fat man knew about the organization made him a dangerous ally.

Vignola glared at Criscolle, his eyes hard as stone. "Find Bochlaine, Nicholas," he said. "Take him alive and bring him to me for questioning. I want to know everything he knows."

"When I get through with him, he'll be glad to see you." Criscolle laughed at his own joke, stood, and started to walk away.

"Nicholas?"

The count's voice stopped Criscolle in midstride. The American swiveled to face Vignola once more, not pleased by his superior's tone of voice.

"Curb your sadistic impulses, Nicholas," the count told him. "Hurt Bochlaine too badly and he'll be of no value to anyone."

"Don't worry, Count," Criscolle returned. "I'll just soften him up."

"And don't let him get away."

Criscolle shrugged and left the count's office. He would catch Bochlaine, he had no doubts about that. And he would force the fat man to sing like a bird—unless he had to kill him. But working out on a big, fat Italian man was not Criscolle's idea of fun. He preferred women.

A prince of the Roman Catholic Church mixed up with an organization that would sponsor killers. Elliot Bradford was stunned after his meeting with Frank Bochlaine.

Brad lacked illusions about the church. Catholic priests in high positions were just as corruptible as other powerful men in the world achieving equal power. The many horror stories served as a testament. Still, the kind of corruption Bochlaine suggested about Massara was hard to imagine, even for a cynic like Bradford.

Bochlaine had been a hundred and eighty degrees away from what Brad had expected. Certainly not a killer. In the army Brad had known plenty of killers. Some actually enjoyed killing while others committed their crimes without remorse by steeling themselves to do so. Bochlaine was neither type, but rather one who would kill with great difficulty. There was strength in the man's big body, and even more in his eyes. His expression was cherubic, but his innocence was only superficial. There was no naiveté there, but no murderous intent, either.

Was Bochlaine telling the truth about Criscolle, Aspis, the theft of the ransom money for the Roman Jews—about the Vatican connection through Vignola and Massara?

Brad could not be absolutely certain, but if Bochlaine was lying, he thought, the man had created a truly masterful web of deceit that read like gospel truth. Every word Bochlaine said had the smell of fact and the man's voice and manner contained a sober sincerity difficult to dispute.

As he drove to his Rome office on the Via Isonzo not far from the Londra, he knew he had to believe Bochlaine. Nick Criscolle sounded much more like Jack's killer than Bochlaine ever could.

Brad wanted to seek out Criscolle, but the fat man begged him not to. Instead, Bochlaine wanted him to quickly fly to London to meet and talk with Suzanne Steelman, an assistant to Count Vignola at Aspis. She, he claimed, had been helping him in his search for the Piedmont Papers.

"How can she help me?" Brad asked him. "I came here to find the man who killed Jack."

"You must talk to Suzanne," Bochlaine had insisted. "She can tell you a great deal about Criscolle—far more than I can, for she has worked with him here in Rome while I have traveled a great deal."

"What can she possibly tell me about him that I don't already know, Bochlaine? I don't see . . ."

Bochlaine's eyes glittered. "Suzanne will tell you something that will shake you to your core, Mr. Bradford," he said. "I promise you."

Bochlaine refused to elaborate further on what he'd said, instead making an urgent plea to Bradford that he help locate the Piedmont Papers.

While Brad rode the elevator up to FINVEST's top-floor office in the five-story Piezarrini office building, he reached into his suit pocket and fingered the single rosary bead Bochlaine had given him for identification.

"Suzanne will know you when you show her the bead," Bochlaine had said. "She'll tell you nothing unless she's sure of your identity, and even after seeing the bead she may not entirely trust you. You must convince her."

"How?"

Bochlaine, who would neither affirm nor deny the possibility that he was not simply in disguise while wearing his Jesuit robes, simply shrugged his wide shoulders. "Your eyes will tell her, Mr. Bradford. Your eyes, your manner—your passion for finding the vermin who killed your friend, Jack Sands."

An idea tugged at Brad's mind as he and Murray Jolles reviewed the preliminary reports FINVEST offices had made on Aspis since yesterday. He asked Murray, a Jew whose influence in the Vatican was little short of incredible, if he would arrange an audience with the Pope for tomorrow.

"The Pope you say, Brad?" Murray replied as the two men sat in FINVEST's conference room reviewing reports on the eight-foot round table that was the room's only furniture other than chairs. "Why not ask me something easy—like making the world rotate the other way? Or get the College of Cardinals to elect an American Pope?"

Brad was serious. "Can you do it, Murray. I'd like to warn the Pope about some disturbing information I've just received. Hopefully he'll believe me and decide how to handle the problem. Maybe I can bring Holly. She needs a lift and getting scheduled for a small audience with the Pope would give it to her. Also . . . there's somebody in Vatican City I want to meet if possible. His name is Cardinal Massara. He is associated with the Vatican Bank. Find out if he's in Rome and available for appointments, but don't make one for me. I want to surprise him. And see what you can find out about Cardinal Massara's finances."

Jolles' expression was incredulous. "You want me to run a financial check on a cardinal?" he murmured. "How in hell can I do that?"

Brad shrugged.

"Don't they take an oath of poverty?"

"They do, but I'll wager they manage to salt away a lira or two anyway. Just check Massara out, Murray."

"You going to turn him in for tax evasion?"

"Not this time. Just let me know the exact source of any wealth he might have, should he turn out to be affluent. Got it?"

Murray would deliver the information, Brad was sure. And it was important. Would it tie the cardinal to the powerful, rich, violent Aspis?

Aspis. From what Bochlaine said, the company was everything Tony Phipps had reported from London—a huge, murky, international financial corporation whose assets were impossible to divine, whose officers were few, whose ownership was unclear. But it was also, if Bochlaine were correct, a two-tiered organization.

At the public level, where Bochlaine had held sway, it was a remarkable company that earned incredible profits and had investments in a maze of industries, all legitimate, or so it seemed. Aspis appeared to have almost unlimited funds at its disposal—even during worldwide recessions such as those of 1973 and 1982 and the one the world was still fighting to turn around now. Rather than staggering in tough times, Aspis had acquired control of many struggling companies, among them a mining company in Alaska incorporated as Precious Metals, which had made a small, but rich, uranium find just last year.

"Uranium?" Brad had questioned.

Bochlaine had not been able to explain why Aspis might be interested in uranium, although he did suggest that the company supplied guns and ammunition to mercenaries around the world.

However, there was an inner core to Aspis, Bochlaine said. Count Vignola had for years walled him off from it—or tried to. Bochlaine had penetrated it here and there, but he had never found the Piedmont Papers.

About five years ago he had accidentally learned from a Japanese computer technician who was repairing Aspis's main computer in Rome that there was a series of secret code symbols needed to pull Aspis's deepest corporate secrets out of the depths of the machine's memory. The technician also told him the symbols had to be fed into the machine sequentially if the computer was to furnish the information in understandable fashion. Otherwise the information would be printed out in an indecipherable code. The man could not be coerced or tricked into furnishing Bochlaine with the codes or sequences, claiming he did not have them.

It was an ingenious system and Bochlaine, whose knowledge of computer systems was minimal, was at a dead end until Suzanne Steelman presented herself to the former weightlifter. Bochlaine had hired her and her expertise in computer programming and systems had led to their cracking of a few of the code symbols. They had learned that Aspis was directly connected with organized crime.

"I'm almost certain that Mafia money is washed within the banks Aspis operates," Bochlaine told Bradford. "But the relationship between Aspis and the Mafia, like the one between Aspis and Massara, is shrouded and unclear. There's no surface contact between the Mafia and Aspis, although I think Nick Criscolle is a Mafioso. I can't prove it, though."

Bochlaine said he learned of Aspis's interest in World Fruit only hours before Walters's suicide. Uncertain what action Vignola would order, Bochlaine took a wait-and-see attitude. When he learned of the suicide he was horrified and he suffered no illusions when the New York coroner made its official determination. He vowed he would not let the same thing happen again.

The telephone interrupted Brad's ruminations, and he took the call in the conference room. Caterina Rossello, Murray's secretary, told him it was Tom Sumereau calling from New York.

"Well, partner," Sumereau said, "glad to see you're still able to walk and talk. You want to know what the New York City police have to say about you?"

"You'll tell me, Tom. Before you do, though, tell me how you're doing with our spy."

"I'm not doing, Brad. Not at all. But I have had a new telephone line put it. It's completely secure—can't be bugged—and I can record everything said during any given conversation with a simple push of a button. Then, if we want, we can feed the data directly into Max."

"Sounds great, Tom, but I'd be happier if you'd been able to find our spy and the missing files. You'll be interested in knowing, by the way, that Aspis is a son-of-a-bitch of a company.

"It's tied in somehow with the Mafia, runs banks and insurance companies, and even owns a mining company. Uranium. With no cash shortages, it does a roaring business washing Mafia money."

There was a long, loud silence on the line before Tom responded. "Jesus, Mary, and Joseph!" he exclaimed.

"All Jewish," Bradford observed, "and none of whom can help us one damn bit."

"Bochlaine—you met him? He told you all this? Can he be trusted?"

"I think so. He's not what I thought he was, though I'm still not

exactly sure what he is. I am sure that he's not an Aspis killer. He was all
set to warn Jack that he was a marked man when Jack was killed. Aspis
is a shady outfit and, I confess, it scares the hell out of me. But that
won't stop me from trying to avenge Jack's death. Bochlaine told me
the killer's name: Nick Criscolle. He can't prove it and neither can I,
but Bochlaine saw Criscolle come out of the TNI building after I'd
chased him down the stairs."

"I need a drink."

"So do I, Tom, but wait till you fill me in on what's been happening.
Did that Lieutenant Burke come back? What is he, an old Irish cop?"

"A young one," Tom corrected. "He's a lot smoother—and
smarter—than I'd have expected. Dresses in plain clothes, sort of Har-
vard preppy, I think. He also likes to ask questions you can't answer with
yes or no. He didn't say much until he realized he wasn't going to get
answers from me unless he was willing to give a few as well."

"What about the autopsy?"

"Nothing there. No drugs, only a little booze—Irish whiskey, no
doubt—death immediate, the cause the bullet from Jack's own gun. The
bullet was lodged in his brain. He had powder burns on his fingers and
Burke wouldn't venture an opinion on why Jack killed himself. That,
he told me, was why he wanted to talk to you and me both."

"You told him I had to go away on business? That I'd be back in time
for Jack's funeral Saturday?"

"Yeah, and he told me you'd almost been killed in an accident on the
way to the airport, but you'd lucked out, made your flight to Rome and
were staying at the Londra."

Bradford whistled into the phone. "He got all that? Did he tell you
Holly Sands followed me to Rome—on the same plane?"

"He did say Holly was with you but left it at that. Is she staying at the
Londra with you?"

"Holly's determined to follow me and pursue possible leads to her
father's killer. She's a pistol! What else did Burke have to say?"

"He asked me what work we'd done for TNI recently, why you had
lunch with Jack Tuesday, what you discussed with Jack before lunch,
where you were at quarter after seven Tuesday night and what your
relationship with Jack's daughter is."

Bradford snorted in disgust at the insinuation. "Is that all?" Brad asked
as he snuffed out the cigarette he'd been smoking in the ashtray on the

conference table—a replica of St. Peter's Square. Smoking was a habit he had acquired during his army tour. He was a situational smoker not a chain smoker, and lit up under stress.

"That was just for starters. I told him the work was confidential—our business—and that your lunch was to talk to Jack about the report on it and listen to an old friend talk about the good old days. I had no idea where you were on Tuesday night or whom you were with, but it wasn't Holly Sands. Then he really let me have it—question after question after question, some of them mentioning familiar names including Bochlaine and Cinema Services."

"How in hell did he get onto CSI?"

"He didn't say, but I absolutely refused to talk about it. You'd have been proud of me, Brad. I was unreadable as a blank piece of paper."

"Burke's not buying the suicide, though, is he? I'm surprised and pleased, Tom. No, I'm in shock! Then again, maybe I shouldn't be. Not all cops are as gullible as they're made out to be on television and in the movies."

"This one's damn good," Sumereau said with admiration. "We should talk him into quitting the force and coming to work for us. We could use a guy like him."

"I'll talk to him when I get back. Better call him and tell him that. The way you talk, Tom, I wouldn't be surprised if he strolled through my door here. I can do without that right now."

"You going to tell him you were outside Jack's office when he was killed? That Jack had help pulling the trigger? That the Mafia, or their pals from Aspis, did it?"

"I don't know what I'll tell him, Tom. I may not decide until I get home."

Before he hung up, Sumereau asked Brad for his ideas about the identity of FINVEST's traitor.

"Take your choice, Tom. Linda, Olga, Murray. They all have access to Max and the files. And there are probably others, too. See if you can use that superb brain of yours to smoke him out."

"Or her?"

"Let's hope it's not a her," Brad observed. He and Tom had both trusted their personal assistants completely over years and had strong bonds with the women.

Holly arrived at the office just as Brad was about to call her at the hotel. The sober expression on her face melted into a warm grin when she saw Brad come through the door from Murray's small conference room into the reception area.

"You're back, Brad?" she said. "No trouble?"

"Disappointed?" he returned, smiling back at her.

She held up a clenched fist. "You're an inconsiderate bastard!" she declared in mock anger. "I've been waiting for you to call me. I've been worried sick."

"I'm sorry," he said. "I just got tied up and—tell you what, I'll make it up to you. I'm trying to arrange a private meeting with the Pope. How'd you like to come along?"

Holly blinked. "I'd love to, Brad, but it's impossible to get an audience with him on short notice. Daddy tried once and couldn't do it." She stared at him. "Do you really think you can arrange it?"

"Hope so," he said. "Let me put it this way, Kitten, I have Murray working on it and if he can't do it, nobody can. He'll know for sure later today. If he pulls it off, we'll see the Pope tomorrow morning, he tells me. That means we can fly home tomorrow afternoon, in plenty of time for the funeral."

At the mention of the grim reality that had prompted their situation in Rome, Holly's mood changed. "What happened at your meeting with this Bochlaine character?" she asked.

"You've got a good memory, Holly," Brad replied, surprised that she'd picked up the name and remembered it. Murray had mentioned the name in her presence during the ride to the hotel from the airport, but she hadn't heard it since.

The anticipation in her eyes begged for an answer.

Brad glanced around the FINVEST reception area, then guided Holly back toward the conference room. Inside it, he closed the door and leaned against the long table as he began telling her a carefully edited version of the encounter.

"I met Bochlaine on schedule," he said, stroking his chin whiskers pensively as he talked. "I had an idea that he might be the one who killed your father, but now I'm sure that he wasn't. He gave me some important information about a very large company that may be involved in the murder."

"He didn't tell you who killed Daddy?"

Brad avoided her eyes. "Not yet, but there's a lady in London—Steelman's her name—who may be able to help. I'm flying there this afternoon, but I'll return late tonight."

The light in Holly's eyes died, then blazed again. "Let me go with you, Brad. I won't feel right here and I won't get in the way. I promise. I want to help. Remember?"

He could have laughed at Holly's eagerness, for she could have no idea how dangerous his meetings were. A short time ago he could easily have been taken out by Bochlaine or a sniper intent on killing Bochlaine. His trip to London to meet Steelman would be no less dangerous, for she was close to the heart of the Aspis organization. If they were onto Bochlaine, they could be ready to expose her as well.

"Trust me, Holly," he said. "I'm not trying to play Father Knows Best. Your father was a very dear friend, and I feel anything but fatherly toward you."

"Well, I'm glad of that anyway," she replied, a dark glitter in her eyes.

He let that pass, recalling with disturbing clarity the supple body she had shown him only a few hours ago. "Did the clerk at the hotel arrange a second room for tonight?" he asked.

She grinned. "We now have a two-room suite. The clerk gave us the room right next door to the other one and there's a connecting door that shouldn't go to waste."

By quarter after five that evening, Bradford was clearing customs at Heathrow Airport, where a rented Austin awaited him.

Following Bochlaine's directions, Bradford drove straight to Audley Street in Mayfair, home of one of the world's great china emporiums, Thomas Goode and Sons. It would be closed by now, but that didn't matter. He was to park and meet Suzanne Steelman near the store about six-thirty. When she approached him, he was to simply show her the rosary bead and identify himself as Bradford.

All the stores were closed when Brad reached the area, so there were plenty of street parking spaces available to him. Coming from Park Lane, Brad passed the Dorchester and was lucky to find a space on Deanery Street.

He was ten minutes early, so he decided to remain in the car and survey the area. He expected no trouble here, but neither could he rule it out. His gun was back in Rome with his holster, for he had carried no baggage in which to conceal it. And the London police were awfully intolerant of firearms.

With the streets dimly lit, there was little to be seen, so Brad hoisted himself out of the compact car and walked slowly to Audley Street. The sidewalk was deserted but when he reached the designated spot he felt eyes on him. Looking around he saw no one. Turning toward Thomas Goode and Sons, he looked briefly at the porcelain display in the window.

"Pardon me, govinor," a voice said nearby as its owner materialized at his elbow.

Bradford swiveled and came face to face with an old man wearing a faded olive drab army jacket—what had once been an ancient American army "Ike" jacket, named after Ike Eisenhower, its most famous wearer.

"And what can I do for you, old chap?" Brad asked the man.

The old timer's eyes were dark and sad as he appraised Brad, sniffed, then nodded as if to say "You might just be the one."

"American are you then? Good, mister. I likes Yanks. My sis had her an American fella durin' the blitz, she did. He was a flier and came to find out what the little corporal's Luftwaffe was doin' to us stubborn limies—and how we were survivin'. That's how I got me jacket. It was his. When he didn't come home from a mission one day—over Antwerp it was—my sis told me I could have it. It's stood up bloody well, hasn't it?"

Brad chuckled at the old man's Cockney speech. He had dropped every "h" and had spoken so fast that it was a blur. He reached into the pocket of his suit coat where he had stuffed the British currency Murray had procured for him, picked out a five pound note, and offered it to the old man. The old timer drew himself up to his full height—a foot shorter than Brad—and declared, "Hey now, I ain't no bloody beggar, I ain't! Just 'cause I look like the devil himself don't mean I got to act like one, too. Would your name be Bradbury by any chance?"

"Bradford," Brad said, suddenly realizing that the man had not sought him out by accident.

"Sounds good, mister. You likely to be looking for somebody special?"

"A lady. Tall, with dark hair."

"Got anything that might prove who you are?"

The old man's eyes were bright as he played out the little game. He was enjoying himself, that was obvious.

"I got a calling card," Brad said, though he did not produce one for the old man. He grinned when a puzzled look came to the old timer's face.

"A bloody business card? You got nuthin' else?" he said.

Brad chuckled, then held out his closed hand in front of the man's face." How about a rosary bead?" he asked, opening the fist.

The old man smiled from ear to ear. "Hey now, dammit, you are the Yank. I knew it from the start. Kiddin' with me, you were! Pullin' me leg. The lady's up the street at Richoux. You go there, and I'll tell you what—you ain't gonna be sorry. She's a bloody looker, she is, and I don't mean maybe. If I were a wee bit younger, I'd have a go at her meself. 'Cept she might just break me back, for she's a good-sized girl."

Brad reproduced the five pound note and this time shoved it into one of the two breast pockets of the Ike jacket. "Buy yourself a pint," he said. "You've earned it."

"Say, you don't have to do that, my friend, but I suppose I'm much obliged." He tipped his dirty old cap and limped down the street.

Richoux was a pastry shop, restaurant, and wine bar all rolled into one and was packed when Brad walked in from the street. The smell of fresh pastry tickled his palate, and he found he was hungry though British Airways had served him supper on the flight from Rome.

Where was Suzanne Steelman? he wondered as his eyes swept the crowded room. She had to be here somewhere. At first, he missed her, but then he spotted her in the front corner of the room, partly hidden by a coat rack. There was a window near the table at which she sat and without looking, Brad was certain she could watch Audley Street from it. In the soft light it was hard to see what Steelman looked like, but she was certainly impressive.

He brushed past a waitress carrying a tray laden with food. The woman gave no sign of recognition as he picked his way among the tables.

When he drew closer Brad saw that her eyes were on him. And he saw something else—something Bochlaine had not seen fit to pass on to him when he was describing Steelman—she was beautiful. No, he decided quickly as he reached the table, she was gorgeous! Her eyes were dark and inviting, her facial features softly feminine, and her flesh glowed. There was a poutiness to her full, pink lips and a natural arch to her eyebrows that could make anyone feel guilty before being proven innocent. She had a long, curvaceous, sultry body, yet her sexiness was curbed by her haughty attitude. Her body was concealed by the fashionable red wool suit she was wearing, but the attitude—that was right out there.

She did not stand when he approached, but accorded him a curious look and said, "Sit, won't you?"

"Suzanne?" he murmured, anxious to end the charade. "Suzanne Steelman?"

"Give me what you showed the old man," she ordered as he took the chair across the table from her.

He handed it across the table and watched her hold the bead up to the light on the wall behind her, study it, then give it back. "Who gave the bead to you?" she asked.

"Frank Bochlaine."

"Your name?"

"Elliot Bradford."

"Your business?"

In spite of the woman's beauty, her snappishness was irritating him and he said, "Look, I didn't come here to go through an interrogation. Bochlaine says you and he have the same objective—the Piedmont Papers. He wants me to help you find them. I'm not certain I want to get involved, or that I will, but I agreed to meet you. My interest here is in only one man—the man who killed Jack Sands. I'm sorry about what happened to your people at the hands of the Nazis, but that's not my problem."

"Then why are you here?" she responded angrily. "Nick Criscolle is probably back in Rome. Go back there and find him—before *he* catches up with *you*. And you'd better be prepared. He's a vicious killer who'll be on your tail soon if he hasn't tried for you already. You're on his list, in case you didn't know it."

"He's on mine as well," Brad replied. "I didn't mean to make you angry, Ms. Steelman. Bochlaine said you could tell me more about Criscolle. And he said there was something else you'd tell me that I'd be terribly interested in."

Suzanne regarded Elliot Bradford coolly. She had felt sorry for the man when Frank Bochlaine told her over the phone what he wanted her to tell him.

"Whatever you do, Suzanne," Bochlaine had said, "you've got to convince him to help us. We need him desperately. If he should be fortunate and somehow get to Nick before Nick gets to him, it won't do our cause any good. We've needed someone like Bradford from the start."

But Bradford seemed entirely uninterested in their cause. All he wanted to do was chart a path to Nick Criscolle. She had to change that.

"Aspis is very unhappy with you and your FINVEST firm, Mr. Bradford," she told him now, as a waiter approached. They ordered rarebit and white wine, then she continued.

"Others have tried to pry into Aspis's business affairs before FINVEST came on the scene and none have succeeded. Frank and I have spent much time and effort trying to expose Aspis for what it is—an abhorrent organization that grew out of blood money and flourishes by aiding and abetting the darkest of causes. Jack Sands wasn't the first to feel the viper's sting."

"I know. Bob Walters was an Aspis victim, too. Bochlaine mentioned him. He told me Criscolle was responsible for that murder, too. That's another reason why I've got to deal with Criscolle."

"Mr. Sands and Mr. Walters were killed on orders, Mr. Bradford. Count Vignola issued those orders. But even killing the count would accomplish little. Whether or not you eliminate Nick or the count, you will do nothing to stop the organization itself. Aspis would simply be taken over by a new chief executive and hire itself another chief assassin."

Bradford masked his thoughts as he listened to her.

"Look, Mr. Bradford," she said, "I'm not just thirsty for the blood of one man. Nick wasn't even born when my grandmother, a Roman Jew, died in a Nazi death camp because Aspis's founders stole the money that was supposed to ransom her people. What Frank and I are after is Aspis's blood. The Piedmont Papers he told you about offer the only chance to drain its vile energy."

"What if you can't unearth them?" Bradford asked. "Bochlaine says you've been trying for years without success."

"We'll dig them up," she said, her voice determined.

Their meal arrived and they ate in silence. She felt his eyes on her, but did not look up. She was, she knew, a very attractive woman and if Bradford liked how she looked—even fancied her—it would make her task easier.

As she sipped her wine, he broke the silence. "Are you sure your grandmother was killed after she was deported?"

He was, she thought, trying to close the gulf that had arisen between them and that was good.

"It's in the records," she replied. "After I read Grandfather Zeisman's letter telling me what had happened in Rome and of his private suspicions of Aspis, I used some of the money he left me to do some investigating. I studied the official records in Bonn and Rome and four years ago I finally got to see the Hauptler memoranda telling of the arrest and deportation—and ultimate destination and disposal—of all the Roman Jews, including my grandmother."

Suzanne paused now and gathered her thoughts. "Those memoranda are locked in a government safe in Germany and guarded constantly, but I have seen them. They say that Hauptler received no ransom money— that he 'couldn't reach' my grandfather, Rabbi Solomon or Massara and finally decided they had chosen to call his bluff. It was no bluff and my grandmother wound up in a German death camp and was exterminated within a month along with a thousand others."

Her words stirred her emotions thoroughly, but she retained the hardness in her expression at the conclusion of her low-voiced monologue.

"If the Hauptler memoranda is locked up and under guard, Suzanne," Bradford asked her now, "how did you manage to see it?"

Suzanne did not hesitate. She met his eyes boldly as she said, "By bribing the guard with my body, Mr. Bradford."

She watched Bradford's eyes as he digested her words and could see that they made him uncomfortable. "Would you like another glass of wine?" he asked, changing the subject.

"You needn't be embarrassed about what I just told you," she observed, ignoring his question. "I'm not ashamed of it. I'd have killed the guard to see the memoranda. As it happened, I only had to fuck him."

"I wasn't embarrassed," Bradford said.

"Then why did you change the subject so abruptly?"

Her question won a smile from him and the admission that he had changed the subject. "You remind me a lot of my wife," he told her. "She was sometimes candid to a fault."

Suzanne's eyes clouded at the mention of Bradford's wife, but she simply shrugged.

"Can we start over?" Bradford suggested. "We both want something badly and, it seems, have pretty good reasons. I've been doing a lot of thinking and can see your point. It's a damn good one. Putting Aspis out of business—if we can bring it off—is a lot more important than simple revenge. I understand that now."

"As important as it would be to you," she hesitated, "if you knew it was Count Vignola who had your wife and sons killed," she murmured almost under her breath.

Bradford's throat was suddenly dry as sand. "What did you say?" he asked her.

Suzanne could have cried for him then, her eyes soft as cashmere, so full of emotion that they looked like they were already wet. "Mr. Bradford," she said, "Aspis was trying to kill you when their assassin, a Mafia hit man procured by Nick Criscolle, ran your wife's car off the road and into that Long Island abutment. He didn't realize you weren't in the car."

Bradford remained stone-faced at the table, his eyes boring into hers. "You're certain of that?"

She nodded.

"How do you know?"

"Frank told me."

Brad paused to think about that for a moment. "Why didn't he tell me himself?"

Suzanne took her time replying, knowing how important it was to her cause. "Because you needed time to realize that you couldn't do what you want to . . . that simply getting Nick Criscolle wasn't the answer . . . that Aspis is the dragon that has to be slain. He hoped the truth about your family's deaths would convince you to help us."

Suzanne signaled the waiter to bring two more glasses of wine. When the wine arrived, Brad was sitting motionless as he absorbed the explosive information.

She reached out to him and covered his hand with hers. "It's hard to be tough about things like this, Brad," she said softly. "I know that too well."

Brad could only shake his head, tears stinging his eyes as a hot, purple anger continued to rage within him.

Recognizing it, she stood and said, "Let's get out of here."

SEVEN

Suzanne did not take Bradford to the Aspis flat, but rather to a place near Hyde Park that belonged to an English friend she'd met in Germany while prowling around in Bonn's dusty archives.

Diane Baker-Trent, who at thirty-five was a year younger than Suzanne, was the daughter of a rich lord and was admittedly spoiled. But Suzanne liked her enormously, a feeling Diane reciprocated.

They got together whenever she was in London, sometimes to shop, occasionally to double date—Diane had a veritable stable of men friends, all young and handsome—but always to chat. Suzanne was a good listener and loved Diane's tales of the dalliances of Britain's royal family, whether true or not. Her friend frequently embellished her stories, Suzanne was almost certain, but it mattered not at all.

Diane was away now, but Suzanne had a key to her place, and Diane had admonished her to use it whenever she was in London and needed a place to entertain an admirer.

As they sat together on the soft, furry rug in front of Diane's parlor fireplace, Suzanne studied this man Bochlaine had sent her—a man Aspis wanted to ruin, kill or both.

Suzanne hadn't immediately liked Bradford. He was sincere, but she had thought that he was too wrapped up in his own motivations to devote or jeopardize his life trying to curb Aspis. Earlier, when he'd announced his objective—to nail the assassin Criscolle—she had no quarrel with his reasons, but she knew that he had to be made to see that Aspis's monster from Brooklyn was only a single piece of the Aspis body that needed to be exterminated. When he began to understand her point of view, the truth about his family would, she hoped, get him to go the rest of the way. So she had sprung it on him. Immediately she hated herself for it.

The truth had hit him hard. She had seen it clearly and rushed him away so he would be free to vent the volcanic anger that was consuming him. Part of that anger overflowed in her car as she drove him to Diane's flat. The rest came out in Diane's parlor.

He looked straight past her as he stormed around the room like a caged lion. He didn't say a lot, but the pain on his face was eloquent. At last he stopped and stood over her. The glaze that had covered his eyes during his half-coherent rambling lifted and his natural warmth reappeared.

"You must have adored your wife and sons," Suzanne said. "I'm sorry I had to tell you. I wish I'd known your family. If only my grandfather had acted more boldly about the ransom money."

"Why hadn't he or the Vatican done something about replacing the ransom after it disappeared?" Brad asked.

"There was little he could do, actually. The Pope had no choice but to accept Massara's statement that the money had been paid to Hauptler and the Nazi Colonel had simply double-crossed them. To replace the money—even if the Vatican Bank could have done so easily, which it couldn't—would have only invited another theft by Hauptler. Or so it seemed, anyway.

"My grandfather could not have been more shocked when he learned that his mistress, my grandmother, was among the Jews Hauptler deported. He was able to hide away their daughter Deborah—my mother, who was twelve at the time—and she eventually married an American and they had me."

"What happened to your mother? You haven't mentioned her."

"She died of labor complications within a month of my birth. My father suffered a massive heart attack two years ago and also died. So I'm alone."

"Did your grandfather try to find out what happened to the money? Surely he approached Massara."

"Grandfather's attempt was ineffectual. Although he was a canny money man—he helped the Vatican achieve financial strength in spite of the war—he was not an investigator. He confronted Massara but the Vatican priest stuck to his story. Because he worked for the Vatican, grandfather could do little more than ask. Then the Allies began their attack on Rome and the world became a different place for everyone. After the war, Hauptler was convicted of the massacre of a hundred civilians just before the fall of Rome. He was sentenced to life imprisonment, but no evidence was ever presented against him for what he did to the Roman Jews—more than a thousand of them!

"When Aspis surfaced and he learned that Massara's half brother was at its head, grandfather swore to get at the truth if it took the rest of his life. It did, and he never found the Piedmont Papers he was certain would prove that Piedmont S.A and later Aspis was founded with blood money."

"You've had no luck since you became Count Vignola's assistant?"

Suzanne smiled ruefully. "The count's no longer a young man and seems uninterested in matters of the flesh, so I can't get close to him. He treats me like a ward who happens also to do a good job in business. I have the run of the place but they try to insulate me from the dirt just like they do with Frank Bochlaine. They haven't kept me from all their garbage, but I haven't come up with what I need, either."

"Bochlaine told me about the codes and sequences that keep Aspis secrets from being pulled out of the computer. It seems to me the count must have them written down somewhere."

"Maybe he does, but where he has them is anybody's guess. He has a great memory in spite of his more than seventy years and I've watched him at the computer keyboard while he was calling stuff out of the sensitive section. He bangs out those codes like they were the ABCs."

"How do you know he was pulling sensitive information out?"

"If he weren't, he'd have told me to do it. Whenever he gets a readout from the computer he takes it into his private office and never discusses it. Data I get for him we sometimes talk about."

"Maybe Piedmont isn't in the computer, Suzanne. What do you think?"

"I think it's there—or at least the location of the papers is in the computer's memory. It almost has to be, if only because the count will eventually die and whoever survives him will need the papers to prove his authority. And that's why I'm certain the Piedmont Papers are what we need."

"I'm beginning to see why Vignola, Criscolle, and company weren't too pleased about having my people sniffing around their trail. To modify an old axiom, I'd say it takes a computer to catch a computer. FINVEST's computer—we call it Max—is as sophisticated as any you'll ever see. My partner Tom Sumereau's a genius at programming it. Maybe he and I can figure out a way to get Max to produce the right codes and sequences that'll open up your computer. It's worth a try, anyway. I'll be flying home tomorrow and can go to work on it. What can you tell me?"

Suzanne told Bradford plenty. She produced a portfolio in which she kept an assortment of papers, sifting among them until she came up with one on which she had recorded, in a code of her own, all the secrets of the Aspis computer that she had either been told or figured out. She spent more than an hour explaining them to Brad, who made his own notes. Then she told him about her mission in London—to procure inside financial information about FINVEST. "I'm to pick it up tomorrow and deliver it back to the count later."

Brad was mildly surprised. "Can you let me have a copy? I'm not sure what they can find out that would let them put the money screws to us, but I sure as hell want to know before they do it."

"I'm not sure it would be wise to try to make a copy of it in London. They haven't followed me—at least not to my knowledge—but I can't be certain."

"I'll meet you at the airport in Rome. Near the TWA Ambassador Club. Pass me the report and I'll photograph it in the men's room and then return it to you. It'll take me less than a minute with the clever minature camera I have."

Suzanne agreed to that and gave him the arrival time of her flight tomorrow. Then she gave him her telephone number and the address of her Rome apartment. "Will you tell me now about Criscolle?" he asked as she drove him back to reclaim his car at nine o'clock. There was a flight to Rome at ten and he planned to be on it. "What he is," she replied, "represents the absolute worst in America. He was born and raised in Brooklyn, probably killed somebody before he had to shave and raped his first girl before other adolescents have their first date. He's tall, dark, and good-looking, as long as you can't see into his head or heart. His heart is as black as Satan's soul. His head's full of depravity and perversion, though I can't tell you from personal experience, thank God. I'm told he can't have sex until he physically abuses his women."

"A modern de Sade," Brad said. "Sounds like a sweetheart. He hasn't tried for you?"

Suzanne shivered. "I'd sooner give my body to the mercies of a lunatic pathologist," she declared. "When Nick looks at me I can see right into his head. I mean I know what he'd do to me if he ever got me in the right position. Thanks to the count, he hasn't tried too hard."

"Vignola holds him in check?"

"Not very much, but some. The count doesn't approve of Nick or his methods, I think. At least Vignola knows how to act like a gentleman when he's not giving the orders to kill someone."

Lost in thought, Bradford stared out the car's windshield for long moments and Suzanne was again sorry she had exposed the truth about his wife's murder. But when she apologized, he told her not to worry about it. "I'm all right," he said. "It's something that'll never be far from my conscious mind, but I can handle it. As long as I know that eventually I'll figure out a way to make the count and his goddamn Aspis pay."

"You will," she said, reaching across the seat to touch his cheek. "We will, Brad. We'll help each other."

When they arrived back on Deanery Street where Brad had parked his rented Austin, Suzanne drove up behind it, pulled up the brake, and turned toward him. She was about to tell him how grateful she was that he had agreed to help when instead she leaned across the seat toward him and offered him her mouth.

Brad hesitated and she thought he would refuse her, but he didn't. When their lips merged a spark raced through her body and her thoughts were fragmented by the electricity. So much so that she did not resist when he gently pulled away, then got out of the car and said good-bye. He headed for the airport, and back to Rome.

Driving back to the Aspis flat at Fountain House, Suzanne derided herself as a fool, for she had wanted Elliot Bradford all night long and should have realized it.

She recalled Brad's bearded face just as she began drifting off to sleep and was overcome with a feeling of passion and a desire to touch him again. She didn't know quite what it was about him that grabbed her, but she felt somehow connected, involved, intertwined with him.

A feeling of excitement and a sense of joy filled her heart and worked its way down to her loins. Suzanne succumbed to the sensation and fueled it with a fantasy about Brad, imagining his lips lingering over her body with soft, sweet, sensual kisses. She touched herself, intimately, and pretended it was Brad.

A wave of pleasure crested and then washed through her body, relieving tension as it did. She slept well, with Brad making guest appearances in her dreams that night.

Holly awakened when Bradford unlocked the door to his room at one o'clock in the morning. She had left the connecting door of the two rooms open and quickly slipped inside. "Brad?"

"Did Murray call?" he asked. There hadn't been any messages for him at the desk.

"Just before eleven," she said. "He still doesn't know if we're going to see the Pope. He said the appointment secretary was trying to work it out. Murray said even heads of state don't get to see the Pope on short notice."

"Any king who had a string-puller like Murray working for him could do it. In the ten years Murray's been with FINVEST he's never failed me. Whatever I ask him to do he manages, though he's always telling me there's no way he can."

Suddenly Holly sniffed the air and accorded him an odd look. Moving closer, she sniffed again, then glared at him unhappily. "How was London?," she asked in a caustic tone. "How was she? Did you sleep with her?"

"What are you talking about?" For a moment Bradford had no idea what Holly was irked about, but then he smiled a bit sickly. "Oh," he said, "you mean . . ."

"I mean the disgusting perfume you're drenched in. It's all over you. Did you take a bath in it?"

He shrugged off her accusation. "I think it's pretty nice," he said mildly. "Sort of like hyacinth, my favorite flower. As for Suzanne Steelman, she was my contact in London, and our meeting was entirely businesslike and productive. And as for sleeping with her, I had no time to sleep with her or without her, not that it's really any of your business."

Holly now drowned him under a flurry of questions about Suzanne. Or she would have, if he'd allowed it. Instead he cut her short and gave her a brief overview of how Suzanne fit into the picture.

"Does she know who killed my father?" Holly demanded.

Brad hesitated, wondering how safe it was for her to hear the truth. He decided he couldn't keep it from her any longer and owed it to her anyway. "His name is Nick Criscolle, Holly," he told her. "I'm told he enjoys his work and is awfully good at it. But, unfortunately, I can't prove that he did it, so don't go passing it around to anyone but your mother."

Her jealousy gone, she studied Brad's face, then asked, "What good is knowing who killed Daddy if you can't do anything about it?"

"A lot of good, Kitten. Now maybe we can find some proof to go with what we know. Suzanne may be able to help us, too. But, of course, if you'd rather I didn't see her or smell of her disgusting perfume . . ."

Holly sighed and made a graceful retreat. "I apologize, Brad. I don't have any right to be jealous. It's just that I'm so attached to you. I always have been, but now, especially, I need you, need to know you care for me. With Daddy gone, I feel so alone and vulnerable. You're the only man left in my life. I couldn't bear it if I lost you."

"I love you, Kitten . . . but like a sister. Maybe that's not how you want it, but let's leave it that way, okay? And I have no intention of disappearing on you—we're friends for life. When this awful mourning period passes, and when you meet some terrific guy your own age, I promise you, I won't look so good to you."

Brad tried to ease the tension with an affectionate wink, but Holly's eyes began to well with tears.

"You'll always look good to me, Brad. I used to be so envious of Nancy I could've . . . oh! I'm sorry. I didn't mean to remind you."

"You're forgiven, Holly. Just leave Criscolle to me. Somehow I'll find the proof we need to get him put away. Trust me. And don't you get involved. I'd hate to have anything happen to you."

"Will you tell the police in New York what you've found out? Will they try to extradite him?"

"Before they can extradite him they've got to prove a crime was committed, Kitten, and they can't do that yet, even if I tell them what I know. So what I've got to do is find proof that your father was murdered."

"Can you do that?"

"I don't know," he said truthfully. "Criscolle's as clever as he is vicious."

Holly's fingers made a small fist. "I wish I could get my hands on him!" she said suddenly. "I'd . . ."

"Forget that Holly. You don't want to get anywhere near him. Suzanne told me he's got a thing for sadistic sex and enjoys raping and punishing his victims."

"I can handle him," she said.

"Please, Holly. Let's get some sleep. I'm tired and need some shut-eye. Just understand one thing. This guy, Criscolle, is a monster like you have never known in your life. People like him make their own rules and don't tell you what they are until after you begin to play their game. By that time it's too late and you're at their mercy. Believe me when I say that mercy isn't what you'd get from the likes of him. Stay away from him—hear?"

He shooed Holly back into her room, latched the door, then fell into an exhausted sleep almost as fast as his head hit the pillow.

It seemed hardly a minute or two later that the telephone on the table between the two beds began shrieking. He groggily reached for it and brought it to his ear.

"Brad?" It was Murray's deep cultured voice. "You and Holly can see the Pope, but you're gonna have to be there at nine o'clock sharp. There was a cancellation and my friend Cardinal Cohen has managed to slip you in as a personal favor to me."

"Cardinal Cohen?" Brad echoed.

Murray chuckled. "His real name's so long and Italian I never could pronounce it, so I shortened it to Cohen. Before he made cardinal he was just my old friend Father Cohen."

Brad was too tired to laugh. "What time is it now?" he asked.

"Just past seven-thirty, so you'd better get your sleepy ass out of bed. You're not going to get in if you aren't there by nine. By the way, we had a call from New York yesterday after you left."

"Burke," Brad speculated, "of New York City homicide?"

"That's the one. He wanted to know . . ."

"What flight I'd be on today. You couldn't tell him, and I'm glad."

"Wrong, boss. I could've told him, but didn't. Your reservations are already confirmed for two o'clock this afternoon."

"He say anything else?"

"Uh huh. Said he'd find out anyhow and not to get frightened when you see him coming toward you at Kennedy. So your tickets are re-served in the name of Caterina and me. As long as you talk to our man Marco at the VIP counter, there will be no problems with your passport and the reservations that I made. How's that?"

That was fine, but as he showered and woke Holly, Brad almost hated his Rome manager. He hadn't had a good night's sleep all week.

An hour later he and Holly drove the rented Fiat across the Tiber River bridge and through the medieval walls that surrounded the mini city known the world over as Vatican City. The size of a small American farm—a very small one—it was located on Vatican Hill on the left bank of the Tiber, and its most prominent feature was St. Peter's Basilica and the round "square" where thousands of Catholics gathered every Sunday to be blessed by il Papa.

Holly, wearing a simple but fashionable black dress, looked like a different person as they reached the Porta Sant'Anna where regally uniformed Swiss Guards stopped them.

Murray had told Bradford that Cardinal Massara was still influential in the Vatican finance and that his office was in the Vatican Bank. "He's a bit of a recluse," Murray said, "and doesn't get many visitors, but you're free to try to get him to talk to you."

"I intend to," Brad had told Jolles. "Have you come up with anything on his finances?"

"Not a thing except that he has a triple-A credit rating and is employed by the Vatican as a part of the Roman Curia that runs the place."

"So what else is new?" Brad retorted. "Try checking out his half brother, by the way. Raffaele Ernesto Vignola, a count I suppose, since he uses that title. But do find anything you can on Cardinal Massara. He's part of the riddle I'm trying to solve."

Now Brad's car was quickly passed through the gates by the Swiss Guards, who had a visitors' permit waiting for them thanks to Murray's great efficiency. Without the permit they might have been delayed and missed the scheduled audience in the papal apartments. As it was, they arrived at the Room of the Evangelists barely in time to take their places before the white-robed Pope was escorted into the room by the Swiss Guard and his personal bodyguard. The Holy Father, looking frail in his advancing years, wore a wan smile as he passed before the fifty or so guests, many of them on their knees, and ascended the throne between the old sculptures of Saints Peter and Paul.

"Peace be with you all," His Holiness said in a steady voice that gave no hint of his years.

"And with you, Your Holiness," came the prompt response from his audience.

Standing on Brad's left, Holly was open-mouthed in awe. She was even more stunned when, after delivering a short, friendly, informal series of comments to the group, the Holy Father of almost a billion Catholics left the throne and began to move here and there around the room. He suddenly appeared beside Holly and greeted her in Italian.

Brad had to admire the Pope's pluck, for he had almost been killed a few years before by a crazed assassin. It was whispered that his state of health was deteriorating badly. "We're Americans, Your Holiness," Brad said as Holly fell to her knees, took the Pope's outstretched hand, and kissed his ring. "This is Holly Sands and I'm Elliot Bradford. We're from New York, where Holly's father, Jackson Sands, a good man and a good Catholic, lies awaiting burial tomorrow."

The Pope's face radiated sympathy as he realized Holly was in mourning. He raised his hand over the young woman and pronounced a few soft words in Latin—obviously a prayer for Jack Sands's soul and for his survivors—then blessed them both in English. "My evening prayers will be for your father, my dear. Do not fear for Jackson Sands; he will know our Father better than us all."

Now the Pope turned to Brad, saying, "Bless you, too, my son, for bringing Holly Sands here today. May peace always be with you and yours."

"Thank you, Holy Father," Brad murmured. For minutes all Holly could do after the Pope and his red-, yellow-, and blue-striped uniformed guards moved on to others in the room was to stare at his back. Then, leaning against Brad, she exhaled with a whoosh.

"I feel as if somehow God himself just touched me, Brad. I'm all goose bumps. Did you hear him? He said my name. And . . . he said he'd pray for Daddy tonight. Isn't that wonderful? Oh, Brad, thank you so much for bringing me!" She hugged him and there were tears in her eyes.

Holly was not the only one in the room brought to tears by the presence and attention of the Pope. As Brad stroked her head, he could see others—including some men—with glassy eyes or weeping openly. As Holly sobbed on his shoulder, he felt like he could have joined her, but he was not a Catholic and he disagreed strongly with much of the

Church's dogma. There was no question, though, of the Pope's personal magnetism and ability to move people. It was difficult to resist.

Following the audience, Brad and Holly went to the Istituto per le Opere di Religione—the Vatican Bank. It was a large stone building directly in front of the Papal Palace near the Porta Sant'Anna.

Inside the bank Brad gave his name to a black-garbed monsignor at the lobby desk and asked for Cardinal Massara. The monsignor gave him an odd look and started to say something, then shrugged and picked up the phone on his desk, punching numbers on the push-button console. He spoke in rapid-fire Italian when the call was answered. Brad understood a little of the language, but not enough to make heads or tails of the exchange.

When the priest hung up the phone and turned to face them, he had an apologetic look on his face. "I am sorry, Signor Bradford," he said, "but the cardinal has a busy schedule today. He says he can perhaps see you tomorrow."

"I'll be back in America tonight. There's no chance that he can give me just a few minutes right now? Tell him I want to talk to him about an organization run by his half brother, Count Vignola."

The monsignor hesitated, but Brad persuaded him to convey the message. This time he spoke more slowly, and Brad was able to understand him as he delivered the message. At the end of his conversation, the priest nodded, then replaced the telephone and told them the cardinal would briefly talk to him.

That was fine with Brad. He commanded Holly to wait in the lobby, then took an elevator up to Massara's private office. As he was met by a young nun, he wondered what he was going to tell Massara, for he still had not made up his mind.

The nun ushered him into the cardinal's office. "Cardinal Massara will be with you shortly, sir," the nun informed him.

While waiting for Massara, Bradford rejected his impulse to move over to the cardinal's mahogany desk to steal a look at the papers scattered there. There were many reasons he decided against this, not the least of them that it was entirely ridiculous to expect that the cardinal might have left anything incriminating on his desk available to anyone who ventured in. Instead Brad kept his distance, contenting himself with looking at the oil paintings and pictures on the wall of the carpeted office. There were several, including an oil of Vatican City itself, another of Pope John Paul I, and a photograph of a crowded St. Peter's Square during a papal coronation.

He was examining the undated photograph and trying to decide which Pope was being installed when Cardinal Massara entered through a rear door of the office and addressed him.

"An inspiring sight, isn't it, Mr. Bradford?"

Brad turned toward the speaker's voice to see a robed cardinal of average height and build who wore a smile on a face that looked like it could have been anywhere between fifty-five and sixty-five years old, though he knew Massara was well past seventy.

"Is this Pope John Paul's coronation, your Eminence?" Bradford inquired, pointing to the picture while watching the cardinal.

"Paul VI," Massara replied. "But it could just as easily have been our dear departed John Paul, or, of course, the second John Paul, whose day that was to shine in the sunshine of Peter's monument. Were you in Rome for either event? I'm told your organization has an office in Rome."

"It does, but I'm afraid I wasn't here," Brad replied smoothly. So that was why the cardinal was absent when he'd entered the office—he was running a fast check on Bradford. Did the Vatican Bank have a computer room with access to names and biographies of people and companies? Or had the cardinal simply phoned Vignola? "I was in St. Peter's Square when John Paul II became Bishop of Rome," Brad continued. "It was an impressive ceremony."

"Won't you sit down, Mr. Bradford? Tell me how I can be of service to you. You mentioned my half brother, Count Vignola, to the receptionist. Are you friends? Business associates?" The cardinal smiled. "Or rivals?"

Bradford ignored the last, though he was sorely tempted to comment on it. "I haven't much time, so I'll stand if you don't mind. Nor will I mince words with you. I'm here because I wanted to know if you were aware of Aspis—your half brother's firm—and the types of activities in which it engages." Brad paused for effect, then pronounced the word that he hoped would shock the cardinal. "Murder, Cardinal Massara."

Massara's bushy black eyebrows raised slightly, but Bradford could detect no other reaction. "Aspis?" he repeated, meeting Brad's eyes. "Murder? I do not understand, Mr. Bradford. I cannot imagine my brother being involved in anything of that kind. He is a man who knows

his duty before God. I am aware of his company, of course. It is Raffaele's business, but I am not privy to its activities." Massara now hesitated, eyeing his visitor with a touch of defiance, Brad thought. "Just
what are you suggesting? That Raffaele has killed someone? That, my
son, is preposterous!" Although his tone had become indignant as he
spoke, the cardinal was still under superb control.

"The count is no better than Hitler," Bradford now declared. "Although he personally hasn't killed anyone, he has an ocean of blood on
his hands, for he has ordered many executions."

"That is a ghastly accusation, Signore. Just whose death has he ordered?"

"For starters, there was an American named Jackson Sands. He was
the head of TNI, an international conglomerate. Jack was murdered in
cold blood, but his death was contrived to look like a suicide."

"How do you know that, Mr. Bradford?"

"Because I was there when he was shot. I chased the murderer after
he killed Jack."

"Obviously you didn't catch him. You say you know who the killer
is? You're certain he is a part of Raffaele's firm? Can you prove it?"

"No, I can't prove it. But I have no doubts at all about the man's
identity or his employer."

"What would you have me do about this, assuming that it is true? I
have little to do with my half brother and nothing at all to do with his
firm."

The cardinal said it so certainly that Bradford was tempted to believe
it. "Perhaps," he said, "you could suggest to the count that his people
should stop their ungodly practices—stop the killing." Brad allowed an
insolent smile to appear on his face as he casually tossed out his audacious
suggestion. He watched carefully for the reaction it drew from Massara.
Brad had already gone a good bit further than he'd expected to. His
original decision had been to make the ground under the cardinal's feet
tremble a little with his allegations. What he'd done was shake it with
volcanic force.

The cardinal's look, however, was benign and unconcerned. "Your
words," he said, "suggest that my half brother's employees spend as
much time committing murder as they do on business." He laughed,
then added, "That is patently ridiculous."

"Is it?" Brad was suddenly irritated. "Nicholas Criscolle, an Aspis operator, has the blood of Jackson Sands, among others, on his hands. He will kill again if he isn't stopped, if Aspis is unimpeded in its grisly endeavors."

A touch of red now appeared on the cardinal's neck. He formed the shape of a steeple with his fingers and stared over them at Bradford, his thick lips now set. "As you say, Mr. Bradford, I can speak to Count Vignola. And I will, you may count on it, although I doubt he will have any knowledge of the murders of which you speak. I'm certain he'll be as upset as I am by the allegation that any of his people are breaking God's laws, and I hope that you realize that slander in our country is a serious violation of the law—it is usually a matter for the police."

With that the cardinal stood and terminated the interview by offering his hand. Brad ignored the hand, and walked out of the office.

As they drove out of the Vatican and back across the Tiber, Holly and Brad were both quiet, though for different reasons. Holly's pensive mood was caused by her vivid impression of the Pope's saintliness. She felt wonderfully reassured by the Pope's words. Bradford was trying to accurately assess the cardinal he had just met.

Cardinal Massara appeared to have no special guilt on his mind. While he had not been especially open with Bradford, he had seemed no more guarded than most bankers Brad had met—or any other high-positioned member of the Roman Curia that ran the Vatican City's affairs. Furthermore, the cardinal had not seemed suspiciously more sensitive concerning Aspis than he should have been simply because of his half brother's involvement with the firm.

Had this cardinal taken part in the merciless slaughter of the Roman Jews fifty-three years ago? Or Jack Sands? Incredible as it may appear, was he the secret power behind Aspis?

Brad's visit to the cardinal had neither answered his questions nor provided a logical course for Bradford to follow in helping Bochlaine and Steelman search for the Piedmont Papers.

Suzanne. She was pleasing to think about, and he smiled now as he recalled that he was to meet her at the airport to copy the report on FINVEST she was delivering to Vignola. He would describe his visit to Massara to her so she would be able to watch Count Vignola for any reaction to the telephone call he would no doubt receive from the cardinal.

The last thought made him wonder if his visit to Massara would result in renewed efforts by Aspis to take him out. It was obvious to Brad now that Criscolle had tried to kill him two days ago, and that a previous unsuccessful attempt on his life had killed his family.

Would a new campaign to kill him prove anything about Massara? Would it prove that the cardinal was not the innocent he appeared to be? That his reaction to Bradford's visit was to urge on Aspis's killers? It might not prove anything at all. Was it possible that the cardinal would call his half brother, speak of the violence earnestly and sincerely to Vignola, and urge the count to stop? And would Vignola ignore the cardinal's plea or simply assure him that it was without foundation?

There were, Bradford thought, no easy answers in this high stakes game.

Holly stayed with him for the balance of the morning. Brad took her with him to Murray's office while he spent an hour sifting through some additional reports produced by FINVEST offices around the world as well as the report Murray made on Cardinal Massara and his half brother. The Massara report showed him to be a virtual pauper in terms of assets. There was a family farm in the mountains of northern Italy, but nothing notable. Vignola, on the other hand, had "assets that had assets," as Murray sarcastically wrote in his report on the count. Like Massara, Vignola had a place in the north of Italy, but the count's was an elegant villa in the heart of ski country and undoubtedly worth a fortune. Vignola's holdings that weren't shielded under the cover of corporate names were substantial. Among them were several banks as well as some rich Roman real estate and some other property holdings in the United States.

With or without Aspis, the count was a very wealthy man, though that fact seemed to have no particular significance.

Suzanne's plane from London was on schedule and Brad met her. So did Holly, whose face fell when she saw the long-stemmed beauty.

While Bradford spirited away the report Suzanne handed him concealed in the folds of a newspaper, Holly and Suzanne got acquainted in an airport lounge.

"I'm sorry about your father," Suzanne told Holly. "It's a lousy thing to deal with and I know how you must feel. Both of my parents are dead."

Holly, surprised by Suzanne's empathy found herself talking about her personal tragedy. The conversation quickly turned to Brad. "I've known him since I was a little girl," she said. "He was a good friend of my father and spent a lot of time with us. My mother loves him almost as much as I do." Holly, embarrassed by her blurted admission, turned away to avoid showing Suzanne the warm blush that quickly spread across her cheeks.

"I can understand that," Suzanne said easily. "He is an attractive man. Unfortunately, he's still head over heels in love with his wife. She must have been special."

"She was. Though I love her husband, I had to love her, too."

"Holly," Suzanne abruptly announced, "this isn't a game. Brad's in danger and so am I. Watch your back and be careful."

Brad's return from the men's room broke up the short conversation just as Holly was deciding that she liked the tall, sensational Steelman.

"All set," Brad said as he returned the report, wrapped in newspaper, to Suzanne. "Can you get a picture of Criscolle for me? It's always nice to know what the guy who's out to land you six feet underground looks like."

"Not likely. He's camera shy for some pretty good reasons and not likely to pose. I've never seen a picture of him, Brad," Suzanne said.

Bradford gave the highlights of his visit to Cardinal Massara that morning. "It may stir up a few things," he said, "and again, it may not. See what you can find out. Can we talk if I call you very late Saturday night from the States? That's Sunday morning for you."

"Let me call you from a pay phone. I think my phone's safe, but since Bochlaine's been disowned from the Aspis family, it's hard to say." She paused. "I'll call you at two in the morning your time Sunday." Having decided that, Suzanne Steelman walked away gracefully, her overnight bag in one hand. Noticing Holly watching her, Bradford wrapped an arm around her waist and gave her a quick hug, then teased her gently. "What do you think about the lady with the perfume now, Kitten?" he asked.

"The question is what do you think?" Holly replied.

"I think she's a terrific woman, as smart as any woman I've met."

"And pretty," Holly added. "So darned pretty! She's nice, too. Sort of reminds me of . . ."

"Of Nancy? You're right, Kitten, she does. She's a courageous woman. Suzanne's risking her life trying to do some things that might one day cut Aspis down to size and stop the murders."

"And you're going to help her?"

"We're going to help each other. It's not just one man who killed your father. The Aspis organization was just as responsible. If we can get at Aspis, we'll get Nick Criscolle, too."

"I hope you can, and I know Daddy does, too."

"I'm sure of it, Kitten."

EIGHT

While Elliot Bradford and Holly Sands were boarding a jet for their return trip to New York, Frank Bochlaine received a note from Cardinal Ambrosiani in Vatican City.

Bochlaine, though still in Rome, was not in the apartment he had maintained ever since he'd made his Aspis connection. He'd always known the day would come when the apartment would be unsafe and so he had made other arrangements.

Bochlaine long ago had befriended the wife and family of Giulio Cardone, a fellow Olympic weightlifter. Giulio had died just eleven months after Bochlaine joined Aspis. Bochlaine had attended the funeral, realized that Giulio's widow would be hard put to support her five little daughters, and offered to help. Over the woman's protests, he had all but supported Teresa Cardone and her brood ever since. In exchange for his kindness, he spent time with them when he wanted to escape from the pressures of his work. Eventually he'd anonymously bought the home Giulio had rented for the family just south of Vatican City.

And now, when he needed a safe haven, Bochlaine had come to roost with Teresa, who asked no questions when he told her two days ago that he would be staying with the family for a while. Only one other person, Ambrosiani, knew where he was.

Ambrosiani's note said Bradford had approached Cardinal Massara at the Vatican Bank that morning. Bochlaine chuckled at the thought that Massara could not have appreciated the visit, no matter what the American had told him, for the cardinal had to be well aware that Bradford was, or might soon be, searching for the Piedmont Papers.

Bradford was bold, Bochlaine thought, as he prowled about Teresa's cellar, where relics of Giulio's weightlifting career were scattered here and there. He would have to be more than bold if he were to stand a chance against Aspis, the fat Italian knew. Suzanne would help him, of course, but even with help from inside Aspis, the odds didn't favor Bradford. Bochlaine knew both Bradford and Suzanne could easily be eliminated.

And so could Frank Bochlaine, although he would gladly give up his life if he could only be assured that in doing so he could bring down the count, the cardinal, Aspis. Bochlaine was not frightened of death. His training as a Jesuit and his great strength perpetually reinforced his deep faith. Had not Cardinal Ambrosiani enlisted his aid years ago, he might well be in a monastery now.

Suddenly he had a chilling thought. In his apartment he had left behind a scrapbook containing newspaper clips of his exploits in the Olympics. It was his lone vanity and he should have destroyed it years ago. But he had not, and now it could betray his whereabouts to Aspis and Nick Criscolle, for in the scrapbook were references to his friend Giulio—his Olympic bronze medal and his obituary. If Criscolle searched his apartment he would surely go through the desk where Bochlaine kept the book. The clipping reporting Cardone's death would have the address of Giulio's widow. Criscolle would have the address where Bochlaine could be found.

Bochlaine would have cursed had he been one to curse. He could not allow Criscolle to follow him here, for if he did, he would find Giulio and Teresa's sweet wonderful daughters. Teenagers now, they were as pretty as only young Italian women could be. If Criscolle came here, he would cut a vicious swath through the entire household.

Ten minutes later Bochlaine was on his way to the bridge across the river in the Fiat he had bought for Teresa a few years ago. Destroying the scrapbook was his only option in order to ensure his safety and the safety of his friends.

Bochlaine's fears were not unjustified, although Nick Criscolle had not yet discovered the connection between Bochlaine and Cardone. Two days earlier, while Bochlaine was meeting Bradford, Criscolle had ransacked his apartment, found the book, and gone though it carefully. But he had not noticed the small newspaper article folded and tucked behind a larger Olympic story pasted into the book.

After his search of Bochlaine's apartment, Criscolle left a man to keep watch and began checking all the places—most of them restaurants and taverns—Bochlaine frequented. But Bochlaine's former habits would not help the man from Aspis locate him, for he now took all his meals with Mama Teresa, as Bochlaine called her. She was an excellent cook and accustomed to cooking for voracious appetites. Like most weight-lifters, her husband had had one and so did her daughters.

Two days spent hunting for Bochlaine had turned up nothing, so Criscolle decided to return to Bochlaine's apartment to search it once more. He was on his way there in his black Porsche when the mobile phone rang. The caller, a little man named Benito, was a sometime gofer for Criscolle. At the moment he was watching Frank Bochlaine's second-floor apartment and it had just had a visitor—Bochlaine himself.

"Bochlaine!" Criscolle exclaimed. "Great. Get ready to follow him if he leaves before I get there. I'm not far away, though. With luck I'll make it."

Now Criscolle floored the accelerator and the Porsche shot ahead, slowing briefly at a street intersection where a traffic light commanded him to stop, then roaring through. Two Rome taxis collided in his wake and both drivers swore at him as he sped away.

Two blocks later he careened around a sharp curve and raced down a long avenue. A pair of streetwalkers saw the handsome Porsche approach and resolved to stop it, but Criscolle paid them no heed. They gave him the forearm as he passed no more than a foot away from where they stood in the street. Moments later he parked near his guard.

Bochlaine, Benito told him, was still upstairs. "Okay, Benito, get the fuck out of here," Criscolle ordered. The little man had his car started and in gear before his boss could cross the street.

Criscolle was carrying a hypodermic needle with which he could ad-minister a mind-numbing drug to a person he wanted to knock out rather than kill, and he was ready to use it on Bochlaine. He also carried a .45 automatic and a stiletto-thin knife. Prepared to surprise and am-bush his prey, he moved stealthily along the wall of the square three-story apartment building toward the rear entrance.

A flagstone walkway ran the short distance from the building's back door to the street behind it. It was lit by a lamp fitted to the side of the building. In the darkness of the moonless night, Bochlaine did not see Criscolle when he emerged from the door, the photo album scrapbook slipped under his vest inside his coat in order to hide it from prying eyes.

Criscolle crouched in the shrubbery as Bochlaine walked right past him, then stepped out and sprinted toward his quarry. Bochlaine heard

the footsteps behind him, but did not turn to find out who was following until he reached his Fiat at the curb.

"How're ya doing, fat man?" Criscolle's voice was a nasty rumble in
the quiet residential street. He held the hypodermic in his right hand,
the stiletto in his left. "See anything interesting in New York?" Criscolle
leaped at Bochlaine, trying to drive the hypodermic into his huge
shoulder.

But Bochlaine jumped aside and struck down at Criscolle's arm,
knocking the hypodermic to the street. Then, Bochlaine seized Criscolle's neck in his enormous hands and began to strangle the assassin. He
never saw the razor-sharp stiletto, but he felt a sharp pain close to his
heart. Criscolle had managed to use his lethal knife.

Still Bochlaine held on with his hands, squeezing with every bit of
strength he could muster. Criscolle held his breath while vainly trying
to break the fat man's grip on his windpipe.

Bochlaine ought to be dead, he thought as a wave of nausea swept
over him and he began to lose consciousness. Dead. Dead, but can a
single knife wound kill such a mountain of a man? He collapsed, unconscious, just as Bochlaine loosened his grip and sank slowly to the curb,
his hands seeking the stiletto buried in his chest. Then Bochlaine's arms
went limp and he fell forward, his head striking the sidewalk.

Minutes passed before Criscolle regained consciousness. When his
blurry vision cleared, he saw the inert mountain of cloth and flesh that
had been Bochlaine lying motionless on the curb. Criscolle still unsteady
and weaving a bit as he tried to clear his head, got to his feet.

Quickly he looked up and down the street. No cars had passed during
his struggle with Bochlaine and none were in sight now. Off in the
distance he heard a church bell begin to sound and he checked his
watch. Ten o'clock? He strained to recall what time it had been when
he had arrived, but couldn't.

He had to move fast, for he had been lucky up to now that there had
been no passersby to witness his struggle with Bochlaine. He bent
towards the unconscious man, intent on retrieving his knife, but found
he couldn't move the man's dead weight, so he decided to abandon the
weapon. He always wore gloves when handling his knives and pistols.
The stiletto could not be traced.

But he had to make sure of Bochlaine; he withdrew his silenced automatic from the pocket of his coat and leaned over the still figure, pressing

the muzzle to Bochlaine's head. But he reevaluated the execution-style murder, so he eased off the trigger just as he was about to pull it. A bullet in Bochlaine's head would change the appearance of things dramatically and perhaps cause an unnecessary investigation, which Count Vignola would not like. With a knife in his heart Bochlaine would appear to be the victim of a simple knife-point robbery, an illusion that his bullet would have destroyed.

Again Criscolle looked around for any observers. He then checked Bochlaine's pockets for a wallet, found one and took it. He reached for the man's wrist to make certain he was dead. He lifted it and searched for Bochlaine's pulse, but had not found it when suddenly the wail of a police car split the cool night air. He dropped Bochlaine's wrist, satisfied that the man was dead, jumped to his feet and headed back to his Porsche. He was almost to it when the police car appeared. It did not slow, but miraculously continued past Bochlaine's car and the man's body.

Criscolle turned the Porsche around and drove it toward Bochlaine's car. Reaching it, he secured a flashlight from his glovebox and focused it on Bochlaine. The big man did not move.

Criscolle smiled as he drove away. "Now for Bradford," he murmured.

His smirk broadened as he remembered the girl he had seen clinging to Bradford's arm as they left his FINVEST office yesterday. Young and pretty, she had stayed with him in his hotel. Criscolle had checked on her and learned that she was Holly Sands, Jackson Sands's daughter. Was she Bradford's lover? She had to be, Criscolle decided, to be staying with him when she should be at home mourning her father.

Could he use her to get to Bradford? He had a feeling he could; the only question was how? He resolved to find out, for the little blonde interested him. If he could somehow make Holly Sands his prisoner, he could use her to get at her lover and kill them both. But not until he had enjoyed her.

A good idea? He laughed to himself. It was great! He was sure of it. Now that the count had given him permission to eliminate Bradford he could go to work on the details.

In spite of a horribly sore and bruised neck from Bochlaine's strangle hold, Criscolle was in rare good humor as he swung the Porsche onto the street where his apartment was located.

Bochlaine lay where he had fallen for more than ten minutes after Criscolle's departure, his blood trickling out of the wound in his chest created by the Aspis assassin's stiletto. Then he came to.

Where was he? Why was he so weary? So weak? Move , . . he had to move. But he couldn't. Was he dreaming?

Vaguely he felt the discomfort of the knife still buried in his chest. He tried to roll away to ease it, but found he couldn't move his bulk far enough. At last he managed to roll over on his back. He blinked as a drop of rain struck his face, then another, and several more. A storm was about to drench him as he remembered where he was. The return trip to his apartment to get his scrapbook, finding it there intact, the retreat down the stairs, then . . . Criscolle! The assassin's voice had come so suddenly, so unexpectedly, that Bochlaine had frozen for the barest of seconds. Then he had hurled himself sideways to avoid Criscolle's attack and lashed out at him. Bochlaine's hands had found Criscolle's throat and he had squeezed with all his might.

Squeezed. But what then? What had happened? Bochlaine shook his head to clear it as more rain splashed down on it, blurring his vision. He blinked and reached up to wipe the rain away from his eyes and that's when he saw the handle of the knife protruding from his chest.

A knife? In his heart? Was he dying?

No. He felt far too strong for that. He stared at the spot on his left breast where the knife was and saw that the handle of the weapon was red with blood. His blood. He mumbled a quick prayer and tried to raise himself into a sitting position, his eyes still on the ugly knife. Then he reached across his chest, seized the knife handle and pulled it straight out. Or tried to, for it did not budge—it was like a miniature Excaliber, unwilling to move for an ordinary mortal.

Sweat rolled down his rosy cheeks as Bochlaine tried again to extract the blade from his flesh. This time it moved, coming out an inch or so. A great sense of relief came to him. Again he tugged at the knife and it resisted him. He could feel warm blood oozing out of his wound. Criscolle had plunged the knife straight into his heart—or so it seemed.

Then he realized why the knife was so hard to remove. The scrapbook! It was thick and heavy and . . . it may have saved his life! Reaching down, he unbuttoned his thin blue-black raincoat and looked inside. Under his vest was the scrapbook, with Criscolle's knife blade buried in it!

"Praise be the Lord!" Bochlaine murmured as he renewed his efforts to pry the knife loose from the album. At last he withdrew it, dropped it into his coat pocket, and inspected the wound it had caused. The gash was bloody, but not too deep, he concluded. Using his handkerchief folded into a thick square, he covered the wound, holding the cloth against it with one hand while he worked to get to his feet.

The effort of raising more than three hundred pounds made his wound smart and burn and spurt fresh blood. He knew he would bleed to death if he didn't get help bandaging the wound soon, so he ignored his pain and staggered around the back of the car to the driver's door.

"Are you all right?" came a voice from his left as he fumbled in his coat pocket for the key.

Turning, he gave a nod and tried to look sheepish. "I slipped," he said to the man who stood watching him from across the street. "Thank you for your concern."

With great relief Bochlaine unlocked the car door and heaved his bulk inside behind the wheel. The drive to Mama Teresa's was not easy. He had to keep his left hand pressed tightly against his wound while changing gears and steering, but he managed it.

On Mama Teresa's street an eternity later he honked for help and was barely conscious when his old friend's wife put on a raincoat against the steady rain and helped him stagger into the house.

Inside, Bochlaine collapsed and it took Mama Teresa and all five of her daughters to get him into the downstairs room he occupied. They giggled among themselves as they watched their mother struggle to get Bochlaine's coat and shirt off, but they gaped in silence when they saw the bloody slit just below his left breast.

NINE

Eleanor Sands and her daughter Holly were dry-eyed during the Saturday morning funeral mass in St. Patrick's for Jack Sands. They did not weep until they reached Jack's ultimate destination—a graveyard in Vermont not far from Winterhaven, the Green Mountain chalet he had loved.

Brad and Tom Sumereau comforted them as they stood and watched the casket being lowered into its grave in the pretty little country cemetery behind St. Francis Church. Only a few TNI officials, among them the new TNI president, flew to New England with Eleanor and Holly Sands, Bradford, and Sumereau.

After a private dinner in a nearby restaurant, Ellie and Holly quarreled over Holly's insistence on taxiing to Winterhaven "to be near Daddy."

"Daddy's gone, darling," Eleanor told her daughter as Bradford and Sumereau watched the pair argue while they waited for a taxi in the restaurant's lobby. "You'll be just as close to him in the city as you would out here."

Holly shook her head, her mind made up. "I think he'd like it if I stayed at Winterhaven for a few days and that's where I'm going. I don't mind staying there alone, although I'd love some company." She turned to Bradford: "Would you stay there with me, Brad?" Her tone was casual rather than sensual.

Brad smiled but refused. "I don't think either of your parents would approve," he said. "Besides, Tom and I have a lot of work to do tomorrow and my system's all screwed up from jet lag."

Although Ellie cajoled and threatened in her attempt to get Holly to fly back in the TNI jet with them, the strong-minded and beautiful blond stayed in Vermont. Brad wasn't at all sure the isolated chalet that at this time of the year looked more like a fancy ski lodge than a private estate was the best place for Holly to be, but at least she wouldn't expect his attention. She wouldn't get anyone's attention at Winterhaven right now, for there was no year-round help there, although the pantry was always well-stocked and the heating system ran automatically, even when the house was unoccupied. The Vermont State Police for years had kept the place free from burglars by doing random helicopter flybys when there was snow hiding the mountain slopes or by having a car check the place out at other times of the year, so it was safe.

During the short flight to Teterboro Airport across the Hudson River in New Jersey, Brad tried to reassure Ellie that Holly would be all right—that maybe she needed some time by herself to mourn. Ellie wasn't so sure, but accepted her daughter's decision gracefully.

Tom told Brad that Lieutenant Burke of homicide would be "around" to see him Monday.

"Just what I need to start the week," Bradford muttered as he stared out the rectangular window beside him just above the plane's wing.

"Tell you what, Brad, he's no typical cop. You won't have to take my word for it. Wait till you meet him.

"I can't wait," Brad said dryly. "Any luck turning up our spy?"

"Not a clue, only hopes."

Because Ellie and the TNI executives who had attended Jack's funeral were on the plane with them, Brad and Tom waited until they were riding in a TNI-provided limousine from Teterboro to Brad's apartment to discuss what Brad had learned during his trip to Rome and London.

When Brad told him about the bombshell Suzanne had dropped on him—that Aspis was responsible for his family's deaths—Tom was too stunned to comfort his good friend. His partner's revelation repulsed him. The nausea rose in his gut, and he ran his hand through his hair as if it would steady him.

"You're sure she's right?" Tom asked, hoping it wasn't true.

"There's no reason not to believe her. In fact, now the whole thing seems to make more sense," Brad responded.

"My God, Brad," he said, shaking his head. "My God they killed Nan and the kids, while trying to get you. It's frightening. It's like a goddamn mobster movie. I'm so sorry. Those lousy sons of bitches."

Brad was silent, his thoughts still jumbled, his course of action entirely unclear. Now that Jack was buried, Brad could concentrate on the problems with Aspis, Nick Criscolle, and the spy at FINVEST. But it was hard to know where or how to begin.

"Let's meet early Monday morning, Tom, before Burke arrives to give me the third degree. There are some things we need to talk about and I've got a computer job that needs your brains. I'll tell you all about it Monday." He did not tell Tom about the Aspis computer codes, mainly because he wanted the weekend to go over his notes and formulate his own ideas free of Tom's influence. There would be plenty of time Monday for them to bounce their ideas off each other and decide what to do about the now-confirmed spy in their midst.

"Hang in there, Brad," Tom told him as Brad climbed out of the TNI limo in front of his apartment building.

Brad waved as the car pulled away and was again submerged in a thick morass of thoughts, the turmoil within him causing a tight feeling in his stomach that reminded him of the ulcer he'd developed the year he returned to civilian life. That had been a tough year. He worked hard to dismiss from his mind some grim and unhappy memories of the killing game that was war and counterintelligence. And now he found himself up to his neck in another such killing game, this one even worse than the first!

Upstairs in his apartment he stripped and stepped into a hot shower to calm his jangled nerves. He lingered there for a long time. At first his mind was blank while the needles of hot water drummed at his flesh. Then his mind began to clear under the steady stream of water and he began to focus on the tasks ahead.

Tom would be the one to crack the computer codes if they could to be cracked, for he was the resident computer genius. And Tom would grapple with the problem of the spy, but would need some input from Brad.

They would have to put their heads together and figure out how to arrange a new and secret line of credit with several large national banks to guard against an Aspis-created credit crunch. FINVEST was a good, healthy firm with few cash problems, but it had become heavily leveraged these past seven years because of its aggressive expansion. Brad's copy of the report Suzanne had delivered to Count Vignola showed that Aspis knew exactly who FINVEST's major credit suppliers were. If Aspis was powerful enough to pull the plug on FINVEST's bank credit, all hell would break loose, Brad knew. Brad hoped Aspis could not pull it off, but he was no longer sure about anything.

In the Aspis/Criscolle matter, Brad had his work cut out for him. He wondered now if Count Vignola's mountain retreat at Livigno might contain any Aspis secrets. He resolved to ask Suzanne when she called tonight. If there was even a chance, he would pay a visit to the count's chalet. It had been a long time since his last "Mission Impossible" intelligence assignment in Vietnam, he thought as he turned off the shower, pushed open the door, and stepped out of the tiled enclosure. Was he still up to it?

He stood in front of the full-length mirror near the bathroom door, sucked in his stomach, and threw back his shoulders. His posture had deteriorated, but his body was still in decent shape.

The telephone in the living room interrupted his thoughts. He pulled a towel around himself and picked up his watch. A glance at it told him it wasn't even one-thirty in the morning yet. Suzanne wasn't due to call until two o'clock New York time. Was she early?

She wasn't. It was Holly on the phone, calling from Winterhaven. "I'm lonely," she said when he picked up. "I miss Daddy, but I miss you, too. Terribly."

"Come on, Holly, get yourself together," Brad chided. "You've good reason to miss your father, but not to miss me."

"How can I help missing you? I'm all goose bumps right now because I was just remembering what happened in Rome."

Brad groaned audibly. "I told you to forget that," he declared. "It shouldn't have happened, and I'm sorry it did."

"I'm not."

"Holly, I have to do some hard thinking about your father's murder. That's why I had to get back here. If you're going to keep me on the phone, I'll get nowhere."

"Are you sure you're not dreaming about Miss Hyacinth?"

"I'm not dreaming about anybody!" he snapped.

He didn't hear her response, for she had already hung up. He gave a quick shake of his head, made himself a drink, put on his robe, and lit a cigarette to help him think. He smoked in silence as he reviewed the events of the past week.

Promptly at two o'clock his phone rang again. It was Suzanne. "Your telephone was busy for a while," she said.

"You called early? That was Holly. She's lonely."

"And wants you, right? I'm not sure I blame her."

Now Brad grinned. "You too? I'm not used to all this attention."

She didn't laugh. "Better this kind of attention than the kind Frank Bochlaine got yesterday. Criscolle waylaid him and knifed him."

"Christ! Is he dead?"

"No, thank God, he was lucky. He'll recover. He's got his own private nurse and he's doing fine, but he's mad as the devil. Luckily, Criscolle believes he's dead."

"Where is Criscolle right now, Suzanne?"

"I'm not sure. He could be anywhere. I haven't seen him since this morning. He was in the office early, conferring with Count Vignola. When he came out he was in a rare mood. Asked me out to dinner, and he hasn't done that in a while. Of course, I told him no thanks. He didn't seem to mind the rejection one damn bit."

"How is the count acting? Do you think he's talked to Cardinal Massara?"

"I don't think he's very happy, but I couldn't find out if the cardinal called. I had a chance to check the pad he doodles on, but couldn't make out anything that confirmed a call from Massara. The only other way I could find out would be to ask his secretary, Felicia, and that would surely get back to the count. She'd do anything for him."

"Did Vignola say anything about the report you delivered?"

"Only a little. He was displeased, I think, because he read that you were in the process of adding BMC to your client list. Then, he actually cursed. He apologized to me before I could get out the door."

"A real gentleman," Bradford said ironically. "No hint of what he might do now?"

"Not a word. But whatever he said to Criscolle must have pleased Nick. He sure didn't share the count's black mood."

"Could it be that Nick just got a sniff of a wounded deer? Maybe the count gave him permission to try to knock me out again."

"He could be in New York right now laying a trap for you."

"That thought has occurred to me. Does it bother you?"

"More than a little, Brad. I need your help, and Nick's as smart as he is deadly."

Brad was a little disappointed in her response, but did not say so. Instead he said, "Don't worry. I'm smart and tough, too. I had intense training while in army intelligence in Vietnam, and the Cong tried its damnedest to put me on ice. For a while I had a pretty good network of spies telling us what they were doing, but then one of my men got caught. They made him spill his guts before they spilled his blood. No genteel torturers the Cong. They cut off his fingers, one by one, and forced him to swallow them. When that didn't work, they dropped his pants.''

Suzanne's gasp was audible over the telephone. "Nick's got an advantage, though," she said. "You're a moral person. And you're not in the middle of a war."

"My morality won't affect me now because I *am* in the middle of a war—a war with him and Aspis. Criscolle's going to lose and so is Aspis. They'll all pay for what they did to Jack, to Nan, and to my sons."

"I hope so. You know I'll help every way I can."

"Tell me, Suzanne, does the count spend much time in his mountain villa? Is it guarded? Could he have a safe there where he might keep written copies of his codes and sequences?"

"The villa is his home most weekends, but I've never been able to find out if it has a safe there. Whenever I'm his guest the place is swarming with bodyguards."

"You go with him often?"

"Most weekends he invites me. This weekend he's still in Rome by the way. I enjoy going to the villa because I like to ski. I have my room there, complete with all kinds of ski clothes that he bought me. He also has the place equipped with a computer terminal and it's networked with our main one in Rome. He could run the operation from there if he had to."

"Do you have any idea how large a staff is on duty when he isn't there? How well it's guarded?"

"You want to break in?"

"That's the idea. See what you can learn about the staff and guards, but don't take any unnecessary chances doing it. Even if you were able to get a roster of every servant and guard the count has and when and where they're on duty, I'd still have to reconnoiter before I tried to get in. So the information will help, but I can do without it."

"If you're going, so am I," she said.

"We'll see about that later," he said.

"No we won't, Brad. This is as much my struggle as yours. Besides, I know Villa Amalfi and the area around it. You don't."

Brad chuckled. "It'll be dangerous," he said, "but I'll be glad to have your company if you're willing."

She was a persuasive and gutsy woman, he thought as he hung up. An hour later he was sleeping soundly.

In spite of his late night, Brad awoke early. The air outside was unseasonably warm, so he put on just a wool fisherman's sweater and slacks before going out for his usual morning walk.

He was strolling slowly down Riverside Drive when he noticed a New York blue and white police cruiser tagging along behind him. Instantly, he became wary and alert. He frowned but took no evasive action right away. Moments later the car swung to the curb just ahead of him and a tall, young-looking man dressed in a kelly green cardigan sweater over a turtleneck shirt and green slacks stepped out in front of him.

Lieutenant Kevin Burke gave Bradford his best Irish smile as he held up his hands. "If you're Elliot Bradford," he said, "I'm Kevin Burke. Lieutenant Kevin Burke, NYPD homicide."

"And if I'm not Bradford? If I'm John Jones or Bill Smith?"

"Then I suppose I'm St. Patrick himself, Mr. Bradford. But you're Bradford, and I'm Burke. I'm glad to meet you." He offered his hand.

"You're early," Bradford observed, accepting Burke's hand. "Tom Sumereau said you were supposed to come by the office tomorrow. Do you guys work on Sundays?"

"Only when we can't avoid it. And never during the football season. I'm a football fan."

"Giants?"

"Jets. I like their green uniforms, of course. Hey, do you mind if I ask you some questions?"

"Your place or mine?"

Burke chuckled. "Good to find someone with a sense of humor. Most of the people I run into in my business don't laugh. They can't. Your place is all right. It's close, and I expect it has a better view."

"Mind if we walk a little? The sun feels good."

Burke didn't mind, and soon they were walking leisurely north toward Riverside Church, whose 400-foot Gothic tower shimmered in the early morning sun.

Brad was quiet, fully expecting a barrage of questions Tom had warned him about. But Burke asked no questions for several minutes as the two men walked along side by side. A uniformed cop in a squad car stayed well behind them in the sparse Sunday morning traffic.

Finally Brad could stand the silence no longer. He stopped and faced Burke, saying, "Jack was murdered, Lieutenant."

"You're certain?" The words weren't challenging, and Burke showed no special surprise at Bradford's statement.

"There were two people in Jack's office just before he was shot. I know because I was there. I was just outside Jack's office door."

"After the shooting you chased the second man—Sands's killer—down the fire stairs." It was not a question, and it surprised Bradford.

"What makes you say that?"

Burke shrugged. "If you were there when Sands was killed and the murderer left the office, you would have followed him down the stairway. Right?"

"He might not have taken the stairs, Lieutenant, and I might have been too scared to follow," Bradford pointed out. "And you said I chased him. Why?"

Burke's chin, a wide, firm one, squared as he smiled and said, "Because my people found a couple of pieces of metal between the TNI offices and the street. One was in the wall, the other one lying on the floor. Both were bullets."

Brad's eyebrows arched high, respect in his expression. He had not believed a police officer would be so fanatically thorough in investigating what must have appeared to the cops to be a straightforward suicide. "What the hell made you check the fire stairs?"

"I could say it was a hunch, but it wasn't, Mr. Bradford. The truth is we had a call from the president of a small securities firm that has offices in the building. He was downtown on the street—Wall Street, of course—until late Tuesday afternoon. When he got back to the TNI building, the guard was nowhere to be found, and he couldn't get inside. It was exactly seven o'clock, and he rattled and banged at the door for ten minutes before he gave up and went home."

Brad knew where the guard had been, but waited for Burke to explain.

"The guard claims he never left the desk in the lobby," Burke continued. They had begun walking again, but now Burke's eyes were on

Bradford as they moved. "That made me a little curious, actually," the cop said. "And so did the fact that everyone I spoke to said there was no way your friend would kill himself. So I began assuming the whole affair was a homicide. And that's why I ordered the fire stairs checked. I was looking for a needle in a haystack, I admit, but it paid off. When we turned up the bullets, I had only a theory how they got there. I figured the killer had been interrupted and had to take the stairs because he was being pursued. He was shooting at you with a silenced gun—right?"

Brad had to laugh. "You're doing fine, Lieutenant. Why don't you figure out who he is and arrest the bastard?"

"I was hoping you'd help me do just that, Mr. Bradford."

Brad's laugh died in his throat. How far could he trust Burke? How much did he dare tell the cop? Telling him who the killer was would open up the whole Aspis mess and that, he knew, was not the kind of dirty dealing over which New York's police had any authority.

"I'm working on it," Brad said, sparring for time. His instincts told him not to say more, although he had never been more impressed by a member of the New York City Police Department. He wasn't yet sure if he liked the smart cop, but Burke had his attention and his respect.

"So am I," Burke said. "Does this killer have anything to do with the outfit your firm just finished investigating on TNI's behalf? Cinema Services?"

Brad was again astonished that Burke had picked that up and wondered if he had gotten the information out of Tom Sumereau without Tom realizing it. Or if he had wiretapped their office. Brad dropped his eyes to a spot on the sidewalk as he tried to figure out what to say.

"Talk to me, Bradford," Burke said finally. "We're both on the same side. And I believe your life is in danger now, just as Sands's was."

Bradford looked up. "It is, Lieutenant. Yes, let's talk. I have some questions too."

It wasn't difficult for Nick Criscolle to learn the details of Jack Sands's funeral arrangements. Aspis had a New York City undertaker on its payroll. The undertaker had been useful more than once, and now he phoned the information that Criscolle wanted to Rome.

On the flight to New York it occurred to Criscolle that Sands's Vermont chalet, built on a plateau miles from the nearest town, would be the perfect place to kill Bradford and his little green-eyed blonde. The question was, how could he lure them there? With Jack Sands being buried in Vermont not far from the chalet, there was a chance that Holly and Bradford would go there after the funeral. But the girl's mother might come along, too, and that would screw things up. Or they might all fly straight back to New York. Perhaps they might separate after the service. There were many possibilities.

But his plan could work. Criscolle arranged for observers at the airport near Rutland where the TNI jet had landed Saturday afternoon. They would tell him the ultimate destinations of Elliot Bradford and Holly Sands.

At nine-thirty that evening, his observer reached him at his apartment with the news that Holly Sands had apparently chosen to remain in Vermont while her lover and her mother flew back to New York. Criscolle was ecstatic. All he had to do to arrange his private "passion play" was to trap Holly at Winterhaven and force her to summon her lover from New York.

It took the Aspis assassin two hours to arrange for a helicopter to take him to Vermont because he was determined to find a good man to pilot the chopper—a man who would follow orders, no matter what they were. Criscolle and his pilot, a swarthy, mustachioed Libyan who had worked for Aspis before, lifted off an hour before daybreak Sunday and got their first look at Winterhaven just before eight in the morning.

The chalet was huge and perched high on a wide plateau south of Rutland. Originally built by an architect for his own use, the front of the chalet had redwood decks on both the first- and second-floors overlooking the steep mountain side. The mountain was tree-lined and broadened out into a valley near the state highway almost three-quarters of a mile below. Inside the chalet, the huge living room had an outer wall constructed entirely of glass rising to the peaked roof some forty feet above the ground. It offered a magnificent view, even without venturing out onto the deck.

The master bedroom, where Jack and Ellie Sands had slept and made love on an enormous four-poster bed of polished cherry, offered an even better view. The bedroom was built directly above the living room, with a glass wall at the bedroom's front that opened up to the mountainside. Through the glass, Jack and Ellie could also peer down into the living room. Direct access to the room could be gained by way of circular "captain's" stairs that rose from the basement-level garage beneath the house. Alternatively, the back stairs could be used. They connected a hall off the kitchen and dining room and a second-floor corridor that led to three other bedrooms, each complete with its own fireplace and private bath.

A short distance from the chalet was a large, red barn that housed snowmobiles and a snowplow along with other maintenance equipment to care for the more than three acres of grass around the house. A neat split-rail fence circled the entire property, with a gate that could be locked or unlocked electronically from the house or family car. Beyond the fence the mountain fell sharply away in front and rose at the rear. The fence was now barely visible on the plateau, for more than three feet of snow had accumulated since winter's beginning three months ago.

Criscolle's pilot circled the house once to get his bearings, then came in low and as quietly as the chopper could to land behind the barn and out of view of the house. The pilot killed the engine a split second before the chopper touched the ground.

Inside the house Holly was nestled snugly beneath the covers of her father and mother's big bed, her sleep filled with dreams.

She was racing her father on brightly colored snowmobiles along the trails of the mountainside. Jack Sands was chastising her for taking an unscheduled holiday from the fashionable girls' school Ellie had gotten her into for a year. And soon her father was kissing her forehead while dropping into her upturned palm the keys to her first car—a snazzy canary yellow Prelude.

Then Brad was there—drinking with her father and grinning at Holly as they all curled up in the living room before a crackling winter fire.

"I'm going to catch you one day, Brad! You'll see."

"Holly! You're embarrassing him," Ellie reproved.

"I don't think so, Mom. Brad's got eyes. I've seen them watching me, and I like it. Wouldn't you like to see all of me, Brad? All you have to do is marry me."

Brad laughed, but her father did not. He began scolding her. Holly's mind moved restlessly from this dream to another.

Or tried to.

Her eyes snapped open wide as a sound from downstairs startled her.

She blinked and listened tensely, but she heard nothing more and so dismissed it as part of her dreams.

Pulling the covers up to her chin, she gazed at the snow-covered mountain outside the picture window. Was it snowing? It seemed like it was, and that was good, for she loved snow. She would have been glad to be alive had she not been so painfully aware of the loss of her father.

Oh, Daddy, she lamented as she closed her eyes. Why did it have to be you? Why couldn't it have been someone else? Somebody else's father?

Before she could find an answer, she was fast asleep again.

Downstairs, Criscolle and the Arab, Abdel, were quietly moving through the rooms, eager to find Holly and ready to take care of any unexpected surprises.

Winterhaven was, Criscolle knew, a big place, but not the type of place where one was likely to encounter a staff of full-time servants. Still he was careful. He was always careful and that was why he was still breathing, for even when he was a teenage gang member back in Brooklyn somebody was always coming at him with a menacing switchblade or a Saturday Night Special. He had survived his teens by learning to dodge the thrusts of his assailants and retaliate swiftly. But he had learned something else in the process as well—that it was safer to be the assailant than the victim. And it was more fun, too.

Now, satisfied that the downstairs was empty, he ordered Abdel to stand guard at the captain's stairway that led straight up to the chalet's main bedroom. That was where the girl would be if she were alone.

As he crept quietly up the rear stairway Criscolle had to wrench his mind away from the image of the pretty young girl he had seen in Rome with Elliot Bradford. He had one hand in the pocket of his ski jacket, his finger on the trigger of a silenced automatic. He doubted he would need the weapon—or even the hypodermic in his other hand—but he was prepared to use them if he must.

Criscolle quickly confirmed that the bedrooms at the rear of the chalet were empty. He removed his hand from his pocket and relaxed, for now he was certain that the girl was alone and defenseless. And sleeping in her father's bed.

The thought made him think briefly about Jack Sands, a portly Irishman who had been gutsy, but dumb, in believing he could talk Criscolle out of killing him. Talk! Jack could never have escaped his fate with mere words.

The Aspis assassin turned the knob of the door leading into the master bedroom and eased it open. He slipped inside.

"Christ, is it only eight-thirty?" Bradford shook his head as he poured coffee into Lieutenant Burke's mug on the coffee table near his living room window.

Standing at the window staring outside, Burke didn't respond.

"How did you figure out I'd be up at this ungodly hour, Lieutenant? Or do you always come calling this early?"

Burke swiveled and faced Bradford, who waved toward the barrel chair next to the low sofa, suggesting that the cop sit. "It wasn't hard to figure. You've got habits, as we all do. One of them is getting up early. Another is taking walks. All I did was wait for you—not that I had to. But I like it better this way. I don't like rousing someone in their home. I'd watch those habits, though. They make it easy for anybody who wants to snuff you."

It was true. Bradford had learned all about habits—man's greatest betrayer and an assassin's best friend. If Aspis was out to get him, he would have to take a long, hard look at the habits he'd acquired in the past ten years. Not even a gun could protect the unwary from a sudden, violent death.

As if reading Bradford's thought, Burke pointed to the slight bulge beneath Brad's sweater. "By the time you could get your hand on that gun," he said, "you could be dead six times over."

"Agreed. I'll be more careful, Lieutenant. Now let's get down to it. What exactly do you want?"

"I want the creep who killed Jack Sands," the cop said in a quiet voice. "I don't like it when somebody tries to get away with murder in my precinct."

Bradford studied the calm cop. "Did you investigate the death of Bob Walters, president of World Fruit, a few years ago?"

Burke stared at him for a second, then snapped his fingers. "Son-of-a-bitch," he muttered, "same MO. Was your firm involved with World Fruit?"

Brad, pleased at having surprised the young homicide officer, went a step further. "Ever heard of an international outfit called Aspis?" he asked.

Burke nodded his head no. He listened quietly as Bradford told him how Aspis had figured in the deaths of Sands and Walters and how they seemed to be involved in myriad suspicious activities around the globe. Brad said nothing, however, of the Piedmont Papers.

"So one of your reports may have gotten Walters killed, Mr. Bradford?" Lt. Burke said. "Have you found out who did it?"

"I know his identity, but proving he killed either Walters or Jack may be impossible. There just aren't any witnesses."

"Give me his name, Bradford."

"What good will it do?"

"Who knows? We've got our own fancy computers nowadays, Bradford. They help us make all kinds of criminals. Maybe I have his name in our computer's memory banks."

"And if you don't?"

Burke sighed. "If we don't know him, maybe we can get him later—after he's arranged your suicide."

Bradford told him the name.

TEN

In her sleep, Holly was suddenly cold and didn't know why. She reached out with her hand to pull up the covers, groping unsuccessfully for them, her eyes still tightly closed. Her hand reached farther down toward the foot of the bed, where her uncovered feet felt cold as ice, but the covers evaded her.

Next to the bed, Nick Criscolle stood watching the girl. He licked his lips at the sight of her flawless, milky white buttocks squirming against the cool air that had been assaulting her since he had gently guided her covers off the bed.

Holly awakened with a jolt as she felt her arms suddenly seized in a steely grip, twisted together behind her back, then gripped by cold steel handcuffs. Her eyes opened wide with fear and she screamed when she saw the tall man beside her bed. The scream was cut short by the man's tough, sinewy hand. At the same time she saw the wicked-looking, blue-black blade of the man's knife.

He held it up to her eyes as he said, "Knock it off, little girl, we've got some talking to do."

Criscolle's mouth curled into an unpleasant smile as he dropped the blade inside the collar of Holly's nightshirt and slit it down the middle.

Stunned and now naked, Holly lay still as Criscolle looked her over approvingly. She vainly tried to cross her legs to cover herself and squirm away from his hands. "Not bad," he said, his smile widening.

Suddenly furious, she kicked out her legs, but he caught them easily, laughing at her ineffectual struggles.

"Let me go, you bastard!"

He laughed harder and at last she stopped, for she was accomplishing nothing with her struggles but tiring herself out. She was terrified, yet strangely calm as she stared up at the man at the foot of her bed whose eyes were drinking in every inch of her.

Brad. If only he'd agreed to stay here with her. If only she hadn't fought her mother's urgings that she go back to the city. If only . . .

But Brad had refused to come to Winterhaven with her and she had disregarded Eleanor Sands's pleas. And thus they were far away. So far away! And Holly was to be . . . what? Raped? No . . . dear God . . . please no!

She shuddered and closed her eyes, as the man put down her legs, then ran his hand slowly along her smooth inner thigh. Without warning, he gripped the sensitive flesh he found there and twisted it between thumb and forefinger. She screamed again.

A satisfied look appeared on his swarthy face, and he gingerly toyed with the ends of her upturned breasts until they stiffened. "They're interested, cutie, even if you aren't." He pinched a nipple until she loosed still another scream. "Do you know why I'm here?" he asked.

"You're going to rape me."

"That scare you?"

"What do you think?"

He slapped her hard across the mouth. "Don't get snotty with me, kid. Answer me when I ask you something."

"It scares me," she said. There was a hardness in the man's eyes that turned her fear into liquid fire. "Who . . . who are you?" she squeaked, shaking all over.

"Want me to kill you, sweetie? If I tell you who I am, I'll sure have to do just that."

"You . . . you'll do it anyway," she stammered, praying he'd deny it.

"Not if you behave yourself. Not if you do what uncle Nick tells you."

Now Holly froze as the man's words penetrated her consciousness. Uncle Nick? Nick who? Nick Criscolle? Could he be the one Brad had told her was the Aspis assassin who had killed her father?

Criscolle, busy examining Holly's body, didn't notice her silence.

Holly tried to blot out the degradation of the man's abuse of her body, but failed miserably. If he was Criscolle, then she would soon be dead. Yet what did he want? Why was he here? How did he get here? Had he followed her—and Brad—all the way from Rome? Brad! The bastard wanted Brad! Fun and games with her, but Brad, too!

It was cool in the big bedroom because Holly had turned down the thermostat before going to bed the night before. Nevertheless, she was sweating profusely as Criscolle now bent over her stomach to seize, with his teeth, the flesh he had pinched so cruelly earlier. Holly prayed he wouldn't bite.

After inspecting Holly's body, Criscolle moved away from her limp body and fished out a fat cigar from the pocket of his yellow shirt, which opened at the neck to reveal a lake of curly black hair. Lighting the cigar, he returned to the bed and said, "Here's what I want you to do. You've got a boyfriend who runs an outfit called FINVEST. Right?"

Holly nodded, afraid to deny it.

"I've got a business deal for him, and I need to talk to him about it. I want you to call him and get him to come up here."

"He wouldn't work for a rapist," she said.

Criscolle chuckled, then stroked her breasts in a circular motion as if trying to arouse her. "Maybe he'd enjoy watching us," he declared. "Anyway, I've a feeling we're gonna make some pretty hot music together. You're not as unwilling as you pretend." With that, Criscolle grabbed the telephone receiver and slammed it against the side of Holly's head.

"I'm not sure I can get him to fly up here," she sobbed, knowing it was the absolute truth.

"He will. You just gotta play it cool. Tell him you hurt yourself—that you need him to hold your hand. Or your crotch!" He laughed and hit her again.

"He'll just tell me to call a doctor."

"Tell him you tried and can't reach one. That you just have to see him. Christ, girl, use your head. You can't be that young."

Holly's mind worked furiously. If she were to pretend they were lovers, Brad would have to know something was wrong. If only she could work something into the conversation that would remind him of Aspis or Criscolle. Could she do it? She must.

"Okay, okay," she said, "I can try, I guess. But I tried to get him to stay, and he wouldn't. Said he had too much work to do."

"A shame you didn't talk him into it. But you're going to convince him now, aren't you, little girl? And you're not going to tell him I'm here—understand?" Criscolle leered at Holly with anticipation. "You know his number?" he asked.

She gave it to him, and he dialed it. For the first time since she'd awakened with a strange man in her room she remembered the end of her previous call to Brad. Would he be angry with her for having hung up on him? So angry that he wouldn't talk to her? She prayed that he wouldn't hang up on her now.

Holly pronounced a couple of Hail Mary's under her breath as her captor punched out Brad's telephone number. She reminded herself to talk fast, so he couldn't give things away.

Beside her Criscolle held the phone away from her ear so that he could hear both ends of the conversation.

It was a little after nine-thirty when Lieutenant Burke arose to leave. There had been some discussion of Nick Criscolle, and the Aspis organization, but Burke still had no positive action in mind except to check out Criscolle on the FBI and CIA computers and to ask Interpol if it had anything on Aspis or its chief assassin. Brad had said nothing of what Bochlaine and Suzanne had told him about the relationship between Aspis and the Vatican.

"I'll be flying back to Rome next week, Lieutenant," Bradford said. "I assume you have no objection."

"None at all. Unfortunately the Sands case is still considered a simple suicide. Until I can change the record, you can go anywhere you want. I'll tell you what, though, if I were you I'd start looking over my shoulder a lot."

"I already am, Lieutenant. Just for the record I saw you and your police car following me. The only reason I didn't run for my life was that I didn't figure you people were owned by Aspis."

"I'm not, but there's a lot of people working for the NYPD. A small army. It wouldn't surprise me a bit if a few of them weren't drawing dollars from Aspis."

"Christ, you're honest! If I were your boss, I'd probably recommend you for promotion and kick you upstairs somewhere to get rid of you."

"If I didn't like my work so much, I'd wish you were my boss."

The sound of the telephone cut short their banter. Brad and Burke had been standing at his door talking. When Brad reached for the telephone, Burke started to open the door to go.

"Wait a minute, Lieutenant. This is probably Tom. I won't be long."

Brad picked up the phone and was greeted with a rush of words—and Holly's voice, not Tom's.

"Elliot? Darling!"

"Holly?" It was all Bradford got a chance to say. As Holly's words flowed into his ear, he turned toward Burke and made a puzzled face.

"Yes, darling, look—I had to call you now because, well, I know I haven't been very loving to you since we came back from Rome and . . . I guess it's just that . . . well, I really didn't like that disgusting hyacinth perfume you bought me. I mean it's just bad news. I'm scared right now that you're mad at me because of it and . . . well, I'm sorry, sweetheart, but I wouldn't be buried in it. And ever since my father killed himself I just haven't felt like . . . you know . . . having sex. Know what I mean?"

Bradford was bewildered by the gist of Holly's words. "What the hell are you trying to say, Holly?" he finally broke in. "I didn't . . ."

Holly broke back. "I need you, Elliot. Oh God, do I need you. If you don't grab a plane and come to me right away I think I'll just die. I will. If you don't believe me, just don't come. You'll see. I'll take a whole bottle of Mama's sleeping pills. Do you hear? Then I'll go to sleep and dream about how you are when you're with me. You just gotta come to Winterhaven. Now."

"Holly, I . . ."

"Please, darling. Come to me, Elliot."

In the Sands bedroom a perplexed and glowering Nick Criscolle listened to the conversation, trying to judge whether the girl was doing what she was supposed to. Then he heard some welcome words from Bradford.

"Well, Kitten, I suppose I can come if you really need me."

Bradford was sweating. Elliot? There was desperation in Holly's voice and her words were mystifying. He hadn't bought her hyacinth perfume. And the comment about "having sex." She was babbling on like a lunatic.

It didn't take him long to realize that Holly had company. Unwelcome company—like Nick Criscolle. All those words she'd been emphasizing—scared, buried, killed, die. They could only add up to one thing. He tried to frame a question for Holly that she could answer even if she had Criscolle listening in.

"I probably won't be able to catch a plane that'll get me there before the middle of the afternoon," he said. "Suppose I call you when I get to the airport in Rutland?" If Criscolle knew he'd be calling, he wouldn't dare kill Holly. And nothing could be more important to Brad right now.

There was a moment's hesitation before Holly answered and Bradford, his senses fine-tuned for additional signs of trouble, held his breath.

"What time, Elliot? Can you give me some idea?" Elliot. She never called him that.

"Maybe three or four. That's the best I can do until I call the airport. Want me to call you right back?"

With his hand covering the receiver, Criscolle ordered: "Tell him he can call when he gets to Rutland. Then end it."

"All right, darling, but get here soon—okay? You won't be sorry and neither will I. Call the minute you get to Rutland."

"I will. Is it snowing up there, by the way? If so maybe I'll have to call Ted Pryor, that friend of your father's in the state police. Remember, he brought me up there in a police chopper once."

Criscolle shook his head and, again, covered the telephone receiver. "No way," he said. "Tell him, then get off."

"That would just delay you, darling. By the time you reach the police barracks, get a hold of him, and get the helicopter ready, you could already be here in bed with me. I just can't wait that long. I'll have the bed all ready for you. Okay? God, I just can't wait!"

"Neither can I, Kitten. Now just lie there and think of how we were in Rome. Everything will be all right."

Holly's spirits took a quantum leap upward. There was no question that Brad had understood her. She was sure of that now. "Mmmm. If you were here right now I'd go to pieces. You know how I am."

Criscolle held the knife to Holly's throat.

"Gotta go now. My bladder's full and I have to pee. Don't forget. And be careful."

When he replaced the phone on the stand, Bradford was sweating heavily. "That son-of-a-bitch!" he roared. "Criscolle's in Vermont. He's with Holly and wants to get me there, too. That's why he had her call. I could tell she was scared and she kept saying all the wrong things to tell me she couldn't talk."

Burke listened as Bradford quickly related all the warnings Holly had managed to work into the conversation. "She was telling me that the one who's got her is Nick Criscolle. He's a sadist who likes to play rough with young women."

"We can fly up by police chopper, Bradford. Okay?"

"We? Vermont's a little out of your territory, isn't it?"

"You need my help. Besides, if Criscolle's our murderer I can chase him anywhere. Can I use your phone to arrange it?"

Bradford handed him the phone and in a few moments the police lieutenant was carrying on a one-sided conversation with his headquarters.

"Have a chopper meet us at the 63rd Street heliport," Burke told the dispatcher. "Get it there within twenty minutes. Make sure the pilot has a full tank of gas. We're going to Vermont." Then Burke hesitated for a minute as he listened to the dispatcher.

"Burke, damn it," he roared. "Homicide. And I don't give a good goddamn about that! Roust out another pilot to fill in. I need him for the rest of the day. And it's my responsibility where I take the chopper. No, damn it, don't worry about that. You can call the inspector after that chopper's in the air, understand? I've got a murder on my hands— one that's sure as hell going to happen if you don't get on the stick. I'm ordering you, Sergeant!"

Burke wore a thin smile when he hung up. "Dumb, namby pamby regulation-crazy bastard! 'You can't take one of our machines out of the city,' he whines. 'It's Sunday and we only have one pilot on duty. Can't it wait till tomorrow?' If I had my way I'd send him back to pounding the pavement."

Bradford thought about calling Tom Sumereau but decided against it. With the police chopper they could make Winterhaven in two hours or so. If they landed on the side of the mountain just west of the house they could take Criscolle by surprise. That was important if they were to save Holly and keep Aspis's killer from using her as a hostage to get away.

"We're going to need snowshoes or skis, Lieutenant," Bradford told Burke. "If we land far enough away from the chalet to avoid alerting Criscolle, we'll have to make it a good thousand yards or so. And the ground's covered with deep snow this time of year."

"We can't land on a road?"

"Not without being spotted from the chalet. The Green Mountains aren't exactly New York City. There aren't any skyscrapers to block the view."

"The Vermont State Police can get us what we'll need," Burke said. "The question is where shall I have them meet us?"

"Can you get them to help us and still stay out of things until we need them, Lieutenant? If they go storming in on Criscolle, Holly will be dead in seconds."

"They'll cooperate. I'll personally guarantee it."

"All right. There's a highway that passes just south of Winterhaven. I'm not sure of the number, but they'll know it. They can meet us there. Better have them bring their own chopper to give chase in case Criscolle gets away."

"Let's hope we can flush the bastard, Bradford. From what you've told me, Sands's daughter isn't in for a pleasant time of it."

"Don't remind me," Brad growled unhappily. "Let's just get moving."

While Bradford and Burke were racing across town toward the East 63rd Street heliport in Burke's police car, Holly's terror was taking a new direction.

After her captor hung up the telephone, he tied her legs to the bottom posts of the four-poster bed. Holly did not protest. Criscolle's expression was black now as he looked down at his captive. "So how come you're not all hot to trot, girlie?" he asked her. "That's what you were telling Bradford."

Holly answered him with a look of defiance. "I was just trying to get him to come here like you said. I . . . I was just doing what you asked me to do." As she said it, Holly prayed that she could focus her mind on Brad while Criscolle was raping her. She tried not to think about exactly what the sadist might do to her.

Now Criscolle sat on the bed next to his captive's slim waist. He smiled a little as she blinked. "You like being tied like this?" he asked with frightening gentility. Ignoring her response, he continued tormenting Holly. "Did you do everything that you were supposed to?"

Fear of what lay ahead caused her to repeat herself. "I was doing what you asked . . ."

A ringing slap turned her head to the other side. "Don't lie to me!"

he roared. "I can read your goddamn mind. You were trying to warn him somehow, weren't you?"

"No."

"Tell the truth, and I won't hurt you, kiddo."

Tears appeared in Holly's green eyes as she slowly shook her head. "No!" Tears flowed now and Holly didn't have to work hard to bring them on or keep them coming. The thought of what Criscolle planned for her made it easy.

"Will ya knock it off!" Criscolle said. "Christ, I can't stand a crying bitch!"

But she couldn't stop.

He got to his feet and watched her for a moment, stroking his chin reflectively. "Well, if you're going to cry, you might as well have something to cry about." He walked from the bed to the top of the captain's stairs and called down for Abdel.

Holly's eyes became big as coat buttons. Abdel? Who was Abdel? She soon found out. When the heavy-set, dark-skinned man appeared at the top of the stairs, she stared at him, terrorized.

Criscolle's face twisted into a sick grin. "What do you think, Abdel? She worth a roll in the hay? Yeah, walk over and check her out. Cop a feel. She won't stop you."

The Arab man flashed a glance at Criscolle to make certain he was serious, then moved quickly across the carpeted floor and stared down at Holly, who closed her eyes against the leering face above her. She drew in a breath and that was a mistake, because her breasts swelled in an attractive fashion.

Abdel sat on the bed and began running his hands slowly all over the helpless Holly. He ogled her flesh as his hand eagerly explored it.

The Aspis assassin just laughed. "What do you want for breakfast, Abdel?" he said.

His large hand groped between her thighs. He ran his fingers through her soft, blond pubic tuft. Holly gasped in despair as she watched the dark hand press against her pale flesh.

Criscolle watched for a minute, then snapped off an order. "Enough, Abdel. It's time for breakfast. We'll let our hostess cook us something. Afterward, she'll be my dessert."

Abdel looked disappointed as he sprang to his feet, his hands covering the bulge in the front of his khaki trousers. "As you wish," he replied sullenly. He knew Criscolle could be just as cruel and dangerous to his own sex as he was to women.

"Don't worry," Criscolle assured. "You'll get some of her."

"I can't wait," Abdel said with a mischievous smile.

Holly could. Released from the handcuffs and having gained a reprieve, she didn't mind being naked—Criscolle wouldn't let her put anything on—as she began preparing breakfast for the three of them. Abdel was with her at every step as she took her time making coffee and cooking eggs.

When at last Holly couldn't stall any more and had to deliver their food to the breakfast nook in the kitchen, Criscolle applauded, grinning. "It better be good, baby," he said. "It took you an hour to get this shit ready."

Holly wasn't hungry, but forced herself to eat, knowing she would very probably need the strength once her ordeal continued upstairs. As she ate she prayed Brad had truly understood her message and that he was coming to Winterhaven in a helicopter or plane. That somehow he could stop the orgy of sex and pain Nick Criscolle was planning. One part of her brain told her not to worry, that Brad could not possibly have misunderstood her meaning. But doubt lingered in Holly's mind and she thought that she would never survive this day. Despair had plagued her the entire time she was making breakfast for them while trying to avoid the roving hands of Criscolle's dark assistant.

The flight to Vermont was agonizingly slow. Elliot Bradford's mind filled with graphic, frightening pictures of a nude and helpless Holly Sands being sexually assaulted by Criscolle. He stared at civilization below as the NYPD helicopter flew north at a slow hundred and fifty miles an hour. Would they be in time to do more than pick up the pieces?

When the chopper passed over Bromley Mountain, south of Winterhaven, Bradford was both pleased and sorry. He was glad the NYPD pilot had coaxed the chopper over the nearly 300 miles in record time for the relatively slow-moving machine, but miserable because he knew that in an hour and forty-five minutes Criscolle could have put Holly through absolute hell. He attempted to convince himself she was smart enough to stall him and that his statement to Holly that he couldn't get there before midafternoon would help her do so. He prayed he was right on both counts.

Vermont was smarting from its snowiest winter in years and even the highway on which Burke's pilot set them down was covered with frozen snow. The Vermont troopers were already there, with a half dozen vehicles containing all the necessary snow equipment for Burke and Bradford to make their clandestine approach to Winterhaven.

Burke did the talking as Brad loaded two pairs of cross-country skis and snowshoes on board. The NYPD lieutenant apprised a burly, parkaclad Vermont officer of the problem and what they proposed to do about it. He had to talk fast to get the Vermont trooper to agree to await a summons from the out-of-staters.

"We can do the job better than you, Lieutenant," the Vermont cop told Burke. "My people know snow like they know their own kids. They were born and raised on skis."

"The woman won't survive a second if we don't take them by surprise," Burke countered. "Bradford knows the chalet like the back of his hand and that's his friend in there. He's a trained army intelligence man and knows how to handle himself in combat. Now, we're ready to go in. Criscolle is our man!"

In the end, Burke prevailed and he and Bradford were soon on their way. When the chopper got close to Winterhaven, Bradford ordered the pilot to swing to the west, where the mountain rose high above the chalet. They approached almost at ground level to keep down the noise.

While the pilot looked for a level place to set down, Bradford laid out a plan of attack. "They'll no doubt have Holly on the second floor in the big bedroom just behind the living room," he told Burke. "There are two ways to reach it, a captain's stairs from the garage and a back staircase that leads to a second-floor hallway. Once in, you go for the back stairs and I'll head up the captain's stairs."

"Captain's stairs?"

"Yeah. It's the circular staircase that Jack Sands loved. When he returned home from New York, he felt like an old New England ship captain returning from a long voyage. He would ascend the stairs to his bedroom and a loyal wife."

"A throwback to another era, Bradford," Burke observed.

"He was a damn good man. I liked him as a person because he never forgot his humble beginnings, but wasn't ashamed of his success, either.

He could be tough in business, but was fair, too. The world was a loser when he died, along with Ellie and Holly."

"What about Holly? Can she think on her feet?"

"If she couldn't, I'd be walking straight into a trap right now. What she did to tip me off was worth an acting award. At least I hope so. If Criscolle caught on . . ." He didn't finish the statement. He didn't have to, for Burke understood perfectly.

As the chopper approached the plateau the pilot had spotted for landing, they noticed for the first time that new snow was falling. It increased in intensity as the machine settled down on a small patch where the mountain's steep slope leveled off on a ridge.

Holly was the last to finish her coffee, goaded by her captors. "Come on," Criscolle ordered, pulling her up out of her chair, "we've got to have our dessert."

Abdel's yellow-toothed smile was unnerving. "Can I be of assistance?" he asked, his eyes on Holly's small, round rear end.

"I should clear the table," Holly said, her teeth chattering. She knew there was no way Brad could have reached Winterhaven yet, but nonetheless strained to hear the sound of a car or helicopter that would announce his arrival. "It'll only take a minute or two."

But Criscolle had a firm grip on her arm and was steering her firmly up the back stairs. "You can clean up after I have my dessert," he said with a harsh laugh. "If you feel like you still want to. Or can."

When they reached the big bedroom, he pushed her down on the bed, nodding to Abdel. "On your stomach, bitch," Criscolle snapped. "Abdel, tie her that way, but put a couple of pillows under her stomach to raise that sweet little ass."

Holly tried to leap off the bed, but the pilot's long arms were too quick. Criscolle had a satanic look on his face as he watched Abdel fit the handcuffs over Holly's thin wrists, cuff them in the back, and then bind her ankles to the posts. By the time Abdel slid two fluffy pillows between Holly's belly and the bed beneath, Criscolle was again in a state of excitement.

Neither man said anything, and Abdel took the opportunity to run his dusky hand over Holly's snow white rump while his boss contemplated the scene briefly.

"Okay, Abdel, make yourself scarce. This is my scene. Go outside and watch the chopper."

Abdel pulled his hand from Holly's flesh and hesitantly followed instructions. As he began to leave the room, a second possibility crossed his mind. "I would like to watch," he said. He was serious.

"Outta here," Criscolle screamed. "Now!"

"You said . . ."

"Later," Criscolle said. "When I'm done you can have her. But for now she's mine."

Abdel stepped away from the bed, a hard look on his face as his eyes met Criscolle's. For just a second the pilot wanted to rebel, but then he squelched his urge to challenge the man from Aspis. He walked slowly toward the rear stairs.

Holly was terrified by the exchange. She was not anxious to have Abdel present to watch Criscolle degrade her, but if the Arab went outside to watch the helicopter he might also witness the arrival of Brad and the Vermont police she hoped would be with him. She had to do something to keep Abdel here.

"Why not let him watch us," she said, almost choking on the words. "I sort of like the idea of him watching. He can learn from it, right?"

Abdel stopped in his tracks, eager to oblige.

"Out!" roared Criscolle. "I don't want you for an audience."

Holly was desperate, certain that her rescue depended on her succeeding in keeping the Arab here. "Look," she said, "why don't you both come into bed? Both at once. I once saw that in a movie . . ."

"No!" Criscolle took a threatening step toward Abdel, his eyes hard as granite.

"Could he just stay downstairs and listen?" asked Holly. "Hearing what you do to me will really get him horny."

"I'm gonna shut your fuckin' mouth permanently!" Criscolle bellowed. Turning back to Holly, he pulled her head up by her hair and stung her with a series of open-handed blows on her face and neck. Her body jerked backward and then fell forward from the force.

The door to the bedroom slammed as Abdel made himself scarce.

When they were alone a half smile curled Criscolle's lips back over straight teeth and he slipped his narrow black leather belt out of his pants, stepped out of his rust colored slacks and dropped his red bikini briefs.

Caressing the belt as if it were an old friend, he doubled it then raised it high in the air and brought it down brutally across Holly's buttocks. Holly screamed. And Criscolle's flaccid manhood came to life.

Soon the Aspis assassin was alternately raining blows on Holly's back-side and stroking the pink-striped flesh with his hands. After her outcry, Holly focused her mind on Brad and used every ounce of mind power to try to dilute the pain.

But, in less than a minute, she was praying Criscolle would tire of whipping her and simply rape her.

Bradford, a good skier, reached Winterhaven's western slope at eleven-fifteen in the morning as large, fluffy snowflakes continued to blanket the countryside. Before moving through the split-rail fence, he thumbed open the switch on one of the two walkie-talkies he and Burke had obtained from the Vermont troopers and spoke quietly to Burke, who was making slower time on snowshoes. A city cop, he had never learned to ski well enough to manage a steep mountain trail.

"I'm at the chalet," Bradford said. "There's no sign of life, but I didn't expect there to be. Criscolle's a loner and probably has just a chopper and a pilot with him. It's probably hidden behind the barn to my left so I'll avoid that area. I'm going in now. How far are you?"

"Not more than a couple of hundred yards, Bradford. Wait for me, will you? You can't take on two men alone."

"You'd be surprised what I can do, Lieutenant. The army showed me how, and did a pretty good job of it. Cover the enemy's chopper, Burke. I'm going after Holly."

"Good luck," was the cop's final message.

Bradford muttered a barely audible "amen" and moved quickly through the fence beyond which stood the barn far to his left and the house about fifty yards from the mountainside to his right.

The falling snow would make approaching the house unobserved a great deal easier, though by no means a snap, for the area he had to cover was wide open to view by anyone watching. He hoped Criscolle wasn't expecting company and so wouldn't have a guard posted.

He soon lost that hope. Abdel, Criscolle's pilot, was sullen and angry as he paced the snowy ground around the helicopter near the barn, his dark eyes glaring at the rear of the Sands chalet, visualizing what was going on with the fair-skinned girl in the front bedroom. The Arab got just a quick glimpse of Bradford as he ducked through the fence and sprinted toward the house.

Both men heard a loud scream—almost a mournful wail—coming from the chalet.

Bradford was paralyzed for a second by the sound; but then he all but flew the rest of the way to the lower of the two porches running the length of the chalet's front. He leaped the railing and reached the door in a single stride. He had a key and quickly unlocked the door and charged inside, his gun raised and ready.

He encountered no one and heard only the sound of his own foot-steps, but he wasn't stopping to listen. He couldn't think about what was happening to Holly right now. He could only focus on what he had to do to save her. He raced across the soft carpeting of the entrance foyer to the captain's stairs.

Criscolle, who was enjoying his domination of Holly as he repetitively raised and lowered himself while his hands were mauling Holly's firm, young breasts, was close to orgasm when the sound of gunfire startled him.

He withdrew and leaped off the bed, racing to the window. Seeing nothing, he pulled on his pants then retreated out of the bedroom when he heard the sound of Bradford's feet on the captain's stairs. In the hall he stumbled and almost fell while buckling his pants, then raced down the back stairs. His gun was in his jacket downstairs. He had to get to it.

Bradford was ready for anything when he burst around the final curve in the captain's stairs and up into the Sands bedroom. Anything but what he actually saw—a sight that he'd half expected, but still was not ready for.

Holly was naked and spread out on the four-poster bed, her rump held high in the air by pillows propped beneath her. Her back and but-tocks were red and pink-striped, with an awful purple hue beginning to rise amid her bruises. She was unconscious.

Criscolle was no longer in the room, Brad quickly confirmed, but that didn't mean he wouldn't be back so he took only enough time to make sure Holly was breathing before forcing himself to leave her. To attend to her now was to invite her sadistic attacker to kill them both.

He eased himself out into the hallway, kicking the door open with his foot. No shots rang out, so he ran toward the stairs.

Criscolle secured his jacket and weapons, then looked outside to find Abdel engaged in a gun fight with someone out of the sight of the house. Although raging over this development, his instincts told him that with just a little luck he could eliminate Bradford, if indeed that's who was upstairs. Too bad he didn't have the opportunity to execute Bradford with care in order to avoid an unnecessary investigation into his death. And of course if he killed Bradford he would have to kill Holly, too. Alive, she was dangerous to him. But to stay was to chance capture and risk too much for Aspis. No, he would have to get Bradford another time. Criscolle had to flee.

Criscolle burst through the backdoor of the house, running in a low crouch and screaming at Abdel to start the helicopter motor.

Burke was too far away to get a good shot at the chopper, which was partly shielded by the barn. When the pilot had fired two warning shots after spotting Bradford, Burke had been just about to seek a position behind the barn from which he could cover the chopper. He never made it.

After Abdel's shots, Burke was certain Bradford had been spotted and was under attack, and so he loosed several wild shots in the direction of the chopper to draw off the fire of whoever was there.

Burke issued quiet orders into the walkie-talkie, telling his chopper pilot to radio the Vermont troopers to move in fast. As an afterthought, he added, "Bring our chopper up to the house, but watch out for fire from the ground. Land near the front and have your gun ready."

Just then Burke saw another figure emerge from the chalet and run toward the barn to the right of where he was crouched. He got off two shots from his .357 magnum before the figure disappeared from view.

Brad was on his way down the backstairs when he heard the shots outside and Criscolle screaming to his pilot to get their chopper going.

Throwing caution to the wind, Brad raced through the house and followed the Aspis killer through the back door. He had to dive for the snowy turf as Criscolle reached the chopper, seized a machine gun, and began spraying lead at him from the right-hand seat. Abdel already had the chopper blades whirling. In moments, the pilot yanked on the vertical pitch stick and sent the chopper soaring straight up.

Before either Burke or Bradford could get an effective shot at the chopper, it was out of gunshot range.

Burke's helicopter began giving chase but was forced to give up quickly when Criscolle's machine gun went into action. Burke's pilot radioed the Vermont troopers to give chase to the white chopper in which Criscolle was escaping. Then he landed next to the chalet.

Brad and Burke were already inside freeing Holly from her bondage. Brad forced open the handcuffs that held Holly's wrists behind her back and untied the ropes that held her to the bedposts so he could carry her outside to the NYPD helicopter. Holly suddenly groaned and opened her eyes.

"Brad? Oh God, Brad, is it really you?" Tears filled her eyes as she looked up at him.

"Easy, Kitten," Brad murmured, reaching down to wipe her eyes with a corner of the sheet. "It's all over now. You're going to be all right."

"Criscolle . . . did you catch him?" Holly's words were barely a whisper, and she winced as she spoke. Even the soft blanket felt harsh against her raw flesh.

Brad shook his head. "No. But the Vermont police have a helicopter chasing him now," he said. "Maybe we'll get him yet."

"He's a monster!" Holly hesitated as a new spasm of pain swept over her. "I tried to warn you that he was here, but didn't know if you understood."

"I read you loud and clear, Kitten," he said. "You made it easy. I got here as fast as I could."

"Criscolle was going to kill you, Brad. I couldn't let that happen."

Brad bent over her and brushed his lips against her cheek. "I wish I could've gotten here sooner and kept him from . . ."

"So do I, but the important thing is that you're okay."

"We've got to get you to the chopper. Forgive me if it hurts a little. I'll be as gentle as I can."

Holly nodded. She gritted her teeth as she felt herself lifted off the bed by Bradford and Burke.

As they carried Holly's battered body down the main stairway and outside to the helicopter, hatred for Nick Criscolle and the Aspis monsters who sponsored him welled up within Bradford. The emotion made his hands tremble, his blood rage through his veins. If only he could get his hands on Criscolle right now! And if not Criscolle, he'd settle for the man's boss, Count Vignola!

An animal-like cry came from Holly's mouth as they lifted her into the cockpit of the helicopter. Brad looked down at her pale face and was devastated by the pain he saw there. "We'll get him, Holly. I swear to you we will," he told her.

As the chopper swooped skyward and left Winterhaven behind, Bradford held her hand, but his mind was focused on the sounds coming over the machine's radio—reports from the pilot operating the Vermont police helicopter.

By the time the NYPD chopper landed in front of the emergency entrance to the Rutland Hospital, it was apparent that Nick Criscolle had eluded his pursuers.

ELEVEN

"What now, Lieutenant? What are you going to do about Criscolle?" Bradford leaned forward in the chair behind his desk as he met Burke for the first time since their mad dash to Vermont to rescue Holly Sands.

Nick Criscolle had escaped the police helicopter that chased him in the swirling snowstorm, a storm that had deposited a foot of snow on New England in less than twelve hours.

"I wish I could tell you I was about to have the SOB picked up," the homicide cop said. His uniform today was a dark blue turtleneck and matching slacks under a light blue cardigan with an embroidered polo pony on the left. "The problem is there's no record of his entering or leaving the States, so I can't prove he could have done it."

Brad said nothing for a moment. What Burke related did not surprise him, but he had hoped for better news. "So you'll do nothing," he declared, his voice tight, his words charged with the emotion inspired by recent events, especially Holly's torturous ordeal.

"I didn't say that," Burke replied in his usual calm voice. "How's Holly?"

"A lot better than she might be. That bastard really did a number on her. Thank God we got there in time to keep it from being worse. The doctors treating her say there was no damage to any internal organs and she probably won't have any scars on her body from Criscolle's brutality. It's her head I'm worried about, although she seems to be hanging in there."

Burke nodded sympathetically. "She's home now with her mother?"

"Do you have to talk to her?" Brad replied, reading Burke's intentions.

"I'll go easy on her, Bradford, but I can't put it off any longer. What she can tell me may help catch Criscolle. She may be able to furnish

171

information that can help you as well—remember, you were his real target. You were damned lucky that she had the guts to try to tip you off and you were luckier still that she succeeded. All things considered, she was lucky, too. He could have easily killed her. And you, too."

"I'm not worried about me, Lieutenant."

"You said you were going back to Rome?"

"Tomorrow.

Burke stroked his chin reflectively, an idea forming in his head. "How would you like a traveling companion? I've never been to Rome and it's about time I went."

"I don't need a bodyguard."

"I'm glad to hear it. The NYPD wouldn't go for that. I just thought it might be a good idea to nose around a bit over there."

Bradford wasn't convinced. "Around Aspis? Around Criscolle? What good would it do? You just got through telling me you can't prove Criscolle was even in the States."

Burke shrugged. "Maybe I can scare him into a mistake. Who knows?"

"You might make a mistake, Lieutenant, and wind up at the bottom of the Tiber River."

"Perhaps. Then again, you could be doing the same if he gets to you." Burke grinned. "Or maybe our Mr. Criscolle could become the fish bait."

"You've got no authority in Rome. I doubt if the Italian police would be too thrilled to have you wandering around the Holy City scaring the nuns."

"Well I don't like having their people shooting my people over here," Burke growled, his grin vanishing. "New York may be a bit of a jungle at times, but that doesn't mean I have to put up with traveling killers from Rome."

"Criscolle's an American, I understand. Born and raised in your city."

"He's not any more. He lives and works in Rome, and as far as I'm concerned that makes him theirs, not mine."

"He also works here, unfortunately," Bradford said. His anger was rising and he fought to keep it down, for he knew he had to stay objective. He needed to assess the effect Burke's presence in Rome would have on the plans that were even now taking shape in his mind. He wanted to meet Nick Criscolle face to face and confront the bastard. He also wanted to see the "gentleman" brother of Massara—the man who, Suzanne had said, had ordered Brad's death and wound up killing Nancy and the boys. And he would soon pay Vignola's mountain villa a visit, for it might hold the secrets of the Piedmont Papers. The trouble was, he could not be certain that any one of his plans—or their sum—would cause his twin objectives to be achieved: to see Criscolle dead or behind bars and to find the papers Suzanne and Bochlaine were so certain could bring Aspis to its knees.

As Burke had suggested, he could wind up at the bottom of the Tiber, his body weighted down by chains, never to be seen again. But others had tried to kill him, and they hadn't succeeded. Perhaps having Burke around might not be such a bad idea. The young cop was shrewd and competent and seemed to share Brad's urgent desire to get Criscolle.

"I'm not sure we should be seen together in Rome, Lieutenant," Brad said in answer to the questions in Burke's eyes. "It might just win you a spot on the Aspis hit list."

"Which is precisely what I want. Let them know who I am and what I'm doing. Unless they are aware of me, I can't hope to convince them I'm dangerous. I want to draw their heat."

"You figure on dying in the Holy City?"

"Not on your life. I know how to avoid high city windows and Italian bullets. And I'm not a bad marksman, either."

"Have you ever killed anybody?" Bradford asked.

"I'm a good shot, and I've always hit what I aimed for—my assailant's shoulder, not his heart. I've wounded a few—eleven to be exact—but didn't kill a one." Burke's smile now became a little thin as he added, "Frankly, though, my aim has been a little off lately. It just may be that if I get a chance to shoot Criscolle, I might not keep up my perfect record."

Bradford wasn't convinced that the Lieutenant's light bragging made him a match for Criscolle, but Burke's confidence was welcome. He stood and offered his hand as Burke rose from his chair. "I'm booked on Alitalia at seven o'clock tomorrow night. If you're serious about going to Rome with me, get a seat on the same flight."

"First-class?"

"Always. And call me Brad, will you? I can't stand being 'mistered' by somebody I like."

"You like me? A cop?" Burke chuckled. "That makes two New Yorkers who do, Brad."

"Who's the other one, your wife?"

"That'd be the day. My wife couldn't stand me. Ran away with a cemetery plot salesman. But I've a good friend in the department. We play a lot of racquetball." He paused, grinning widely. "He always wins."

"Good thing Criscolle won't be playing racquetball, Lieutenant."

Before repacking his suitcase and heading back across the Atlantic, Bradford had a lot to do. He spent the afternoon working and later conferred with his partner. "Things may get really tough now that they know we're onto them," he warned. "Don't let yourself be caught alone or unawares, Tom, or I may have to go looking for a new partner."

"You think they'll go after us that openly?"

"They may. I've got a feeling it'll be table stakes from now on. They're out to break us and they don't care how they do it. By now they know we have our people investigating Aspis all over the world. Did you see the stuff Tony Phipps fed into Max from London?"

Sumereau's usually cheerful face was grim, his expression worried as he chewed on the stem of a dead pipe he was using as a crutch while trying to give up the big cigars he habitually smoked. "I saw it," he said, "but don't understand it. How can the Vatican Bank be dealing with or through Aspis? If Tony's analysis is even close to the mark, Aspis is plugged into both organized crime and organized religion as well as international terrorism. Is Israel's Knesset crawling with Aspis people, too?"

"I doubt that, Tom. Remember, Cardinal Massara may not be the official head of the Vatican Bank now, but he might as well be. For years after Zeisman's death Massara served as president of the bank. When be became a cardinal, he stepped down, but Archbishop Crasta, who succeeded him, came out of nowhere—with no banking background at all. Tony says he's nearly a phantom, that his name almost never comes up in connection with the Vatican's business dealings. But Massara's still does."

"Do you think a cardinal would let the bank get involved with a group of killers? That he'd use the Vatican Bank to fund illegal operations?"

"I'm not sure what I think yet, Tom, but if Massara was the one who ripped off the ten million that was supposed to ransom the Roman Jews in 1943, I guess he'd do just about anything. I do know that Vignola runs Aspis, and Aspis is up to its *ass* in all sorts of dirt, including international crime. Now it seems the Vatican Bank is holding hands with a dozen firms and banks that are either controlled by or have strong financial dealings with Aspis. Vignola is Massara's half brother, after all."

"Unless you find the Piedmont Papers there's no way to prove Massara was in on the ransom," Sumereau pointed out.

"I'll find them, Tom," Brad replied. "I'm going to help Bochlaine and Suzanne Steelman ferret them out if it takes every ounce of nerve and skill I have. And speaking of tracking things down, did you plant those little tidbits we discussed?"

Sumereau made a face. They had only yesterday decided to plant different items of false information that would be of interest to Criscolle and Aspis with each person who had access to FINVEST's computer room. "I feel like I'm putting my mother on a medieval rack," he declared. "It's difficult to imagine any of our people as an Aspis spy."

Brad said nothing. He felt the same way, but knew they had no other choice. There was a mole in their operation, and until they found out his identity they had to guard all new information that came in from all personnel.

If their spy took the bait, his special piece of information would wind up in Aspis hands within twenty-four hours. Brad had to find out which of the four seemingly important, yet fictional pieces, wound up in Aspis headquarters in Rome. Suzanne might be able to help him determine that. Or perhaps Brad himself could do it in a confrontation with Vignola and Criscolle. The thought excited him. The last thing the count or his chief assassin would expect would be that their prey was running right up under the barrels of their guns!

On his way to the Sands home on the upper East Side to see Holly, he wondered if Sumereau and Max could solve the riddle of the Aspis computer codes and sequences. They'd gone over the notes he'd made from his conversation with Suzanne but had reached no conclusions. Tom was going to work seriously on the problem beginning tomorrow, now that his business at BMC had concluded.

Holly, clad in a green cotton nightgown that only partially covered her bandages, was sore but in good spirits when her mother escorted

Brad into her bedroom. She was lying on her bruised back when she saw her visitor, but sat up immediately and reached out for him.

"Brad!" she cried, hugging him. Then she winced, as the painful state of her buttocks made itself evident. But it didn't stop her from raising her face to kiss him on the mouth.

Brad stole a glance at Ellie and was surprised to see her beaming.

What followed was difficult for Bradford. Holly could not have been more cooperative as he questioned her about Criscolle, but she became very upset when he admitted he was going back to Rome tomorrow.

"Please stay away from Criscolle, Brad," she pleaded. "He'll kill you just like he killed Daddy, and I couldn't take losing both of you!"

"Calm down, Kitten," he said, squeezing her hand. "I'm not about to let him do anything to me. Your father was taken by surprise, but I won't be." But deep inside, Brad knew he would be in great danger.

That night after he returned to his apartment, Brad checked the security guards in the lobby of the high-rise to make certain there'd been no unusual activity in the building—no visitors or strange "servicemen" to his apartment.

There had been none. His apartment door was fitted with a lock that could not be opened by any known method of lock picking; he was taking no chances these days. After a shower he called Suzanne in Rome. He got no answer.

He sat and smoked a half dozen cigarettes as he studied the already bulky file on Aspis he had established along with the files on Nick Criscolle, Count Vignola, and Cardinal Massara.

T W E L V E

Tuesday had been a scary day for Suzanne Steelman. She was summoned into Count Vignola's office to find an angry Vignola and a glaring Nick Criscolle. On the count's desk in front of him was the report she had delivered to him on FINVEST.

"Where's the rest of this report, Suzanne?" Vignola asked, his anger shattering his usual reserve.

She picked up the manila folder and looked inside, truly puzzled by his question. "That's all there was," she said. "I was told me there might be more later, but that was all there was on short notice."

The two men exchanged glances, then the count dismissed her.

After the meeting broke up, Criscolle had come to the office she used when working with the Aspis computer, which was right next door. He seemed oddly subdued as he asked her to have dinner with him. She was about to brush him off when it occurred to her that perhaps she could learn something about the count's villa from him. It was dangerous, but . . .

"I'm not trying to get you in the sack, Suzanne," Criscolle said, breaking into her thoughts.

She screwed up her face as if trying hard to overcome her normal reluctance, then forced a smile. "Well, I am free." she said. "And hungry. But just for dinner, right?"

He agreed and tried to hide his surprise along with his pleasure. She wondered if his tastes were changing—for she was no teenage Lolita. But she hoped not, for the thought of his touch repulsed her.

It was with great effort that she kept her nerves under control as Criscolle drove her to Giarosto Toscano, a restaurant near Via Veneto.

After penne all'arabiata and veal lombatina, they sipped Sambuca and she tried to coax him into talking. She chatted about business, so as not to arouse his suspicion and so that he would not think she was interested in him personally. She had to approach the subject of the count's northern retreat with care.

Criscolle reached across the wooden table to hold her hand and succeeded in spite of her fleeting efforts to withdraw. She could feel the strength in his hands, and she became aware of a sinister element in his eyes.

"I thought you promised you wouldn't try to lure me into bed," she said as his other hand came to rest on her knee.

"Christ, Suzanne, you're a great-looking chick and, well, I'm a great-looking guy," he reasoned. "You ought to be glad I want to touch you. You've got a great ass, too, in case you don't know it."

"What's this thing you have for women's anatomy?" she asked. "I've seen you looking over the backsides of the women at the count's villa." Before Criscolle could respond, she changed the subject. "That's super ski country, isn't it? I wish we'd gone up last weekend. I'd love to spend a month there. Does anyone use it during the week? Do you think the count would let me sneak up there?"

Nick's right hand squeezed Suzanne's knee as he leaned forward bringing his face only inches from hers. He replied. "What do you say about going there, Suzanne? There are only a couple of guards to keep out intruders, and we're sure as hell not intruders. Come with me, and I'll show you a time you won't forget."

"I can imagine," she murmured, still trying to break his grip on her knee. "You'd probably strip me, whip me, tie me and invite the guards in to make it an orgy. I've heard about some wild sadistic tastes of yours."

If she hoped to anger him, she didn't succeed. "Not a bad idea," he said. "I'll bet you'd look great getting it from two guys at once. But don't worry about the guards. They patrol the outside. The count doesn't let them use the house. Not with our computer terminal there. They don't even have a key. Anyway, I don't need any help with you. I'd keep you busy." The way he said it made her shiver with revulsion.

"I'm not into whips and chains," she said, fighting to keep her control. "I've heard about your perversions."

"Experiencing is a lot better than hearing, Suzanne," he said, a glazed look in his eyes. "Don't knock what you haven't tried. There's a certain sensation you can get when your flesh is sweetly tortured and bruised. It's a thrill that can only come from feeling pain."

"Take me home, Nick. I didn't come out here for this."

"Okay, okay, don't get on your high horse. If the count wasn't around you'd get it whether you liked it or not. With an attitude like yours, you're just askin' for it."

"Just try it, Nick," she said, finally withdrawing her hand. "I'll cut off your balls."

He drove her to her apartment, and she was surprised that he didn't seem angry. There was, she thought, something that could have passed for respect in his eyes as she started to get out of his Porsche.

"You've got guts, Steelman," he declared. "A shame you're not going to try me."

"Good night," she muttered, fleeing up the walk to the front door of her apartment.

Tonight, Suzanne had scored on Criscolle. She had learned that the count's villa was not guarded as closely as it might be. If she and Brad could reach the house without being detected by the guards, there would be no one inside to hinder their search for the count's safe. That was good news.

She was sitting at her writing desk drawing a map of the Villa Amalfi when she heard a news bulletin on her radio. The Pope was critically ill.

In his room at Mama Teresa's, Frank Bochlaine learned of the Pope's grave illness at the same time. Teresa saw an announcement about it on television and came in to tell him. Bochlaine had met the Pope and knew him as a good man and fine father to his flock. It was an opinion shared by Cardinal Ambrosiani and most others throughout the Roman Curia. The Swiss Guards, who swore allegiance to any Pope, would have fought each other for the privilege of dying for this Pope.

"Let us pray for him," Bochlaine said as he and Teresa exchanged unhappy looks. He heaved his bulk out of the double bed and fell to his knees beside it, ignoring his still painful wound. Afterward Bochlaine turned on a small bedside radio and tuned it to Vatican Radio to keep track of the pontiff's condition. He soon learned it was deteriorating.

Late in the evening, a priest came to Teresa's door bearing a sealed envelope from Cardinal Ambrosiani. Bochlaine's big hands trembled as he opened it and unfolded the note inside. Ashamed that he had let

Criscolle find and nearly kill him, he had not informed Cardinal Ambrosiani of what had happened. Had the cardinal somehow learned of it?

Bochlaine scanned the note:

"Imperative you meet me tomorrow—nine-thirty A.M. at the usual place. The Holy Father will not resume his Papacy. He is dying."

There was no signature, but Bochlaine knew who had sent it. Why the meeting was so important was hard for him to comprehend, though it surely must be connected with the Pope's medical condition.

When Bochlaine asked Mama Teresa if she would drive him to his scheduled meeting, she urged him not to go.

"Your wound, it is too severe, Franco. You must give it the time it needs to heal. Because you would not let me get you a doctor, I can't be sure it is getting better."

"Then I will have to walk," Bochlaine said. Teresa swore at him and called him a fool. Bochlaine answered her in the same language, chiding her for taking the name of God in vain.

"I am a fool," Bochlaine continued, "but I do what I must. Would you have me turn my back on those who count on me?"

Bochlaine had told Teresa nothing of his quest except that his work was important to the Vatican and to the entire outside world. The woman, a small but robust figure in the sweaters and skirts she still wore because her Giulio had always liked them, knew only that her benefactor received messages from the Vatican itself and was important enough that someone had tried to kill him. And she knew that Franco, as she called him, had made it possible for her and the girls to not just survive her husband's death, but to prosper—even though her earnings as a seamstress were meager. So was the money her girls more recently brought home from selling the carnations and Easter lilies they raised in the small heated greenhouse Giulio had built behind the house years ago.

Gratitude for all Bochlaine's help during the past years propelled Teresa to reassure him. "Don't think badly of your Mama Teresa," she cried. "I only want what's good for you. What hurts you hurts me also."

"Then help me keep my appointment," Bochlaine said.

She did.

Wednesday morning Teresa carefully rebandaged Bochlaine's wound and eased him into her car, then drove him through the busy Rome streets to St. Paul's Outside-the-Walls.

In the confessional, Bochlaine was standing when Cardinal Ambrosiani entered. When the cardinal learned why Bochlaine couldn't kneel, he muttered a fervent prayer. "I fear for your life, my dear, loyal son. You have already gone through so much for the cause we both serve. Yet I fear for the Church, too. The Holy Father lies close to death and the Inner Circle even now speaks of Massara as his successor."

"Massara, Father? Dear sainted Jesus! It can't be. They would not do such a disservice to our faith."

"If only I shared your conviction that they would not elect Massara, but I know now what I should have realized right along—that the Inner Circle has been working to gather the power to elect one of their number to Peter's throne."

"You've never mentioned this Inner Circle to me before, Father. What is it? Who are they?"

"I can only guess, for they are a faceless group, their numbers as yet uncounted. They do not meet, yet can act in concert when necessary. I know this for, over the years, I have seen many demonstrations of their power. It was the Inner Circle which put Massara in the Vatican Bank originally—to learn of the inner workings of Vatican finances and assure access to funds they wanted for their secret endeavors.

"And it was the Inner Circle, I believe, which had a hand in the Piedmont Papers. They sponsored Massara in his monstrous theft of the Jewish ransom. They caused the birth of the infamous Aspis!" The cardinal's anger was near rage by now and he stopped to gain control of himself.

"They are cardinals, my son, and would that they were not, for they seek to steer the Holy See in a different direction. A poisonous direction. I shudder to know what unholy ambitions could be embraced by the Inner Circle. And that they will soon place Massara in the Apostolic chair of the Holy Father to carry out their wishes to realign the Church's policies here and around the world."

"But it must not happen, Father. We must prevent it!"

"I fear we cannot. I had hoped the Piedmont Papers would be found before the worst happened—that the papers might expose the reality of the Inner Circle as well as Massara's infamy."

"Would the Piedmont Papers name these men?"

Cardinal Ambrosiani shook his head. "None of them were cardinals when the papers were executed. But the exposure of these papers would almost certainly make them rethink their immediate plan and wait for another chance long after we are dead."

Bochlaine's spirit sagged, his head full of misery at the cardinal's incredible new revelation. "Woe to us all, Father," he declared. "What shall I do now?"

"We must pray that Our Father will not allow His Church to be mortally wounded by such an insidious cancer as the Inner Circle and its puppet Massara."

They prayed, but Bochlaine's thoughts were not on the prayer. He must, he decided, renew his efforts to uncover the secrets of the Piedmont Papers. If he must die to find them, then he must die. And if Massara was elected Pope, then . . .

But Bochlaine's mind would not let him complete the thought. He prayed he would not be forced to resort to such a horrible alternative.

THIRTEEN

The Alitalia flight back to Rome was uneventful. Neither Burke nor Brad were able to sleep even after consuming too much liquor. They arrived at Fiumicino early in the morning. Despite Brad's insistence, Burke refused the offer to use the FINVEST apartment north of Rome. Instead Burke booked a room at a modest hotel on Via Flaminia.

Brad called Suzanne Steelman from the airport. Fortunately, she had not yet left for work. Without identifying himself he asked for Paula. When Suzanne responded that the caller must have the wrong number, Brad asked if he had called 37-66-47. Suzanne hung up. Brad remained at the pay phone and held down the receiver until the phone rang a few minutes later. Suzanne told him briefly what she had learned from Nick Criscolle.

"You went out with him?" Brad asked incredulously.

"It seemed the only way to find out what he knew about the villa guards. I can assure you that I didn't do it because I wanted to, and I did my best to discourage his bizarre advances."

"You've got nerve, Suzanne," Brad said. "I'm glad it turned out all right. The information you got may be important." He told her what Criscolle had done to Holly in his attempt to trap him.

Suzanne was horrified. Her voice shook a little when she asked Brad, "Will she be all right?"

"The doctors say she will, but it'll take time. He tore her up pretty badly before I got there. The bastard got away from the Vermont police clean as a whistle, but I intend to get him!" Then Brad told her that he would pay Count Vignola a visit later that day. "What do you think of that?"

"I think you'll give him the best surprise he's ever had," she replied, "if they allow you to enter. We don't have the sort of office just anyone can walk into. There's a high, locked gate and a stone wall around the property. A guard is always on duty at the gate, and he won't let you in without orders from inside. And even if you're admitted, I wonder if you can get anything out of the count. He's rather crafty."

"It's worth a try, Suzanne. It'll give me a chance to appraise the opposition up close. Is Criscolle in Rome? Do you think he'll be at your office today?"

"He was in yesterday, but I don't have any idea about today. Sometimes he's in the office every day for a while, then he might be out for weeks. He could be on his way somewhere right now. If he's coming in, it'll be early, though. He never comes in later than nine o'clock and is usually gone by noon."

She gave him directions to the Aspis main office, then described the building in which it and the count were housed. "It's a three-story, stucco palazzo surrounded by a courtyard," she said, "and it is several hundred years old. The building has stone balconies jutting out from the second floor, where the count's palatial quarters are. There are surveillance cameras and floodlights positioned under the eaves of a terra-cotta tile roof."

"Trusting bastards, aren't they? Is one camera focused on the gate so they can identify visitors?"

"Yes. We don't get too many traveling salesmen or thieves, I can tell you that. The place is very secure, and the count's suite is well guarded, too. It's a treasure house of antiques, for he's quite a collector. Downstairs only the office equipment and computer terminals are worth much, but they're easily replaceable. The main computer's in a vault-like room that you'd have to literally blow up to get into. Reaching it to put it out of commission wouldn't do you any good, though, because there's a backup computer in Tokyo that's linked to ours by satellite. It has all the data locked away safely so it can't be lost by accident or computer breakdown."

"And there's no way to get at the company's computer database without the right codes. A damn sophisticated operation, Suzanne. Tom's working on how we can get Max to help. He says it won't be easy!"

"Tell me about it. I've been wrestling with them for nearly a year, and you know how little progress I've made. I'm still at square one."

"That's the hardest square to get off. Look, I want you to meet me today after you finish work. We must talk. Have you got any pictures of the count's Villa Amalfi?"

"I have quite a few, Brad, but meeting you could be dangerous for both of us. Is anyone following you?"

"Not so far. Why don't we meet at the Piazza Navona—near the north entrance to the square. Make it about five-thirty."

"Better make it six, Brad," she told him. "I've got a bunch of work on my desk and want to clean it up."

It was eleven o'clock when Bradford drove up to the gate barring entrance to the courtyard of Aspis's headquarters. He wondered what kind of reception he'd receive inside. Or would they let him in at all? Brad gave the guard his card and tried to respond in Italian to the man's question about why he was there. When he mentioned the name of Cardinal Massara the guard's eyebrows shot upward and he hurried away to a small kiosk adjacent to the gate. Brad watched as the man talked animatedly into an intercom. Then the gate swung open in front of him, operated by the guard from his cubicle.

Bradford was watchful as he drove through the gate into the courtyard Suzanne had described. In a month the flower beds along the drive and around the court would be cheerful with flowers from the well-tended gardens, but now it was drab gray and brown.

On the far side of the main building was a small parking lot and he left the rented Fiat there—parked next to Nick Criscolle's expensive black Porsche. Brad's heart began to pound in his chest. Would he get to see Criscolle, he wondered, or would Count Vignola prevent their confrontation in his office?

A male receptionist whose double-breasted suit hid neither his well-developed chest nor his rippling biceps did not smile when Brad presented himself. The large reception area contained a black marble desk, severe modern Italian chairs, and a stainless steel coffee table with a few newspapers and magazines thoughtfully laid on it.

The receptionist frisked Brad quickly with his eyes, and Brad was glad he had chosen to simply tuck his Beretta into his belt beneath his gray suit rather than wear his shoulder holster. He didn't know what to expect from Vignola, but whatever happened, he wanted to be ready for it. The man at the desk waved Brad to a chair, saying, "Just a moment, Signor Bradford," in a surprisingly high, cultured voice.

Brad picked up the *Herald Tribune* on the coffee table and began flipping through it while the receptionist disappeared through a door behind his desk. Two headlines caught his eye. The first headline announced in big black letters: POPE CRITICALLY ILL, RECEIVES LAST RITES. Bradford was sober-faced as he visualized the Holy Father he had met and talked to just last week. How frail and old he had looked. And now he was dying. Brad felt a genuine sadness entirely unrelated to the religious significance of a dying Pope. The second headline—in much smaller type and buried in the middle of the paper—was nonetheless significant to Brad: BANCO VECCHIO PRESIDENT COMMITS SUICIDE OVER MISSING FUNDS.

Brad knew the name of the bank and its president because they had both been mentioned in Tony Phipps's recent report on Aspis. It was a bank that had reputedly been involved in some questionable loans to a South American oil exploration company that had gone bankrupt and in the process cost its investors a fortune. The company's majority shareholder had been the Vatican Bank, but apparently its shares had been unloaded on the market the day before the company declared bankruptcy. Banco Vecchio had bought heavily into the company that very same day.

And now Pepe Romanazzi, the bank's chief executive officer, was dead. Romanazzi, according to the newspaper story, had hanged himself leaving a note telling the world he had been guilty of speculating with the bank's money in the shares that had turned so sour.

Brad swore at the certain knowledge that another suspect suicide had now taken place. He made a mental note to have Murray check with Tony Phipps on the Banco Vecchio affair and try to determine the extent of probable Aspis involvement.

Interrupting Brad's thoughts and plans, the muscular receptionist and eyed Brad speculatively. "Count Vignola," the man announced, "will see you now." He watched Brad get to his feet, then motioned for him to follow, leading Brad through the door behind the desk into a huge room that had once been a high-ceilinged salon but was now simply a clerical section.

A dozen desks were carefully placed around the red-carpeted room and along one wall were several large copying machines. All the desks in view were occupied by men except one. The lone female was Suzanne Steelman, who looked up when Brad approached but gave no hint of recognition.

Behind the room was a large, sunny office with several oil paintings lining the walls, one of them an oil of St. Peter's Square filled with a throng of people. A wiry, fastidiously dressed man with a mustache but no beard sat behind a massive, uncluttered rosewood desk. His small, ferret-like eyes were on Brad, his expression one of anxiety. Or was it pure astonishment?

Gall! Count Vignola thought as he eyed the tall, bearded Elliot Bradford approaching his desk. To walk, unescorted, into his enemy's camp required the sheerest sort of gall.

"What can I do for you?" the count said evenly.

"Didn't your half brother Cardinal Massara call you to warn you I'd be coming?"

"He did. Your visit disturbed him greatly, Mr. Bradford, for as you must know, the suggestions you made to him are not palatable to a man of the cloth—a man important and very high up in the Holy See. You, sir, should be thrashed."

"Or killed? You've been trying to get that done for quite a while now. Long before I had the temerity to talk to your brother."

The count frowned, wondering how much Bradford knew. Did he suspect that the man who'd taken Holly Sands prisoner last week was an Aspis assassin?

"You can believe that if you wish," Vignola said. "Why are you here? I'm a busy man, with much to accomplish."

"So I'm told," Bradford said. "My people say your organization has made a bundle from all sorts of barely legal activities. You know we're on your trail, don't you?"

Vignola seethed with rage, though his face now displayed only a wan smile. "It is my understanding," he said, "that FINVEST is wasting a good deal of time and money investigating our business transactions. It's your loss of time and money, not mine."

"It's no waste of time, Count Vignola. I have evidence that your half brother's bank—the Vatican Bank—is dirtying its hands dealing with you."

"Absurd!" Vignola snapped. "The Vatican Bank is the most respectable and respected bank in the world."

"It was once," Bradford returned. "But that was a long time ago. Simon Zeisman was the Vatican's banker then."

Vignola's throat was suddenly dry and a flicker of surprise visibly passed over his face like a fleeting shadow. What did this arrogant American know of Simon Zeisman? "The Vatican Bank remains so," Vignola said. "Its assets have increased tenfold since Zeisman retired."

"So, it seems, has the scope of its activities. I wonder how much the Pope knows of Cardinal Massara's dealings with Aspis and you, its director. Do you think he would condone the Holy See having ties with a Mafia-linked organization such as yours?"

Vignola, though reeling under Bradford's piercing attack, forced himself to chuckle to emphasize how ridiculous the man's allegations were. "Really, Mr. Bradford, you have seen too many gangster movies. The Mafia is real enough, but we certainly have no connection to it. What would the Mafia want from us?"

"To wash dirty money? To invest it? Hide it? To finance new activities—say revolutions here and there around the globe? Mercenaries? Drugs? All sorts of things, I would think."

While Vignola was thinking over Bradford's rapid-fire series of assertions—which weren't far off the mark—a sharp knock sounded at the door. Without waiting for a response, Nick Criscolle sauntered in. He was grinning like a man who had just won the Irish sweepstakes. For a change Vignola was glad to see Criscolle. "Nicholas," he said as the Aspis assassin stopped beside Bradford and looked him over, "this is Elliot Bradford."

As Bradford stood next to Criscolle, he had to squelch the urge to avenge the murder of Jack Sands and Holly's assault by shooting a hole in the middle of the assassin's grinning face.

He and Criscolle made searing eye contact, and Brad knew instinctively that, demented sadist or not, Criscolle was as formidable an opponent as he would face. Everything about the man stated it clearly. Criscolle had developed a hard, sinewy body an inch or two shorter than Brad's that would have been at home on a circus trapeze or in a boxing ring, hands that looked strong enough to bend steel as they flexed at the waist of Criscolle's tailored navy blue Italian suit.

But it was the strength and confidence reflected in Criscolle's steel gray eyes and the high-cheekboned face that impressed Brad the most. Strength, confidence, and harsh cruelty. Brad had the feeling that Criscolle should have been born a few hundred years ago. He would have been completely within his aggressive element during the Middle Ages—as a dungeon torturer.

"Tortured anyone lately, Criscolle?" Brad heard himself snapping at the killer. "Was it you who arranged the neat little suicide in Rome yesterday? You know, the banker's?"

The gauntlet was laid down and Bradford tensed, alert for any possible hostile reaction by Criscolle. Any, that is, but the one he got, for now the Aspis killer threw back his head and laughed, his eyes sparkling with glee. "You sure as hell are a piece of work, Bradford," he said. "First you go over to the fuckin' Vatican . . ."

"Nick!" broke in Count Vignola sharply.

But Criscolle paid him no heed, continuing, ". . . and try to shake up one of the head honchos in the place, then you got the balls to . . ."

"Enough!" roared the count. "Mr. Bradford, you've wasted enough of our time. As I told you, I'm a busy man and so is Mr. Criscolle . . ."

"Yeah—busy as hell whipping defenseless women!" Bradford's eyes were on Criscolle. A frown now replaced the smile on Criscolle's face.

Vignola's expression was venomous as he was ignored by the two sparring warriors before him.

Brad lost control as painful memories resurfaced. "I'm going to take you out, Criscolle! Count, you'd better start looking for a replacement triggerman for your unholy consortium. And I'll tell you something else, when I'm finished with the two of you, Aspis will be floundering in its own blood."

If Bradford thought his challenging tirade would arouse fury in his rival, he was wrong. Criscolle's frown vanished when Brad finished, and he was beaming a moment later, though Count Vignola was not.

"You're on, Bradford," Criscolle replied, his voice a nasty rumble. "Who the fuck do you think you are? Superman?" With that a stiletto leaped into his hand, its razor-thin blade a deadly gleam little more than a foot from Brad's breast.

Bradford had expected it and had his Beretta out almost in the same instant of time. "Not Superman, but ready for you!" he declared.

Criscolle's eyebrows shot up in surprise. "Not bad, Bradford, but pull that trigger and you'll be just as dead as I am."

Brad knew the killer was telling the truth. "Let me see your weapon go down, and mine is history too," he said.

Criscolle chuckled, then palmed the knife deftly and it disappeared from view. "That's a good idea, Bradford. The count don't like blood on his carpet. It ruins expensive Orientals, right, Count?"

Before Vignola could respond Suzanne Steelman appeared in the doorway. "Is everything all right?" she asked. Not until later did Brad learn from her that a camera hidden in a compartment behind the one-way glass of a mirror over the doors was monitored by Vignola's secretary and one of his bodyguards. Today Suzanne was watching the television monitor on the secretary's desk and she had beaten the guard into the count's office to defuse the confrontation.

Vignola, quickly recovering his calm, nodded. "Mr. Bradford was just about to leave, Suzanne. Show him to the door."

Brad knew there was little to be gained by prolonging the meeting so he preceded Suzanne out of the office without comment. When the pair reached the outer doors of the building, she bid him an icy good-bye, as she had told him she would.

Not that it mattered, for Brad was in no mood for small talk. The emotional meeting made his hands shake as he seized the handle of the door and strode out. It had taken every ounce of willpower he possessed to keep from attacking Criscolle in Vignola's office. As Bochlaine and Suzanne Steelman had told him though, Criscolle was simply a pawn of the greater evil represented by Count Vignola and Aspis.

Vignola, the sleek, well-mannered gentleman, could find a hundred animals like Criscolle to do his bidding, although Brad doubted any of them would be more cold or efficient than the American, who obviously relished his work as an assassin.

Recalling the speed with which the Aspis killer had produced his knife, Brad knew he could give Criscolle no advantage in hand-to-hand combat. To do so would guarantee his death.

Brad was deep in thought as he slid behind the wheel of the Fiat and drove it around the courtyard circle, then past the main building and toward the gate. Only when he had turned the car onto Via Toscana did the tension he had felt throughout his visit to Aspis dissipate. He found himself keeping an eye on his rearview mirror for sign of a trailing car of any description as he headed toward FINVEST's Rome headquarters.

Would Kevin Burke manage to locate Criscolle's living quarters by following him from Aspis today? Bradford wondered. There had been no evidence of Burke or any Roman police vehicle near the entrance gate to Aspis either when Brad arrived or just now when he'd left. It mattered little then, for Brad was committed to his next move—a clandestine visit to Villa Amalfi perhaps aided by whatever Burke might learn.

Lieutenant Burke was pleasantly surprised by the cooperation he was obtaining from the Rome police. After leaving Bradford he had sought out Captain Enrico Parente, a man whose police assignment in Rome was similar to Burke's in New York.

Captain Parente was a chance acquaintance Burke had made when the Italian visited New York with his wife and twin daughters several summers earlier. Kevin had been at precinct headquarters when Parente wandered in, identified himself and asked if he could talk to an American detective to compare methods. The desk sergeant thought Parente, whose English was heavily-accented but more than passable, was a certifiable fruitcake and would have sent the Italian packing had Burke not interceded and led Parente away. After four hours of seeing Manhattan from inside a NYPD squad car, Parente had bubbled over with goodwill toward his "brother" police officer and issued a sincere request that Burke let him one day show Rome to him.

Not until his sudden flight to Rome with Bradford had Burke even thought about the offer. When Burke showed up at Captain Parente's Italian police headquarters, Enrico embraced the Irishman so excitedly that Kevin was certain he'd suffered a broken rib.

After they each drank an espresso, Parente ushered Burke out of the building and into a beige Fiat van that looked like an ordinary delivery vehicle but whose side panels were constructed of one-way glass made to look like sheet metal. Used for surveillance, it was equipped with radio and electronic equipment that could be used to pick up and record conversations as much as a thousand feet away through directional microphones and amplifiers.

Burke knew of Bradford's intention to confront Criscolle and Vignola at Aspis headquarters, for Brad had told him the story of the Piedmont Papers during their flight to Rome. It had been Burke's idea to follow Criscolle after the Aspis meeting, aided by Captain Parente. The Italian had suggested the surveillance.

When Parente showed off the van with its electronic marvels, Burke could not have been more pleased—especially with the power of the equipment. Parente's driver-technician parked the van down the road from Aspis headquarters, then demonstrated the ability of the gear to pick up conversations by focusing on a pair of women walking slowly along the street so far away that it was hard to see their mouths. The result was an unintelligible blue streak of Italian streaming out of the van's speakers. Parente laughed when he heard it, then translated it. "One woman," he said, "complains that her husband is too attentive. That all he wants to do is make bambinos. The other complains that her husband turns the other way when she takes off her nightie and gets into bed."

"My wife was both of them," Burke observed with a laugh. "When we were both in law school I was too ready—for her taste—to make love, but later, when I had to work long and hard for the police department, she suddenly wanted me all the time—or so she claimed."

Parente chuckled. "I don't have that problem, Kevin," he said. "My wife and I make love no more, no less than we ever did—once or twice each week. During the week, however, I visit my mistress twice. She is so exciting and sexy that I cannot be too tired to love her. So I hear only the complaints of my children, I am glad to say."

"And they complain all the time," Burke observed dryly.

"Of course," Parente replied, "but at least one can beat one's children without fear for his life if the complaining becomes too loud."

Burke got a kick out of the Italian's logic and did not ask what Parente's wife thought of his keeping a mistress. Perhaps in Italy that was the accepted thing.

Parente and Burke arrived at Aspis headquarters just before ten in the morning, but the van's directional mikes picked up nothing of interest until Bradford arrived an hour later. They chuckled over his language difficulties with the Italian guard, then listened in on the guard's intercom exchange with Count Vignola.

Parente translated it: "Bradford? Elliot Bradford?" The count's voice, Parente said, showed surprise.

"I'll bet," murmured Burke.

"He wants to talk to you about Cardinal Massara," the guard told Vignola.

There was a momentary silence on the line, but then Vignola told the guard to admit Bradford. Before the guard shut off the intercom, however, Vignola's muffled voice was heard to say: "We have a visitor, Nicholas. The same man you missed twice."

"Nicholas Criscolle, Enrico," Burke declared. "He's our boy. I have a rough description of him and I'm told he drives a black Porsche. We'll follow him when he leaves."

There was nothing they could do while Bradford was inside the Aspis office but wait and wonder since the directional mikes couldn't penetrate the building's stone walls. Burke was greatly relieved when Bradford appeared at the entrance, escorted by a tall, attractive dark-haired woman who stiffly bid him good-bye, then strode away. The exchange between Bradford and the woman could be heard clearly in the police van.

When Brad reappeared a few moments later driving through the gate, Burke wondered if the woman who had just brushed him off was the one Bradford had mentioned to him—Suzanne Steelman.

On the plane Brad had said that he had been vaguely familiarized with life at the Villa Amalfi, Vignola's retreat in Italy's ski country near the Swiss border. "I think we may find some of Aspis's hidden secrets there." Brad had said. "It makes sense that Vignola would lock papers and evidence in the house. Most likely in a safe."

"Then don't go without me, Brad," Burke had told him. "I'm not bad with safes."

"A cop safecracker?"

"I learned it from a reformed second-story man who became a cop and . . ."

"Your racquetball partner, no doubt?"

"An adept conclusion, Brad. He's good at many things and likes to talk after he's won a few games."

"And you like to listen?"

"Never learned a thing with my mouth open, Brad. All you can do is eat and show your ignorance."

A short time after Bradford's departure from Aspis headquarters, Burke and Parente saw two men, one of them too big to fit Criscolle's description, but the other one just right, emerge from Aspis's front entrance. Burke watched the two exchange a few words before parting and the mikes confirmed Criscolle's identity.

Several minutes later a black Porsche emerged from the gate. When Criscolle turned left, he was headed in the same direction as the police van, which was already running and ready to begin pursuit.

"I've told our driver to pull up alongside him at a light so we can get his picture," Parente said after issuing quick instructions to his man in front and returning to the rear.

"Good idea," Burke said, more impressed with his Italian friend than ever.

It took the driver only about two minutes to seize an opportunity to pull up beside Criscolle's Porsche and allow his boss to take two pictures with an old Polaroid camera.

Seeing the results made Burke ask why Parente didn't have a high resolution, digital camera. He was astonished to learn that the Rome police had many but that they were all unavailable right now.

"Unavailable? Why?" Burke asked.

Captain Parente flashed him a toothy grin. "They are constantly being borrowed to take pictures of mistresses."

Burke might have laughed at that, but missed the opportunity. He and Parente were suddenly interrupted by their driver as he floored the accelerator in hot pursuit of the Porsche, which had bolted away from the light.

It took them only a few moments to realize that they'd lost Nick Criscolle's car.

FOURTEEN

After spending a good part of the afternoon reviewing Aspis reports with Murray Jolles at his Rome office, then talking with Tom in New York and Tony in London, Bradford realized that he had only thirty minutes before he was supposed to meet Suzanne.

Soon after he pulled his Fiat into traffic he saw another car tagging along behind him, in no apparent hurry. He made a few turns and lost the other car, but it—or another just like it—showed up behind him not long afterward and he decided to make certain it wasn't a tail by getting rid of his car.

It was late afternoon and rush-hour traffic was at its usual Rome worst, so he simply drove until he came upon a free space on the street. There he pulled up on the curb and watched the other Fiat pass him. He waited for the other car to make a right turn around the corner, no doubt with the intention of parking there to wait for him. He removed the keys from the ignition, got out of the car, and locked the door. He would pick up the car later. Then he began walking back down the street in the direction from which he'd come, seeking a taxi. He found one two blocks away and completed his trip to the piazza without incident.

Suzanne arrived in her slightly battered Alfa only moments after he'd paid the taxi. She was smiling when he got in.

"Your visit shook things up a bit," she said as she released the clutch and pulled the small car out into traffic. "He kept Nick with him for quite a while after you left and was in a bitter mood the rest of the day."

"Did you overhear anything?" he asked.

"Not a thing. You scared me in there, Brad. I was watching on the television monitor in the count's secretary's office when Nick pulled a knife on you. That's why I broke in on your meeting."

"I'll admit it would have scared me, too, Suzanne—if I hadn't been expecting a move like that. And if I hadn't been so busy trying to keep from attacking him right then and there!"

"He'd have killed you, Brad."

"Maybe. But that's not what stopped me. I want that bastard dead, Suzanne, but I also know now that you and Bochlaine are right about Aspis. Your boss, Vignola, is an unctuous, venomous snake and the organization's far worse than that. Killing Criscolle would make no difference at all to the count or Aspis."

Suzanne half-turned toward him and gave him a pleased look, then had to brake hard to keep from crashing her car into the back of a big, Mercedes tour bus that stopped abruptly in front of her. "Then you're going ahead with the trip to Amalfi?" she asked after she had maneuvered the car around the bus.

For the first time that day Brad managed a genuine smile. "I am if you don't ram into any buses."

Suzanne turned red, then laughed. "I had that coming," she said. "Don't worry, we'll make it."

They drove to the FINVEST apartment on Via Cassia north of Rome. They were almost there when Suzanne told him that Criscolle and the count had confirmed that Bochlaine survived Criscolle's attack.

"How do you know?"

"The count's secretary was checking hospitals. I overheard her and asked about it. She said the count was concerned because Frank had disappeared. Concerned, hell!"

"How is Bochlaine?"

"I haven't heard from him lately, but he's been recovering all right. He gave me a number where I could reach him, but I haven't tried it yet."

"Let's give him a call when we get to the apartment. My line is safe and I have to talk to him."

"You're sure your apartment isn't bugged?"

"It better not be. I pay a lot to keep it free of bugs that might be planted there by unfriendly people, including your boss and his little army. It's a nice place, by the way. Has a great view of the rolling hills north of the city and it's big, well-furnished, and comfortable. There are two bedrooms, and one of them is fixed up with its own private computer terminal plugged into our Max."

Suzanne made a face. "Just what I always dreamed of," she declared, "sleeping with a computer. Ugh!"

Brad said nothing, his eyes on her, but his mind back on the interview with Criscolle and Vignola.

"Turn here," Brad ordered as they reached the turnoff to the apartment complex that housed the FINVEST corporate apartment.

They drove up to the gate, the only opening into a fenced-in property with a tree-lined asphalt drive leading toward a cluster of three balconied, four-story buildings several hundred yards ahead. It was dark now, so only the lights on the sides of the buildings could be seen.

The gate was closed, and a gatekeeper approached them. Brad carried an identification card and handed it out the window of the car to the thin young man. The youth checked the card over carefully then nodded and pressed the button on a remote control electronic unit to unlock and open the gate. As the gatekeeper returned his card to him, Brad told him that he should allow no one to visit him without first calling on the intercom.

Five minutes later Suzanne and he were on an elevator to the top floor of the first apartment building. Suzanne liked the place immediately and said so. Bradford's corporate apartment had wooden slat shutters like the cover of a rolltop desk, to give the residents a good measure of privacy if they desired it, was roomy and comfortable as well as tastefully furnished by Murray.

There was little to be seen outside at night, so Brad didn't bother to open the shutters, which were kept shut when the place was empty.

The phone rang as Brad finished showing Suzanne around the place. It was Jolles. "Your friend just called, Brad," the Rome office manager told him. "Bochlaine. He wants to talk to you as soon as possible."

Bradford's eyebrows shot up. "Bochlaine?" he repeated for Suzanne's benefit. "Did he leave a number?" Murray rattled off a number, and Brad repeated it while scribbling it on a scratch pad.

"Call him back in the next five minutes, Brad. He says it's a pay phone, and he can't stay there long. Also, that New York cop called. I gave him your number, but not the address of the apartment. Okay?"

"Good man, Murray," Brad said, and then hung up the phone, glad to know there were many people in his organization he could trust.

Immediately after hanging up, Bradford dialed the number Bochlaine had given Murray. "Bradford?" was all Bochlaine said when he answered.

"You want to know who my kindergarten teacher was back in California?" Bradford asked.

"You didn't go to school in California, Mr. Bradford," came the prompt response. "Is Suzanne with you?"

"Are you a priest?"

"I have a robe that says so. Let me talk to Suzanne, Mr. Bradford. Suzanne and I need to talk about the Pope's imminent death."

"I know. I've read about it in the papers. What's that got to do with . . .?"

"Everything," Bochlaine broke in. "His successor will be Cardinal Massara."

Bradford, astonished, stood in place for a moment, then instructed Suzanne to pick up the phone in the second bedroom, the door of which was across the way. As she disappeared into the room he asked Bochlaine, "Are you certain about Massara? How do you know?"

"As certain as anyone can be. The College of Cardinals makes the papal choice and I've just learned that there's a strong group within the College that will sponsor Massara. They have been behind Massara since the war."

Bradford heard a cry of surprise from Suzanne, who was now on the line. "Were they involved in the disappearance of the ten million dollars?" she asked.

"Probably, but only through Massara. And only the Piedmont Papers can confirm that," Bochlaine responded. "Now it has become more imperative that we find the paper trail. Once the Holy Father dies and begins his pilgrimage to our Father, the cardinals will meet and the Inner Circle will push forward Massara's name against all the rest."

"The Inner Circle? What's that?" Brad asked.

"That's what they call themselves, although no one knows who they are or how they operate."

Bradford told Bochlaine of his idea to visit the count's villa in Livigno in search of hidden documents.

"If there're at the Villa Amalfi," Bochlaine said, "they're surely well-hidden for I've been there often and managed to thoroughly check his private rooms while visiting with him socially. I've seen no indication of any papers. Yet wherever the cursed papers are, they must be close to him and accessible enough so that he can produce them if he has to." He paused for a moment, thinking. "If you can get in unobserved, try the computer room. It's never unguarded while the villa's occupied, so I haven't been able to take a look."

"We'll do that, Bochlaine," Bradford said.

"How's your wound, Franco?" Suzanne asked.

"Better now," the fat man said. "My appetite is returning. Tell me, has the exterminator resumed his hunt for me?"

"Nick knows now that you're alive, Franco, but I've no idea whose trail he's on—yours or Brad's. He set a trap for Brad in America last Sunday, but thanks to Jack Sands's daughter, Holly, Brad managed to avoid it."

Bochlaine's reaction to Suzanne's quick summary of Criscolle's most recent activities in Vermont was a murmured Hail Mary and a vow. "That man, Suzanne, is the devil himself!"

"I hope he doesn't find you, Franco. Are you safe where you are? How did he locate you before?"

"It was my fault, but now there's no way he can find me. Only one man knows where I am and he would die before betraying me. I haven't told you, Suzanne, so that the sadist cannot rip the information from your throat."

"Can we reach you at the number you gave me once? You'll want to know the results of our trip to Livigno."

"The number is good, though there are things I must attend to. Someone will be there to answer—a woman. Should a man answer, hang up immediately; do not trust him. It is an unlikely event, but do not talk to him lest you give yourself away. If I answer and am unable to talk because of a personal danger, I will tell you that I am not the party you seek."

When Bochlaine hung up, Brad and Suzanne stared glumly at each other. Finally, Brad broke the silence. "Massara—the new Pope?" He shook his head in disgust. "Even a suspicion that he was involved in the theft of the Jewish ransom would make it impossible for any responsible person to vote for him as pontiff."

"Yet no one suspects that except Franco, you, and me, Brad. And no one in the College of Cardinals would give credence to such an allegation, except this Inner Circle Franco mentioned."

"Not without the Piedmont Papers to back it up." Bradford stared at Suzanne, who was now sitting beside him on the sofa.

Suzanne was unaware that Brad's eyes did not see her. Nor did she care, for she was imagining the coronation as Pope of the man who had killed her grandmother—or at least had been responsible for her death.

"We've just got to find those papers, Brad," she murmured. "Got to!"

The phone rang again. Burke was in excellent spirits, in spite of what he called his abject failure in shadowing Nick Criscolle.

"We lost him almost as fast as we got on his trail," Burke told Bradford. "That's some fast car he's got, let me tell you. And he knows Rome's streets damn well. But we got lucky in the end when a traffic cop found him for us and followed him to the apartment he keeps under an assumed name. We now know where the apartment is and to whom it's leased. How do you like them apples?"

"I like them a lot, Burke. Suzanne told me Criscolle's apartment is almost as mysterious as the Piedmont Papers. That even Count Vignola has no idea where it is."

"We also got a couple of pictures of your buddy Nick, Brad. Captain Parente, an Italian police officer I befriended in New York a couple of years ago, took them with an old Polaroid. They're not as sharp as they could be, but good enough."

"Have you told your Italian cop about Aspis or why we're so interested in Criscolle?"

"I told him a little bit about both, but he's promised to keep it under wraps, and I think he will. He's a pretty honest sort, and competent, too. By the way, I think he can arrange with a friend of his to get us snow equipment to use when we go to Livigno."

"Did you tell him we're going to Vignola's mountain retreat?"

"I had to, Brad. I also told him that we'd be doing a little high-class breaking and entering—with the aid of Suzanne's key. He wasn't pleased, but I convinced him that it's necessary and he's given me a letter of authority that'll help if we run into any police problems we can't handle up there."

"Let's hope we won't need it. What I want to do is get into Amalfi, look it over carefully, then get out nice and quietly, whether or not we find the Piedmont Papers. I'm not looking for a shoot-out at the O.K. Corral or anything like it, and I sure don't want to wind up in some dusty Italian jail."

Bradford told Burke where to have Captain Parente drop him off the next day—a private airport north of Rome—and then hung up.

Suzanne cooked them veal chops found in the apartment's well-stocked freezer while Brad went over maps of the Livigno area he had obtained from the Italian Tourist Bureau earlier in the day. After dinner she showed him pictures she had taken of the count's villa on weekend trips she had made there with Vignola and his entourage.

North of Milan, Livigno was a winter resort only a few miles east of St. Moritz, more than three hundred miles north of Rome in the Alps. It was much too far to travel easily by car, so Brad had chartered a Gulfstream GIV jet from a Saudi charter outfit that operated out of metropolitan Rome. Specializing in very wealthy tourists and business people, Tourways International was a client of FINVEST and Brad had often used it to make business trips all over Europe from Athens to London. It saved money only because it saved time, and it saved Brad plenty of that.

The last of the pictures Suzanne handed somewhat hesitantly to Bradford was of her in the diamond-shaped swimming pool in the basement level of Amalfi. She wore a revealing two-piece bathing suit and sported a magnificent tan as she stood atop a diving board.

"Who took this?" Brad asked.

"The count has a photographer come in from Saint Moritz on weekends when we're there. He takes pictures of every guest."

Brad looked back down at the picture on the cluttered table in the apartment dining room, then up at the real life woman whose image was in it. For the first time since they'd met in London, he really saw her. "You could have been a model," he said. "You are a beautiful woman."

She stood and stretched wearily before him, her shoes discarded on the floor beneath the table. "Thank you, kind sir," she said, rendering him a quick curtsy.

He did not laugh at her attempt at humor. Instead he stood and moved up against her. A quizzical look flashed across her face and she matter-of-factly asked, "How many women have you made love to since your wife died?"

"Does it matter?"

"Maybe, maybe not," she persisted.

"I've been with two, but . . . well, it was more physical than anything. A release."

"Holly obviously adores you. You must know that. There isn't anything going on between the two of you?"

"She's just a kid and much too young to know what she wants. I love her and find her as tempting as a sizzling steak when I'm starved. But I won't sleep with her. She's not what I'm looking for."

"Do you know what you really want?"

His reply was to kiss her as gently as if he were brushing her lips with a feather. Her eyes remained open for just a moment, but then they closed as she felt his body against hers.

Time stopped. The glowing warmth of the kiss seemed to have no end. Neither withdrew from what had become a silent yet vibrant communion. Brad remembered the feeling—it had once been like this with Nan. Suddenly, the passionate man he had once been came into being again.

As the warmth grew and radiated downward, the reaction of their bodies became instinctive. Brad's hands lightly traced Suzanne's back and shoulders. The subtle scent of her perfume was intoxicating. The kiss deepened, until it was not enough to express what was happening between them.

The moment was inspiring! Brad carried her effortlessly into the main bedroom. There, in silence, they undressed each other. Suzanne's slim, elegantly manicured fingers opened the buttons on Brad's shirt, then continued down to his belt and zipper. She touched him there, gently, with soft, sensual sweeps of her hand. Then she pulled away, gazing steadily into his eyes as she removed her own blouse.

She wore no bra to conceal or constrict her well-formed, milky white breasts. As she dropped her blouse to the floor, Brad's sight set upon the softly sensual pair, his eyes gazing admiringly at the slight pink rise of her erect nipples. His hands automatically reached for her there, and caressed her. Then, his hands went to the zipper of her skirt and slipped it past her hips; the last major barrier between their flesh was removed.

He knelt, bringing the skirt to the floor so she could step out of it, and looked up at her long legs and the inviting cleft between them. She was covered now by only a pair of bikini panties. Brad slid a hand beneath their elastic band and removed those too.

He stopped to gaze thoughtfully at the woman before him. "God, you are perfect," he whispered, the words passed his lips before he even realized he was speaking them. "And I want you so much."

His hands explored all of her, caressing the curves of her flesh, enjoying the feel of her, the scent of her, the sight. She was warm, soft and so alive.

She pulled him to her and helped him remove his shorts. Then their two bodies embraced, with arms entwined and flesh kissing flesh. They held each other for what seemed to be both exasperatingly brief and arousingly long.

"Dance with me, Brad," she whispered. Brad heard faint music from the tape deck in the living room. He took her in his arms and they swayed to the music. Suzanne's arms were around his neck. Slowly she slid her hands down his back to the base of his spine and pulled him to her, pressing his flesh to her own.

There was no need for either to speak. They sank down on the thick carpeted floor of the bedroom and the rest unraveled like a slow motion dream. They teased and tasted each other with growing passion and then, unable to delay any longer, their bodies joined in deep, sensual and spiritual union.

Later, they lay side by side in silence, until Suzanne spoke.

"Thank you," was all she said.

Brad's dreams that night were wonderfully visual as he slept with this beautiful woman in his arms, her long, lustrous dark hair fanned out on the pillow. Suzanne was the star of his dreams, but she was joined by a smiling Nancy Bradford, Kevin Burke, and Frank Bochlaine. Holly Sands was a part of it, too. But Holly was not smiling.

Unlike Bradford, Count Raffaele Ernesto Vignola slept poorly that night in his ornate apartment over Aspis headquarters.

Nick Criscolle was complacent about Elliot Bradford and FINV-EST—an attitude that the count could not share. The American's visit had unsettled him more than anything since his half brother initially approached him about forming Piedmont S.A.

There was, of course, the problem of the debt owed to Piedmont's original "investor," but, in those early years, the relationship was manageable. In the years that passed since, though, the organization, its name changed to prevent any speculation about its Vatican connection, became more complex. Once Massara and the others had agreed that Aspis could serve as a private banker to its original "lender" and to other clients with very special needs, all limits to its prosperity had dissolved.

It had become one of the richest and most powerful organizations in the world. Even most of the world's banks did not have assets that could match those of Aspis. The organization was, of course, much more than a bank and always had been, right from the start.

It served as owner of record for hundreds of companies operated by shadowy clients who could not afford to let their identities be known or even hinted at to more honest banks. The count himself was no longer certain of the actual numbers, although he could summon the information quickly enough from the computer systems. The managing directors of Aspis operations around the world, though they took orders from Rome, dealt directly with representatives of their clandestine clients, but not one of them had even the vaguest notion of the total extent of Aspis operations or power.

None ever would, for that information was the golden key to continuing Aspis's power.

Nick Criscolle fancied himself the successor to the Aspis throne, Count Vignola knew, although that would never come to pass, for, Mafia connections or not, he was simply a hired hood, good at what he did but not management material. When the time came for the power to pass, Cardinal Massara and the Circle would select and install the count's successor quietly and without fuss. As for Criscolle, he would be removed from the scene just as quietly, for the new Aspis leader would most certainly sweep the organization clean to assure the loyalty he would require from his people. Nick was loyal only to himself and his goals and an asset to the organization only as long as he remained an effective force.

Now his effectiveness was questionable, for not only had he failed to eliminate Bochlaine, but he had also missed Elliot Bradford, an infinitely more important target.

As Count Vignola breakfasted in a large sunny room overlooking the courtyard below, he reflected on the Bradford problem and what to do about it. Would Criscolle finally succeed in taking out the audacious Bradford? The count couldn't believe Nick could not soon finish the assignment. For as much as he disliked Criscolle personally, the sadistic assassin was by far the most dangerous man who had held the position in the past twenty years.

Bradford, the count now thought, was getting awfully arrogant, first visiting Cardinal Massara in the Vatican Bank, then presenting himself here at Aspis. What had he hoped to accomplish? It was still a mystery to Vignola.

The count had been genuinely shocked by Bradford's reference to Zeisman, for by connecting the Jewish banker who served under three Popes, he was getting too close to the source of Aspis's original capital. Far too close. There was, after all, no possible way Bradford could prove Aspis's connection to the Jewish ransom money. Only Cardinal Massara, the Circle and he, Count Vignola, knew the truth about what had happened. Colonel Hauptler was still in prison, a senile old man whose words made no sense, and Cardinal Ambrosiani, Massara's Vatican superior, had never suspected the truth. More than eighty years old now, Ambrosiani was no one to be concerned with anyway.

Only the Piedmont Papers could now link the stolen ransom and Aspis and its investor with Massara. They would never come to light, for they were, in their way, buried and not available to anyone but the few who might need them to prove their power—the power of Aspis's inheritance.

Bradford, Vignola concluded as he left his apartment and strolled down the sweeping circular stairway that led to his first-floor office, was simply charging around in the dark like a blinded bull, desperately seeking someone to gore.

FINVEST had no doubt come across evidence of Aspis's spider web of business dealings—among them the sorry Cinema Services affair—and from that Bradford had begun checking Vignola personally, a search which led ultimately to Cardinal Massara.

A superficial smile greeted Giuseppe, the receptionist, as Vignola entered his office through his private entrance. His half brother, the count thought, would one day be the Pope and ruler of a billion Roman Catholics around the globe. It was a stirring thought, and he had often toasted the new Holy Father privately.

Vignola's pleasure lasted only until mid-morning, when he got a call from an Aspis informant who was high up in the Rome polizia. "I thought you'd better know that one of my people is assisting an American homicide police officer in investigating you and your organization, Raffaele," the informant told him. "He had a surveillance vehicle parked outside your offices yesterday."

"There is little here for him to survey," Vignola replied. "We're a business organization, as you know. Nothing more."

"I understand that, of course, Count. But there is something else, though I cannot be certain that it is significant. My captain, Enrico Parente, has been in touch with the polizia in the north and he has arranged for a snow rescue vehicle to meet the American officer, Lieutenant Kevin Burke, in Livigno. Since I have had the honor of being your guest at Villa Amalfi, I know you will be interested in that."

The count was indeed very interested. Nick Criscolle walked into the office just as Vignola thanked his caller.

"I think I'm onto Bochlaine, Count," Nick told him. "He had a private charity he was supporting—the widow of a friend. I have her name, but I am still trying to find out where she lives."

"Never mind him, Nick," Vignola said. "We may have trouble at Amalfi. Burke, the American police lieutenant who helped Bradford avoid your trap in Vermont, is on his way up there and he's arranged to have an SRV meet him in Livigno. Bradford may be with them. Amalfi has to be their target."

Criscolle's smile was brilliant. "Christ! What balls on that guy! Well, Nicky's about to cut them off, Count. I'm on my way."

An Aspis-owned helicopter picked Nicholas Criscolle up fifteen minutes later and flew him to da Vinci Airport, where an Aspis-owned jet awaited him.

FIFTEEN

Even though the sky was overcast with threatening dark clouds, Brad's flight to St. Moritz was fast and spectacular, as the sleek, twin-engine Tourways Gulfstream jet soared past the seven hills of Rome toward the north country with its three- and four-mile high, snow-covered Alpine mountain peaks. They were approaching the small St. Moritz airport.

Burke enjoyed himself the most, since he had never before seen any part of the awesome Alps. Brad now instructed his pilot, a quietly competent sort who'd become "the" pilot for Brad and his company in recent years, to bank to the right and fly over Livigno. Whenever FINV-EST people needed a charter, they asked for Robert Brockway. Perhaps they trusted American pilots more. Robert always obliged them with a safe flight, no matter where they were traveling or what the weather was.

As Robert banked the jet smoothly to the east, Suzanne Steelman stood behind him to direct him over the Villa Amalfi, which was surrounded on all four sides by steep, tree-covered slopes. There had once been a road—a terribly treacherous mountain road—up to Amalfi, but several successive mountain slides had buried it a few years ago, leaving it little more than a ski trail through the trees. On the far side of the mountain from Amalfi were public ski trails used by tourists and a lift that rose all the way up to the ten thousand-foot top of the mountain. Only a few skiers were brave enough to try the upper trails.

Suzanne told Brad they were steep and awesome. "It'll make you wet your pants just looking downhill!"

Brad chuckled.

Between the villa and the public ski trails was a series of narrow trails used by Vignola's guests who wanted to do some downhill skiing, among them Suzanne, who was an expert skier. "There it is," Suzanne said as she pointed toward the mountain. Robert applied full flaps to slow the plane and gave his passengers more time to view the villa.

Below them was a large, rambling structure more Swiss than Italian in architecture. It was tucked almost precipitously against the side of the mountain on a snowy plateau.

Bradford sat next to Suzanne, a pair of powerful field glasses held to his eyes as he carefully looked over the buildings on the plateau. It was a huge, well-kept place that clearly announced that its owner had great wealth. "There's no sign of life down there," Brad observed.

"The guards are probably inside one of the two service buildings near the fence by the trail leading across the mountain. Each of them has living quarters and one—the one nearest the villa—has a big kitchen that includes food pantries and refrigeration units for their supplies."

"Is that the one where the guards would be?" Burke asked.

"I doubt it. The quarters in the other building are nicer," Suzanne said. "The skis are kept there, and there's a game room with pool tables and two or three arcade games."

"No surveillance cameras?" Brad said.

"Not unless they've just installed them. Amalfi is very secure due to its position. The trail we'll be taking up the mountainside is only a little wider than a cross-country ski trail and it'll be a slow trip even with snowmobiles."

Brad's glasses were focused on the forested slope south of the villa. As Suzanne explained that they'd have to zigzag through the forest. "It's not hard to see why the SRV won't be able to get closer than a thousand yards from the villa," he said. "Has your friend Parente arranged snow-mobiles for us, Kevin?"

Burke nodded. "I told him I'd prefer a quiet helicopter," he said with a laugh. "He told me there's no such thing."

A few minutes later Robert landed at the airport in St. Moritz and they were picked up by a young Italian police officer named Carlo Cervi, Parente's friend. Cervi had all manner of equipment aboard the SRV, a truck-like vehicle that could travel either on tires or tank-tread and had the power of a bulldozer. On occasion, the SRV could achieve speeds of up to twenty-five miles an hour, which it did in driving from St. Moritz to Livigno. When it headed up the mountainside toward the Villa Amalfi, however, it was considerably slower and traveled along like a tank as Cervi maneuvered it through the snow and among the trees.

Soon the vehicle had reached the heavily-forested part of the mountainside nearly a half mile below the villa, and there Cervi parked the SRV between two tall pines and announced, in surprisingly good English, "This is as far as we can climb with the vehicle."

Cervi helped them unload three white snowmobiles, each equipped with an electric motor and a police radio set. He demonstrated how to use the equipment and added, "If you get into trouble up there, contact me, and I can arrange for a helicopter to pick you up," he said.

Burke's face expressed concern as he looked from the snowmobiles toward the narrow trail they would follow up the mountain.

"You don't have to come, Burke," Bradford said ceremoniously.

"I don't have to breathe, either," the New York cop retorted. "Don't worry about me, I'll make it."

"I'm serious, Kevin," Brad said. "You're only after a killer. We're after his organization and what we're doing up here is only . . ."

"Pipe down, Brad!" the cop growled. "Criscolle and Aspis are tied together. Anything we can get on Aspis will help me with their assassin."

Bradford was comforted by Burke's presence, for anything could happen in the next two hours. Turning toward Cervi, he said, "If we're not back by three o'clock, you'd better send for that chopper even if we haven't radioed you to do it. Okay?"

The Italian smiled. "It will be done," he said.

Burke was about to climb aboard his snowmobile when he turned to Cervi and said, "I know Captain Parente told you we were up against dangerous killers, Lieutenant Cervi, but I should warn you that they might attack you too—if they should spot us and give chase. So keep on your toes."

Cervi nodded. "I am always on the alert," he assured Burke.

Now the three snowmobiles moved silently up the trail, with Suzanne leading the way, weaving her machine in and out as she followed the contours of the mountain and avoided the clusters of trees that surrounded them. Behind them Burke brought up the rear, managing to avoid the ruts left by Suzanne and Bradford with the aplomb of a veteran snowmobiler.

As they ascended the slope, Brad's head was a veritable whirlpool of thoughts, not the least of them the memory of his unplanned sexual liaison with Suzanne the night before. It had been spontaneous, he thought, perhaps a needed release from the immense tensions that had been building up in both of them. It was odd, but they had been so comfortable together that it seemed as if they'd made love before. Few lovers were ever that compatible with each other.

She had touched him with her passion, for she was a strong, self-sustaining woman who might desire a man, but didn't *need* one. Making love to her had been good for him and, he was sure, for her as well. He found himself liking Suzanne more with each passing day.

Now, as Suzanne's snowmobile veered to the left to pass between two stout pines, then shot up a short open stretch, Brad ordered himself to clear his mind for the serious business that lay ahead. So he shifted his mental gears and reacted quickly when Suzanne suddenly had to slow to a halt just short of a tree that blocked the trail. Brad and Burke dragged the tree aside so they could continue.

As they climbed higher and higher up the mountain, the air grew crisper and the twenty-six degrees of the low country dropped into the teens, in spite of a hot, high afternoon sun. The nylon ski suits they wore were warm though, and only their faces felt the biting cold.

"How much farther?" he called out as she stopped and surveyed the trail ahead, which was suddenly becoming much more narrow. Brad could see a low, rocky outcropping ahead.

"We're there, Brad," she replied. "We've got to leave the machines now and go the rest of the way on foot. The edge of the property is only about fifty yards from here, but we've got to climb the rocks to get there."

It took the trio almost ten minutes to negotiate the rocky cliff-like outcropping and another five to cover the thirty snowy yards to the villa's east-facing front porch. There were no guards in sight as they reached their destination.

Suzanne's key got them inside quickly and without complications. Burke and Bradford, both with drawn pistols, made a quick tour of the downstairs part of the house to make sure it was empty. Suzanne then led them up to the count's suite on the western side of the villa. His office and private computer room were located there.

They were stymied briefly at the door to the count's suite. It was locked, but Lieutenant Burke stepped forward and picked the lock with a deftness that would have qualified him as a pro. "Wait till you see what I can do with a safe," he boasted.

"Let's hope we can find one for you to crack," Brad observed tersely.

The count's suite was orderly and exquisitely furnished. Through the large windows that looked to the southwest, they searched for the guards. The only sign of them was smoke issuing from the chimney of the service building Suzanne had said housed the skis and recreation rooms.

"So far, so good," muttered Burke. "Let's get to work locating what we're after."

For more than half an hour the lieutenant supervised a thorough, professional search of the suite, which yielded nothing.

Then Suzanne led them into the small computer room furnished only with a heavy oak desk on which the computer console was bolted and a low, straight-backed leather chair.

"Bochlaine said that the count may have a secret compartment in here somewhere," Bradford told his companions, his eyes sweeping the small, mostly empty room. "Any ideas?"

"None at all," Suzanne declared, "unless they've concealed the papers somehow in the computer console. The walls are flush with those of the rooms adjoining these. I've checked them before."

Bradford and Burke quickly realized she was right, then began a close examination of the computer console itself. But Brad soon realized that there was no possibility that the papers they were seeking could be concealed there. As he sat in the chair behind the console, Brad's forehead furrowed and he stared at the computer's dark screen.

"Can we operate this terminal without alerting Vignola?" he asked Suzanne.

She nodded. "I don't see what good it'll do," she said, "unless you've come up with the code to unlock its secrets."

"Negative, Suzanne," Brad said, "but maybe my partner in New York might have some ideas. Do you think the phone's working?"

"You're not going to call New York from here, are you?" Suzanne asked, her expression entirely incredulous.

"Why not? Italian phone bills never itemize the calls; and anyway, it takes them months to send a bill."

Burke chuckled. "One thing I've got to say for you, Brad," he declared. "You've sure got brains—and balls!"

"I'd trade them both right now for the code," he said.

Silence settled in the room as Brad picked up the phone on the table next to the computer terminal. It was past working hours in New York, so Brad direct-dialed Tom's apartment. His wife Jane answered the phone.

When Jane Sumereau picked up the phone in New York, Nick Criscolle was less than fifteen minutes away from St. Moritz, hurtling northward in a sleek jet. A helicopter awaited him at the airport, stocked with several machine pistols and a supply of grenades. Two Aspis sharp shooters from Geneva were already with the chopper.

Criscolle's pilot had contacted the craft by radio, and Criscolle had learned that a Tourways jet from Rome had landed there little more than an hour ago. Two men and a woman were on board.

The woman's presence mystified Criscolle. Bradford probably had his buddy, Kevin Burke, in tow, but who could the woman be? Had Bradford's girlfriend Holly Sands returned to Rome?

The thought of the young blonde excited his imagination for just a moment before he brought his thoughts back to the matters at hand. With the aid of the helicopter, he had no doubt that he could surprise them. The question was, could he take them alive so that he could find out what the hell they were up to? The count had told him only he thought they'd be looking for anything they can find out about Aspis, but Criscolle thought that they had more definite plans.

Criscolle shrugged. There was nothing in the villa that would tell them anything about Aspis, so it mattered little whether he took them alive or dead. But he would like to keep the woman breathing for a while, if only to determine if she was worth anything. If she was Holly Sands, he would finish what he had started with her. If she was someone else, she might serve just as well before she died.

Staring out through the window of the small plane, he looked for familiar landmarks in the snowy mountains below. A few minutes later he recognized lofty Piz Bernina and the adjoining Bernina pass straight ahead. Moments later he brought his field glasses to bear on Count Vignola's villa.

Everything at the villa looked peaceful enough, he thought as he scanned the grounds surrounding Amalfi. But then it should, for Bradford would hardly announce his presence by sending up a display or rockets.

Bradford! Criscolle had to smile at the thought of his enemy. "I'm going to take you out," the cocky son-of-a-bitch had said to Criscolle's face. And he hadn't even flinched when faced with a deadly stiletto in Nick's hand. Not that Nick would have killed him then and there, for Vignola didn't like to be confronted with violence. Bradford's gun had evened things out.

Could Bradford take Criscolle out? The thought only served to widen his smile. Criscolle thought he knew all there was to know about Bradford.

Bradford's army record said he'd killed, that he was smart, capable, and courageous. An Aspis mole in the American CIA had furnished the information that the CIA had once tried unsuccessfully to recruit Bradford.

But none of that worried Criscolle, for he believed that he was, one on one, as good a killer—an eliminator as the count would put it—as anyone who ever lived. Given the edge he always enjoyed because of the information-gathering power of Aspis, Nick was impossible to defeat. He did not handle all Aspis eliminations personally, only the most difficult and challenging ones.

And as Nick had learned in New York and Vermont, Bradford was certainly a challenge. The assassin was philosophical about his earlier losses, chalking them up to bad luck. As Nick had assured Count Vignola, Bradford's demise was inevitable—it was only a question of when it would come.

Below Criscolle saw skiers skimming over the slopes west and south of the villa like water bugs skating downhill on blinding white water. But there was no sign of Bradford, his New York cop, or his female companion, whoever she was.

The plane banked westward toward St. Moritz just as Nick's binoculars caught a glimpse of something partially concealed by trees far down the mountainside from Amalfi. He had his pilot come around for a second look, and he confirmed the presence of a blue and white snow rescue vehicle parked among the trees. It took little mental effort to connect the SRV with Burke, Bradford, and company, but his search of the forested east slope was fruitless. There was no sign of them.

Criscolle began to formulate a plan, the heart of which was the capture of the SRV and the incapacitation of any snowmobiles he and his men might find parked below the villa, where they would surely be found. After which . . . Criscolle smiled. There was time enough to contemplate the rest.

Tom was in the shower, Jane said. When he came to the phone and learned where Bradford was phoning from, he screeched at his partner. "Christ! Are you determined to get yourself killed, Brad? I don't want to lose my partner and another good friend."

"I hope you won't have to. Look, I don't have time to play word games with you. Tell me anything you've figured out about how to access the Aspis computer. Right now I'm sitting at Count Vignola's private keyboard console which has a modem attached."

"We need to interconnect Max," Sumereau said after a moment's silence. "Max is the best hacker—he's never failed us before."

"OK. Tell us what to do."

"For starters, turn on the computer and disconnect the telephone. Then, plug the phone cable into the computer modem. If we're successful, I'll be communicating with you through the computer in about five minutes."

Exactly three minutes later, black letters on the gray screen announced:

TOM AND MAX HERE. WE'RE IN. NEED MORE TIME FOR MAX.

The computer console flashed line after line of unintelligible computer code at lightning speed for the next few minutes.

Thousands of miles away, Tom Sumereau was staring at the same code on his computer screen. Max was very busy.

Suddenly, the desk on which the computer terminal sat raised three inches and swiveled away to the right, almost knocking Burke off his feet. Below the spot where the desk had been was a metal plate and it now sprang up and outward to reveal a large file box two feet square. Inside it were several manila folders bulging with paper.

The dizzying lines of computer code had stopped, and Brad typed a message to Tom that Max had succeeded.

Carlo Cervi never had a chance against Criscolle's cunning. Nick's men approached the SRV on snowmobiles out of the trees ahead and Cervi, who had been sitting safely in the driver's seat of the big machine, made a mistake. A fatal one. He grabbed a machine pistol, opened his door and stepped outside to cover the pair—without checking his rear. It was Cervi's final mistake. Before he could even ask the men who they were, he felt the impact of Nick Criscolle's knife, hurled at him from less than ten feet away.

The Italian crumpled to the ground even as he ordered his finger to pull the pistol's trigger. His order was disobeyed by a body robbed of its ability to act or react by the razor-sharp knife. He died instantaneously.

Leaving one of his two men to guard the SRV and monitor its radio, Criscolle and the other man, an expert mechanic, boarded snowmobiles and moved up the mountainside following the same trail taken by Bradford's party. They reached the three parked snowmobiles in less than ten minutes. Criscolle's mechanic disabled two of them and was moving toward the last when Criscolle shook his head.

"There's a girl with them, Rudi," he said. "I want her alive. They'll let her take the one working machine. As soon as she's gone, we'll kill the others, and Werner can take her when she reaches the SRV."

With that Criscolle radioed the guards on duty at the villa, using their private frequency known only to Aspis's director and his chief assassin. In less than a minute the guards—there were two on the premises at the time—took up positions on each side of the villa. Both carried machine pistols and one of them also had a battery-operated megaphone.

Inside the villa, Brad, Suzanne, and Burke were going through the papers they'd found, but they quickly discovered that all of the documents were written in Latin. Only Suzanne had any knowledge of the language, and it would take her far too much time to try to translate the papers into English.

"We haven't the time to spend with them now," Brad told her and Burke. He handed Suzanne a small document camera and produced a second camera for his own use, saying, "We'll take pictures of them and translate them later."

"You two are having all the fun," complained Burke as Brad and Suzanne worked on the papers.

"Don't worry," Brad replied, "the game's not over yet."

That fact was confirmed a few moments later as an amplified voice from outside chilled them all. "All right in there, come out with your hands up. We know you're there," the voice boomed in English.

SIXTEEN

"Hurry up, Suzanne," Brad urged, working fast on his stack of papers with the other camera. "Go check it out, Burke."

Burke was already at the rear window of the count's suite. Seeing no sign of the owner of the voice, he raced out of the room to check the other side of the villa. He returned just as the voice sounded again, this time punctuated by the sound of a chattering machine gun.

"Wherever he is, he's out of sight of the house, Brad," Burke reported. "Are you almost done?"

Brad snapped a picture of the last document just as Suzanne did the same. He put the papers together in the same order they'd been in when he lifted them out of the compartment, then went back to the computer room to replace them. Then he sat at the keyboard and asked Tom to instruct Max to close the hidden compartment. Immediately the trap door closed again and the desk and console swiveled back into place. Brad reconnected the phone.

With their weapons drawn and cocked, the trio left the computer room and raced out of the count's suite, and Suzanne locked the door behind them. They started down the stairs just as the voice—and a burst of machine gun fire—sounded again, demanding that they surrender.

Suzanne stopped short on the stairs. "I have a couple of pairs of skis up in the room I use when I'm here. We might need them out there if they've got the villa surrounded."

"Get them," Brad said. He and Burke now took the stairs three at a time and checked outside through the downstairs windows.

"You don't have a chance," came the voice from outside.

"Come out now or die. You have one minute. Refuse and we'll slaughter you." Then the guard fired the machine gun again.

Brad couldn't locate the guard, though his voice sounded as if it was originating from the rear of the house.

Burke confirmed it. "I'm not sure why, but it looks like they're covering the rear rather than the front," he told Bradford. "There seems to be only two of them. At least that's all that are firing. They either don't believe we'll want to go down the mountainside . . ."

"Or that's just where they want us to go, Burke," Brad said. "Straight into a trap. See if you can reach Cervi on the radio."

Burke took the pocket-sized walkie-talkie from his jacket and thumbed open the mike. He spoke urgently into it, opened the receiver awaiting a response, but got none. He repeated his call twice, but there was no answer. "Nothing!" he muttered. "Son-of-a . . ."

"Bitch!" Bradford finished for him. "Cervi said he could get a police chopper here pretty quickly if we needed it. I wonder if he tried before they got him."

"I hope to heaven that he did, Brad," Burke said.

Brad said nothing, but Suzanne now appeared with two pairs of cross-country skis. "It's a good thing you've got them," he told her. "It looks like whoever set Amalfi's guards on us must have taken Cervi, too." He looked at Burke. "What do you think about trying to phone the local constable, Burke?" he asked.

"Try it, but I'll be surprised if the phone's still working," Burke replied.

It wasn't.

"That means they're downslope and probably have the snowmobiles guarded as well as the SRV," Burke said. "They won't expect us—you and Suzanne anyway—to have an alternative to the machines. If I can get their attention, maybe you can get past them."

"Which leaves you in the soup, Burke," Bradford said. "You wouldn't have a chance with your pistol against their machine guns."

"I might have a better chance than you would. If I'm right, that's your friend Nick Criscolle down there. And he wants you, not me. He'll kill me in an instant if he can, of course, but if he thinks you're getting away, he might drop me like a hot potato. Even if he leaves someone to finish me off, I may be able to hold out until you get help." He didn't add "if you get help," though he might have.

Brad nodded. "You've got a point," he said, "though I can't imagine how the hell Criscolle got onto us being here."

"Your time is up!" the voice outside boomed. "Throw down your weapons, and we won't hurt you, Mr. Bradford. You, too, Lieutenant Burke."

Brad scowled. "Sounds like our man Criscolle. It has to be him. That's his way of letting me know he's accepting my challenge. All right, Suzanne, let's move out. If we can reach the SRV safely, we'll try to radio for help."

"If you make it, Brad," Burke said, "try to reach either the Italian or the Swiss police. Mention Cervi's name or Captain Parente's."

"We can get down a different way, Brad," Suzanne said. "There's an opening in the trees barely wide enough to ski through on the side away from the trail we took coming up. It's scary and longer, but we won't be ambushed going down."

"I'll try for the snowmobiles, Brad," Burke said. "Once they see me, they'll figure we're all coming down, so they aren't likely to shoot me until they're sure you're with me. It might give me just the edge I need."

Bradford stopped the New York cop with a hand on his arm. "Be careful, Kevin," he said seriously. "I'd miss you."

"I'll be as careful as a quarterback sitting on a fourteen-point lead, Brad," Burke said, grinning. Then he was out on the porch and gone, running low on the hard-packed snow as he covered the short distance between the villa and the rocky edge of the mountain like the sprinter he'd once been in high school. As he reached the edge, the roar of a machine gun was audible and Burke dived over the edge, half-sliding, half-climbing down the outcropping. He prayed Criscolle and his crew would now hold their fire until they saw the whites of Brad's and Suzanne's eyes.

Burke was as easy a target as a rubber duck in a tub as he jumped the final six feet to the snowy base of the outcropping and grabbed for a nearby cedar tree to stop his fall. He waited for a bullet to tear into his chest, but none came.

From his vantage point in a stand of pine trees some twenty-five yards below the three snowmobiles, Criscolle saw Burke clamber down the side of the mountain and race for the machines without waiting for his companions. Through his binoculars he saw that the man was neither Bradford nor the girl who was with them. He swore, wondering why the three of them had not stayed together.

He raised a gloved hand to signal Rudi across the way to hold his fire. There was, he knew, plenty of time to kill the New York cop. If he had any kind of character, he wouldn't take the only working snowmobile and leave the others stranded.

Still Criscolle would not let the cop get away if he chose to strand the others, so he took a grenade from the bag he carried on his shoulder and was ready to pull the pin and hurl it if Burke took the working machine down the mountain.

He watched as Burke boarded one of the disabled snowmobiles and tried to start it. Finding it dead, the cop went to the second machine as Criscolle fumed over the absence of Bradford and the unknown woman. Where the hell were they, he asked himself. Had they tried the sheer, densely-forested other side of the villa? That was insane.

Unless they somehow knew a trail down. Unless they knew of an opening among the trees that led away from the rocky cliffs. Was there an opening? Criscolle wasn't sure. He didn't think so, but . . .

A thought now clawed its way into his head as he watched Burke try unsuccessfully to start the second machine. Suzanne Steelman! She was always exploring the mountainside alone on skis when they were here for a weekend. He had several times watched her set out down the mountain carrying cross-country skis and a walkie-talkie in case she got into trouble. She would know if there was a trail. And only the other day she had seemed awfully interested in Amalfi's security when Vignola was absent!

Could the woman with Bradford be Steelman? Had he somehow gotten to her? Now Criscolle smiled, remembering the tall, curvaceous lines of Suzanne's body. She was older than his usual fare, but her haughty attitude would make up for it. Nick had always found her stimulating and tempting, in spite of the count's order to stay away from her.

He had no time to dwell on the thought. If Suzanne had indeed joined forces with Bradford, then the two of them might already be halfway down the mountain to the SRV.

Suddenly he realized that Burke had jumped on the only operative snowmobile and keyed it to life. There was only one way to stop him quickly and Criscolle was prepared to do it. He pulled the pin on his grenade and hurled it, then signaled Rudi to attack.

But Burke already had the snowmobile in motion and was hurtling downward—away from the trail where Criscolle waited and into the trees on the other side. The grenade exploded harmlessly in Burke's wake.

"After him!" Criscolle screamed at Rudi.

Bradford followed Suzanne through the thick forest, down the steep slope. She was an excellent skier and followed the trail she had previously explored without difficulty. Twice in the first several hundred yards they had to stop, take off their skis, and clamber down steep rock formations.

They were gradually moving back toward the main trail when the muffled sound of an explosion reached them. It took only a second for Brad to recognize it as the sound of a grenade.

He focused his attention back onto the hazardous trip down the mountain and what they would do when they reached the SRV, which was obviously in Criscolle's hands now. Could he and Suzanne retake the vehicle? They might have a chance if Criscolle had left it unguarded or with only a single guard. The last was not a bad possibility, Brad thought, for he was now certain that Criscolle was a lone wolf sort. In Vermont he had only a single helper along. In New York he had been alone in killing Jack Sands.

Brad grit his teeth. He hadn't thought about his "father" in days, but Jack was a long way from forgotten!

Criscolle would want to kill Bradford personally, Brad was sure of that. And that explained why the guards at Amalfi had been content to drive them down the mountain. There was a second reason, too, since no doubt Count Vignola would not take kindly to having the valuable antiques and furnishings he kept in the villa destroyed in a firefight.

Another explosion sounded far above them and Bradford's hopes for Burke's safety were both raised and lowered. A second grenade suggested that Burke had managed to avoid the effects of the first but was under attack again. Brad smiled grimly when he heard the sounds of machine gun fire answered by single shots. Burke's single shots, no doubt.

If Suzanne was aware of the uproar from the mountainside above them, she gave no indication of it. She was devoting her full attention to steering them through the trees that surrounded them like stately guards.

Only a few minutes had passed since they left Amalfi, though it seemed much longer. They were nearing the main path and skiing more than ski-skating, as they had been forced to do on many of the upper stretches. Suzanne suddenly snowplowed to a halt, her hand upraised to warn Brad to do the same. He did, then moved up beside her to follow the direction of her gaze.

The SRV was barely a hundred yards ahead, half-hidden by trees. They were in luck, for they could see only one guard.

Brad outlined an idea he had been considering. It would put Suzanne in jeopardy, but she—and he—were already up to their necks in trouble. If she could get the attention of the guard and keep it for a half minute or so, they had a chance. At least they had a chance if Burke could continue to keep Criscolle occupied farther up the mountain, where the sound of gunfire was continuing.

Burke had swerved the snowmobile away from the trail as much by instinct as for any other reason. Criscolle had to be there. It would make no sense for him to lie in wait anywhere else. He knew it as well as he knew he was a good Irish Catholic.

As the snowmobile plowed through its quick turn he thought he detected sudden movement across the way and made a second turn to avoid what he figured would be a quick burst of machine gun fire. Instead the surprising explosion of a grenade acted on the snowmobile like wind on a sail—propelling him even faster on his path.

A moment later Burke's machine sideswiped a stout oak tree and he was knocked off. Then the world turned upside down as he began tumbling over and over in the snow. He didn't see the snowmobile continue its driverless way down the slope. Just as he flip-flopped to a halt, Burke heard a second explosion. He raised his eyes and looked down the mountain to see the snowmobile blown up in a shower of snow and fire.

Suddenly realizing he was out in the open and vulnerable, Burke scrambled on all fours toward a large boulder not more than a dozen yards away. He hurled himself behind it just as Criscolle and his man spotted him and opened fire with automatic weapons.

When the firing ceased for a moment, Burke crawled to the far side of the boulder and peered across the way, where his two attackers were conferring behind a stand of trees. Burke thought that Criscolle had witnessed by now that Bradford was not with him and that he would be backtracking down the mountain after Brad, so he took dead aim with his nine millimeter pistol and began firing. In return he got a new fusillade of bullets from the machine guns of Criscolle and his man.

No more than a minute later Burke heard a new, ominous sound—the flap of helicopter blades whipping through the frosty mountain air not far off. The firing had stopped now and again he stuck out his head for a cautious look. He saw the chopper hovering over his attackers' position.

It was time, Burke thought, to look for a safer position. Throwing caution to the wind, he fled the boulder and bolted away toward a thick patch of tall evergreens west of his position. He reached the safety of the trees, but not before being grazed by a machine pistol slug. It barely broke the skin beneath his sweater and ski parka, though, and after stanching the flow of blood with his handkerchief he ignored it. Taking up a sitting position next to a cluster of four trees he took his five spare clips of ammunition out of his jacket and lined them up in a neat row beside him. If Criscolle and his friend wanted a fight, they would sure as hell get one!

Blitz all you want, you dirty fucks, he thought. I'll be ready for you.

Suzanne and Bradford heard, then saw, the Aspis chopper that had brought Criscolle and his assistants to Livigno. That, Brad thought unhappily, might well be the hawk that would swoop down and devour all three of them. They had to work fast. If they could take the SRV, they could radio for help. "Go," he said to Suzanne, and he watched her head for a position ahead of the SRV.

Then he edged his way to a spot west of the vehicle, where he knelt in the snow and studied the SRV through his glasses. The single guard was sitting in the driver's seat, a pair of field glasses raised to his eyes as he scanned the area ahead of the vehicle. An Uzi's ugly barrel protruded out of the opened window.

Brad dove for cover as the guard turned his glasses toward the rear of the vehicle. He held his breath as the guard kept the glasses steady for a moment, then relaxed when the guard straightened and again studied the mountainside ahead of the SRV.

Brad regained his feet and watched as, far up the slope, Suzanne skied into view of the SRV. The guard saw her at the same moment Brad did. Holding the Uzi, he opened his door to cover her as she approached the machine.

Edging his way closer to get a clear shot at the guard, Brad prayed he could bring him down with a single bullet so he would not have the chance to fire at Suzanne. He had not fired a pistol in several months and even then his marksmanship had been lacking. He needed every advantage he could get right now.

Suzanne had snow-plowed to a halt to the right of the vehicle, flashed the guard a smile and a salute. Then she stepped out of her ski bindings and began talking to him, pointing animatedly toward the ski slopes to the west and shaking her head—as if unhappy with herself for getting lost.

As Brad drew within thirty yards of the SRV going from tree to tree, the guard took the bait and stepped out onto the running board, his Uzi in his hand.

Closer, Brad told himself, and darted forward to the shelter of a cedar tree twenty yards from the vehicle. It was now or never, he knew, for there were no closer trees to shelter him. He raised his pistol, stepped out from behind the tree, and sucked in a deep breath, steadying the gun with his left hand beneath it. Just as he was squeezing the trigger he caught a glimpse of a snowmobile far above them, hurtling down at a good speed.

The guard noticed the machine as well and was turning toward it when Brad's shot took him in the stomach.

Suzanne grabbed his weapon by its barrel, wrenching it loose as he fell off the running board and into the snow. Racing for the SRV, Brad stumbled over Cervi's dead body buried in new snow. He pitied Cervi but could do nothing for him.

"Criscolle," Suzanne declared as they got in the SRV and Brad started it. She pointed up the mountain.

"It sure as hell isn't Kevin Burke. Let's get out of here!"

In the snowmobile, Criscolle screamed into his radio for help from the chopper. "Leave Rudi to finish off Burke," he roared. "Get your god-damn ass down here fast. Bradford's getting away in the SRV!" He swore as he saw the vehicle turn to its left and come roaring out of the trees and head straight down the mountainside.

Criscolle's snowmobile could travel faster than the lumbering SRV, but the Aspis killer had to fall back when Suzanne Steelman began firing at him with the Uzi she had taken from the guard. He was not surprised to recognize Suzanne as the tall, feminine figure wielding the weapon.

"Get on the radio," Brad instructed Suzanne after she had driven off Criscolle. "See if you can raise Cervi's chopper."

It took her a few seconds to locate the switch to activate the SRV's powerful radio, but she finally found it and began calling for help in Italian in the name of Lieutenant Cervi, giving their position and asking for an armed helicopter. She was in the middle of repeating their position when she and Bradford heard a foreboding flapping noise above them.

"Hold onto your hat," Brad yelled, "we've got company!" He wrenched the steering wheel to the left, just as the front of the SRV was sprayed with machine gun fire from the Aspis helicopter that was hovering at treetop level above them.

Suzanne, the radio headphone held to one ear, held open the transmit switch to let Cervi's chopper hear what they were up against—if their possible rescuers were on their wavelength at all. She was crouched on the floor, fighting to keep her balance during Bradford's evasive actions.

"We have your message, SRV," came a voice in Italian when Bradford moved between several tall trees and the Aspis chopper swooped away. "Our chopper is on its way to assist you. Where is Lieutenant Cervi and who are you?"

Suzanne explained as quickly as she could, but had to break off the transmission as Brad whipped the vehicle into another tight turn to avoid a new attack from Criscolle's chopper, which now began to dog the SRV like a cowboy on the back of a bucking bronco.

Criscolle's chopper pilot began throwing grenades at them. One narrowly missed and sent the SRV careening, but Brad managed to maneuver the vehicle away and into a denser cover of trees. Criscolle and his pilot peppered the trees with grenades.

"We're going to have to get out of here, Suzanne," Brad yelled. "This thing's no tank. They'll blow us off the mountain with one direct hit. There's an open stretch up ahead and a few scrub pines shielding a rocky plateau just before it. When we reach it, jump. As soon as you're out, I'll jump, too. I'm going to tie the wheel and pull the hand throttle all the way out."

One of Criscolle's grenades exploded with a loud boom near the rear portion of the SRV and the vehicle suddenly showed daylight above it. Bradford got it moving and steered it out of the trees, his hand on the door handle as the vehicle continued down the flattening mountainside with the helicopter in hot pursuit.

"Now!" Brad ordered as the SRV reached the plateau.

"Save yourself," she yelled, and then she pulled the door handle and jumped out, hanging onto the Uzi as she went.

Bradford yanked on his door handle and was about to jump when the helicopter caught the SRV. Criscolle hurled two grenades. They caught the vehicle dead center and the SRV was torn apart in a fiery explosion, its remains rolling end over end like a football as it continued down the mountain. A second blast turned it into a funeral pyre as its fuel tank exploded.

In the Aspis chopper Criscolle was exultant, but not yet satisfied that Bradford and Suzanne were dead. Before the SRV was demolished by the grenades, he thought he had seen someone jump out. He had to determine who.

A low-level sweep around the area covered by the SRV in its death throes revealed no bodies, alive or dead, and Criscolle ordered his pilot to return to the burning vehicle. But, as he was leaving, he saw what looked like a body, sheltered by some pine trees on a rocky plateau.

"Down," he yelled, pointing to the plateau. The pilot complied, putting the machine down twenty yards from the trees shielding the plateau.

Criscolle, a machine gun in his hand, jumped out of the chopper and trudged through the snow toward the crumpled figure of Suzanne Steelman. The woman had struck her head in her escape from the SRV and had lost consciousness. Curled up in a ball on her stomach, the Uzi beneath her, she awoke just as Criscolle reached her, her eyes seeing nothing but the snow beneath her.

"Well, bitch!" Criscolle declared smiling. "Did you and your boyfriend Bradford have a good time shacking up at Amalfi? Or were you there for some other reason?"

Dropping his weapon, he reached down and seized her to pull her to her feet. His smile faded when he saw the weapon poised in her hand.

Although out-gunned and out-manned as well as out-machined, Kevin Burke gave no ground in his fight for his life. He peppered the helicopter with accurate pistol fire each time the pilot tried to fire at him from atop the trees in which he was sheltered. His shots did the chopper no particular damage, but it did keep the man in the machine from finishing him.

When suddenly the helicopter roared away and headed down the mountain and left Burke alone with but a single attacker to worry about, he would have been elated except for the sobering thought that the chopper would probably return after it had helped Criscolle finish off Brad and Suzanne. He had to draw his lone attacker out into the open. But how?

Curiosity, he knew, could be a potent weapon. His attacker knew where he was and would be keeping a sharp eye over here, though he would be unlikely to risk an all-out attack unaided. If Burke could pique his curiosity . . .

He moved around a bit, just to confirm to the attacker that he was still alive. Then he let his pistol gleam in the afternoon sun for several seconds before holding it up as if he were about to shoot himself in the head.

The shot that sounded when he pulled the trigger was deafening, the gun was so close to his head. Now he pretended to fall away from his position, the top of his green and white wool cap just visible to his attacker across the way.

Burke was tense while waiting, his eyes fastened on his attacker's last position, his gun now carefully shielded from the sun.

A minute went by. Another. Off in the distance he heard machine gun fire. Had Brad and Suzanne escaped? Or were they being slaughtered by Criscolle? Muffled explosions could be heard and Burke fought off the fear that they might well signal the end of this intense battle.

A third minute passed. His "suicide" ruse hadn't worked. Burke sighed. Well, it had been worth a try, he thought.

A cop he had once known had died when he'd fallen for a similar ruse. Had Criscolle's gunman read about it somewhere? He was about to give up the ghost when he heard the sound of automatic weapon fire and slugs whistled through the air over his head.

Suzanne's head was aching and still groggy so she was hardly aware of the reason Nick Criscolle had backed away—the machine pistol in her right hand.

Bradford? Amalfi? What was he talking about? Then she regained her senses just as Nick saw her confusion and again reached for her. "No!" she hissed. "You bastard."

"That's me," he said carefully. "Back in Brooklyn they used to make it a 'Wop' bastard, or a 'Guinea' bastard. But it doesn't matter because . . ." He grabbed for her gun, but she now leveled it at his midsection, her finger on the trigger.

"Not this time, Nick," she said. "It's time for you to die, you lousy . . ."

But she had waited too long. Her words were cut off in the middle of the sentence by the knife that Nick somehow produced from his jacket and rammed straight into her chest in one lightning motion.

Staggering backward against the tree, she looked down at the knife buried in her chest, her finger still on the trigger of the Uzi. Criscolle was grinning—the infuriating grin she had learned to hate.

Suzanne's life was ebbing. She could feel it, and Criscolle knew it. But she pulled the trigger of the pistol a split second after she regained her balance. She was weak, however, and the quick burst of lead that spat from the Uzi's snout made it jerk upward. Then the weapon fell harmlessly to the snowy turf.

Suzanne's eyes closed briefly and her senses were dulled so she didn't hear Criscolle's outcry. Then she smelled the expensive cologne he always wore and became aware that he was there before her again. She opened her eyes, just in time to receive a vicious slap from him.

When she saw him she had the mad desire to laugh, for the ruggedly handsome face he was so proud of was handsome no more. Her shots had raked his face with bloody gouges, the bullets scoring it from chin to brow. As she watched, they filled with thick purple blood. A wave of regret swept over the young woman, filling her with a great ache. For though her bullets had hurt him and scarred him, they had not killed him. He would survive.

Suzanne again closed her eyes and thought about Brad. Brad! He had been so wonderful last night. So sure, so tender, so loving. Never in her life had she enjoyed a man more. And now? What now? Was he dead? She hoped not—hoped that Brad would survive and take the photographed papers they had found in Vignola's secret compartment back to Rome for translation. The Piedmont Papers!

That was Suzanne's final thought, for Nick Criscolle began to beat her with practiced punches as she lay dying in her blood before him. "Whore, slut, bitch! Die! Die!" he screeched as he battered her limp body with both his hands and feet, unleashing his wrath like a beast in the wild.

As a strange sort of peace came into her waning consciousness, Suzanne felt the pain leave her body, replaced by sorrow for the crazed monster beating on her dead corpse.

Burke said a Hail Mary as the slugs fired by his assailant sailed just above his cap. He tensed, his grazed side aching, his nerves taunt, as he waited for the other man to show himself. And he would if he had bought Burke's apparent suicide. Were the slugs he fired at Burke meant to make sure he was dead? Or were they designed to tell Burke that the other side hadn't bought his dumb stunt?

He would never find out, for his attacker did not show himself until the Aspis helicopter settled to the snow behind his attacker's position, then lifted back off with the assailant on board.

Burke crossed himself again and murmured a few more Hail Marys as he scrambled unsteadily to his feet and wondered why Criscolle and his killers hadn't bothered to finish him off.

He made his way carefully back to the trail down the mountain and prepared himself for a long trek—wishing he was almost anywhere but here.

Hope returned when he saw that Criscolle had left a black snowmobile. Finding it operative, he drove it down the trail, his eyes watching for signs of Bradford and Suzanne. It was only a few minutes later that he learned why Criscolle's chopper had departed so prematurely—an Italian police helicopter was hopping around the mountainside like a honeybee.

The Italian cops were grim when the chopper swooped down on Burke, having already found the bodies of Carlo Cervi and Suzanne Steelman. They were ready to manacle him if he couldn't properly identify himself.

"Is there anyone unaccounted for?" the officer in the chopper asked Burke after they'd shown him the bodies of Cervi and Suzanne.

Burke swallowed hard at the sight of Suzanne's brutalized body. A maniac had gone to work on her. "One more," he managed to say at last.

A short time later they found Bradford, his body covered with snow, bruised and unconscious, but alive.

SEVENTEEN

"Suzanne . . . dead?" Elliot Bradford stared vacantly at Kevin Burke, a huge, heavy feeling in his heart over what Burke had just told him.

Bradford lay in a hospital bed in St. Moritz, his body a mass of contusions, a bandage over the lacerations on the back of his head. He had suffered a concussion when Criscolle's grenades had destroyed the SRV, his body coming to rest in a deep snowdrift. The last had saved him from more serious injury, but the concussion had been bad enough to keep him unconscious for more than thirty-six hours. When he'd finally come to, a sober-faced Kevin Burke, himself sporting a bandage beneath his turtleneck shirt, was at his bedside.

"It was Criscolle. He must have gone berserk. But we think she might've wounded him because there was a trail of blood leading away from her body."

Brad drew no comfort from this news. Suzanne dead? He wanted to scream out a denial. She couldn't be. He could still see her face. It was burned into his very soul. Alongside Nan, Jack and the boys.

"It won't help much, I suppose, Brad," Burke said, "but for what it's worth, the doctor says she died quickly. She didn't suffer."

"And he got away," Bradford murmured, acknowledging Burke's attempt to ease his pain.

Burke nodded. "I unloaded your document cameras," he said, trying to change the subject. "After what happened back there, I don't trust anybody. Not even Captain Parente, although I'm positive he didn't knowingly tip off anyone. But someone he talked to did us in. I'm positive."

"I'll get the film developed when we get back to Rome. Murray Jolles, my man there, can get it done. Then I'll have to arrange for translations. Murray's a linguist, but I doubt he knows Latin. Have you talked to my doctor?"

Burke nodded his head affirmatively. "He says you're pretty beat up. Told me you might have brain damage."

"The only damage thus far is Suzanne's death, Kevin! I'm so angry, I could . . ." He trailed off, knowing his wrath would do him no good.

They were interrupted by a white-clad nurse. "How are you feeling?" she asked Brad in English.

"I'm alive," he observed. "Will you ask the doctor to visit me? I've got to talk to him about getting out of here."

"That's a little premature," the nurse said. "You were in pretty bad shape when you arrived. The doctor was here when you came out of your coma. Do you remember that?"

Brad had to admit that he didn't.

"Well, don't worry about it too much. It's normal under the circumstances. Do you feel up to seeing visitors? You have two."

Brad and Burke exchanged surprised looks. "Who?" Brad asked.

"A Mr. Sumereau and a Miss Sands."

Brad looked questioningly at Burke, who appeared uncomfortable and said, "I was afraid you might not come to so I thought I'd better notify somebody. Your partner and Holly seemed the nearest thing you have to family."

Brad frowned. "Tom was all right," he said. "It's just that I don't want anything more to happen to Holly. She would have been far better off to stay in New York."

Burke now grinned. "When she found out you'd been hurt there was no holding her back. Anyway, Criscolle isn't likely to go after her again."

Moments later Holly stepped into the hospital room and sat on the bed next to Brad when she realized that he was alive and alert. "Oh, Brad," she declared, "I was so worried about you. Lieutenant Burke said you were in a coma."

"I was, Kitten, but I'm not now. I'll be all right."

"I'm glad to see you, too, partner," Tom Sumereau said cynically as he stood next to the bed.

"I'd be more pleased to see you, Tom, if you hadn't brought Holly. This isn't a picnic we're having, you know."

"I had to come, Brad," Holly said. "I'd have come alone. It's the least I can do for my 'brother.'" She made a face.

Tom now cleared his throat and rolled his eyes at Brad. He had some news that was confidential and Brad read his partner's hesitation correctly. "You have something for me, Tom? Is it anything Holly and Burke can't hear?"

Sumereau thought for a moment, then reached a negative decision. "I doubt if it'll make any real difference, Brad. It's about our mole. I think it's come to the surface."

Brad groaned as he searched his partner's face trying to read his thoughts.

"I'd never have believed it, but . . . well, it was Linda. I found the missing papers concealed in her desk. She had a file labeled personal and that's where they were—together with a First National City Bank passbook savings account that shows a very hefty balance: one hundred thousand dollars, all deposited since 1992. We pay her pretty good, but not that good. And all that money was deposited into the bank in four equal installments."

"How'd you find out? Did the information we planted with her on our new investigation into Aspis's uranium connections cause some scurrying around in Alaska?"

Sumereau shook his head. "None of the stuff we planted panned out," he said. "I found out about Linda by accident. I had to go through her desk yesterday afternoon after I identified her body in the city morgue. She's dead, Brad. Killed by a hit-and-run taxi driver while crossing Fifth Avenue on her way to work. I'm sorry."

Brad reeled under this latest piece of news. Linda—dead? Linda—their spy? He could hardly believe it.

"I know what you're thinking, Brad, and I don't blame you. If it had turned out to be Olga," Tom said, "I'd feel the same way about it."

Burke, who'd been paying close attention to the conversation, now broke in. "That only proves that your Linda may have been selected as a fall guy—excuse me—woman, a long time ago. Aspis could simply have opened the account in her name at the same time it put the real spy on its payroll, so that it could deliver to you an apparent traitor when it needed to."

"You're right, Lieutenant," Sumereau said slowly, his expression sad, "but it's also possible that Linda was the spy."

"I can arrange to have her telephone bills checked to see if she made any calls to Aspis or any of their people," Burke said. "The trouble is, the checking could only prove that she looks guilty. It won't clear her, for I've no doubt Aspis could have paid someone at the phone company to slip in a couple of long-distance calls to Aspis offices."

Enraged, Holly now interrupted. "Criscolle is an animal!" she shouted. "Isn't there anyone who can do something about him? Everyone knows he killed my father, and I can testify to what he did to me. And now he's hurt you, Brad. Can't he be arrested?" She directed the last question to the New York City police officer.

"I wish we could arrest him, Holly," Burke answered for Brad. "But it isn't as easy as that. We don't have the kind of proof that would convict him in a court of law. We know he tried to kill us and succeeded in killing Suzanne Steelman. But . . ."

Holly's eyes grew immense at Burke's reference to Suzanne. "Suzanne?" she repeated. "She was with you? Criscolle killed her?" Holly looked confused as she glanced from Burke to Brad and back, searching for a disclaimer. Then she dissolved into frightened tears and, overwhelmed, sat miserably alone amid the three men.

The next day, the competent Indian doctor released Brad from the hospital without a long argument. But he warned Brad that he should rest before undertaking any more strenuous activity. "Your body has been through a great deal, Mr. Bradford," Doctor Desai declared. "And but for good luck, you might be dead now. As it is, you suffered a severe concussion and may still have dizzy spells."

"If so, I'll put up with them," Brad replied, "but back in Rome. Not here."

After arranging to have Suzanne's body taken for burial in the same cemetery where her grandfather, Simon Zeisman, was buried, Brad flew to Rome Sunday night with Burke and a still-dazed Holly. There was no time, even, to arrange a proper funeral for Suzanne; Brad would somehow say his spiritual good-byes later.

Sumereau jetted off to London to confer with Tony Phipps, who was conducting a painstaking and intense examination of Aspis's business dealings around the world. Phipps had been ordered not to pass his information along by conventional methods due to the possibility that there was still a spy in FINVEST's midst. Tom would return to Rome with Phipps's report next Tuesday or Wednesday.

Brad begged Holly to go home to her mother in New York, but she steadfastly refused. "I need to be here with you, Brad," she told him. "You may not need me, but I need you. You're the nearest thing I have to a father now and I'm not going to lose you like I did Daddy." In the end, Brad agreed to let her stay with him in the FINVEST apartment he had shared with Suzanne only five nights earlier, although Holly again occupied separate quarters.

Burke went directly to see Captain Parente and learned that he had already tried to bring Nick Criscolle in for questioning—without success. Parente had people watching both Criscolle's apartment and Aspis headquarters.

Murray Jolles delivered the prints of the Piedmont Papers Bradford and Suzanne had photographed at Amalfi. FINVEST's super-efficient Rome manager had arranged to have the film developed and the prints ready within hours of Brad's arrival in Rome.

While Bradford and his party were fighting for their lives on the mountainside at Amalfi Thursday afternoon, Frank Bochlaine was listening with trepidation to the periodic announcements over Vatican Radio of the Pope's unchanging critical condition. With each passing hour his resolve to kill the Pope's successor, if it were Massara, grew.

But how? He had no idea. If he could, he would gladly have wrung the cardinal's neck. Yet he knew no one except Massara's most trusted aides and the College of Cardinals would be allowed close to him once he was elected Pope.

No, Bochlaine decided, he would have to use an assassin's weapon—a firearm. Which one he could not know until he had paid a visit to Vatican City to refresh his memories of St. Peter's Square and the Basilica.

As Suzanne Steelman was dying and Kevin Burke's siege was lifting, Bochlaine, back in his Jesuit robes, strolled in sunny St. Peter's Square with Mama Teresa for more than an hour. He was searching for a place from which he could get a clear shot at Massara should he be named Pope.

Silent and unquestioning as always, Teresa had driven him to Vatican City. Her never-expressed love for the man who had been her benefactor for so long was only a tiny pinpoint of light in her eyes each time she looked at him, but it was there. She would do anything for Bochlaine. Anything. She didn't understanding why he was hiding, or who or what he was hiding from. And she did not ask him why he wished to come to the piazza today. She only knew that she must help him in any way she could, for without him her life would have been a void, even worse than it had been when her Giulio had been taken from her.

Bochlaine strolled around the square beside Teresa, hardly aware of her because of the vision in his mind. He was both remembering and imagining—happy in the memory of the last papal installation, yet experiencing only horror in imagining the next to come.

The square, wider than an American football field at its mouth beneath the steps of the huge Basilica, curved gracefully out into a huge open-ended ellipse. It was enclosed by two arms of a quadruple colonnade and measured over 200 yards at its widest point.

Many thousands of people could and did crowd into the piazza for papal installations. Even hundreds of thousands, Bochlaine thought, recalling what the newspapers had reported years ago about the ceremonies for Pope Paul VI and the two John Pauls.

The fatal question lingered in his thoughts. Could he, a Jesuit, who regarded God's laws and commandments as seriously as the most zealous of priests, carry out the deed he had come here to plan? Had he the right, or the duty, as he had been telling himself ever since Cardinal Ambrosiani informed him of the certainty of Massara's election, to kill that new Pope? An involuntary shudder raced over Bochlaine's huge frame and Mama Teresa looked at him through suddenly worried eyes.

"Are you all right, Franco?" she asked.

They had stopped their walking and stood at the precise point, a hundred feet or so in front of the huge four-hundred foot high dome, where the platform would be erected on which the new Pope would be installed. Bochlaine nodded when Mama Teresa broke into his thoughts to repeat her question.

Bochlaine eyed the tall Egyptian obelisk that rose like a gunsight in the middle of the elliptical part of the Piazza, flanked by twin fountains.

A gunsight? Bochlaine bit his lip, appalled by the murderous state of his thoughts. The idea of looking through the telescopic sight of a rifle at a fellow human being, then ending a life with a quick pull on a trigger, was sickening.

How, he wondered, did one human being justify destroying another? Yet a Pope with the dark depths of Cardinal Massara—one who was a mere pawn for the immoral Inner Circle, if Cardinal Ambrosiani's beliefs were correct, one who had founded and remained closely tied to Aspis—was simply intolerable.

Perhaps, he thought, the Circle would fail to elect Massara Pope. Perhaps the Circle's brothers had not yet achieved the power to do it. Perhaps the others, the moderates of the College of Cardinals, would band together to name a second successive non-Roman to replace the wonderful pontiff who presently lay on his deathbed, one whose name was not Massara.

But even as the last thought surfaced, Bochlaine had no doubt that it was a forlorn hope and that Cardinal Ambrosiani's judgment was probably correct—that the Circle's power was at its zenith.

Bochlaine shook off these morose thoughts and forced his mind back to the task at hand—to find a place that would be accessible to him at the proper time and from which he could aim his gun on Cardinal Massara's evil head.

Evil. Yes, that was it. He had to think only of the evil mind Massara carried around with him; of the blood of the Roman Jews that despoiled Massara's hands; of the unholy and murderous activities of Aspis and the ambitions that were so dangerous to the whole world. Bochlaine's composure returned, and he again focused on his grim task.

Swiveling away from the gunsight obelisk, he scanned the famous dome of the Basilica and along the thirteen Bernini statues of the saints on the rim of the facade. Finally his eyes rested on the center balcony from which Popes had for hundreds of years addressed the faithful in the square with the benediction Urbi et Orbi.

A thought occurred to him now and he turned back to the piazza and stared at the huge statue of St. Peter off to the left. While the cardinals of the College of Cardinals were debating the identity of the next Pope, workers would erect a tall, spidery web of metal pipe behind the statue and top it with a wooden platform for the paparazzi—the infamous Italian photo corps who would train long-nosed cameras on the new Pope the instant he appears on the balcony. Long-nosed cameras that might hide a sniper's rifle.

Bochlaine stared at the statue and tried to picture the way it had been for the last papal installation. He was convinced that from the statue one would have an unobstructed view of the Pope. He gnashed his teeth in sudden passion—he'd uncovered a view from which he would have a clear shot at Massara, the father of evil!

Bochlaine now led the way as he and Teresa walked straight toward the massive bronze doors of the largest church in all Christendom. When they were even with the statue of St. Peter, Bochlaine turned abruptly, and began to pace the distance to the statue.

At the statue he turned and stared at the Loggia of Benedictions, the balcony below the tympanum of the church of St. Peter. It was about fifty yards to the balcony, he estimated, adding height to the distance he had just paced. From the stand with an accurate rifle, a good sharp-shooter could easily hit his target.

During the drive back to Mama Teresa's home, Bochlaine didn't even notice his growing hunger, immersed as he was in a new worry. Could he relearn a skill he had acquired in his childhood many years ago? He had not touched a rifle since he was sixteen years old.

His uncle, who had raised him after his father's death in the war and his mother's remarriage, had insisted that he learn how to hunt and Bochlaine had obeyed. But he had never been truly good with a rifle and had felt nothing but revulsion for the slaughter of innocent animals.

He would have to relearn the motions, he knew, just as he would have to use some contacts he had made while working for Aspis to acquire the right weapon and the camera to conceal it. Moreover, he would have to seek Cardinal Ambrosiani's help in acquiring press credentials, for they would be far more difficult to obtain since the recent increase in terrorist activities.

His biggest worry was the last, for he knew Cardinal Ambrosiani was not likely to be pleased with assisting in a murder, even one so justifiable as this one.

Sunday, Bochlaine secured his weapon—a short-barreled, stockless rifle with a super-accurate telescopic sight—from a terrorist group Aspis supplied with munitions. He then phoned Bradford's apartment.

Bochlaine's first words when Bradford answered were an expression of relief that he had finally reached the American. "I've been trying to get Suzanne as well and neither of you have been answering your telephone. Is everything okay with you? Were you successful in entering Villa Amalfi?"

Bradford paused before answering and Bochlaine's body began to perspire with renewed anxiety. Before he could ask more questions, Bradford told him about Suzanne's death.

Tears came to the big Italian's eyes as he realized that he would never again see beautiful, brave Suzanne Steelman. He had come to respect her greatly during her time with Aspis and had often wished she had not become involved.

"At least she didn't die in vain," Brad told him, sensing Bochlaine's grief. "We may have the Piedmont Papers—or photographs of them." He explained what they'd found at Amalfi, adding that they were in Latin and would have to be translated.

"I can help you do that," Bochlaine said. "When will you have them?"

Bradford was glad to have the help and promised to phone Bochlaine at Mama Teresa's the moment Murray Jolles delivered the papers.

A few hours later, Bochlaine was settled at the dinning room table in the FINVEST apartment translating the documents. Soon Bochlaine gave some disheartening news to Bradford, Holly, and Burke, who crowded around him.

"These documents," he said, "are coded. They make no sense at all. Listen." Bochlaine rattled off a string of words and numbers, illustrating his point.

"What about the signatures, Bochlaine? Can you make them out?"

"Many are mere scribbles, Mr. Bradford. The ones that can be read are meaningless without understanding the contents of the documents. I recognize none of them."

A short time later, however, Bochlaine cried out excitedly. "Here's something!" he declared. "It's a letter dated in early April 1944, written by Monsignor Vincenzo Massara to his half brother, Count Vignola. Much of it is of only social significance, yet listen to the final paragraphs.

" 'Would you help us in forming a new financial organization to handle certain investments for the church and our Circle? We do not trust the Jew who has for years fooled our Holy Fathers. Did you know that he would have given Vatican funds to Hauptler had we not interfered?

" 'We simply cannot entrust the financial future of the Holy See to such a man. That is why I have recommended you to head an organization we shall call Piedmont S.A. It must operate at our bidding rather than that of the Pope—at least until the right pontiff is selected. There is a substantial fund in Swiss accounts that can be turned over to you for investment as soon as the war ends and you have established the corporation. Do visit me at the earliest.'"

"Our Circle?" Burke queried, his eyes on Bochlaine.

"It is a radical faction inside the Vatican, Lieutenant," Bochlaine said. "I've been informed that the Inner Circle is composed entirely of cardinals who have been patiently preparing for many years to return the church to the dark ages. They cannot succeed until they elect one of their own as the Holy Father. That man, we believe, will be Cardinal Massara."

"Then Piedmont is now Aspis? And it's controlled by this Inner Circle?" Burke asked.

"Through Count Vignola, Massara's half brother," Brad said. "That reference to giving money to Hauptler is pretty damning, Bochlaine. And so is the reference to the money in Swiss accounts. But it doesn't prove what we have to prove—that Aspis sprang directly from the stolen blood money—though it certainly confirms that there's a conspiracy in the Vatican to turn the church clock back to the days of papal political power."

"It also leaves no doubt that Massara was the creator of Aspis and is a member of the Circle."

Burke's expression left no doubt to his feelings. "It makes me ashamed to admit I'm a Catholic," he declared.

"Me, too," chimed in Holly. "I shudder to think that a cardinal or priest could be involved with killers like Nick Criscolle! Can you believe the Pope, who seemed so kind when we met him, could tolerate someone like that, Brad?"

"Do not blame the whole Roman Catholic Church, my friends," Bochlaine begged. "In our Father's church there are many pews. Some, I'm afraid, are occupied by men in red miters who have Satan in their hearts."

"Let's get on with it, Bochlaine," Bradford told him. "There must be a more solid piece of evidence than that in this stack of documents."

Holly, who had behaved circumspectly since she found herself again occupying Brad's quarters, stood beside him as Bochlaine turned back to the documents on the table.

Brad accorded her a smile. She was, he thought, growing up fast. Faster than a young woman should have to, he thought. It reminded

him of what Suzanne had calmly told him the first time he'd met her—
that she, too, had grown up fast.

Suzanne. It was hard to think of her now—yet impossible not to. The
grief of this loss was reminiscent of the pain of losing Nan and the boys.
But Brad resolved that he would let nothing get in the way of his mission—a mission he had shared with Simon Zeisman's granddaughter.

While Bochlaine was busy with the papers, Burke told Brad and Holly
that Captain Parente was enraged by the possibility that Aspis had spies
within the Roman police.

"In New York we aren't really surprised when we find some of our
cops on the take," Burke said, "though we sure as hell don't like it
much. It's damn hard to prove—no matter that a cop has been living
like a prince on twenty-five or thirty G's a year. By the time we've
nailed a cop, a dozen more are on the take. But Parente's damn mad.
He's on a short fuse and I'd hate to be working for him right now."

Brad said nothing, for there was little to be said. Whoever had tipped
off Aspis and Nick Criscolle to their expedition to Villa Amalfi had
killed Suzanne as surely as if he'd wielded the knife. Catching him
wouldn't bring her back, but maybe it would save someone else's life
one day.

In his Rome apartment above Aspis headquarters Count Vignola's
phone rang. The caller did not identify himself, but the count knew the
voice, for he had heard it before. "The Pope is dead," declared the
caller, "long live the Pope!"

"Amen!" murmured Vignola into the phone as his caller hung up.
For the first time since Nick Criscolle, sporting bandages on the entire
left side of his face, had returned from Amalfi, the count was pleased.
Soon the new Pope would be in place and it would be his half brother;
that meant the beginnings of a new order of things, both inside the
Vatican and elsewhere.

But Vignola's glee soon departed and he began to pace the floor of his
bedroom, a hundred thoughts muddling his mind. Suzanne Steelman
was dead and she had been a spy. He still found it difficult to believe and
wondered again if Nick had simply spirited her off somewhere to satisfy
his sadistic passions before flaying her with one of his knives.

Yet he knew Suzanne had died in Livigno, for certain Italian authorities had checked into her death for him, and had confirmed it.

Only his good breeding kept him from spitting out an epithet, for he hated the fact that Bradford was alive and Suzanne was not. He'd rather have Suzanne still alive, spy or not, than dead in a casket meant for the audacious Elliot Bradford.

"Bradford must die!" the count snapped at Nick Criscolle. "You know my half brother will soon be elected Pope and you also know Bradford has somehow connected Cardinal Massara to Aspis, so it's possible he may try to interfere. Kill him or . . ." Vignola did not finish his threat, but he saw momentary fear in Criscolle's eyes.

Now, he thought, Criscolle had reason to experience fear, for he had become an embarrassment to Aspis by bungling his recent assignment. Soon, the count thought, Nick must be eliminated. But only after Bradford was slaughtered. If Criscolle failed again . . . The last thought did not please him. Never before had he used the term *if* regarding a task given to Criscolle.

The count wondered why Suzanne had betrayed him and Aspis. There was no possible way Bradford could have known her before, of that he was certain. The break-in at Amalfi made little sense unless Bradford knew about the secret compartment beneath the computer terminal—or suspected it. No one knew of the compartment except the count and his secret contact within the Circle, a man whose identity was not even known to Massara.

Bradford could not, therefore, have reasonably suspected its existence, and there was little chance that he could solve the computer code that would expose its secrets.

Or was there? A single concern gripped the count. Could Bradford's FINVEST, a modern investigative firm with a computer system reported to be as advanced and sophisticated as any in the world and with experts to program it, have cracked the code? The possibility made him sweat even though he had flown to Livigno and gone through the documents in the secret compartment immediately after the break-in. They seemed undisturbed, but who could be sure?

Still there was only a single paper in the compartment that was not coded in the private cipher given Vignola years ago by the man from the Circle. The signatures on the papers, most of them mere scrawls, would mean little to anyone. Only the letter his half brother wrote him many years ago was not in code. Vignola had kept it for strictly sentimental reasons because it represented the very conception of Aspis.

After rereading it, he decided at last to put the torch to it, for it was far too suggestive in content, though not truly damning. There was the reference to the Jew who watched the Vatican finances and his desire to pay off Hauptler, but neither Elliot Bradford nor Suzanne Steelman could have any direct knowledge of that affair. They would not yet have been born.

Feeling relieved after burning the letter, he concentrated on the possible reasons for Suzanne's treachery. Her background had been investigated thoroughly after she'd come to work for Aspis and everything had checked out. Yet the count remembered that it had been Bochlaine who recommended Steelman. He had to be the one who had turned Suzanne against him, just as Bochlaine had begun to bite the hand that was feeding him. Vignola railed at himself for not having realized sooner that Suzanne was a risk.

The count nurtured a special fondness for Suzanne, a paternal feeling that made him quite protective. Perhaps it was because she was so beautiful and strong yet vulnerable, or because he had no daughter of his own. For a man of very few emotions when it came to murder and the destruction of human life, sadness ran surprisingly deep through his venomous system. He suffered the loss in silence.

EIGHTEEN

St. Patrick's Day in Rome was not a happy one for the Italian Catholics or for Elliot Bradford.

The dead Pope lay in state on a catafalque beneath the cupola of St. Peter's, watched over by the Swiss Guards as he was gazed at and prayed for by thousands of tearful mourners.

Cardinals from all over the world were in the air—en route to Rome for the College of Cardinals' conclave that would elect a successor to the beloved Holy Father.

Bradford was morose. The Piedmont Papers, or whatever they were, provided no evidence against Massara. Of all the documents Burke, Suzanne, and he had risked their lives to photograph at the Villa Amalfi, only one—the letter from Massara to Vignola—had revealed anything damaging, but even it was not conclusive. The other documents were indecipherable. Most bore more than one signature, but the names meant nothing to him.

Were they now at a dead end? It seemed so, for Brad had seen codes like this one before. They often took thousands of work hours to break, for they were usually keyed to a particular book or text, of which there were only a few copies in print. Unless you had one of the books or texts, the code represented a nearly impossible morass of words, even to an expert cryptographer.

Bradford berated himself for risking Suzanne's life—and losing it—with the Amalfi gamble.

Bochlaine laid a huge hand on his shoulder. "Do not feel guilty, Mr. Bradford. You did what you had to and so did Suzanne. She willingly took a chance for what she believed. You and Lieutenant Burke could have died at Amalfi and she might have lived."

"If so, she'd feel just as badly as I do," Bradford pointed out.

Bochlaine shrugged. "No one can dispute that," he said. "Yet we cannot dwell on it. We must continue to try to defeat the monster Massara and his evil organization. If we do not, then Suzanne will have died in vain."

The next morning the Pope's death remained the subject of conversation for millions of people around the world, including Brad, Holly, and Burke.

Brad had decided that Bochlaine was right—he would have to continue to try to find the key to the coded papers or Suzanne's death would be in vain. He told Burke he was going to have a "heart to heart" chat with Count Vignola.

"He'll hardly agree to talk to you, Brad," Burke observed, for the moment missing Bradford's meaning.

"I mean to break into his apartments over Aspis headquarters, Kevin," Bradford said, "and persuade him to tell me about his codes and code book. With drugs, if necessary."

Holly was petrified by the suggestion. She stared at Bradford in horror and fascination.

"He'll have guards," Burke said. "And the grounds are covered by camera surveillance. It'll take a lot of planning and won't be easy to carry out. You'll need help."

"I can manage," Brad said. "Too many cooks . . ."

"Help to get the meal ready on time," Burke broke in.

"You can't do it by yourself, Brad."

"I can't ask you to help, Burke. You're a cop and what I'm going to do is patently against the law."

"So was our jaunt to Villa Amalfi. Anyway, I'm still investigating a murder and sometimes you have to bend a few laws to be successful. Captain Parente will help, I'm almost sure of that. So you've got yourself an accomplice or two—whether you like it or not." Burke frowned, then added, "But you've got to put off doing it for a couple of days. I need to fly back to New York and try to get my superiors to put me on official business. It'll help if we run into any trouble at Aspis. And I'm sure I can get some of the barbiturate thiopental sodium, or whatever they're using nowadays, from some of my connections at the police lab."

"We could use some guns that fire anesthetic darts, Burke. They'd help with the guards."

A grin illuminated Burke's face. "Then you'll wait for me to get back?"

"I'll be as patient as Job, Kevin. But hurry back. We don't have all the time in the world. I'll check with Bochlaine on the physical layout of Count Vignola's quarters."

Burke called from New York the following day to give Bradford his flight number and arrival time. He would have the drug with him when he arrived Sunday morning. They could hit Vignola Monday night.

Brad agreed to pick him up at da Vinci Airport.

By Saturday Brad's spirits were high. Bochlaine had given him detailed plans of Count Vignola's second-floor apartment with information on the guards. Brad had devised an attack plan, which depended on Captain Parente's being able, as he had said he could, to cut the power to the Aspis headquarters. Brad would have less than thirty seconds to scale the wall, cross the courtyard and climb to Vignola's bedroom balcony before the emergency diesel generator would activate.

After going over the lengthy report Tom Sumereau had brought back from London, Brad was more convinced than ever that Massara's ascension to the papal throne had to be truncated, for as Tony Phipps put it in his summary, Aspis's silent partner was the Vatican Bank. The only question in Brad's mind was whether Cardinal Massara directed the Inner Circle at the Vatican or the brothers of the Circle directed him. In either case, it was imperative that he be stopped before the conclave of the College of Cardinals, which was slated to begin in less than a week.

As Brad and Holly watched the televised funeral services for the dead Pope, Brad wondered what the world's Roman Catholics would think if they learned that their Sunday offerings were underwriting Aspis's murderous activity. Would they reject their Church in horror?

That would be tragic, for the Church itself was not to blame, only inhuman, misguided members like Massara and the brothers of the Circle. Brad resolved to lay the facts not before the entire world, but only before the College of Cardinals. Was it possible? Only Count Vignola knew that.

Holly was terrified by what Brad was planning and told him so. But she had made no effort to talk him out of it or otherwise interfere and he was glad of that, although it would not have mattered. She had slept in the second bedroom of the FINVEST apartment, cooked meals for them when they did not go out, and made no overtures toward him. The events of the past weeks had stunned her into submissiveness. After losing her father and being critically injured by his assassin, Holly lacked the strength to combat Brad's plan of action.

Brad's dreams had for days been haunted by visions of Nan, Suzanne, and Jack Sands, all urging him to continue his private war against Aspis and Nick Criscolle. Suzanne's part in each dream was to love him and reassure him with her strength and conviction. It was as if she were alive and they were in bed together, her long, beautiful body curled up beside him, her flesh warm against his.

Bradford left Holly in the apartment when he drove to da Vinci Airport that morning. He was early and drank an espresso at the bar while awaiting Kevin Burke's arrival. From where he stood he could see a large board on which arrival and departure information was displayed. He had already ascertained that Burke's flight was on time and would be landing in the next ten minutes.

As he sipped his coffee, he was glad he had not brought Holly to the airport, for he was in a quiet, uncommunicative frame of mind and neither needed, nor wanted, any company. Besides, she was safer at the apartment than she would be with him; Nick Criscolle could strike at any moment.

The thought made him look around the bar for familiar faces. Seeing none, he looked out into the airport rotunda, checking out the unusually heavy crowd. Many travelers were leaving after having come to Rome to bury a Pope. Others had just arrived, wanting to be in the Holy City when a new Pope was chosen.

He checked the screen again and saw no change in the arrival time of Burke's flight.

Arrivals cleared customs on the lower level at da Vinci, so Brad finished his espresso and began the short walk to where he would soon greet Burke. He wondered why the airport architect had designed the building so that one had to go outside to get from departures to arrivals.

Once outside, Brad watched a jumbo jet touch the runway and quickly become a sleek, silvery bird as its speed increased. It raced across his line of vision and Brad saw that it was not Burke's Global Airlines plane, but rather one with the Alitalia insignia upon it.

Brad searched the distant sky and saw another huge plane still several miles away. That, he thought, could well be Burke's plane, for it was due to arrive very soon.

Burke. He smiled for the first time since he'd reached the airport at the thought of the affable, competent young homicide detective. What color turtleneck would he be wearing tonight? Burke was in his thirties, but seemed younger in sweaters and Brad supposed that it was the departure of Burke's wife in favor of a salesman that made the cop dress that way.

Brad could sympathize with Burke. The cop was alone and Brad knew well how it felt to have no one—or virtually no one—to call family.

In the tourist section of the big Boeing 747 jet, Kevin Burke was staring out the window beside him at the rolling hills and small farms that translated peace and beauty into unspoiled agricultural landscapes.

Burke had been surprised at how solidly booked his Global flight was—until he realized what was to take place in Rome in six days. Popes were not chosen often and many people—including more than a few non-Catholics—wanted to be in St. Peter's Square when the white smoke issued from the Sistine Chapel's stovepipe to signal that the College of Cardinals had agreed on a new pontiff.

Now he wondered if he and Bradford would be lucky enough as well as daring enough to achieve success on their dangerous mission to Count Vignola's headquarters.

There were so many details that could go wrong. Little things. Big things. Even if everything went smoothly and they got in, neutralized the guards, and took Vignola prisoner, their success was far from guaranteed. As the lab boys had told him, the truth serum they'd given him, thiopental sodium, was the best of the so-called tongue looseners, but, even so, it did not always work.

"It's like a short pass, Lieutenant," one of the lab people, a fellow Jets football fan declared. "It can go for a touchdown if it fools a bunch of defenders, but it can result in no gain just as easily. The drug's effectiveness depends a lot on the individual's level of resistance."

Burke respected Bradford's determination, and he believed that there was a fair chance they would succeed.

Burke grinned as he leaned back in his seat and recalled his initial meeting with Bradford outside the East Side apartment building where Brad lived. He had liked Brad from the start and was on his way back to Rome as much to help Bradford as to bring Nick Criscolle to some kind of justice. He recalled how hard Brad had taken Suzanne's death. Burke was sure there had been more between them than their mission against Aspis and Criscolle. He could hardly blame Brad, for she was very beautiful and very intelligent.

Now Burke suddenly became aware that his seatmate, an attractive dark-haired woman in her mid-twenties, was eyeing him again, as she had done several times since exchanging seats hours ago. He flashed her a smile, trying not to drop his eyes to her saucy breasts, which were restrained by a bra beneath her blue tank top. Burke was a lover of women; he'd charmed quite a few since his divorce and was always interested in meeting new dates.

"We'll be in Rome soon," Burke now told the woman. "Will you be staying there long?"

"At least a week," she replied. "I'm a journalist, which is why I'll be in Rome. I've got an assignment to cover the papal conclave. I'm Lexie Mathes, by the way." Her smile broadened as she added, "I thought I'd start looking for human interest stuff by checking you out. What's a New York cop doing on a plane to Rome? Are they hiring bodyguards?"

The startling question had been followed by an enjoyable exchange of information during which Burke learned that Lexie had spotted him back at the airport in New York and had made some inquiries about him at the reservation desk.

Kevin was genuinely sorry to see their flight end as the announcement to fasten their seat belts came over the jet's loudspeakers.

"I'd like to see you in Rome if you're not too busy," Burke said. "I've got business that will occupy me until Tuesday. Is there any chance we could get together then?"

"Every chance, Kevin," Lexie Mathes said. "Especially Tuesday. Tomorrow and Monday are completely out. There are three American cardinals flying in first-class, and I've got an interview with one of them tomorrow. I'm hoping he'll introduce me to the others as well. If so, I'll need all day Monday to wrap up my interviews."

Burke, thoroughly captivated by the journalist, was about to find out where she was staying when the importance of what she'd just said reached him. "Cardinals. They're going for the conclave to elect a new Pope! Is there any gossip about it?"

Lexie laughed, delighted that he was interested in her work. "They're on their way to vote in the elections. In my research, I've dug up much factual gossip. These three are a part of the progressive movement in the Catholic Church. They're backing a French cardinal—des Balmat, Bishop of Paris. He's one of the favorites to become Pope. My interviewee, Cardinal Mobley, is also a possible candidate, though he poo-poos talk about it."

"Does their man Balmat have a chance?" Burke asked as the plane slowed noticeably while starting its descent toward the da Vinci runway.

"It's hard to say. I'm told there's a pretty powerful conservative faction in the church that wants a Roman in the driver's seat again. They're pushing Vincenzo Massara, their man with the Vatican Bank."

This pert journalist had done more than simply make his pulse pound with her overt interest in him. She had just confirmed the impending power struggle within the College of Cardinals' papal conclave: The Inner Circle versus the rest.

"Where are you staying, Kevin?" the writer asked. He told her the name and address of his hotel, but his mind was far away.

She leaned across the seat and looked intently into his eyes. As if moved by some force beyond her own mortal desires, Lexie suddenly found herself about to kiss Kevin Burke. Before he realized what she was about to do, she planted her mouth fully on his. The light scent of lilac surrounding her drifted into his nose as he surrendered to the kiss. It was exquisite for reasons neither could comprehend.

And then their whole world ceased to exist as a timer in the baggage compartment in the belly of the plane ticked its final second and sent an electrical spark to an explosive device in a suitcase.

Brad was tracking the plane when he saw the fleeting, brilliant blue and white flash of an explosion illuminate the jumbo jet.

His senses slowly registered the horror of what he was seeing. His flesh crawled as he perceived a streak of fiery red where the plane had been and watched it whistle down to the ground. The muffled sound of a new explosion came into his ears and he stood there transfixed.

The plane was burning now. He could see the flames lighting the sky over the area just below the beginning of the runway. The plane, Burke's plane!

He rushed back into the terminal. A man standing near the only window with a view of the approach area lowered his eyes and stared numbly at Brad. "The plane," he said in Italian, "it just blew up!"

Brad knew enough Italian to understand him. "Was it the plane from New York?" he asked in English. When the man did not immediately reply, he gestured toward the red glow far down the runway and said, "From Nuova York?"

The man now nodded and began to babble—in broken English, "My Claudia—she was avisiting her abrother in America. Ina New Jersey!"

Brad was awash with thoughts and emotions. Was there a chance that Burke had survived the crash? Or that he had missed the plane? People missed planes frequently—and stayed alive because they had. Was Burke one of them? But even as he harbored the hope, he knew it was futile, for if Burke had missed the plane, it would have been hours ago and he'd have surely called Brad to give him the bad news and a new flight number and arrival time.

Burke could have been injured in an auto accident while driving to the airport. If so, he might not have been able to call. There was only one way to find out and little time to do it, for the people at the airline ticket counter would refuse to give out any information at all once the news of the crash had reached them.

He ran to the ticket counter, some distance from where he had been. The uniformed ticket personnel behind the deserted counter were calm, and Brad was certain they had no knowledge of what had just happened.

Brad drew in a deep breath to calm his nerves as one woman approached him. "Can you tell me," he asked, "if all booked passengers actually boarded Flight 840 from New York? I'm meeting a Kevin Burke."

"Just a moment," the light-haired woman said. "I'll check. It ought to be on the ground by now."

As she turned to the computer screen beside her, Brad winced at her innocent words. In the ground was more like it. He glanced away from the counter and toward the window where Claudia's father had stood. He was now striding toward the ticket counter. Behind him were others. A horde of others! The rush was on. He turned back to the woman and commanded her to hurry. Come on, he mentally told her, give me some good news—that Kevin missed the plane.

"All booked passengers were checked in, sir," the woman said.

Bradford's forlorn hope was discarded in that instant. For a moment he just stood there, his eyes locked with those of the Global Airlines woman. Then, his head one huge sad ache, he left the counter, avoiding the clamorous wave of relatives and friends of the people aboard Flight 840.

He thought about trying to get to where the plane had gone down, but decided there would be little he could do if he got there. So he waited in the terminal with the others while fire fighters and emergency crews from the airport dealt with things at the scene. Forty-five minutes later, an announcement in four languages including English instructed all those awaiting Flight 840 to meet in a special area near the passport control. There, Brad heard a meticulously dressed Italian say that there were no expected survivors as he distributed the passenger manifest.

God! Where would it end? A bomb to kill Kevin Burke. A bomb that might have been the work of Aspis. Everyone Brad cared about had been the victim of violence, the latest was Kevin Burke. The only ones left were Ellie and Holly Sands.

NINETEEN

Though it would be months before the pieces of the plane could be fit together and the cause of its destruction absolutely established, the burned and dismembered bodies of the passengers were recovered and accounted for within seventy-two hours. But the fact that the plane's flight recorder confirmed that the plane was functioning properly just before it went down clearly indicated sabotage.

The radio reports Sunday said several dignitaries had died aboard the plane, among them three American cardinals, who were en route to Rome for the papal conclave, and several Italian envoys to the United Nations, who had taken leave from their posts to witness the installation of a new Pope.

As Bradford was trying to decide what to do about his planned incursion into the residence of Count Vignola, the gatekeeper of the FINVEST apartment building announced that Captain Enrico Parente of the Rome Police was there to see him. Brad allowed the gatekeeper to admit Parente.

The Italian police officer was a raging bull over what had happened to Burke. "You must tell me exactly what's going on, Mr. Bradford," the Italian officer demanded as he shook Brad's hand at the door. "Kevin was my friend and he was doing important work and now he's dead. Killed in a plane crash that was no accident! Even after my good friend Carlo Cervi and Miss Steelman were killed in the north, Kevin would not tell me everything. I am asking you to do so now."

"There are spies in your organization, Captain Parente," Bradford said as he led the officer into the living room of the apartment. "One of them tipped off Nick Criscolle, the man we were after, and it was Criscolle who killed your friend and mine. Perhaps he was responsible for the bomb aboard Kevin's plane—if that was what caused the explosion and crash."

"I knew nothing about his return to Rome on that plane, Mr. Bradford," Parente declared, "but somebody did. It is an atrocity that some-one would end hundreds of lives just to get at Kevin."

Brad wondered if Parente would help him as he had aided Burke. He could not decide how much he should reveal to gain the Italian's sup-port. In the end he reached the conclusion that he had to trust someone with what he knew, if only to make sure that it was not lost should he be the next victim.

"Will you assure me that what I tell you will not be repeated, Captain Parente?" He met the Italian's eyes earnestly. "To anyone?"

"After what has happened, how could I refuse, Mr. Bradford?"

Brad started at the beginning of the story during World War II and laid it all out before Parente. Even Holly was shocked at the depths of the conspiracy and by the Vatican's involvement. All Parente could do when he'd heard the entire mystery was shake his head in disbelief. "Incredible," he muttered in a hushed, almost inaudible voice.

"Incredible, yet true," Brad returned. "If I can get Count Vignola to reveal the code, perhaps the Piedmont Papers we copied with the aid of Carlo Cervi can prove it all to be true. Burke was bringing back truth serum for me to use."

"You still intend to try?" Parente asked.

"I have to," Brad said. "It's our only chance to stop Massara."

"Count Vignola's building is well guarded. You could easily lose your life."

"I've been living on borrowed time for years, Captain. This is not the first time I've had to watch my back."

"There is a difference between calculated risks, Mr. Bradford, where danger is certain but death is not, and stupidity. What you face at Aspis headquarters, if your tale is true, is certain death."

"Not if I have an edge—the count won't be expecting me. Not, at least, unless your people tell him I'm coming. And I trust you to guard what I've told you so that it won't happen."

"Even if you escape with your life, Vignola can have you arrested afterward."

"If I don't get killed, I sure as hell won't get arrested," Brad said. "Once Vignola realizes I have copies of the Piedmont Papers, he won't chance the police because I'd scream my head off and have the papers to back me up. As for his Aspis killer, I've had his number one assassin

Criscolle on my trail for several years now and as you can see, I'm still very much alive."

Parente nodded, then stood and went to the window of the apartment, where he silently stared outside for more than a minute before turning back to Bradford. "You won't go alone, Mr. Bradford," he declared. "Two of my very good friends are dead, killed by Count Vignola and his associates. I will therefore go with you and help you persuade the count to cooperate. I can get the truth drug and a syringe for you, as well as tranquilizer guns."

"No, Captain," Bradford said, "I can't let you risk your career. If we are caught . . ."

"We will not be caught," Parente said firmly, "and the risk is not too great for me to take for Kevin and Carlo."

Bradford was not at all chagrined at the captain's insistence.

Parente was true to his word and arranged for all the equipment Bradford needed, including climbing gear.

It was a dark, moonless Monday night when the electric power failed in the Parioli section of Rome. The Aspis headquarters was immediately enveloped in darkness, but the large Caterpillar diesel generator in the basement automatically initiated its starting cycle. The engine's preheaters warmed the cylinders to prepare for ignition. Then the starter motor engaged, but the engine failed on its first attempt. The system recycled and the second attempt to start was successful. The building had power again. Fifty-five seconds had elapsed.

It was enough time for Brad to climb over the wall, sprint across the courtyard and scale the stucco wall of the Aspis headquarters using a grappling hook. He had made it to the balcony undetected.

Parente had presented him with a two-way radio that looked like a wristwatch and Bradford had grinned as he remembered Dick Tracy's comic strip radio of long ago. But he'd put it on without comment and now, as he crouched on the balcony, he pushed the button on the stem that opened the transmitter.

"Are you in place, Parente?" he muttered in a whisper.

He pushed the button a second time and was reassured by a quick affirmative response from the Italian officer, who was outside the gate leading into the Aspis grounds in his specially equipped Fiat van.

Bradford pushed the button again, to reopen the transmitter so Parente could hear everything he did and respond quickly should he find himself in trouble. He had convinced the captain that what he had to do inside was a job for one man, not two, and that his biggest need was for someone prepared to come to his rescue if required.

Brad was clad in dark clothes, including a thin black nylon jacket. In its right pocket was a hypodermic filled with thiopental sodium. In the other was a lock-picking tool and a special pistol Parente had procured to anesthetize the guards.

Now Brad found that Bochlaine had been wrong about the lock on the door of the balcony. Bochlaine had told him the lock was broken, but apparently a new one recently had been installed. Brad inspected it in the light of a small penlight and found that it was a simple spring lock he could easily pick with the tool he'd learned to use in the army.

A minute later he was inside the sitting room of the small suite. The house was quiet as he took out Bochlaine's diagram for another look to orient himself. Then he opened the door out into the hall and crept silently toward the small study Bochlaine said had been converted into a security station to house the television surveillance monitors.

A single armed guard was supposed to be on duty in the room at all times and he posed the most dangerous threat to Brad's survival. Once he was put to sleep with the tranquilizer gun, the gates could be unlocked and the cameras shut off. Only then would Brad and Parente have a clear field.

Brad had no trouble locating the study. Reaching it, he knelt beside the door and listened, his ear up against it. At first he heard only the quiet buzzing of television monitors, but then heard—or thought he heard—the sound of breathing not far from the door. Heavy breathing, if he was not mistaken. Was the guard dozing? That would be a lucky break. Brad held his breath as he gripped the door knob with his left hand. He held the tranquilizer gun in his right as he turned the knob excruciatingly slowly.

He flinched when the door clicked as it opened and stopped to listen. There was no change in the sounds inside and, after a moment, he eased the door open a few inches and peered in. Across the room was a bank of television monitors, each showing a different view of the floodlit grounds around the building.

In front of the monitors a swarthy man with thick, black hair and well-developed arms sat in a high-backed black swivel chair. Only the light snoring Brad detected told him that the guard was indeed asleep.

The man didn't even open his eyes as Brad crept up next to the chair and fired a tranquilizer dart into his arm at close range. He would not wake up for several hours.

Now Brad produced a pair of wire cutters and began clipping the cables to the television monitors so there was no danger of Captain Parente being observed if he entered.

He found the electronic switch controlling the front gate, flipped it and spoke into the wrist radio. "The gate should be opening, Parente. Is it?"

"You've neutralized the guards?" the captain responded.

"One of them. The only one on duty. I'm going after the others now. Stay where you are and be ready to intercept anyone who may show up in the next hour. And keep your tape recorders ready to receive what I get from Vignola."

After tearing out the wiring to the gate switch, Brad retraced his steps down the hall, looking for the rooms where Bochlaine had said the guards slept. During the day when Vignola traveled, there were a pair of brawny, armed guards always at his side or close at hand. But at night in the Aspis headquarters, the guards were lax because of the surveillance system covering the grounds outside. Bochlaine had said that the guards who were not on duty frequently left the premises for twenty-four hours at a time, so there was no telling how many guards there would be in the rooms, and there could be as many as five.

He paused and listened at the door to the first of the guards' rooms. When he heard heavy snoring, he tried the door. It was locked, but he slid his tool into the keyhole and quickly unlocked it. A moment later he slipped inside the darkened room. After his eyes became accustomed to the dark, he crept to the bed and fired another of the nonlethal darts into an Aspis guard.

The second of the guards' rooms was also locked, but it was empty. The third one contained a surprise—two men. Brad put them both to sleep.

All three of the other guards' rooms were empty. One, Brad figured, belonged to the on-duty guard he had taken out first. The others were probably occupied by a pair of guards who were presently prowling around Rome's night spots. He warned Parente about the possibility of their return, then left the last of the rooms to find Vignola.

The small staff of servants Vignola maintained was, according to

Bochlaine, quartered in small rooms on the third floor. The only access was a rear stairway from the kitchen. So there were no other obstacles standing between Brad and his target.

As he moved along the wide hallway in the dim light of two low-wattage wall lamps, Brad prayed the thiopental sodium would work on Vignola. Because there was no foolproof truth drug, torture was still used in the intelligence and espionage business. Brad had never resorted to it, but had seen it practiced. If Vignola did not respond to the drug, he wasn't certain what he would do.

A heady feeling swept over him as he reached the polished mahogany doors that led into what Bochlaine had said was a lavish suite of rooms fit for a king. Vignola's furnishings were exclusive Italian antiques for which Vignola had paid handsomely. There were also fabulous oil paintings, some by renowned artists, some by relative unknowns. All were museum pieces, for Vignola was a connoisseur who had the means to buy the fine art he admired and absolutely no reluctance to spend the money.

Bradford checked the doors carefully for any indication of an alarm, but found none. They were locked, however, and his elation disappeared as he found that the lock, a new design Brad had never seen, was difficult to pick. He sweated over it for several minutes, swallowing the frustration he experienced as he failed repeatedly to open the lock. But finally he managed it, and the doors opened. Brad found himself in Vignola's huge, high-ceilinged living room.

Even in the soft light of the single floor lamp in the room, Brad could see that Bochlaine had not exaggerated the beauty of Vignola's possessions. Nonetheless, he didn't stop to admire them. Taking one quick look around, he listened for hostile sounds and crossed the room to another pair of doors that led to a large foyer and a hallway to the rest of the suite.

He found the count's library next to a large study, both of them on the right, exactly where Bochlaine had said they'd be. Brad gave them a cursory look and was about to go on when a voice from behind made him freeze.

"Welcome to my home, sir," came the calm, cultured voice of Count Vignola. "Is there something special you're interested in? Would you like a guided tour?" Vignola laughed when Bradford did not respond. He thumbed a wall switch to illuminate the study.

"Drop your weapon and turn around slowly," Vignola ordered. "I've a deadly little Beretta pointed at your back, and I can assure you I know how to use it and will, if you should decide to act foolishly."

Bradford had no choice. He let the tranquilizer pistol slip from his fingers and swiveled around to face the count.

"Mr. Bradford!" It was all Vignola could say, his surprise evident on his face. "You should have let me know you wished to see my living quarters," he finally added, recovering his composure. "I would have been happy to arrange it at a more conventional hour."

"How did you know I was here?" Brad asked. "Did I miss one of your guards?" If he did, he'd better warn Parente right now, he thought, wondering at the same time if the Italian would risk his job to come to Brad's rescue.

The count's smile was cold. "Although I am fond of the antiques you see exhibited all around you, Mr. Bradford, I am not averse to a few, select modern toys as well. One of my companies, you see, specializes in security systems that are both effective and undetectable. The one they installed here awakened me by a device I wear on my forearm at night. The moment you touched the special lock on the door I was awakened and warned by electronic impulse. I've been awaiting your arrival ever since."

"Where's your private assassin—Criscolle?"

"Nicholas is supposed to be arranging for your deportation, Mr. Bradford. Not just from Italy, but from this world. It appears he has failed again. I suppose I shall have to show him how to eliminate you myself."

"You'd dirty your hands with murder, Vignola? How does Cardinal Massara justify dealing with you and Aspis? The same way he did the theft of the Jewish blood money?"

Vignola's surprise was evident, but he said nothing, his finger tightening on the trigger of the Beretta he held steadily in front of him, its muzzle pointed at Bradford's chest.

"Massara's not going to make Pope," Brad challenged. "Not even your Inner Circle's strong enough to make a crazy man Pope."

Now Vignola looked stricken. "Sit," he commanded, pointing to a chair beside his desk. "I must think."

"Think about this, Count. My partner knows about you and your organization's activities and so do the Rome Police. I've given them all copies of your Piedmont Papers."

"The Piedmont Papers?" Vignola repeated, an odd look on his face. "What do you know about them?"

"I know you keep them in a secret compartment at the Villa Amalfi," Brad declared. "Did you think Lieutenant Burke and I went to Livigno to admire the scenery? I must say you have a nice setup. And I found your computer fascinating."

Vignola scowled but composed himself quickly, his eyes on Bradford's wrist. "Turn around in the chair," he ordered, "and put your arms behind your back."

Brad obeyed and Vignola came over to jab his gun in Brad's back and grab his left wrist. "Interesting watch," he observed. "How does it work?"

Before Brad could reply, Vignola had pulled off the watch and backed away with it as he looked it over closely. A moment later he tossed it on the top of his polished cherry desk and fell into its leather, executive chair, a disgusted look on his face.

"What shall I do with you now, Mr. Bradford? You are an intruder in my home, and I should shoot you. Who was listening on the other end of the microphone, Mr. Bradford? Not Captain Parente."

It was Brad's turn to be surprised. Vignola knew of Parente? With the radio shut down, Parente would surely move in fast. Or would he? Bradford had no idea.

"Who, Mr. Bradford? Tell me or I'll be forced to kill you here and now. I'm well within my rights to do so."

"In the back, Count?" Brad pointed out, only half-turned in the chair toward his captor.

"Where does one shoot a fleeing criminal, Mr. Bradford? In his chest? Really! Anyhow, I shall have your remains deposited in the Tiber by my guards."

"I've no doubt of that. I wonder, though, if you have the guts to do your own killing. It's one thing to send your hired assassins and suicide specialists to rid you of your enemies, another entirely to watch a man die." He turned around slowly and faced Vignola.

Vignola wasn't fazed by Bradford's suggestion and proved it by squeezing the trigger of his silenced weapon.

Bradford was thrown back in the chair as the bullet tore into his left shoulder. He glanced at the blood rushing out, genuinely surprised by the count's ruthlessness.

"I'm an excellent shot, you see. If you'd like, I can give you an additional demonstration." Vignola raised the gun again and took dead aim on Bradford's other shoulder, then paused, smiling. "Who is your accomplice, Mr. Bradford?" he asked again.

Bradford, the heel of his right hand against the hole in his left shoulder trying to staunch the flow of blood, shook his head. "Kill me, Vignola, and my partner and the American police will be on your ass straightaway. As I told you, I've copied your Piedmont Papers and they're being decoded right now."

"Your American police can't decode those papers, Mr. Bradford, but even if they could, they'd find they had nothing terribly incriminating. Just a bunch of contracts, most of them over fifty years old. The signatures adorning them are of men who wouldn't affix their real names to any truly incriminating documents, and these are couched so as to cause no difficulty for anyone. There are no Piedmont Papers. Not any more. I've destroyed them and only their content remains, but it's buried within my computer system and can't be retrieved by anyone but my successor and me."

"You're lying, Count," Bradford countered, stalling. "The papers you had at Amalfi must be important, to have been put in code. Suzanne was certain . . .

"Suzanne! Ah, yes! How did you corrupt her, Bradford? Why did she ever agree to help you?"

"She was Zeisman's granddaughter. With her legacy from him was a letter telling her of his suspicions of you and Cardinal Massara. She knew about your half brother's part in the theft of the ten million dollars raised in America to ransom the Roman Jews." Brad, his shoulder throbbing with pain, watched Vignola carefully during his revelation, looking for a chance to catch the man's attention flagging long enough to leap and wrest the Beretta from his hand. If he couldn't do that, both he and Parente might well be destined to die shortly, for the captain ought to be here soon. But Vignola remained alert.

"Why did you have Burke killed, Count?" Bradford asked. "And how could you arrange to kill all those others, just to get at one man?"

"Burke wasn't the target," the Count sneered. "His life wasn't worth a bomb of that magnitude. The targets were three men, all cardinals of the Roman Catholic Church, all opponents of my brother. They would have voted for des Balmat, the French Bishop of Paris.

"You don't understand the importance of what we are doing," he continued. "Of what we have done. Until we took action and used Zeisman's funds for a proper purpose, our church was on the verge of insolvency. Do you know what that would have meant? It won't happen again. We will never permit our church to follow the path to ruin."

Vignola stared at Bradford, his eyes revealing his total commitment to the message. "Do you expect the Roman Catholic Church to raise money on television, Mr. Bradford, selling religion like soap powder? For two thousand years it has survived. Have you ever considered the financial foundation of the Crusades? The sources of the gifts of gold which the Church received from centuries of monarch's patronage? And you object to *our* partners? Who else would step forward and provide for the Church. They are a powerful temporal force, and we deal in reality. Let him without sin cast the first stone, Mr. Bradford."

The enormity of the count's announcement made Bradford dizzy. A whole plane full of innocents killed—to get rid of three votes! The room began to spin. He had to shake his head to clear it. Vignola laughed and shifted his eyes momentarily to his captive's blood-drenched shoulder— just as Brad summoned all his remaining strength and leaped.

The force of Brad's leap knocked Vignola's slim frame off balance, and his gun arm came up in the air as the American seized his wrist in an iron grip. In spite of his weakened condition Brad hung on, desperately trying to thwart the count's efforts to wrest the gun away and bring it to bear on him.

Brad suddenly bent, threw Vignola over his shoulder, and sent the count crashing into his desk. The Beretta fell to the carpeted floor and Brad kicked it under the desk as Vignola dove for it. "You murdering bastard," Bradford roared, fighting off a mounting wave of nausea as he stalked the weaponless Vignola around the study, "I'm going to wring your goddamn neck!"

The count evaded Bradford's reeling lunges and slipped through the door, but Brad caught him just outside. His hands were closing around Vignola's neck, both thumbs in the Italian's windpipe, when suddenly the strength drained out of Brad's body and a great feeling of weariness swept over him. His senses dimmed and his concentration failed. Choke him . . . must choke him. His mind took forever to form the thought and when it was whole, Vignola shook off the American's hands and pulled away.

Vignola watched Bradford collapse in an unconscious heap to the floor; then he left the lifeless body and raced inside the study to retrieve his gun. He had to get down on all fours to reach where Bradford had kicked it under the desk.

Then, panting from the exertion, he returned to his fallen adversary and stood over him, the gun held to Bradford's head. "Good-bye, Mr. Bradford," he murmured. "It has not been a pleasure to know you."

A shout—in Italian—made Vignola look up. At the end of the hallway, Vignola could see a tall, thin man in the uniform of the Rome Police kneeling on one knee, his automatic held solidly in both hands as he aimed at Vignola's chest.

"Drop your weapon, Count Vignola," Captain Parente ordered.

"Who are you? How dare you threaten me in my home?"

"I am a member of the police," Parente shot back. "Now drop your gun or I'll shoot it from your hand."

"You have no right! I'll see to it that you are demoted. I have many friends with the Rome Police. Good friends!"

"I have every right, Count," Parente said, and quickly squeezed off a shot that all but parted Vignola's hair.

The count lowered the Beretta to the floor beside him, his eyes remaining fixed on Parente. The captain watched Vignola release his hold on the weapon and straighten up, apparently surrendering. But then, as Parente stood and began walking toward him, the count suddenly dropped to the floor, reclaimed the gun, and fired at him twice.

Both shots were off the mark, but Parente's single bullet was not. He was expert with a pistol and now put a shot straight into the Count's right wrist, shattering the wrist bone. Vignola dropped the gun and fell to his knees in agony.

When Parente saw Bradford's bloody condition, he was grim and furious. The American, he could see, had lost a great deal of blood and a growing pool of it was soaking the carpet beneath him. If he were to survive, Bradford must have swift medical attention.

Parente seized Vignola by the collar of his silk robe and yanked him to his feet, dragging the man with him as he went into the study to find a telephone.

"Your career is over, Captain," Vignola threatened. "I promise you that!"

Parente ignored the count's threats until after he'd called his headquarters and ordered an ambulance. Then, replacing the telephone on its stand, he slapped the count with four vicious blows across the face. "I only wish that I could kill as easily as you and your assassins," Parente declared.

Vignola cowered as the Italian police captain raised his open hand again. "No, no!" he cried. "I'm hurt. Please don't hit me again!"

Captain Parente turned away in disgust.

An hour later both Bradford and Count Vignola were in a Rome hospital undergoing surgery to remove bullets from their bodies.

TWENTY

Elliot Bradford had come through surgery early Tuesday morning without difficulty and was recovering nicely as Friday dawned. Today the papal conclave of the College of Cardinals in Vatican City would open, but Bradford had other problems. There were guards outside his hospital room, for Count Vignola had succeeded in having him placed under arrest and charged with burglary.

The count had remained in the hospital only a single day after an operation to repair his shattered wrist before returning to the splendor of his Aspis apartment. He had made good his vow to Parente—the Italian police captain had been officially suspended from his post pending a complete investigation of the burglary of the count's apartment and of Parente's role in it.

Parente had been sad-eyed when he related the news of his removal to Brad, Holly Sands, and Tom Sumereau, who had flown back to Rome when he learned of his partner's hospitalization.

"I am sorry they've placed you under arrest, Mr. Bradford," Parente had told Brad. "I wish I could have prevented it."

And so there was a police guard stationed outside Brad's room, and there were no clothes in the closet so that he could not dress and escape.

Brad was able to get up and move around the day after his surgery and had grown stronger quickly. Holly had stayed with him every day until the hospital staff ordered her to go home.

There was a television set in Bradford's room and all channels were focusing exclusively on the activities at the Sistine Chapel.

Now, in the early afternoon, the cardinals had already held one ballot for the new Bishop of Rome. It had not produced the two-thirds majority that was required to elect a Pope.

Brad, wearing nothing but a hospital gown and sitting up in bed, felt helpless as he watched the proceedings at the Vatican and thought of his abject failure in trying to prevent Massara's election to the papacy. Murray Jolles was with Brad giving an almost instantaneous translation of the commentary.

"If Divine Providence truly plays a role in the selection of the Bishop of Rome," a stern-faced narrator related as the television cameras panned around St. Peter's magnificent square, "nowhere is that intervention more apparent than in the unsummoned, yet rapid massing of the faithful in the great square before St. Peter's Basilica today. Even before the earliest wisps of smoke marking the results of the cardinals' first ballot of the afternoon arise from the chimney of the Sistine Chapel, more than a hundred thousand people have come here as pilgrims, following some internal imperative that told them the cardinals would not long tarry over a successor for the dead Pope."

It was true, Brad thought, as the cameras clearly showed the wall-to-wall people clustered across the piazza between the long arching Bernini colonnades.

When the first of the watchers saw black smoke coming from the Sistine chimney, there were loud groans although few of the veterani di fumate—those who had for many years attended papal pilgrimages—had expected white smoke so early in the balloting.

Rome had been filling up all week with tourists who hoped to be there when a new Pope was named and the coronation ceremony performed. They came from all over the world and were met in the age-old Roman streets by the persistent hawkers who sold images of past Holy Fathers and rosaries in addition to countless other religious souvenirs. It didn't matter that internal Vatican politics had often caused previous papal conclaves to take many days and even weeks and months to agree on the identity of the man God wanted to head the church. Human reason was not the cornerstone of the Roman Catholic faith.

An immense, mostly Italian, crowd descended on the Vatican. Shuffling bureaucrats of the Roman Curia were present, along with taxi drivers and street sweepers, nuns in habits of black and white, mothers and grandmothers who'd left pasta drying over the backs of chairs, prostitutes who'd forsaken eager customers in hotel lobbies, soldiers and judges, clerics and drunks. The old were there and the young; the common and the important; the devout and the curious. Like a steadily flowing brook of human water they crowded as close to the Basilica as they could.

But Bradford was aware of none of that. In his head were images of people he loved—people who were now dead—people who could only be comforted by God. Nan, Jack, Suzanne, Burke—they were all with him in spirit as he stared at the television set and cursed his failure.

If the count had told him the truth, the Piedmont Papers were irretrievable and would not bring about the destruction of Aspis. And now, if Bochlaine is right, the Inner Circle of cardinals was at work in the discussion chambers adjacent to the Sistine Chapel, pushing Cardinal Massara to the forefront of the papal candidates. The television analysts were saying Cardinal Jean des Balmat, Bishop of Paris, was the favorite to become the next pontiff, but Bradford had little hope that they were correct. He looked away from the set as Murray continued translating the most ponderous sort of speculation.

"Will the College of Cardinals elect an intellectual such as Papa Montini? Will the new Pope have the warmth, the humility possessed by Papa Roncalli and Papa Luciani? Or will he be more like his predecessor, a strong, healthy man who will travel far and wide, recognizing the internationality of Catholicism? Will he rather be satisfied simply to act as Bishop of Rome, as have so many of his predecessors? Whoever the new Pope is, the masses will love him, they already know that. The question is, who will he be? Who will be our new Pope?"

Again the cameras focused on the rude stovepipe over the Sistine Chapel. Its outline was clear against the suddenly blue sky that had seemed to shed its early morning clouds as the afternoon was born. The sun was welcome, but would, the commentator now observed, make it difficult to "read" the color of the smoke and learn if it was the black of indecision or the white of rebirth.

There had always been confusion over the smoke that issued from the chimney to signal the results of the cardinals' vote. One newscaster in tongue-in-cheek fashion had put the question of whether the tradition ought to be updated. "Why," he asked, "is it that more than a hundred of the world's most powerful men, attended by a large staff, acting under the direction and guidance of God to select a leader for nearly a billion people, can't figure out how to make a simple fireplace work?"

Bochlaine. Brad had not spoken to him since he had obtained from him the detailed diagram of Count Vignola's apartments at Aspis headquarters. Holly had, though. He had called Tuesday night, and she told him what had happened. Bochlaine had been very disturbed.

What was the big man doing right now? Brad wondered. Suzanne had told Brad once that Bochlaine would give up his life to prevent Vignola's half brother from being named Pope. She had also told Brad that Bochlaine was, or had been, a Jesuit before accepting his mission to thwart Aspis.

"I believe Frank would even kill if he had to, rather than see Massara as Pope," she had told Brad.

"He's big and strong enough to do it," Brad had replied, "but it takes more than strength to kill. As a Jesuit, I doubt if he could."

Suzanne, though, had disagreed. "He's a dear, sweet, lovable person," she had said, "but if he believes God wants him to kill, he will. You can bet your life on it."

As he reviewed the conversation with Suzanne, Brad's eyes moved back to the TV screen. He was suddenly startled, for a camera apparently stationed on the roof of the north colonnade of the Basilica had zeroed in on the platform next to St. Peter's statue where other television cameramen and paparazzi were stationed. At the far end of it, Brad could plainly see a massive man in the black robes of a Jesuit. A long-nosed camera was clutched in the Jesuit's hands. Even without seeing a close-up view of the man's face, Bradford was certain who it was. Frank Bochlaine.

Long after the camera had left the press platform to show views of the growing crowd and return to the stovepipe, Bradford stared at the receiver and saw only Bochlaine and the long-nosed camera he held; a camera that could easily accommodate the barrel of a rifle. Was Suzanne Steelman right about Bochlaine? Would he try to kill the new Pope if it turned out to be Cardinal Massara? Was that why he had joined the paparazzi?

Nick Criscolle's face was still bandaged from the plastic surgery he'd undergone five days ago, but he felt a great deal better than he had, knowing that soon he'd be as handsome as ever.

On the day before the opening of the papal conclave in Vatican City, Criscolle had left the small private hospital just outside Rome where he'd been operated on. He did so for two reasons: his men had finally located Mama Teresa, the woman who had been sheltering Frank Bochlaine, and he heard about what had happened at Count Vignola's apartment Monday night and Elliot Bradford's subsequent confinement in the hospital.

Criscolle did not try to hide his pleasure when he called the count and learned what had happened. "So you had Bradford cold and you blew it, too?" he declared. " I told you the bastard's no easy target!"

"He was dead, had the police captain not intervened," Vignola replied. "Now the important thing is that he is under guard and ready for elimination. When will you do it?"

"As soon as I've taken out Bochlaine. I know where he is now, and all I've got to do is take a little ride to see his keeper."

When Criscolle reached the house occupied by Mama Teresa Cardone and her daughters, however, it was Friday morning, and Bochlaine had already departed for Vatican City. Teresa was alone with her eldest daughter Elena, who had taken the day off from her job to go to St. Peter's Square later in the morning.

Criscolle did not knock on the door. He simply picked the lock and burst in on Teresa as she was cleaning the kitchen after breakfast.

"Where is Bochlaine?" Criscolle demanded, holding his knife to the woman's throat.

"Please, I know no one by that name," Teresa gasped.

"Tell me or I'll cut your fuckin' throat!" Criscolle growled, drawing blood from the woman's throat with a slight increase in pressure.

"I'm alone," she said. "A widow. I don't know . . ."

"Mama, I . . ." Elena, wearing only a thin cotton nightgown, appeared in the doorway of the kitchen.

"Run, Elena! Run for your life!" Teresa screamed. But she was too late.

"Come over here, honey," Criscolle ordered, forcing his captive around so the girl could see that he held a knife at her mother's throat. "If you don't want me to kill your mama, you better do what I say."

"Don't listen to him, Elena!" Teresa said. "He's . . ."

She never finished her warning, for Criscolle slashed her jugular vein and let her fall to the floor. He grabbed the young girl before she could escape.

Elena told Criscolle everything she knew about her "Uncle Franco" before he ruthlessly killed her. But she didn't tell him where he was, because she simply didn't know. Criscolle was so furious that she couldn't or wouldn't tell him where Bochlaine was that he slashed her in a dozen places before allowing her the peace of death with one cold jab into her heart.

But Criscolle soon learned where Bochlaine was. He was eating in a restaurant that had a television set tuned to the happenings at St. Peter's Square when he, like Bradford in the hospital, noticed the bulk of the Jesuit on the press platform.

"Jesus Christ!" he muttered, recognizing the large figure of Frank Bochlaine. "What the hell is he doing there?" Then he remembered. Count Vignola had told him Bochlaine was in league with Bradford and they both knew of the strong connection between the new Pope-to-be and Aspis.

Criscolle noticed the camera Bochlaine was holding and an astonished look crossed his face. He was certain that the camera wasn't what it seemed. He, like Bradford, sensed that it was a sniper's rifle.

Criscolle paid for but didn't finish his lunch. His task was clear. If he allowed Bochlaine to kill Massara, then Aspis would lose its power and the throne he so dearly wanted would be worthless.

On the press platform, Bochlaine was not aware of the attention he was getting from the television cameraman, a red-haired Italian-American named Anthony with an eye for the unusual. His lens was focused on the large-sized Jesuit with a camera.

Bochlaine was alert as he waited and watched for the telltale white smoke above the Sistine Chapel. But in his heart and mind was a fervent prayer different from any other in St. Peter's Square today: "Please, dearly beloved God, do not let it be him. Let it be des Balmat. Or anyone else! Anyone. But not him."

Bochlaine fought back the urge to eat another of the sandwiches Mama Teresa had fixed for him before driving him to Vatican City early that morning. A vote was due soon, he knew, and his stomach was roiling at the prospect.

The commentator on Vatican Radio had been telling the world for nearly an hour that the French Cardinal des Balmat appeared to be gaining recognition rapidly. Bochlaine had a tiny radio in his robes turned to the Vatican station, with an ear plug running to his left ear so he could hear it over the roar of the crowd.

"Let it be the Frenchman," Bochlaine murmured again. But he sensed in his heart that it would be Massara, and he knew he would have to destroy him.

Cardinal Ambrosiani had been shocked when he learned of Bochlaine's plan to assassinate the new Pope if it were Massara, but Ambrosiani had not forbidden him to carry it out. Instead they had both fallen on their knees before the Holy Virgin and prayed together that it would not be necessary—that Bochlaine would be spared the need to perform the deadliest sin. Even the thought of it made Bochlaine feel like the devil. How, he wondered, could Nick Criscolle perform such heinous deeds so matter-of-factly without regret?

Shocked as he was at Bochlaine's intention to kill Massara, should he be chosen as Pope, the aged cardinal also found himself doubting the big man's ability to see it through. Bochlaine had in the past week practiced with the deadly weapon now concealed by his camera, and he had achieved a high level of accuracy. But he was still not certain he could pull the trigger when his gun was trained on the figure of the new Pope. Obtaining the weapon had been far easier than using it would be. And even the extreme accuracy of the gun could not guarantee that he would not waver at the last moment and miss his target.

His target! He swallowed, a lump the size of an apricot seeming to grow in his throat. In the shopping bag beside him was a container of red wine and now he uncorked it and took a quick gulp, while trying to shield his action from the crowd in the square.

Then, his eyes on the stovepipe atop the chapel, he thought about Mama Teresa who had looked after him these past few weeks. She was a wonderful woman, he knew. His friend Giulio had been fortunate indeed to have her love. In his way, Bochlaine loved her, too. He felt, rather than knew, that Teresa shared his great affection. If things had been different, he thought, he might have asked her to become his wife. But he could not, for the Church was his true calling. And he would not survive the horrible murder he was about to commit, for he would most likely be killed within seconds of firing upon Massara. He was prepared for the bullets that would end his life. He prayed for them.

He would not attempt to escape, but had already carefully composed a long, coherent letter explaining his actions, copies of which he had sent today to an old friend in Spain where he had served the Church as a young man. He had begged his friend to mail the copies to all of Italy's major newspapers should he read of Bochlaine's death after assassinating the Pope.

The original letter, like its copies signed with both his real name, Francesco Bergamo, and the name he'd assumed before infiltrating Aspis, would be found on his body. In the missives he had detailed everything he knew about the Piedmont conspiracy, from its beginnings with Massara's theft of the blood money to the formation of Aspis, including Aspis's deadly dealings with and its connection to Massara and the sinister Inner Circle of cardinals.

"Unfortunately," Bochlaine wrote, "I cannot prove these accusations, for the cardinals are a brilliant lot and totally secretive in their scheming. Massara is monstrous, and I am carrying out God's will in destroying him as any prudent man would kill a snake that threatened his safety. I pray that the rest of the world will make the Inner Circle—the most potent part of the infamous Piedmont snake—curl up and die by exposing it for what it is."

Bochlaine's death after his act as a papal assassin was necessary to give substance, if not validity, to the charges he was making. Cardinal Ambrosiani had already blessed him and prayed for his soul. Both hoped Bochlaine's plan would work, for it was now their only hope to stop Aspis and the Inner Circle.

Shortly after Bradford recognized Bochlaine, two events that captured the world's attention transpired within minutes of each other. First came the hesitant puffs of smoke from the chimney as ballots were burned inside the Sistine Chapel's stove, the traditional, if antiquated method of announcing the success or failure of the cardinals' efforts to choose a Pope.

An erratic breeze, blowing between the chapel and the Papal Palace next to it, through Marshal's and Parrot's Courts, past the slender stovepipe, seemed possessed by a will of its own—to make the announcement entirely unclear. It forced the smoke over the red-tiled roof of the chapel and away from the square, making it impossible to be sure of its color. Then the wind shifted and pushed the smoke down toward the crowd, its color masked this time by the dark shadow of the chapel itself.

At last the breeze dissipated and a trail of smoke could be seen going straight up from the pipe. It appeared black, then white. The crowd roared for a moment, but then groaned, as the color became unquestionable. It was black. No Pope had been chosen.

In his hospital bed Bradford heaved a relieved sigh as the TV analyst called attention to the chorus of groans across the piazza. Then the analyst brought some more startling news to his audience. Cardinal des Balmat of France had fallen gravely ill in the chapel just before the last ballot and was being treated by Vatican doctors while the cardinals continued meeting to elect a Pope.

"Obviously," the commentator concluded, "des Balmat is out of contention now, whether or not he recovers. It appears that the new favorite must be Cardinal Massara of the Vatican."

Bradford's mind now contained an ugly idea—that des Balmat's sudden illness might well have been caused by the cardinals of the Inner Circle in order to guarantee Massara's election. If so, it appeared the die was now cast. No one could stop Massara. Unless Bochlaine did it violently! Although he still thought the possibility insane, Brad had to give credence to it.

"Looks like they've won the ball game, Brad," Sumereau observed, his eyes on the television receiver. "Another ballot and Massara comes up Pope."

Holly shivered. "Do you think des Balmat's sudden illness was caused by the Inner Circle? Could holy men do such a thing, Brad?" She paused, seeing the answer to her question written on Brad's face. "Can't anything be done about them?"

"Tom and I sure won't stop trying to find evidence to prove the Piedmont conspiracy, Holly," Brad said, "no matter who becomes Pope."

"I hope not, Brad," she interrupted. "Somebody's got to stop Aspis and Massara from killing more innocent people. I hope nobody has to experience the hell I've been through because of Aspis and Nicholas Criscolle. Nobody deserves to live through a father's violent death."

Brad nodded, his eyes back on the TV set, which again showed a growing sea of humanity swirling around St. Peter's Square. When the cameras scanned the press platform, he saw Bochlaine again. Brad scowled.

"What is it?" Holly asked.

"Look at the press platform, Holly. That's Bochlaine dressed in a Jesuit robe. He's up to something. I think he's going to try to kill Massara."

Holly gaped and so did Tom Sumereau, though Tom knew Bochlaine only by his size. "Can he do it, Brad? Kill Massara?" Holly asked.

"I don't know," Brad replied truthfully. "It's been said that it's impossible to keep a public person like a president or the Pope completely safe, but even so it takes a competent assassin to kill him. A random killer who lacks apparent reason to try can get to within a few feet of the Pope on some occasions, Holly. Like you and I were when we had our papal audience. Bochlaine is at least a hundred fifty feet and maybe as much as two hundred from the balcony where the new Pope will appear to greet the crowd. At that range, an inexperienced killer would need a miracle."

"Whatever Bochlaine has inside that camera snout will have to be accurate as hell, Brad," Tom said. "And he'll have to know how to use it. Even the best rifle can't aim itself."

"True," said Brad. "And I don't see how Bochlaine can qualify. Of course I know almost nothing of his background, but I doubt if target practice with rifles or anything else was a required subject when he was studying to become a Jesuit. Look. There he is again, on the far left of the platform."

The colonnade camera had again focused on the huge, robed Jesuit, his eyes raised toward the stovepipe of the chapel.

Now a new picture replaced the old one. It was a view provided by a hand-held TV camera whose possessor had just clambered up on the platform and had to be standing alongside Bochlaine as it zeroed in on the papal balcony, the center of three balconies overlooking the square.

The commentator began speaking rapidly about the origins of the square and how it had evolved into its present, elliptical state at the far end, but Brad, Holly, and Tom weren't listening. They were staring at the papal balcony.

Sumereau whistled. "That's quite a distance, Brad, and at a pretty good angle as well. I don't think Bochlaine has a chance. And he'll never get away afterward. The crowd's so thick, the guards will box him in."

"I wish I could disagree with you, Tom, but I can't. As for his getting away, though, I doubt if he wants to. He's prepared to die once he's killed Massara. That's the kind of person he is. He'll be more than willing to pay the price of his life to do what he thinks is right."

"Then he'll die for nothing if he fails, Brad," Holly said.

Brad nodded. "Probably," he said. "Unless . . ." Abruptly he pushed aside the sheet on the bed and, heedless of Holly's presence, swung his bare legs over the edge of the bed. He stood and walked around to the other side of the bed where Tom stood. "Unless I can stop him," he said. "There may still be time to convince him to wait for a better chance. As Pope, Massara won't be able to be a recluse and that means there will be other chances far better than this one. I'm going over there to try."

"You can't, Brad. You're under arrest—remember? I've got requests in at our embassy to squelch the charges and get you released, but they haven't pulled it off yet."

A curious smile lit Brad's face as he looked over Sumereau's custom-made navy gabardine suit, white shirt, and striped tie. It was noticeably more luxurious than Brad's traditional look.

Reading him correctly, Tom backed away, saying, "Oh, no you don't, Brad. You're not thinking what I think you are!"

The two men were not exactly the same size and height, but Brad could fit into Tom's clothes, though Tom's neck size was larger and his arms shorter. "Take everything off," Brad said. "It's for a good cause. Holly, do you think you can distract the Italian guard over there long enough for me to get past him?"

"If he's got eyes I can," she said. Before leaving the room she reached down to open two buttons of her blouse to expose more cleavage. "I've got a rental car down at the hospital entrance, Brad," she said.

"C'mon!" protested Sumereau. "I haven't agreed to this. I've got to get back to the office."

"You can call in from here, Tom, but don't do it until after I'm gone. You're going to have to convince the guard I'm still in bed and asleep when he checks the room after we all leave."

Sumereau was still cursing Bradford when his partner finished dressing and sneaked out of the room past the back of the Italian cop, whose eyes were exploring Holly's bosom as they talked near the window.

TWENTY-ONE

It was nearly three o'clock when Nick Criscolle began picking his way slowly through the masses in St. Peter's Square. He was carrying a press camera and a professional-looking pass, the last hastily arranged for him by Count Vignola when he learned of Bochlaine's threat against his half brother. Criscolle made painfully slow progress, for the crowd had grown enormous since the news of Cardinal des Balmat's illness had been made public.

Criscolle had barely edged his way into the square when the shouting began again. He stopped to look up and saw smoke beginning to trickle out of the Sistine Chapel stovepipe. A hush came over the crowd for several seconds as the smoke thickened. Its color unclear, the brightness of the midafternoon sun made it difficult to read. But then shouts rose from the watchers as the most discerning ones decided that the smoke was white. "E bianco!" they roared, "E bianco!"

The noise in the piazza became a thunderous roar, then a chant shared by all: "E bianco, è bianco, è bianco!" as a huge cloud of smoke billowed forth from the chimney—white without a doubt.

Criscolle might have celebrated with the crowd except the news of the Pope's election would make it more difficult for him to get through the crowd in the square and reach Bochlaine. People around him were already jumping with joy, hugging each other, kissing each other. Next to him a nun, caught up in the excitement of the papal election, threw her arms around Criscolle's neck and kissed his cheek. "Peace and joy be with you this day!" she cried. "We have a new Holy Father!"

Criscolle's answering smile was sickly, for he was embarrassed by the gray-haired nun's attention. An old prune, he thought as he moved away.

Bradford heard the official announcement of the new Pope's election over the Vatican's English radio station while driving toward Vatican City.

"The roar of the crowd in the piazza is deafening right now," the Vatican radio announcer declared unnecessarily as the city's bells began a concert. In huge invisible concentric circles centered on the largest church in Christendom, the peals cried out the joy of the people. It started at the six other churches inside the Leontine walls of Vatican City and raced across the Tiber and through the city until the joyous noise was everywhere.

Inside the square a contingent of Swiss Guards in their bright orange- and blue-striped uniforms marched smartly across the piazza through an area kept free of people by other security guards. They were cheered by the crowd every step of the way as they took up posts near the steps of the Basilica. Band members hurried to muster for their part of the activities.

Bradford was silent, listening to the announcer relate how the new Pope, yet unnamed, would even now be at the sacristy in the Sistine Chapel where the white papal robes waited him. Who is he? Brad de- manded mentally as he maneuvered the Fiat through incredible traffic on Via della Concilizione—much of it headed for Vatican City.

"The new Pope's ceremonial aide," the radio announcer droned on, "will help him pick out the right size from the assortment the Vatican tailors will have laid out, and then the dressing of His Holiness will begin."

Bradford fumed as the announcer began describing "the white pon- tifical stockings so rich with gold embroidery they have to be tied above the knee to prevent their weight from dragging them down to his ankles" and "the white cotton soutane and white silk falda with intricate and delicate lace that will cast changing shadows on the soutane as the Pope moves about."

In the Sistine Chapel a grave, though inwardly beaming, Cardinal Vincenzo Massara was in fact in the midst of shedding his cardinal's red for the papal adornments. Over the falda he had put on a white linen and lace alb, then girdled the body-length tunic with a white and gold cincture—a sash fourteen-feet long. Once tied, it hung from the left of Massara's thick waist, the delicately embroidered crosses and crowns shining crisply despite the dim light of the sacristy.

This was it, then, the new Pope thought, as his aide helped him into the fanon, a circular cape of silk with two gold and red stripes and an embroidered cross in the front. This was the finale—the crowning moment he had so long dreamed about while the others maneuvered to make it possible. It had taken many more years than Massara had expected, but at last the day had arrived. His day. He was the Holy Father and soon the whole world would know it!

His aide looked critically at the layered arrangement of his garments—each of them supposed to show a little beneath what lay above it. The aide nodded his approval, then placed over the vestments the pallium, a narrow circular band of white, ornamented with small crosses.

Now Massara stepped into a pair of white silk slippers, each of them bearing the symbol of the Church in gold embroidery. Then, putting on the white gloves and pulling the large gold cross around his neck, he stood, tall and stately, a tentative smile on his face. His aide and two other attendants draped over the rest a long, flowing mantle of white silk, elaborately woven with gold thread and bearing the icon-like images of Christ and the Virgin Mary.

He blinked. Robed in the vestments ordained for centuries, the new Pope longed to cry out his joy. He moved out of the sacristy with confidence, sureness—arrogance—trailed by the attendants who held the twenty-foot long mantle off the floor.

In the chapel, the assembled cardinals—the one hundred ten princes of the Church—watched in silence as the new Pope moved without hesitation to the ornate throne that had been erected in his absence.

It was time for him to receive the cardinals and he did, smiling as each approached the throne, dropped to one knee, and leaned forward to kiss his hand. He embraced each in turn, though there were many who had opposed him bitterly and would, he had no doubt, continue to do so as he tried to turn the Church around and develop it into the worldwide power it had once been.

When at last the final cardinals had been received, the Vatican Secretary of State, serving as Cardinal Chamberlain, knelt at Massara's feet and spoke softly in Latin as he placed on the pontiff's hand the piscatorial ring, which bore the image of Peter the fisherman. The ring was a shade too small but the Chamberlain managed to get it on Massara's finger anyway. It was only temporary and would soon be replaced with one bearing the new Pope's chosen crest, one that would be worn throughout his papacy.

Cardinal Ambrosiani's voice shook as he joined the other cardinals in singing Te Deum—the hymn of thanksgiving to God. In his heart was a prayer for Franco Bochlaine, who was in place somewhere outside awaiting the new Pope's appearance and first blessing.

"Please, Father," Ambrosiani prayed silently, "let us quickly rid the Church of the monster the others have mistakenly chosen, for he can only preside over the fall of your Church."

The cardinals formed lines for their walk with the Pope to greet the waiting faithful assembled in the piazza. Outside the chapel they walked slowly behind the Pope toward the second-floor balconies at the front of the Basilica.

Preceding the entourage were three papal attendants carrying a large velvet tapestry bearing the seal of the last Pope. They carefully unfurled it over the stone railing, securing it with the hooks it bore, their appearance increasing the noise in the square tenfold.

The tapestry displayed the seal of Gregory, a shepherd's crook and candle against a background of seven gently sloping hills—a simple Roman sign of a belief in helping others through knowledge and faith.

When the tapestry was secure, the attendants set up the microphones that had been stored inside the massive French doors.

As the cardinals moved to the balconies on each side of the papal center balcony, the roar of the crowd again increased. Then the Cardinal Chamberlain appeared on the central balcony, moving straight to the microphone and leaving the Pope in the corridor inside, for the moment alone.

It took several minutes for the Chamberlain to quiet the crowd, but finally he did. Then he spoke the words the crowd had been waiting for. "I bring you great joy," he declared in an emotional voice, "for we have a Pope!"

Nick Criscolle heard the Cardinal Chamberlain's announcement from a position directly behind the press platform, the huge statue of St. Peter shielding him from the eyes of Frank Bochlaine while he worked out a plan of escape.

The piazza was too full of people to allow a quick escape. He had realized that as he worked his way slowly toward the Basilica. His press pass and camera would get him through the police lines that barred people from positions closer to the Basilica than the barriers behind the statues, but he would need a little luck to get out without alarming anyone. What he had to do, he decided, was to pitch Bochlaine head-first over the platform after killing him. That would get everyone's attention and allow him to make his escape from the platform. Once he had done that and passed through the police lines, he simply had to lose himself in the crowd. There were, he noted, no uniformed guards on the press platform itself, though two were on duty at the stairway up, checking press credentials. Hundreds of other guards were stationed throughout the square, but only at barriers and gates that had been set up to divide the square into sections to maintain control of the people.

Criscolle began making his way toward the temporary gate workers had entered earlier in the day, not far from St. Peter's statue and the press platform. He had just passed through the police lines when the crowd's cheers increased as the attendants draped the tapestry over the railing of the balcony high above the square.

Again the noise increased as Criscolle showed his pass to a guard at the press platform. As he was waved through and climbed up on the platform through the assembled paparazzi, he heard the voice of the Cardinal Chamberlain booming throughout the square over loud-speakers:

"We have a Pope," the Secretary of State declared. "Cardinal Vincenzo Massara."

The crowd in St. Peter's Square reacted with glee, the sound rising like the thunder of thousands of immense cannons fired at the same precise moment. No matter that Italy's newspapers, who had speculated on the new Pope's identity ever since the former Pope's death, had shown little enthusiasm for Cardinal Massara's candidacy. Or that, though Massara's name was well-known because of his imposing presence in the Vatican Bank's ever-increasing financial dealings, few knew his face or the kind of person he was. "Cold" and "calculating" were terms often used by the writers who met him and described him later; not "humane," or "warm," or "humble," terms the papers insisted ought to be appropriate to describe any pontiff, whatever his stripe.

God had directed the cardinals to choose Massara, the people reasoned, so how could the new Pope be ill-chosen? He was their Papa and they would follow his lead faithfully, just as they now cheered his election.

"Eminentissimum ac reverendissimum dominum" the Cardinal

Chamberlain said when the roar subsided following his declaration of the election of a Pope "who has taken the name Peter Deum!"

Bochlaine recoiled in horror as he heard the Cardinal Chamberlain tell the entire world that not only had Massara been elected Pope, but that the monster had arrogantly taken the name of Peter, upon whose great rock the entire Church had been built!

"Oh, dear God!" Bochlaine exclaimed through tightly-set lips. "Help me to carry out what you've put me on this earth to do. Give me the sharp eye to find my target through this infernal weapon and the strength of will to pull the trigger. And I beg you to forgive me and make me once more pure of such sin after I've done it. Purge me and allow me to die quickly."

He busied himself with his camera, which he had cloaked from the view of anyone who came close to him on the platform. When Bochlaine had the camera braced on the wood rail in front of him, he removed the lens cover, which actually covered the barrel of the gun. Bending at the waist, he put his eye to the sight and slid out the trigger mechanism, then locked it in place.

The square was rocking with cheers and yells now, as the flock awaited the appearance of Pope Peter Deum on the balcony. Bochlaine sighted easily in on the Cardinal Chamberlain, his big hands concealing the stockless trigger mechanism, the telescopic sight of the weapon bringing the cardinal's chest close enough to reach out and touch.

But Bochlaine's hands were shaking and he knew he had to calm himself if he hoped to hit Massara—Pope Peter Deum. Even the slightest tremor in his hands would cause his shot to go wild and he knew he would not be allowed more than a single shot.

He also knew the infamous Pope must die this day and he must be responsible for the pontiff's death. His soul could never return to the Father if he failed. So he focused all his energies on calming his trembling hands before placing his finger on the trigger. He tensely awaited the appearance on the balcony of the monster Massara. This man was not the Holy Father, he told himself to calm his jangling nerves, he was only the blasphemous Massara.

Bochlaine did not notice Nick Criscolle as he appeared at his elbow.

Bradford had made it to the middle of the square, near the colonnades when he heard the Cardinal Chamberlain confirm the Pope's identity.

He had finally left the Fiat with Holly, bogged down in traffic, and walked the remaining distance to the square after ordering her to find a place to park and wait for his return. She had been unenthusiastic about the order, but had seemed to accept it, though cautioning him to be careful.

Before he was out of sight, however, she had found a tiny place to squeeze the car into and squeeze it in she did—shoving another Fiat slightly ahead in the process. Then she got out of the car and without hesitation began following Bradford into the square.

Bradford had mixed feelings as he worked his way through the happy men, women and children mobbing the piazza, none of them with the slightest idea of the kind of man whose election they were celebrating, the kind of monster who was about to become the power of the Holy See.

On the one hand, Brad had no desire to see the Catholics crown Massara and would have welcomed his death. On the other, as Brad saw it, the big Italian had little chance of succeeding and would almost certainly wind up dead himself while Massara would live. Bochlaine's death would be ignominious, for Brad had come to know, like, and respect Bochlaine as a sincere and purposeful good man working hard for a good cause.

Could Brad prevent Bochlaine from making his ill-fated attempt on Massara's life? It surely didn't look like it, for the new Pope was scheduled to make his first appearance very soon, and he was still far, far away from Bochlaine's position.

He propelled himself forward with renewed conviction while straining to see the balconies of the Basilica where the new Pope would appear any moment.

As Pope Peter Deum was delayed for a moment in the Vatican hallway by the last of the cardinals to make his way to the adjacent balconies—Cardinal Ambrosiani—a staff aide to a television anchor in Rome found a quotation from Saint Malachy, the twelfth-century Irish cleric, concerning the possible papal ascension of a second Pope Peter.

Without reading the quotation all the way through, he thrust it under the nose of the anchor during a live broadcast, as the monitors before the man showed the panorama of the crowd at St. Peter's Square, the cardinals on the balconies beside the papal balcony and Cardinal Chamberlain at the microphones.

Mistaking the sheet his aide had given him for a new voice-over, the anchor began reading it—a prophecy of doom.

"In the twelfth century" he began confidently, "there was an Irish cleric and scholar who wrote that Peter Deum will reign in the final persecution of the Holy Roman Church. He will lead his flock through many tribulations, St. Malachy predicted, after which the seven-hilled city will be" the newscaster hesitated, frowning as the importance of what he was saying began to penetrate his fevered brow . . . "destroyed and the dreadful judge will judge the people."

His smile suddenly vanished and he lapsed into a stunned silence as he pronounced the last part of the prophecy of doom. Then, covering his mike with his hand, he half-turned toward the control room behind him and glowered as he mouthed in a hoarse whisper, "Who the hell is responsible for this?"

"An offering of peace and love, Holy Father," said the cardinal kneeling before the new Pope as he held out a glass of the sweet white wine from Livigno. "As you know, I opposed your election in the conclave. But that was before. Now we must unite behind Your Holiness."

Pope Peter Deum's eyes narrowed at this symbolic act of contrition and demonstrated loyalty. Cardinal Ambrosiani had been fiercely outspoken against him from the moment the debate began over the identity of the new Pope and had been the principle reason why the College was poised to name des Balmat only a short time ago. Had not the brothers of the Inner Circle intervened to change things, des Balmat would be standing here rather than Massara. Who among the cardinals would have believed that another cardinal had slipped a mild form of poison into des Balmat's wine glass to bring on his sudden illness only moments before balloting that might well have elected him?

Was Ambrosiani's offer sincere? He had chosen a moment when only the two of them bore witness to it, but that could mean only that he did not wish to humble himself before the others. Regardless, Pope Peter Deum could afford to be gracious; he didn't need anyone's support now other than that of the Inner Circle and Aspis.

"I thank you," the new Pope said, smiling at the aged Ambrosiani and accepting the glass from his hands. He brought the glass to his lips for one small sip. "I am a little thirsty," he said as he handed it back to Ambrosiani.

Now, Pope Peter Deum thought as he watched Ambrosiani's withdrawal, my victory is truly complete.

Still savoring the wine, he moved through the door leading to the balcony and the faithful flock in the square awaiting his entrance and first blessings as Pope.

Peter Deum grinned broadly as he listened to the loving cheers the crowd directed toward him. He stood tall and erect as he gave his version of the traditional papal greeting—elbows bent, palms up, but moving his arms in a side to side motion—as if reaching out to each—before making the usual pulling motion to bring them back to him. That the crowd liked his slight adaptation was immediately obvious, for they began waving back, imitating him.

Was Raffaele watching? he wondered, noticing the TV cameras far below on the press platform near St. Peter's statue. He sent Vignola a mental message: "Look at me now!"

Then Cardinal Chamberlain held before the new Pope a large, leather-bound, gold-embossed folio, its half-inch Latin characters easily readable to even the most far-sighted.

"Blessed be the name of the Lord," Peter Deum read aloud, his voice strong and clear, a voice of power.

"Now and forever!" roared the crowd.

Bochlaine blinked back tears as the crowd roared its undeserved affection for the new Pope who had just appeared on the balcony high above the square. "Forgive them, Father," he muttered. "They know not for whom they cheer."

He sucked in a deep breath of air as he bent over his weapon, then held his breath as he tried to sight on the heart of Pope Peter Deum. But his vision was blurred by the moisture in his eyes and he had to exhale and start again.

"Now and forever!" cried out the crowd in response to the papal "Blessed be the name of the Lord!"

And a voice sounded at his elbow. A familiar voice.

"Teresa sends you her best, fat man."

Bochlaine heard Nick Criscolle's words at the same moment that the Aspis killer drove his knife deep into the left side of the big man's back.

He grunted as he tried to comprehend the meaning of what Criscolle said. Mama Teresa? What did he know of her?

"She and her kid Elena made me work hard to find out where you were, but they also gave me great enjoyment before they died—especially the girl."

No! Bochlaine seemed to drown in the horror at the thought, as his "camera" dropped from his hands and fell off the twenty-foot high platform to the cobblestone paving below. He swiveled in his agony and surprised Criscolle by wrapping his massive arms around the killer's thin waist, then locking them in place.

"You killed Mama and Elena?" Bochlaine screeched at the attacker. His rage and pain made his eyes as red as the blood coursing out of his veins. "Then die with me, you vermin!" With that he leaned his full weight forward and pushed with his feet, at the same time hanging on to Criscolle.

Slowly the two men toppled over the side of the platform.

Bradford was too late to stop it. His progress was impeded when Pope Peter Deum made his appearance before the crowd; Brad could barely move let alone break through the throng of bodies to get to the press platform.

"Viva il Papa!" the crowd roared, as they strained to see the Pope with telescopes, cameras, and their naked eye. Because of his height, Brad was able to see over their heads somewhat to catch a glimpse of what Bochlaine was doing. But he was still thirty yards away.

A nun stood next to Brad in the crowd, eagerly watching the new Pope through a pair of opera glasses. Brad, noticing this, charmingly asked in broken Italian if he could borrow the glasses for one moment, so that he might feast his eyes upon his Holiness. After the Pope pronounced his holy words, "Blessed be the name of the Lord," the nun handed the glasses over.

Mumbling a thank you, Brad brought the glasses up to his eyes, just in time to see Nick Criscolle appear at Bochlaine's elbow. He tensed. Pain and helplessness could be read on his face as he watched the killer knife the fat man in the back. He saw the blood gush from the massive body, watched Bochlaine's huge form turn and embrace his attacker like a wrestler, and then saw the two figures topple forward to the cobble-stone below.

The two bodies seemed to hang in the air for an endless moment before falling, and Brad felt he was watching a slow motion movie as he observed the shocking sight of their descent. The two twisted figures did a swimmer's somersault in mid-air that put Criscolle's body beneath Bochlaine's—and then they flipped around. When they struck the pavement, not far from the spot where the big man's camera and gun had fallen, it was Bochlaine who hit first, his huge bulk helping to break Criscolle's fall. From Brad's vantage point he could see through the opera glasses that the fight was not yet over. It looked like Criscolle was getting away.

On the cobblestone, a shaken and bruised Criscolle was trying to get to his feet; his right shoulder and hip had taken a pretty good hit in the fall. Unable to escape the fat man's steel-like embrace, he'd plunged over the side with Bochlaine, his heart in his throat as they plummeted down-ward. The former weightlifter was clinging to life by a mere thread, but he still would not relax his grip on Criscolle, who was feverishly trying to get out of the body lock. A very brief struggle ensued and finally Bochlaine inhaled his last breath; his body went limp and Criscolle leapt to his feet. Looking down at the dead figure, he spat at him in disgust. Then he grabbed hold of his knife, pulling hard to dislodge it from Bochlaine's flesh. Ignoring the dull ache in his shoulder, he fled. Brad-ford thrust the opera glasses back to the nun and went after him.

Criscolle did not know Elliot Bradford was following him, nor did he know that in the square the winds of fate would turn the white smoke of the papal choice to dark clouds.

The new Pope had noticed the scuffle between Bochlaine and Cris-colle from the corner of his eye as he stood on the balcony. He had no idea who they were or what was happening, and he didn't care—for he was intoxicated by his sudden power and wanted only to enjoy these moments in the papal sun at St. Peter's Square.

He turned his eyes to the crowd and turned his mind to his new position of authority. It was a heady feeling. In fact, he felt lightheaded and physically faint as he went through the ritualistic Latin words before the loyal flock massed below him in the square that over endless time had hosted millions—including emperors and conquerors as well as priests and Popes.

Conquerors! He felt like one today. He felt he had come into power as no man in history ever had. He felt more than a Pope; he felt like a king.

As self-aggrandizing thoughts sped through his mind, he continued with the ritual. "Our help is from the Lord . . ." he spoke, when suddenly, his voice trailed off.

He stopped speaking and moving altogether when his reverie was interrupted by an immense, searing pain that racked his body. At the same moment, he felt the need to retch and he couldn't catch his breath. A violence he could not understand attacked his body. He clutched his throat and fell heavily to his knees before the Cardinal Chamberlain, a choking "aaaggghhh" issuing from his wide open mouth as he went down. Within moments, the new Pope was dead.

Only in his final moments did Pope Peter Deum realize the irony of his impending death. The wine he had accepted from Cardinal Ambrosiani had been poisoned. He had been taken by the same ruse that had cost des Balmat the papacy!

Hysteria and panic ensued as the throngs of people gathered in the square realized something had happened to the Pope. As the awareness swept through the masses and rumors of the Pope's collapse were confirmed by those in the crowd carrying radios, a madness of sorts seemed to overtake Vatican City.

And through it all, Nick Criscolle was trying to get away from the scene of Bochlaine's demise, not knowing that the pontiff was dead as well. He noticed the heavy commotion, but he could not care less; he was interested only in saving himself.

As he reached the police lines in the square, the intensity of the situation became too searing to ignore. There was crying, screaming, wailing, and wild confusion. The guards barely noticed him; their eyes were fixed on the papal balcony, where the Pope's aides were trying desperately to revive him.

As he began to pick his way through the crowds, Criscolle did not see the grimly determined figure of Elliot Bradford stalking him.

In the television control center in Rome, the director whose aide had dug up the St. Malachy doomsday prophecy and had had it read over the air now found himself with the most bizarre dilemma ever. His cameras had, of course, recorded the Pope's open-mouthed swoon at the microphones on the papal balcony and were zoomed in on efforts to revive the Pope. But he had just as sensational a picture on a different monitor, this one taken by the young redheaded cameraman whose vantage point was high over the north colonnade.

The youth's camera had caught the apparent murder on the press platform of a big Jesuit by an assailant wielding a knife. Looking for the unusual in the crowd below him, the cameraman had seen the two figures through his lens. His camera had captured the knifing as well as the desperate fall over the railing.

When the attacker survived the fall, the cameraman began stalking him with his lens as the killer retrieved his knife, passed through police lines beside St. Peter's statue, and began weaving through the crowds of the piazza.

"What shall I do?" the cameraman asked his director, yelling into the mouthpiece of his headset from his post on the roof of the colonnade. He still had his lens on the fleeing Nick Criscolle.

"Stay with him, Anthony," the director declared. "We'll go live with the whole sequence in a few seconds. Follow the killer as far as possible. Try to get a close-up of his face if you can so he can be identified later."

Soon a worldwide TV audience that included Tom Sumereau and Murray Jolles in Bradford's hospital room, Count Vignola in Aspis headquarters, and Eleanor Sands in New York witnessed a videotaped rerun of the murder of Frank Bochlaine followed by the stalking of the killer by the television camera.

Sumereau watched the scene in shocked silence, seeing first the apparent death of the new Pope—but not from a rifle bullet—then Nick Criscolle's knifing of Bochlaine and now something new. Another familiar figure had just shown up on his television set—Elliot Bradford, who had just begun to close in on Criscolle.

What a crazy bastard my partner is, Sumereau thought, his eyes glued to the action. Then he spoke in the silence of the room "Get him Brad. Kill the son-of-a-bitch!"

Next to the bed, Murray stared.

TWENTY-TWO

Bradford paid scant attention to the Pope's final swoon in the middle of his blessing, though it made him wonder if somehow Bochlaine had gotten off a shot—a silenced shot—and miraculously hit his target before Criscolle stabbed him.

Criscolle! When Brad saw that the assassin had survived the fall off the platform and was making his escape, he knew what he had to do. Although he had no weapon—the police had taken his Beretta along with his clothes—and there was blood oozing out of his bandaged shoulder, he had to head Criscolle off, catch him unawares and . . . and then what?

Bradford had taken karate training in the army and learned how to kill with his hands, but that was long ago and he had never had occasion to use the training in hand-to-hand combat. He wondered whether he could still use it now. If he surprised Criscolle and could manage to hit the right spot with the right force, he might be able to down the deadly assassin. Brad knew the right spot—the carotid arteries at the base of the neck. There were two of them, one on either side.

He had to try. He knew it as well as he knew he was consumed with hatred for Nick Criscolle and that he would find no peace until the Aspis killer was dead. If Aspis was out of his reach, Criscolle was not. His mind clear about the path he must pursue.

The people in the square were milling around devastated over what was happening, and it took Brad great concentration to keep his eyes glued to the figure of Criscolle while simultaneously avoiding collisions with others in the crowd. Brad stumbled several times as he moved on an intercepting course with Criscolle, who was heading for the mouth of the piazza. Brad figured he could head the killer off near the first of the colonnades.

Intent on his quest, Brad did not see Holly Sands, who also had seen Bochlaine's demise on the press platform. She was only a short distance behind him then and she was only ten or fifteen yards behind him now.

Like Brad, she had seen Criscolle, but she had seen the killer without the benefit of opera glasses and had not recognized him. Thus, the small .22 caliber pistol she had bought in New York and had managed to get through customs in her luggage remained in her purse. She had never fired a gun, but the man in the shop where she'd bought it had coached her on how to shoot it, emphasizing the need to remember to lock and unlock the safety before storing or firing.

When Holly suddenly got a better look at Criscolle as she followed Brad through the crowds in the square, her adrenaline pumped with hatred and her mind flooded with horrific images as she recognized Aspis's executioner. Realizing now what Brad was up to, and knowing that he could not possibly be armed, she removed the petite pistol from her purse and jammed it into the pocket of the light jacket she wore. Her thumb went to the safety catch and she carefully unlocked it.

Holly's lip quivered as she flashed back to how Criscolle had brutalized her, and she wondered only for a moment if she could actually shoot him. She knew she could. And to protect Brad, she could and would do anything. She increased her pace, dogging Brad's footsteps, as he headed for his rendezvous with a killer.

The eyes of millions of television watchers saw the continuing drama as Brad drew closer to Nick Criscolle in the jammed square.

In his trailer outside the square, the TV news director had sent staff assistants to alert the Swiss Guards, though his eyes told him there would be more violence before the guards could intercede.

A second camera was now focused on the chase, and so was a third—both of them on the roof directly across from the fleeing Nick Criscolle and his pursuer. It was one of these cameramen who noticed and zoomed in on the young and pretty blond woman who had a small gun in her hand and was circling to the killer's right, her eyes on his every move.

The television commentator began a low-voiced speculation on Holly's role in the deadly scenario, as a close-up of the woman and her weapon appeared, big as life, on television screens all over the world.

In New York, Eleanor Sands gasped when she recognized her daughter. From the hospital room in Rome, Tom Sumereau groaned with fear for Jack Sands's daughter.

They saw Bradford break through a trio of bearded old men who'd drifted into his path just as he closed to within a yard or two of Criscolle. They watched as Bradford hurled himself on the killer, his right hand upraised in a typical karate attack.

Now! Bradford thought. He startled the three sad-faced old men by shoving them rudely to one side. A snarl formed in his throat as he launched himself at Criscolle, his eyes welded to the carotid artery of the killer's sinewy neck, his mind focusing all his strength in his raised right hand—especially in its sharp edge, which had to strike "through" its target to be effective. Once he had shattered a few boards with that edge of his hand, but never had he used its force against a human. Not until now. On the other side of Nick Criscolle, Holly saw Brad leap, just after she'd positioned herself within five yards of the two men.

She brought her gun up, her finger tightening on the trigger as she sighted on Criscolle's back. Then she moved closer still, to be sure of her aim. She stopped when she heard Bradford's sudden roar and saw Criscolle swiveling toward his attacker to parry the blow.

Criscolle had sensed, rather than saw, Bradford coming at him. He only had time to react, and his reaction was both swift and immediate, his left forearm coming up to ward off Bradford's deadly blow, while he reached for his knife.

Criscolle's fingers closed around the knife's handle at the same instant that Bradford struck his forearm a paralyzing blow. But the killer only grunted and swore, then grappled with Bradford.

"You're going to die, you murdering snake," Bradford declared, his face only inches from Criscolle's. "I told you I'd kill you."

Criscolle sneered. Then he tore himself suddenly loose from Brad's grasp and backed away, his knife glistening in the sun.

The two men faced each other, Criscolle in a half-crouch ready to spring. Bradford, his advantage of surprise gone, was weaponless and on the defensive.

"C'mon, motherfucker," Criscolle growled, heedless of the dozens of bystanders who surrounded the two gladiators. Any one of them could have interceded in the battle, but none did, all instead shrinking back in terror.

For the first time Brad became aware of the bandage on Criscolle's face. "What happened to your face, killer?" he snapped. "Is that what Suzanne did to you?"

Criscolle glowered and took a threatening step forward, his knife drawing invisible circles in the air. Then he stopped. "She got lucky, the bitch," he said. "But she paid for what she did to my face. Paid damn good. How'd you get out of the hospital, Bradford? I was going to bring you flowers tonight. Flowers and a dose of this!"

The killer now rushed Bradford, his knife held out before him, ready to be plunged into Brad's chest. But Brad sidestepped him and lashed out with a fist, cuffing Criscolle on the bandaged side of his face. The Aspis assassin roared in pain but didn't stop his assault. Again, he lunged at Bradford.

Bradford backed away. And both men stopped at the sound of a new voice—that of Holly Sands, who stood only a few yards in front of Criscolle, her legs slightly splayed, the small gun in her hand pointed at Criscolle's gut. "Drop the knife, you bastard!" she screeched.

Criscolle, despite his surprise, did not obey. Instead he feigned a move to his left, then dove at her legs in a flying tackle.

"Watch out, Holly!" Brad yelled, but it was too late. Holly was on her back, the gun clattering to the cobblestone pavement in front of her as Criscolle drove her back. Brad rushed for the gun, as Criscolle scrambled to his feet, dragging Holly with him.

Brad seized the gun, took quick aim and fired, just as Criscolle was struggling to pull Holly in front of him to serve as a shield. The bullet took him in the stomach and he staggered back, still clutching both the knife and Holly, the knife at the woman's throat.

"Get out of the way!" Brad thundered, as the edge of Nick's blade drew blood from Holly's flesh.

Then Criscolle's strength was gone. His fingers could no longer hold the blade, and it dropped to the pavement in front of Holly as he sank slowly to his knees.

Holly, a scream in her throat at the sight of her own blood, pulled loose and rushed into Bradford's arms.

Now Criscolle crossed himself, his body facing the Basilica, as if worshipping the deceased Pope Peter Deum.

Brad hugged Holly with his left arm in a protective embrace. He was tempted to fire again, to make sure Criscolle would die, but instead resisted his vengeful impulse and passively watched Criscolle meet his death. Die, you bastard. He railed inwardly, as Criscolle surprisingly remained on his knees as if praying. Die! For Nan, for Jack, for Suzanne, for Burke, for Bochlaine. Die!

Then, finally, Criscolle fell forward, face down on the pavement of St. Peter's Square.

TWENTY-THREE

It took the College of Cardinals nearly a month of nonstop wrangling to name a replacement for Pope Peter Deum, whom Vatican doctors certified as having died of a massive heart attack. Although many were certain he'd been poisoned, the Vatican would not permit an autopsy.

Cardinal Ambrosiani, the only person in the world who knew the truth, pronounced a fervent prayer for the dead Pope at his funeral. He meant every word of it.

"Dearly beloved Father," he said in a strong voice that had gained strength with Peter Deum's death. "No man who walks this earth is perfect lest you decree that he become the Holy Father of your church. Pope Peter Deum, like all who passed before him as our pontiff, achieved that perfection, so we pray today not for the perfect Pope that he was, but the imperfect mortal man he was before. Let Vincenzo Massara account to you for his life, as we all shall one day have to. Be merciful to him as you will to us all."

In silence, he prayed also for Frank Bochlaine, who gave his life in his attempt to save the Church. Cardinal Ambrosiani had poisoned the new Pope, even though he knew Bochlaine was poised to assassinate him with a bullet. Perhaps it was divine guidance that moved him to eliminate the new pontiff when the opportunity arose, for he knew, in his heart, Bochlaine would have never succeeded.

Elliot Bradford was taken into custody by the Swiss Guards within seconds after he'd put an end to the life of Nick Criscolle. The whole world knew Bradford's actions were justified, however, for what had taken place in St. Peter's Square—from the time Criscolle stabbed Frank Bochlaine until Bradford shot Criscolle with Holly's pistol—had been recorded by television cameras. Millions of people saw videotape replays of the events.

The burglary charges against Bradford were dropped in the aftermath of the investigation when Count Raffaele Ernesto Vignola went into seclusion after his half brother's death and refused to appear in court to press charges. Captain Enrico Parente's police suspension was summarily ended when the pressure brought to bear by Vignola was similarly withdrawn.

Back in New York, Brad finally had time to breathe—and to mourn for Suzanne. Her body had already been buried next to her grandfather's, and Brad made sure that there had been a rabbi to say a traditional prayer. But Brad could not be there. So he arranged a private memorial service once he got home, and had a local rabbi lead a special prayer for Suzanne. Holly Sands stood next to him for the emotional moment.

"We can have someone plant hyacinths over her grave in the fall," she suggested sincerely, tears in her eyes. "The scent can stay with her forever."

Later that day, Brad went alone to visit the Long Island cemetery that was the final resting place for his wife and sons.

"Nan," he said, standing close to her grave. "Maybe you and the boys really can rest now. I wish it could have been me they killed, that you were all still alive, free and thriving. But I have to believe in my heart that you are somehow with me always. I've lost a lot of good friends, Nan, so you're in good company. I love you."

He walked away from the grave feeling his heart and spirit lift. Finally, Brad had found closure to the unsolved mystery of his family's unexpected deaths.

The next day Brad and Tom Sumereau sat in Tom's office for the first time since his return.

"So what now, partner?" Tom said. "Jack's killer is dead and so is Massara."

"Aspis is still out there, Tom," Brad replied. "So's Vignola and that secret Vatican fellowship—the Inner Circle. They're all a part of this horror story and I'm afraid it's not over yet."

"Maybe so, but we've got to get back to business or FINVEST will go bankrupt. Tony's reports on Aspis leave no room for doubt on one score—it would take forever to get the kind of evidence against Vignola and company that would really hurt them. And we can't afford to do much more investigating than we've already done."

Brad nodded. Tom was right. "I'd like to follow up on the Piedmont Papers—or whatever they are. If we could only crack that code . . ."

"Tearing down the great wall in China and replacing it with one made of diamonds and rubies would be easier and cheaper, Brad," Tom observed. "Turn the damn papers over to that government cryptographer you told me about and let him give it a try on federal money and time. They can afford it."

Bradford finally agreed that they'd have to put the Aspis problem aside, but the future threat of a spy in their organization caused them to become much more secretive with their staff and feed voiceprints into the computer system so that no one but themselves could withdraw their most secret information.

Criscolle's death did not, Brad knew, preclude the possibility that a new Aspis assassin might be on his trail, so he exercised extreme care.

EPILOGUE

Eleanor Sands with great regret sold Winterhaven in Vermont that summer and purchased a place in the Pocono mountains of Pennsylvania. She and Holly spent the entire summer there, especially since Holly was now dating a police sergeant she met in Manhattan after her return from Rome.

Bradford was a little dismayed to find the sergeant, a superb physical specimen in his early thirties, vacationing with Holly and her mother in the Poconos that August.

"Mick plays a mean game of tennis," Holly told Brad when she introduced him as a friend of Lieutenant Kevin Burke's.

Accepting the cop's proffered hand and eerily recognizing a man he had never met, Brad asked Sergeant Mick O'Rourke if he had been Burke's favored racquetball partner.

O'Rourke, a personable cop with flashing dark eyes, nodded. "Not a very good one," he said, "but we played a lot because we both enjoyed the game. He'd let me win as often as not, but it wasn't easy. He was good. And a helluva nice guy."

Watching Holly on the diving board by the swimming pool, Brad found it hard to believe she was still only twenty-two.

She had grown up this past year, and become even more striking than she'd been before. Later, as Holly and her new friend danced on the flagstone patio near the pool, a twinge of jealousy came over Brad, and he had to remind himself that she was still too young for him. But that night the memory of the saucy and hungry young Holly who had slept in his arms in a Rome hotel bed haunted Brad's dreams. He did nothing about it, however, until Christmas, when he spent the holidays in the Pocono mountains with Eleanor and Holly Sands.

They had said goodnight just after midnight Christmas Eve, with kisses all around, then retired to the upstairs bedrooms in the large house.

Brad could not sleep, though, and after an hour of tossing and turning in bed, he got up and crept downstairs to the study, where a fire flickered in the fireplace. He threw a log on it and was lying on a furry rug staring into the blue-yellow flames licking at the unburned log when Holly suddenly dropped down beside him. She looked very much a woman in her formfitting and silky black negligee.

"I couldn't sleep," she said in a low voice. "Not alone," she added, and snuggled next to him, turning on her back so she could look up into his eyes.

The silky black material was taut across her round breasts and he could clearly see her charming outline—the swell of her stomach, the rise of her pubic mound, the V space between her thighs.

When he returned her look, he felt himself overcome with emotion and passion that was far from brotherly. And he was pulled toward her flesh as if by magnetic force. His arms went around her shoulders and upper torso and his mouth sought hers. He kissed her deeply with an impatient tongue, and she returned his kiss with a fiery response. And yet she seemed so quiet, so controlled—as if she were presenting her possibilities to him and allowing him to take her at his will. She simply received his attentions—and this made him want to give her so much more.

Beneath the sexy nightgown was a body covered by smooth, creamy skin that Brad suddenly wanted to know better. He slipped the straps from her shoulder, and then removed the nightgown entirely, until she was completely nude and open to him. Then his hands, his mouth, his skin explored every inch of her, every sensual place within her, until Brad's blood boiled over with his need to have even more of her.

He quietly and quickly removed his clothes and joined her, flesh to flesh. Her legs quivered slightly and tiny beads of sweat slid from her body as Brad caressed her thighs with kisses and soft touches and then finally opened her to his love. She never even placed a hand on him, she simply surrendered. He glided inside her softly, slowly, until they created a special rhythm of love that swept them to the heights of passion. The two lovers, brought together by their hearts and their desires, became one as they made love into the night.

When the sex was over, the warm feelings of love and respect remained. Brad held Holly in his arms until they awoke to greet the new day, together.

Early in the new year several events reminded Bradford of the perpetual threat of Aspis precisely when his life promised peace and serenity.

Count Vignola had died in a skiing accident in Livigno on New Year's Day. Vignola's death made him wonder if it had been truly an accident. Or, was it a result of foul play, as Jack Sands's death and those of Nan and the kids had been?

A young Catholic monsignor showed up in the lobby of Brad's apartment building one evening in mid-February. Brad invited him upstairs only after the monsignor offered him a Rosary bead, saying, "Once a bead like this was given to you by a now dead Jesuit named Bergamo— you knew him as Frank Bochlaine. It was used to identify you to a young woman in London named Steelman."

Monsignor DiLello had been sent, he claimed when they sat together in Bradford's living room, "by the same man who caused Bergamo to seek the truth about Cardinal Massara and Aspis. He is the only man who knows for certain that Pope Peter Deum died from poison because he himself administered it."

Bradford did not ask why DiLello had come. He didn't have to.

"Bochlaine was an extraordinary human being to put his life in danger in order to stop Aspis. But I am a simple man who cannot help your cause like he did."

"Mr. Bradford," the priest returned. "Count Vignola's death was not an accident. He was killed. His death was the first of a reign of terror committed by a new regime at Aspis. His successor—a Spaniard—is colder and more deadly than Count Vignola or Nick Criscolle. His name is Fernando."

Brad's initiation to the vicious world of Aspis had forever altered his perception of international events; Monsignor DiLello reawakened his hatred of Aspis's abominable transgressions.

A week after Brad's meeting with DiLello, the recently-elected president of the National Bar Association suspiciously killed his wife and three children, then himself. The woman who was named his temporary replacement—the NBA's first woman president—had once served as an envoy to the Vatican.

In late March the president of the Hong Kong Stock Exchange stepped into an open elevator shaft after coming out of the directors' restaurant forty-two floors above the exchange. His successor was an Englishman—another first—whose name had appeared in the maze of reports on Aspis that Tony Phipps had assembled. He had once been in charge of Aspis's Far Eastern investments.

Bradford had never denied the priest's assertions, but neither had he agreed to involve himself again. As he finished reading the *New York Times* account of the elevator accident at the Hong Kong Stock Exchange and the identity of its new president, he asked himself what he could, or should do, about these new outrages.

He had no answer.